W9-BUD-840

Large Print Lan
Lansdale, Joe R., 1951-
The bottoms

THE Bottoms

JOE R. LANSDALE

THE Bottoms

WHEELER
PUBLISHING, INC.
ROCKLAND, MA

★ AN AMERICAN COMPANY ★

Published in Large Print by arrangement with The Mysterious Press, an
imprint of Warner Books, Inc., in the United States and Canada.

Wheeler Large Print Book Series.

Set in 16 pt Plantin.

A considerably different version of this story first appeared in 1999, edited
by Al Sarrantonio (Avon Books, 1999).

Library of Congress Cataloging-in-Publication Data

Lansdale, Joe R.
    The bottoms / Joe R. Lansdale.
        p. (large print) cm.(Wheeler large print book series)
    ISBN 1-58724-093-9 (hardcover)
    1. Category—Fiction. 2. Category—Fiction. 3. Category—Fiction. 4.
Category—Fiction. 5. Category—Fiction. 6. Large type books. I. Title.
II. Series

[PS3562.A557 B68 2001]
813'.54—dc21
                                                                2001nnnnn
                                                                    CIP

This is dedicated to the loving memory of my mother and father, A.B. (Bud) Lansdale and O'Reta Lansdale. They weathered the Great Depression, recessions, plain old hard work, and difficult times without complaint. I wish there were more like them.

Prologue

◆

News didn't travel the way it does now. Not back then. Not by radio or newspaper it didn't. Not in East Texas. Things were different. What happened in another county was often left to that county.

World news was of importance to us all, but we didn't have to know about terrible things that didn't affect us in Bilgewater, Oregon, or even across the state in El Paso, or up northern state way in godforsaken Amarillo.

All it takes now for us to know all the gory details about some murder is for it to be horrible, or it to be a slow news week, and it's everywhere, even if it's some grocery clerk murder in Maine that hasn't a thing to do with us.

Back in the thirties a killing might occur several counties over and you might never know about it unless you were related, because as I said, news traveled slower then, and law enforcement tried to take care of their own.

On the other hand, there were times it might have been better had news traveled faster, or traveled at all. Then again, maybe it wouldn't have made one whit of difference.

What's done is done though, and even now in my eighties, as I lie here in the old folks home, my room full of the smell of my own decaying body, awaiting a meal of whatever, mashed and diced and tasteless, a tube in my shank, the television tuned to some talk show peopled by idiots, I've got the memories of then, nearly seventy years ago, and they are as fresh as the moment.

It all happened, as I recall, in the years nineteen thirty-three and thirty-four.

Part One

1

I suppose there were some back then had money, but we weren't among them. The Depression was on. And if we had been one of those with money, there really wasn't that much to buy, outside of hogs, chickens, vegetables, and the staples, and since we raised the first three, with us it was the staples, and sometimes we bartered for them.

Daddy farmed some, and where we lived wasn't so bad for growing things. The wind had blown away most of North and West Texas, along with Oklahoma, but the eastern part of Texas was lush with greenery and the soil was rich and there was enough rain so that things grew quick and hardy. Even during dry periods the soil tended to hold some moisture, and if a crop wasn't as good as it might be, it could still turn out. In fact, when the rest of Texas was tired out and gone to dust, East Texas would sometimes be subject to terrific rainstorms and even floods. We were more likely to lose a crop to dampness than to dryness.

Daddy had a barbershop as well, and he ran it most days except Sunday and Monday, and was a community constable because nobody else wanted the job. For a time he had been justice of the peace as well, but he finally decided it was more than he wanted, and Jim Jack Formosa took on the justice of the peace position, and Daddy always said Jim Jack was a damn sight better at marrying and declaring people stone cold dead than he ever was.

We lived back in the deep woods near the Sabine River in a three-room white house Daddy had built before we were born. We had a leak in the roof, no electricity, a smoky wood stove, a rickety barn, a sleeping porch with a patched screen, and an outhouse prone to snakes.

We used kerosene lamps, hauled water from the well, and did a lot of hunting and fishing to add to the larder. We had about four acres cut out of the woods, and owned another twenty-five acres of hard timber and pine. We farmed the cleared four acres of sandy land with a mule named Sally Redback. We had a car, but Daddy used it mostly for his constable business and Sunday church. The rest of the time we walked, or me and my sister rode Sally Redback.

The woods we owned, and the hundreds of acres of it that surrounded our land, was full of game, chiggers, and ticks. Back then in East Texas, all the big woods hadn't been timbered out and we didn't have a real advanced Forestry Department telling us how the forest needed help to survive. We just sort of figured since it had survived centuries without us it could probably figure things out on its own. And the woods didn't all belong to somebody back then, though of course timber was a big industry and was growing even bigger.

But there were still mighty trees and lost places in the woods and along the cool shaded riverbanks that no one had touched but animals.

Wild hogs, squirrels, rabbits, coons, possums, some armadillo, and all manner of birds and plenty of snakes were out there. Sometimes you could see water moccasins swimming in a school down the river, their evil heads bobbing up like knobs on logs. And woe unto the fella fell in amongst them, and bless the heart of the fool who believed if he swam down under them he'd be safe because a moccasin couldn't bite underwater. They not only could, but would.

Deer roamed the woods too. Maybe fewer than now, as people grow them like crops these days and harvest them on a three-day drunk during season from a deer stand with a high-powered rifle. Deer they've corn-fed and trained to be like pets so they can get a cheap free shot and feel like they've done some serious hunting. It costs them more to shoot the deer, ride its corpse around in a pickup, and mount its head than it would cost to go to the store and buy an equal amount of beefsteak. Then there's those who like to smear their faces with the blood after the kill and take photos, as if this makes them some kind of warrior. You'd think the damn deer were armed and dangerous.

But I've quit talking, and gone to preaching. I was saying how we lived. And I was saying about all the game. Then too, there was the Goat Man. Half goat, half man, he liked to hang around what was called the Swinging Bridge. Up until the time I'm telling you about I had never seen him, but sometimes at night, out possum hunting, I thought maybe I heard him, howling and whimpering down there near the cable bridge that hung bold over the river, swinging with the wind in the moonlight, the beams playing on the metal cables like fairies on ropes.

He was supposed to steal animals and children, and though I didn't know of any children that had been eaten, some farmers claimed the Goat Man had taken their livestock, and there were kids I knew claimed they had cousins taken off by the Goat Man, never to be seen again.

It was said he didn't go as far as the main road because Baptist preachers traveled regular there on foot and by car, making the rounds, and therefore making the road holy. We called it the Preacher's Road.

It was said the Goat Man didn't get out of the woods that made up the Sabine bottoms. High land was something he couldn't tolerate. He needed the damp, thick leaf mush beneath his feet, which were hooves.

Dad said there wasn't any Goat Man. That it was a wives' tale heard throughout the South. He said what I heard out there was water and animal sounds, but I tell you, those sounds made your skin crawl, and they did remind you of a hurt goat. Mr. Cecil Chambers, who worked with my Daddy at the barbershop, said it was probably a panther. They showed up now and then in the deep woods, and they could scream like a woman, he said.

Me and my sister, Tom—well, Thomasina, but we all called her Tom 'cause it was easier to remember and because she was a tomboy— roamed those woods from daylight to dark. That wasn't unusual for kids back then. The woods were darn near a second home to us.

We had a dog named Toby that was part hound, part terrier, and part what we called feist. Toby was a hunting sonofagun. But the summer of nineteen thirty-three, while rearing up against a tree so he could bark at a squirrel he'd tracked, the oak he was under lost a rotten limb and it fell on him, striking him so hard he couldn't move his back legs or tail. I carried him home in my arms. Him whimpering, me and Tom crying.

Daddy was out in the field plowing with Sally Redback, working the plow around a stump that was still in the field. Now and then he chopped at its base with an axe and set fire to it, but it was stubborn and remained.

Daddy stopped his plowing when he saw us, took the looped lines off his shoulders and dropped them, left Sally Redback standing in the field hitched up to the plow. He walked part of the way across the field to meet us, and we carried Toby out to him and put him on the soft plowed ground and Daddy looked him over.

Unlike most farmers, Daddy never wore overalls. He always wore khaki pants, work shirts, work shoes, and a brown felt hat. His idea of dressing up was a clean white shirt with a thin black tie and the rest of him decked out in khakis and work shoes and a less battered hat.

This day he took off his sweat-ringed hat, squatted down, and put the hat on his knee. He had dark brown hair and in the sunlight you could see it was touched with streaks of gray. He had a slightly long face and light green eyes that, though soft, seemed to look right through you.

Daddy moved Toby's paws around, tried to straighten his back, but Toby whined hard when he did that.

After a while, as if considering all possibilities, he told me and Tom to get the gun and take poor Toby out in the woods and put him out of his misery.

"It ain't what I want you to do," Daddy said. "But it's the thing has to be done."

"Yes sir," I said, but the words crawled out of my throat as if their backs, like Toby's, were broken.

These days that might sound rough, but back then we didn't have many vets, and no money to take a dog to one if we wanted to. And all a vet would have done was do what we were gonna do.

Another thing different then was you learned about things like dying when you were quite young. It couldn't be helped. You raised and killed chickens and hogs, hunted and fished, so you were constantly up against it. That being the case, I think we respected life more than some do now, and useless suffering was not to be tolerated.

In the case of something like Toby, you were expected to do the deed yourself, not pass on the responsibility. It was unspoken, but it was well understood that Toby was our dog, and therefore our responsibility. And when it got right down to it, as the oldest, it was my direct responsibility, not Tom's.

I thought of appealing to Mama, who was out at the henhouse gathering evening eggs, but I knew it wouldn't do any good. She'd see things same as Daddy.

Me and Tom cried awhile, then got a wheelbarrow and put Toby in it. I already had my twenty-two for squirrels, but for this I went in the house and swapped it for the single-shot sixteen-gauge shotgun so there wouldn't be any suffering. Kids back then grew up on guns and were taught to respect and use them in the manner they were meant. They were as much a part of life as a hoe, a plow, and a butter churn.

Our responsibility or not, I was nearly twelve and Tom was only nine. The thought of shooting Toby in the back of the head like that, blasting his skull all over creation, was not something I looked forward to. I told Tom to stay at the house, but she wouldn't. She said she'd come on with me. She knew I needed someone to help me be strong. I didn't try hard to discourage her.

Tom got the shovel to bury Toby, put it over her shoulder, and we wheeled old Toby along, him whining and such, but after a bit he quit making noise. He just lay in the wheelbarrow while we pushed him down the trail, his back slightly twisted, his head raised, sniffing the air.

In a short time he started sniffing deeper, and we could tell he had a squirrel's scent. Toby always had a way of turning to look at you when he had a squirrel, then he'd point his head in the direction he wanted to go and take off running and yapping in that deep voice of his. Daddy said that was his way of letting us know the direction of the scent before he got out of sight. Well, he had his head turned like that, and I knew what it was I was supposed to do, but I decided to prolong it by giving Toby his head.

We pushed in the direction he wanted to go, and pretty soon we were racing over a narrow trail littered with pine needles. Toby was barking like crazy. Eventually we ran the wheelbarrow up against a hickory tree.

Up there in the high branches two big fat squirrels played around as if taunting us. I shot both of them and tossed them in the wheelbarrow with Toby, and darned if he didn't signal and start barking again.

It was rough pushing that wheelbarrow over that bumpy ground, but we did it, forgetting all about what we were supposed to do for Toby.

By the time Toby quit hitting on squirrel scent, it was near nightfall and we were down deep in the woods with six squirrels—a bumper crop—and we were tuckered out.

There Toby was, a cripple, and I'd never seen him work the trees better. It was like Toby knew what was coming and was trying to extend things by treeing squirrels.

We sat down under a big old sweet gum and left Toby in the wheelbarrow with the squirrels. The sun was falling through the trees like a big fat plum coming to pieces. Shadows were rising up like dark men all around us. We didn't have a hunting lamp. There was just the moon, and it wasn't up good yet.

"Harry," Tom said. "What about Toby?"

"He don't seem to be in pain none," I said. "And he treed six squirrels."

"Yeah," Tom said, "but his back's still broke."

"Reckon so," I said.

"Maybe we could hide him down here, come every day, feed and water him."

"I don't think so. He'd be at the mercy anything came along. Darn chiggers and ticks would eat him alive." I'd thought of that because I could feel bites all over me and knew tonight I'd be spending some time with a lamp and tweezers, getting them off all kinds of places, bathing myself in kerosene, then rinsing. During the summer me and Tom ended up doing that near every evening. In fact, ticks were so thick they gathered on weed tops awaiting prey in such piles they bent the weed stalks over. Biting blackflies were thick in the woods, especially as you neared the river, and the chiggers were plentiful and hungry. Sometimes, late in the afternoon, the mosquitoes rose up in such a gathering they looked like a black cloud growing up from the bottoms.

To ward off the ticks and chiggers we tied kerosene-soaked rags around our ankles, but I can't say it worked much, other than keeping the bugs off the rags themselves. The ticks and chiggers found their way onto your clothing and body, and by nightfall they had nested snugly into some of the more personal areas of your person, sucking blood, raising up red welts.

"It's gettin' dark," Tom said.

"I know."

I looked at Toby. There was mostly just a lump to see, lying there in the wheelbarrow covered by the dark. While I was looking he raised his head and his tail beat on the wooden bottom of the wheelbarrow a couple of times.

"Don't think I can do it," I said. "I think we ought to take him back to Daddy, show how he's improved. He may have a broke back, but he can move his head and even his tail now, so his whole body ain't dead. He don't need killin'."

"Daddy may not see it that way, though."

"Reckon not, but I can't just shoot him without trying to give him a chance. Heck, he treed six squirrels. Mama'll be glad to see them squirrels. We'll just take him back."

We got up to go. It was then that it settled on us. We were lost. We had been so busy chasing those squirrels, following Toby's lead, we had gotten down deep in the woods and we didn't recognize anything. We weren't scared, of course, least not right away. We roamed these woods all the time, but it had grown dark, and this immediate place wasn't familiar.

The moon was up some more, and I used that for my bearings. "We need to go that way," I said. "Eventually that'll lead back to the house, or the road."

We set out, pushing the wheelbarrow, stumbling over roots and ruts and fallen limbs, banging up against trees with the wheelbarrow and ourselves. Near us we could hear wildlife moving around, and I thought about what Cecil had said about panthers, and I thought about wild hogs and wondered if we might come up on one rootin' for acorns, and I remembered that Cecil had also said this was a bad year for the hydrophobia, and lots of animals were coming down with it, and the thought of all that made me nervous enough to feel around in my pocket for shotgun shells. I had three left.

As we went along, there was more movement in the thicket next to us, and after a while I realized whatever it was it was keeping stride

15

with us. When we slowed, it slowed. We sped up, it sped up. And not the way an animal will do, or even the way a coach whip snake will sometimes follow and run you. This was something bigger than a snake. It was stalking us, like a panther. Or a man.

Toby was growling as we went along, his head lifted, the hair on the back of his neck raised.

I looked over at Tom, and the moon was just able to split through the trees and show me her face and how scared she was.

I wanted to say something, shout out at whatever it was in the bushes, but I was afraid that might be like some kind of bugle call that set it off, causing it to come down on us.

I had broken open the shotgun earlier for safety sake, laid it in the wheelbarrow and was pushing it, Toby, the shovel, and the squirrels along. Now I stopped, got the shotgun out, made sure a shell was in it, snapped it shut and put my thumb on the hammer.

Toby had really started to make noise, had gone from growling to barking.

I looked at Tom, and she took hold of the wheelbarrow and started pushing. I could tell she was having trouble with it, working it over the soft ground, but I didn't have any choice but to hold on to the gun, and we couldn't leave Toby behind, not after what he'd been through.

Whatever was in those bushes paced us for a while, barely cracked the leaves it stepped on, then went silent. We picked up speed, and didn't hear it anymore. And we didn't feel its presence either.

I finally got brave enough to break open the shotgun and lay it in the wheelbarrow and take over the pushing again.

"What was that?" Tom asked.

"I don't know," I said.

"It sounded big."

"Yeah."

"The Goat Man?"

"Daddy says there ain't any Goat Man."

"Yeah, but he's sometimes wrong, ain't he?"

"Hardly ever," I said.

We went along some more, found a narrow place in the river, crossed, struggling with the wheelbarrow. We shouldn't have crossed, but here was a good spot to do it, and I was spooked and wanted to put some space between us and it.

We walked along a good distance, and eventually came up against a wad of brambles that twisted in amongst the trees and scrubs and vines and made a wall of thorns. It was a wall of wild rosebushes. Some of the vines on them were thick as well ropes, the thorns like nails, and the flowers smelled strong and sweet in the night wind, almost sweet as sorghum syrup cooking.

The bramble patch ran some distance in either direction, and encased us on all sides. We had wandered into a maze of thorns too wide and thick to go around, too high and sharp to climb over; they had wound together with

17

low-hanging limbs, making a thorny ceiling above.

I thought of Brer Rabbit and the briar patch, but unlike Brer Rabbit, I had not been born and raised in a briar patch and it wasn't what I wanted.

I dug in my pocket, got a match I had left over from when me and Tom tried to smoke some corn silk cigarettes and grape vines, struck the match with my thumb and waved it around, saw a wide path had been cut into the brambles.

I bent down, poked the match forward. I could see the brambles were a kind of tunnel, about six feet high and six feet wide. I couldn't tell how far it went, but it was a good distance.

I shook the match out before it burned my hand, said to Tom, "We can go back, or we can take this tunnel."

Tom studied the brambles. "I don't want to go back because of that thing. And I don't want to go down that tunnel neither. We'd be like rats in a pipe. Maybe whatever it is knew it'd get us boxed in like this, and it's just waitin' at the other end, like that thing Daddy read to us about. The thing that was part man, part cow."

"Part bull, part man," I said. "The Minotaur."

"Yeah. It could be waitin' on us, Harry."

I had, of course, thought about that. "I think we ought to take the tunnel. It can't come from any side on us that way. It has to come from front or rear."

"Can't there be other tunnels in there?"

That I hadn't considered. There could be openings cut anywhere. And if it grew tight in there, all a person, animal, Minotaur had to do, was reach out and grab me or Tom.

"I got the gun," I said. "If you can push the wheelbarrow, Toby can sort of watch for us, let us know something's coming. Anything jumps out at us, I'll cut it in two."

I picked up the gun and made it ready. Tom took hold of the wheelbarrow handles, wiggled it through the split in the briars, and me and her went on in.

2

The smell of roses was thick and over-whelming. It made me sick. The thorns sometimes stuck out on vines you couldn't see in the dark. They snagged my old shirt and cut my arms and face. I could hear Tom back there behind me, cussing softly under her breath as she got scratched.

The bramble tunnel went on for a good ways, then I heard a rushing sound, and the tunnel widened and we came out on the bank of the roaring Sabine River. There were splits in the trees above and the moonlight came through strong and fell over everything like milk that had thickened, yellowed, and turned sour.

Whatever had been pacing us seemed to be good and gone.

I studied the moon, thought about the river. I said, "We've gone some out of the way. But I can see how we ought to go. We can follow the river a bit, which ain't the right direction, but I think it's not far from here to the Swinging Bridge. We cross that, we can hit the main road, walk to the house."

"The Swinging Bridge?"

"Yeah," I said.

"Think Mama and Daddy are worried?" Tom asked.

"Yeah," I said. "Bet they are. I hope they'll be as glad to see these squirrels as I think they'll be."

"What about Toby?"

"We just got to wait and see."

The bank sloped, and there was a little trail ran along the edge of the river.

"Figure we got to carry Toby, then bring the wheelbarrow. You can push it forward, and I'll get in front and boost it down."

I carefully picked up Toby, who whimpered softly, and Tom, getting ahead of herself, pushed the wheelbarrow. It, the squirrels, shotgun, and shovel went over the edge, tipped over near the creek.

"Damnit, Tom," I said.

"I'm sorry," she said. "It got away from me. I'm gonna tell Mama you cussed."

"You do, and I'll whup the tar out of you. 'Sides, I heard you cussin' plenty."

I gave Toby to Tom till I could get a footing and have him passed to me.

I slid down the bank, came up against a huge oak growing near the water. The brambles had grown down the bank and were wrapped around the tree. I put my hand against it to steady myself, jerked back quick. What I had touched hadn't been a tree trunk, or even a thorn. It was something soft.

When I looked I saw a gray mess hung up in brambles. The moonlight was shining across the water and falling on a face, or what had been a face, but was more like a jack-o'-lantern now, swollen and round with dark sockets for eyes. There was a wad of hair on its head, like a chunk of dark lamb's wool, and the body was swollen and twisted and without clothes. A woman.

I had seen a couple of cards with naked women on them that George Sterning had shown me. He was always coming up with stuff like that 'cause his Daddy was a traveling salesman and sold not only Garrett snuff, but what was called novelties on the side.

But this wasn't like that. Those pictures had stirred me in a way I didn't understand but found somehow sweet and satisfying. This was stirring me in a way I understood immediately.

Her breasts were split like rotten melons

cracked in the sun. On closer examination I realized the brambles weren't brambles at all, but strands of barbed wire tightly wrapped around her swollen gray flesh.

"Jesus," I said.

"You're cussin' again," Tom said.

I climbed up the bank a bit, took Toby from Tom, laid him on the soft ground by the riverbank, stared some more at the body. Tom slid down, saw what I saw.

"Is it the Goat Man?" she asked.

"No," I said. "It's a dead woman."

"She ain't got no clothes on."

"No, she ain't. Don't look at her, Tom."

"I can't help it."

"We got to get home and tell Daddy."

"Light a match, Harry. Let's get a good look."

I considered on that, finally dug in my pocket. "I just got one left."

"Use it."

I struck the match with my thumb and held it out. The match wavered as my hand shook. I got up as close as I could stand to get, due to the smell.

It was even more horrible by matchlight.

"I think it's a colored woman," I said.

The match went out. I righted the wheelbarrow, shook mud out of the end of the shotgun, put it, the squirrels, and Toby back in the wheelbarrow. I couldn't find the shovel, figured it had slid on down into the river and was gone. That was going to cost me.

"We got to get on," I said.

22

Tom was standing on the bank, staring at the body. She couldn't take her eyes off of it.

"Come on!"

I pulled her away. We went along the bank, me pushing the wheelbarrow for all I was worth, it bogging in the soft dirt until I couldn't push it anymore. I bound the squirrels' legs together with some string Tom had, and tied them around my waist.

"You carry the shotgun, Tom, and I'll carry Toby."

Tom took the gun. I picked Toby up. We started toward the Swinging Bridge, which was where the Goat Man was supposed to live.

Me and my friends normally stayed away from the Swinging Bridge, all except George. George wasn't scared of anything. Then again, George wasn't smart enough to be scared of much.

The bridge was some cables strung across the Sabine from high spots on the banks. Some long board slats were fastened to the cables by rusty metal clamps and rotting ropes. I didn't know who built it or how old it was. Maybe it had been a pretty good bridge once. Now a lot of slats were missing and others were rotten and cracked and the cables were fastened to the high banks on either side by rusty metal bars buried deep in the ground. In places, where the water had washed the bank, you could see part of the bars showing through the dirt. Enough time and water, the whole bridge would fall into the river.

When the wind blew, the bridge swung. In a high wind it was something. I had crossed it only once before, during the day, the wind dead calm, and that had been scary enough. Every time you stepped, it moved, threatened to dump you. The boards creaked and ached as if in pain. Little bits of rotten wood came loose and fell into the river below. Down there was a deep spot and the water ran fast, crashed up against some rocks, fell over a little falls, and into wide, deep, churning water.

Now, here we were at night, looking down the length of the bridge, thinking about the Goat Man, the body we'd found, Toby, it being late, and our parents worried.

"We gotta cross, Harry?" Tom asked.

"Yeah," I said. "I'm gonna lead, and you watch where I step. The boards hold me, they're liable to hold you."

The bridge creaked above the roar of the river, swaying ever so slightly on its cables, like a snake sliding through tall grass.

It had been bad enough trying to cross when I could put both hands on the cables, but carrying Toby, and it being night, and Tom with me, and her trying to carry the shotgun... Well, it didn't look promising.

The other choice was to go back the way we had come. Or try another path down where the river went shallow, cross over there, walk back to the road and our house. But the river didn't shallow until a good distance away, and the woods were rough, and it was dark, and Toby was heavy, and there was something out there that had been tracking us. I didn't see any other way but the bridge.

I took a deep breath, got a good hold on Toby, stepped out on the first slat.

When I did, the bridge swung hard to the left, then back even more violently. I had Toby in my arms, so the only thing I could do was bend my legs and try to ride the swing. It took a long time for the bridge to quit swinging. I took the next step even more gingerly. It didn't swing as much this time. I had gotten a kind of rhythm to my stepping.

I called back to Tom. "You got to step in the middle of them slats. That way it don't swing so much."

"I'm scared, Harry."

"It's all right," I said. "We'll do fine."

I stepped on a slat, and it cracked and I pulled my foot back. Part of the board had broken loose and was falling into the river below. It hit with a splash, flickered in the moonlight, whirled in the brown water, went over the little falls, and was gone.

I stood there feeling as if the bottom of my belly had fallen out. I hugged Toby tight, took a wide step over the missing slat toward the next one. I made it, but the bridge shook and I heard Tom scream.

I glanced over my shoulder as she dropped the shotgun and grabbed at the cable. The shotgun fell a long ways and hung between the two lower cables. The bridge swung violently, threw me against one of the cables, then to the other side. I thought I was a goner for sure.

When the bridge slowed, I lowered to one knee on the slat, pivoted, and looked at Tom. "Easy," I said.

"I'm too scared to let go," Tom said.

"You got to, and you got to get the gun."

It was a long time before Tom finally bent over and picked up the gun. After a bit of heavy breathing, we started on again. That was when we heard the noise down below and saw the thing.

It was moving along the bank on the opposite side, down near the water, under the bridge. You couldn't see it good, because it was outside of the moonlight, in the shadows. Its head was huge and there was something like horns on it and the rest of it was dark as a coal bin. It leaned a little forward, as if trying to get a good look at us, and I could see the whites of its eyes and chalky teeth shining in the moonlight. It made a high keening noise, like a huge wood rat being slowly crushed to death. It made the noise twice and went silent.

"Jesus, Harry," Tom said. "It's the Goat Man. What do we do?"

I thought about going back. That way we'd be across the river from it, but then again, we'd have all that woods to travel through, and for miles. And if it crossed over somewhere, we'd have it tracking us again, because I felt certain that's what had been following us in the brambles.

If we went on across, we'd be above it, on

the higher bank, and it wouldn't be that far to the Preacher's Road. The Goat Man didn't go as far as the road. That was his quitting place. He was trapped here in the woods and along the banks of the Sabine.

"We got to go on," I said. I took one more look at those white eyes and teeth, and started pushing on across. The bridge swung, but I had more motivation now. I was moving pretty good, and so was Tom.

When we were near to the other side, I looked down, but I couldn't see the Goat Man anymore. I didn't know if it was the angle or if it had gone on. I kept thinking when I got to the other side he would be there, waiting.

But when we got to the other side there was only the trail that split the deep woods. It stood out in the moonlight and there was no one or nothing on it.

We started down the trail. Toby was heavy and I was trying not to jar him too much, but I was so frightened I wasn't doing that good a job. He whimpered some.

After we'd gone on a good distance, the trail turned into shadow where the limbs from trees reached out and hid it from the moonlight and seemed to hold the ground in a kind of dark hug.

"I reckon if it's gonna jump us," I said, "that'd be the place."

"Then let's don't go there."

"You want to go back across the bridge?"

"I don't think so."

"Then we got to go on. We don't know if he might have followed."

"Did you see those horns on his head?"

"I seen somethin'. I think what we oughta do, least till we get through that bend in the trail there, is swap. You carry Toby and let me carry the shotgun."

"I like the shotgun."

"Yeah, but I can shoot it without it knocking me down. And I got the shells."

Tom considered this. "Okay," she said.

She put the shotgun on the ground and I gave her Toby. I picked up the gun and we started around the dark curve in the trail.

When we were in deep shadow nothing leaped out on us, but as we neared the moonlit part of the trail we heard movement in the woods. The same sort of movement we had heard back in the brambles. Something was pacing us again.

We reached the moonlit part of the trail and felt better. But there really wasn't any reason for it. It was just a way of feeling. Moonlight didn't change anything. I looked over my shoulder, into the darkness we had just left, and in the middle of the trail, covered in shadow, I could see it.

Standing there.

Watching.

I didn't say anything to Tom about it. Instead I said, "You take the shotgun now, and I'll take Toby. Then I want you to run with everything you got to where the road is."

Tom, not being any dummy, and my eyes

probably giving me away, turned and looked back in the shadows. She saw it too. It crossed into the woods. She turned, gave me Toby, took the shotgun, and took off like a scalded-ass ape.

I ran after her, bouncing poor Toby, the stringed squirrels slapping against my legs. Toby whined and whimpered and yelped. The trail widened, the moonlight grew brighter. The red-clay road came up. We leaped onto it, looked back.

Shadows and moonlight. Trees and the trail.

Nothing was after us. We didn't hear anything moving in the woods.

"It okay now?" Tom asked.

"Guess so. They say he can't come as far as the road."

"What if he can?"

"Well, he can't...I don't think."

"You think he killed that woman?"

"Figure he did."

"How'd she get to lookin' like that."

"Somethin' dead swells up like that. You know that."

"How'd she get all cut? On his horns?"

"I don't know, Tom."

We went on down the road, and in time, after a number of rest stops, after helping Toby go to the bathroom by holding up his tail and legs, in the deepest part of the night, we reached home.

It wasn't an altogether happy homecoming. The sky had grown cloudy and the moon was no longer bright. You could hear the cicadas chirping and frogs bleating off somewhere in the bottoms. When we entered into the yard carrying Toby, Daddy spoke from the shadows, and an owl, startled, flew up and was temporarily outlined against the faintly brighter sky.

"I ought to whup y'all's butts," Daddy said.

"Yes sir," I said.

Daddy was sitting in a chair under an oak in the yard. It was sort of our gathering tree, where we sat and talked and shelled peas in the summer. He was smoking a pipe, a habit that would kill him later in life. I could see its glow as he puffed flames from a match into the tobacco. The smell from the pipe was woody and sour to me.

We went over and stood beneath the oak, near his chair.

"Your mother's been worried sick," he said. "Harry, you know better than to stay out like that, and with your sister. You're supposed to take care of her."

"Yes sir."

"I see you still have Toby."

"Yes sir. I think he's doing better."

"You don't do better with a broken back."

"He treed six squirrels," I said. I took my pocketknife out and cut the string around my waist and presented him with the squirrels. He looked at them in the darkness, laid them beside his chair.

"You have an excuse," he said.

"Yes sir," I said.

"All right, then," he said. "Tom, you go up to the house, get the tub and start filling it with water. It's warm enough you won't need to heat it. Not tonight. You get after them bugs with the kerosene and such, then bathe and hit the bed."

"Yes sir," she said. "But Daddy..."

"Go to the house, Tom," Daddy said.

Tom looked at me, laid the shotgun on the ground, and went on toward the house.

Daddy puffed his pipe. "You said you had an excuse."

"Yes sir. I got to runnin' squirrels, but there's something else. There's a body down by the river."

He leaned forward in his chair. "What?"

I told him everything that had happened. About being followed, the brambles, the body, the Goat Man. When I was finished, he sat silent for a time, then said, "There isn't any Goat Man, Harry. But the person you saw, it's possible he was the killer. You being out like that, it could have been you or Tom that he got."

31

"Yes sir."

"Suppose I'll have to take a look early morning. You think you can find her again?"

"Yes sir, but I don't want to."

"I know, but I'm gonna need your help."

Daddy took his pipe and knocked out the ash on the bottom of his shoe and put the pipe in his pocket. "You go up to the house now, and when Tom gets through, you get the bugs off of you and wash up. I know you're covered. Hand me the shotgun and I'll take care of Toby."

I started to say something, but I didn't know what to say. Daddy got up, cradled Toby in his arms, and I put the shotgun in his hand.

"Damn rotten thing to happen to a good dog," he said.

Daddy started walking off toward the little barn we had out back of the house by the field.

"Daddy," I said. "I couldn't do it. Not Toby."

"That's all right, son," he said, and went on out to the barn.

When I got up to the house, Tom was on the back screened porch, what we called a sleeping porch. It wasn't real big, but it was comfortable in the summer. There was a swinging seat held by chains to the beams, and there were two pallet beds and a tin tub that hung on the wall till it was needed.

Like right then. Tom was in the tin tub and Mama was scrubbing her hard and fast by the light of a lantern hanging on a porch beam directly above them.

When I came up, Mama, who was in an old green dress, barefoot, her sleeves rolled up, was on her knees. As I came through the screen from the outside, she looked over her shoulder at me. Her raven black hair was gathered up in a fat bun and a tendril of it had come loose and was hanging across her forehead and eye. She pushed it aside with a soapy hand, looked at me.

I didn't understand it then, her being my mother and all, but any time I looked at her I found myself staring. There was something about her that made you want to keep your eyes on her face. I had just begun to have a hint of what it was. Mother was pretty. Years later I was to learn that many thought her the most beautiful woman in the county, and looking back on the handful of photos I have of her then, and even into her sixties, I would have to say that such an evaluation was most likely true.

"You ought to know better than to stay out this late. And scaring Tom with stories about seeing a body."

"I wasn't all that scared," Tom said.

"Hush, Tom," Mama said.

"I wasn't."

"I said hush."

"It ain't a story, Mama," I said.

I told her about it, making it brief.

When I finished, she asked, "Where's your Daddy?"

"He took Toby out to the barn. Toby's back is broken."

"I heard. I'm real sorry."

I listened for the blast of the shotgun, but after fifteen minutes it still hadn't come. Then I heard Daddy coming down from the barn, and pretty soon he stepped out of the shadows, onto the porch and into the lantern light. He was carrying the shotgun, smoking his pipe.

"I don't figure he needs killin'," Daddy said. I felt my heart lighten, and I looked at Tom, who was peeking under Mama's arm as Mama scrubbed her head with lye soap. "He could move his back legs a little, lift his tail. You might be right, Harry. He might be better. Besides, I wasn't any better doin' what ought to be done than you, son. He takes a turn for the worse, stays the same, well... In the meantime, he's yours and Tom's responsibility. Feed and water him, and you'll need to manage him to do his business somehow."

"Yes sir," I said. "Thanks, Daddy."

"I fixed him up a place in the barn."

Daddy sat down on the porch swing with the shotgun cradled in his lap. "You say the woman was colored?"

"Yes sir."

Daddy sighed. "That's gonna make it some difficult," he said.

———◆———

Next morning just as it grew light, I led Daddy to the Swinging Bridge. I didn't want to cross the bridge again. I pointed out from the bank the spot across and down the river where the body could be found.

"All right," Daddy said. "I'll manage from here. You go home. Better yet, get into town and open up the barbershop. Cecil will be wondering where I am."

I went home by the slightly long way, not frightened of the Goat Man during the day, feeling, in fact, somewhat brave. Hadn't I encountered him and lived?

I went by Old Mose's shack, but I didn't stop in to visit. He was sitting on the bank of the river in his dry-docked boat wearing a straw hat that was starting to unravel. He was whittling a stick. I called out, "Mr. Mose." He turned his face toward me and waved.

I had no idea how old Mose was, but I knew he was ancient. His red-black skin was wrinkled like a raisin and most of his teeth were gone. His eyes were red-streaked from strain and cigarette smoke. He was always smoking cigarettes, mostly the kind he made from rolling paper and corn silk. They burned up fast and another had to be rolled almost as fast as the first was lit. Mose used to take me fishing, and Daddy said that when he was a boy Mose had taught him to fish.

I went along the bank of the river, stopping long enough to poke a dead possum with a stick so as to stir the ants on it, then I hurried on to our place.

I went out to the barn to check on Toby. He was crawling around on his belly, wiggling his back legs some. I gave him a pat, carried him to the house, and left Tom with the duty to look after him being fed and watered, then I got the barbershop key, saddled up Sally Redback, and rode her the five miles into town.

Marvel Creek wasn't much of a town really, not that it's anything now, but back then it was mostly two streets. Main and West. West had a row of houses. Main had the general store, courthouse, post office, doctor's office, the barbershop my Daddy owned, a drugstore with a nice soda fountain, a newspaper office, and that was about it. There were potholes on Main Street, and there was limited electricity in the courthouse, doctor's office, drugstore, and general store.

Another staple of Marvel Creek was a band of roving hogs that belonged to Old Man Crittendon.

The hogs were tolerated most of the time, but once a big one got after Mrs. Owens and chased her down West all the way into her house. Being how she was a little on the fat side, the general talk of the men around town— who didn't care much for Mrs. Owens because she was a Yankee and apt to remind folks constantly that the North won the war—named this momentous event the Race of Two Hogs.

Anyway, Mrs. Owens's husband, Jason, who wore a beard and dressed in stiff clothes, shot the hog on his front porch with a shotgun, but not before he blew off the porch steps, knocked down a support post, and dropped the roof on the hog and himself. The hog recovered, Mr. Owens didn't.

Mr. Owens was missed, and Old Man Crittendon missed his hog, but Mrs. Owens, who moved back up North with the rest of the Yankees, was not. Mr. Crittendon made a special effort to keep the hogs home for a week or two, but soon they were loose again, roaming about, getting yelled at and chased off by rock-tossing pedestrians. The hogs accepted this, and had perfected a kind of sideways jump upon hearing anything that might be a missile whizzing in their direction.

Our barbershop was a little one-room white building built under a couple of oaks. It was big enough for one real barber chair, and a regular chair with a cushion on the seat and a cushion fastened to the back. Daddy cut hair out of the barber chair, and Cecil used the other.

During the summer the door was open, and there was just a screen door between you and the flies. The flies liked to gather on the screen, which was the only barrier between you and them. Daddy preferred the main door open. The reason for this was simple. It was hot and the wind came through and cooled you some. Though that time of year the wind was often hot. It's the kind of weather where you learn to move as little as possible, seek shade, and stay low to the ground.

Cecil was sitting on the steps reading the weekly newspaper when I arrived. There wasn't any set time for opening the barbershop, but usually Daddy opened it around nine. It was most likely later than that when I showed up.

Cecil looked up, said, "Where's your Daddy?"

I tied Sally to one of the oaks, went over to unlock the door, and as I did, I gave Cecil a bit of a rundown, letting him know what Daddy was doing.

Cecil listened, shook his head, made a clucking noise with his tongue, then we were inside.

I loved the aroma of the shop. It smelled of alcohol, disinfectants, and hair oils. The bottles were in a row on a shelf behind the barber chair, and the liquid in them was in different colors. Red and yellow and a blue one that smelled faintly of coconut. When the sunlight shone through and hit the bottles, it lit them up like the jewels from King Solomon's mines.

There was a long bench along the wall near the door and a table with a stack of magazines with bright covers. Most of the magazines were detective stories. I read them whenever I got a chance, and sometimes Daddy brought the worn ones home.

When there weren't any customers, Cecil read them too, sitting on the bench with a hand-rolled cigarette in his mouth, looking like one of the characters out of the magazines. Hard-boiled, careless, fearless.

Cecil was a big man, and from what I heard around town and indirectly from Daddy, ladies found him good-looking. He had a well-tended shock of reddish hair, bright eyes, and a nice face with slightly hooded eyes. He had come to Marvel Creek not too long ago, a barber looking for work. Daddy, realizing he might have competition, put him in the extra chair and gave him a percentage.

Daddy had since halfway regretted it. It wasn't that Cecil wasn't a good worker, nor was it Daddy didn't like him. It was the fact Cecil was too good. Daddy had learned his barbering by hit or miss, but Cecil had actually had training and had some kind of certificate that said so. Daddy let him pin it to the wall next to the mirror.

Cecil could really cut hair, and pretty soon, more and more of Daddy's customers were waiting for Cecil to take their turn. More mothers came with their sons and waited while Cecil cut their boy's hair and chatted with them as he pinched their kid's cheeks and made them laugh. Cecil was like that. He could chum up to anyone in a big-city minute. Especially women.

As for the men, he loved to talk to them about fishing. He'd strap his rowboat on top of his car and drive off to the river every chance he got. He enjoyed dropping off work for a couple days to camp. He always brought back a lot of fish and sometimes squirrels, which he loved to give away. He always gave the biggest ones to us.

Though Daddy never admitted it, I could see it got his goat, way Cecil was so popular. There was also the fact that when Mama came to the shop she wilted under Cecil's gaze, turned red. She laughed when he said things that weren't that funny.

Cecil had cut my hair a few times, when Daddy was busy, and the truth was, it was an experience. Cecil loved to talk, and he told great stories about places he'd been. All over the United States, all over the world. He had fought in World War One, seen some of the dirtiest fighting. Beyond admitting that, he didn't say much about it. It seemed to pain him.

If Cecil was fairly quiet on the war, on everything else he was a regular blabber-mouth. He kidded me about girls, and sometimes the kidding was a little too far to one side for Daddy, and he'd flash a look at Cecil. I could see them in the mirror behind the reading bench, the one designed for the customer to look in while the barber snipped away. Cecil would take the look, wink at Daddy, and change the subject. But Cecil always seemed to come back around to it, taking a real interest in any girlfriend I might have, even if I didn't really have any. Doing that, he made me feel as if I were growing up, taking part in the rituals and thoughts of men.

Tom liked him too, and in fact had a girlish crush on him, and sometimes she came down to the barbershop just to hang around him, and if he was in the mood he'd flatter her a bit and now and then give her a nickel. Which was good. It meant I'd probably get one too.

What was most amazing about Cecil was the way he could cut hair. His scissors were like a part of his hand. They flashed and turned and snipped with little more than a flex of his wrist. When I was in his chair, pruned hair haloed around me in the sunlight and my head became a piece of sculpture, transformed from a mass of unruly locks to a work of art. Cecil never missed a beat, never poked you with the scissor tips—which Daddy couldn't say. When Cecil rubbed spiced oil into your scalp, parted and combed your hair, spun you around to look in the closer mirror behind the chairs, you weren't the same guy anymore. I thought I looked older, more manly, when he was finished.

When Daddy did the job, parted my hair, put on the oil, and let me out of the chair (he never spun me for a look like he did his adult customers), I was still just a kid. With a haircut.

Since on this day I'm talking about, Daddy was out, I asked Cecil if he would cut my hair, and he did, finishing with hand-whipped shaving cream and a razor around my ears to get those bits of hair too contrary for scissors. Cecil used his hands to work oil into my scalp, and he massaged the back of my neck with his thumb and fingers. It felt warm and tingly in the heat and made me sleepy.

No sooner had I climbed down from the chair than Old Man Nation drove up in his mule-drawn wagon and he and his two grown boys came in. Mr. Ethan Nation was a big man in overalls with tufts of hair in his ears and crawling out of his nose. His boys were red-headed, jug-eared versions of him. They all chewed tobacco, probably since birth, and their teeth that weren't green from lack of cleaning were brown with chaw. They carried cans with them and spat in them between words. Most of their conversation being tied to or worked around cuss words not often spoken in polite company in that day and time.

They never came in to get a haircut. They cut their own hair with a bowl and scissors, and it looked like it. They sat in the waiting chairs and read what words they could out of the magazines before their lips got tired, or they complained about how bad times were.

Daddy said they had bad times mostly because they were so lazy they wouldn't scratch bird mess out of a chair before they sat in it. Customers came in for a haircut, they wouldn't move and give them the chairs, even though they didn't have any interest in a trim. They had, as Daddy said, the manners of a billy goat. I once heard him say to Cecil, when he thought I was out of earshot, that if you took the Nation family's brains and wadded them up together and stuck them up a gnat's butt and shook the gnat, it'd sound like a ball bearing in a boxcar.

Cecil, though no friend of the Nations, always managed to be polite, and, as Daddy often said, he was a man liked to talk, even if he was talking to the devil about how much fire was going to be set between his toes.

No sooner had Old Man Nation taken a seat than Cecil said, "Harry says there's been a murder."

I wondered what Daddy would think of my big mouth. Daddy was a man liked to talk himself, but it was usually about something. When it wasn't any of your business, you didn't hear it from him.

Once the word was out, there was nothing for me to do but tell it all. Well, almost all. For some reason I left the Goat Man out of it. I hadn't even told Cecil that part.

When I was finished, Mr. Nation was quiet for a moment, then he said, "Well, one less nigger wench ain't gonna hurt the world none." Then to me: "Your Pa's lookin' in on this?"

"Yes sir," I said.

"Well, he's probably upset about it. He was always one to worry about the niggers. He ought to leave it alone, let them niggers keep on killin' each other, then the rest of us won't have 'em to worry with it."

I had never really thought about my father's personal beliefs, but suddenly it occurred to me his were opposite of those of Mr. Nation, and Mr. Nation, though he liked our barbershop for wasting time, didn't really like my Daddy. The fact he didn't, that Daddy had an opposite point of view to his, made me feel good, and at that moment, measuring the contrast between the two, I think my views and my Daddy's, at least on the race issue, became forever welded.

In time, Doc Taylor came in. He wasn't the main doctor in Marvel Creek, he was working with Doc Stephenson, a grumpy old man that had tended to me and my family a few times. Stephenson, with his sour puss and white

43

hair, reminded me of how I thought Scrooge in that story about the Christmas ghosts should look.

Doc Taylor was a tall, blond man with a quick smile. The ladies liked him even better than Cecil. He always had a good word for everyone, and was fond of children. He always treated Tom like a princess. Once, out at the house, stopping by to check on her when she had a bad cold, he brought her a small bag of candy. I remember it well. She didn't share a one of them with me. Next time I saw Doc Taylor I said something to him about it, and he laughed, said, "Well now. Women, they got their ways. You got to admit that."

He didn't offer to explain that comment in depth or to fix me up with a bag of candy of my own, so I bore him the smallest of resentments.

Around his neck Doc Taylor wore a French coin on a little chain. It had been struck by a bullet and dented. The coin had been in his shirt pocket, and he credited it with saving his life. One night when Mama mentioned it, talking about how lucky Doc Taylor had been, Daddy said, "Yeah, well, I figure he banged it with a hammer and made up that cock-'n'-bull story. It gives him somethin' to tell the ladies."

Anyway, I was glad to see him come in. It took some of the edge out of the air, and he and Cecil went to talking about this and that while Cecil snipped at Doc Taylor's hair.

Reverend Johnson, a Methodist preacher,

came in next, and Mr. Nation, feeling the pressure, packed himself and his two boys in their wagon and went on down the road to annoy someone else. Cecil told Reverend Johnson about the murder, and the Reverend clucked over it and changed the subject.

Late in the day, Daddy arrived. When Cecil asked him about the murder, Daddy looked at me, and I knew I should have kept my mouth shut.

Daddy didn't add any new information however. "I just soon I didn't see nothing like it again, and I sure hate Harry and Tom seen it."

"I seen some stuff in the war, all right," Cecil said. "But it was war, not murder. I was fifteen. Lied about my age, and I was big, so I got away with it. I had to do over, wouldn't have done it."

Cecil, without saying a word, took a comb from the shelf, walked over to me, reparted and arranged my hair.

4

hung around for a while, but Daddy didn't get but one customer, and no one was talking about anything that interested me. There weren't any new magazines I wanted to read, so after I had swept up the cut hair, Daddy gave me a couple pennies and sent me on my way.

I went over to the general store, spent a long time looking at bolts of colored cloth, mule harnesses, and all manner of dry and soft goods, geegaws and the like. It came down to a Dr Pepper out of the ice barrel, or peppermint sticks.

I finally zeroed in on the peppermint sticks. My two cents bought four. The storekeeper, Mr. Groon, bald, pink-faced, and generous, winked, gave me six sticks, wrapped them and put them in a sack. I took them back to the barbershop, left them for picking up later, then, with no hair to sweep, and nothing to do, I went roaming.

From time to time I liked to visit Miss Maggie. That's how she was known to most. Not as Maggie or Auntie, as many elderly colored women were called, but simply Miss Maggie.

Miss Maggie was rumored to be a hundred years old. She worked every day and somehow managed to plow a little crop with a mule named Matt. Matt was as tame a mule as ever drew a plow down a corn row, even more than Sally Redback. Maggie said hardest part to plowing Matt was hitching up the rig. After that, it was Matt done the work. Considering the couple of acres she plowed were deep sand and Miss Maggie had legs about the size of hoe handles, and wasn't overall bigger than a large child, some credit had to go to her.

She was black as midnight, wrinkled like eroded land, and the twisted hair on her head had gone sparse. She dressed in faded cotton shifts made of potato or feed sacks, wore men's socks and cheap black shoes she ordered out of the Sears and Roebuck catalogue. Outside, she wore a big black hat with the brim left flat and the crown of the hat uncreased. Story was the hat had belonged to her husband, who was prone to beat her and had run off with a Tyler woman.

The land she owned had once belonged to Old Man Flyer's father. After the Civil War and the freeing of the slaves, he kept Miss Maggie on at the farm as a servant. Later, for her dedication, he willed her a parcel of land, twenty-five acres in size. She kept five acres of it for a house, a barn, a bit of a farm, and sold the rest to the town of Marvel Creek. It was rumored she kept money from the sell buried in her yard in a fruit jar. A number of would-be robbers had dug spots in her yard, but after a few shotgun blasts over their heads, the investigation stopped, and it came to be said that her money had been all spent up.

Outside her house was Matt's pen. It consisted of a rope tied tight to posts to form a square. Matt had a shed inside the rope and inside the shed there was always plenty of fresh water, grain, corn husks, and the like. Matt worked on the honor system, stayed inside that rope. He had a pretty good deal and knew it.

There was also a hog pen with a little shoat roaming about in ankle-deep stinky mud, nosing an empty number ten tub.

Tied to the house, stretched out with the other end tied to a chinaberry tree (everyone I knew called them chinerberry trees) was a rope clothesline on which hung sheets and what the women I knew called unmentionables, meaning underwear.

Miss Maggie's house was a simple weathered shack with a loose tarpaper roof, a short narrow porch under which a number of chickens and the occasional stray dog liked to rest in the heat of the day. On the porch was a rocking chair made of warped cane. The house leaned slightly to the right. It had one door and a dusty screen. There were yellow oilskin shades she pulled down over her three patched screen windows when sunlight or privacy warranted it, and the glass itself was fly-specked. In the summer all the windows were raised to let air come in through the screens, which were essential to keep out the flies. If you kept stock, especially that close to the house, they were twice as bad.

I went to the screen door and chased away

all the flies that were lit on it. Miss Maggie was at her wood stove, taking biscuits out of the oven. I could smell them through the screen, and they made my mouth water. I called her name, and she turned and greeted me like she always did, her braided hair whiter than when I had seen her last. "Hey, boy. You git in here and sit down."

I shooed the flies again, went inside. I sat at her little table in a slightly tippy chair. She put some biscuits on a battered tin plate and poured me up some sorghum syrup from a can she heated on the stove, told me to eat. I did.

Those biscuits were so soft they melted in the mouth, and the sorghum, which she had most likely traded some corn for, was as good as any ever ground by a mule-operated mill and cooked down sweet by human hands.

As I ate, I looked at a double-barreled shotgun hung over two huge nails driven into the wall, and her black hat hung up next to it. She sat across from me and ate, then said, "I think I'm gonna fry me some salt pork. You want some?"

"Yes'm."

She opened the oven's warmer, took out some salt pork. It was smoked already and could have just been warmed, but she put a little lard in a pan and stoked up the wood in the stove and set to frying it. It wasn't long before it was ready. We ate the pork and more biscuits. She said, "I can tell you're just 'bout to burst, dyin' to tell me somethin'."

"I don't know I'm supposed to," I said.

"Well then you don't need to tell it."

"But I ain't exactly been told not to tell it."

She grinned at me. She had two good teeth in the top of her mouth and four on the bottom, and one of them didn't look so good. Still, they managed to chew biscuits and tear salt pork.

I figured whatever I told Miss Maggie didn't matter. She wasn't gonna get back to Daddy with it, so I told her about finding the colored woman down in the bottoms and about there being something in the woods following me and Tom.

When I finished she shook her head. "That a shame. Ain't no one gonna do nothin' about it. It just another dead nigger."

"Daddy will," I said.

"Well, he only one might, but he probably ain't neither. He just one man. They'll ride him down, boy. Best thing can happen 'bout all this is be gone on and forgot."

"Don't you want them to catch who done it?"

"It ain't gonna be. You can rest on that. My people, they like chaff, boy. They blow away in the breeze and ain't no one cares. Whoever done this have to kill a white person if he gonna get the big law on him."

"That ain't right," I said.

"You better not be sayin' that too loud, or them Kluxers be comin' to see you."

"My Daddy would run them off."

She cackled. "He might at that." She studied

me for a long moment. "You best stay out of them woods, boy. Man do something like that, he ain't got nothin' 'gainst hurtin' chil'ren. You hear me?"

"Why would someone do something like that, Miss Maggie?"

"Ain't no one but Gawd knows reason 'hind that. I think what we got there is a Travelin' Man."

"Travelin' Man?"

"That's what they calls a man like that, does them kind of things to womens. Anyways, what my Daddy called 'em."

"What's a Traveling Man?"

Miss Maggie eased out of her chair, walked over to the cabinet, took out a little green tin and brought it to the table. She opened the tin, removed a pinch of snuff and poked it between cheek and gum.

I knew she was about to tell me a story. The snuff, the comfortable position, it was her way. It was how she had first told me tales about the tar baby and the big snake of the bottoms that was killed in nineteen and ten. It was said to be a water moccasin forty-five feet long, and when it was split open a child was found inside. When I told my Daddy that one, he just snorted.

Outside a cloud moved over the sun and darkened the greasy windows and the light through the screen door. I watched as the flies regrouped on the screen, lighting slowly, clustering together in a dusky wad, as if they too wanted to hear Miss Maggie's story; their accumulation

51

made a shadow on the floor and across the table, like a rain cloud.

Off in the distance I heard a wagon clatter, followed by the sound of a car. It was a hot day and even warmer in the shack because of the stove and the tight space. I felt cozy and almost sleepy.

"Dat ole Travelin' Man, he someone you don't want no truck with, boy. They's folks wants to have anything at any ole price. Wants it so bad, they makes 'em a deal."

"What kind of deal?"

"With the debil."

"Uh uh. No one would do that."

"Would too. They was this colored man named Dandy back in the time the numbers turned to nineteen and ought. It was the year that big ole hur'a'cun blowed Galveston away. I had a sister down there and she was drowned durin' that."

"Really?"

"Uh huh. They gathered up all them bodies and burned 'em, boy. I don't know nothin' other than she had to have drowned, and if her body got found, then she got burned up. That's what they had to do, was so many dead-'ns. Coloreds. Whites. Womens and chil'ren."

This was interesting, but I didn't want her to stray too far away from her story about the Travelin' Man and Dandy. I said, "What about Dandy?"

"Dandy," she said. "Well, he loved to play a fiddle, but he weren't no good at it. He couldn't make that fiddle talk. He wanted to

52

be like them could, but 'ceptin' for a tune or two he could play to kinfolks, and them puttin' up with it, he weren't no good at all. So you know what he done, Little Man?"

"No ma'am."

"He got him some whiskey, and he drank him a little of it, then made water in it. You know, pee-peed in it."

"In the whiskey?"

"That's what I done said. Just let it go in that bottle till it fill on back up. Put back what he drunk, guess you could say. He put the cap on it and shook it up. You know why he done that?"

"No."

"'Cause they says that's the way the Old Man likes it. He think a man's water spices it up."

"The Old Man?"

"Old Man got other names. Satan. Beezle-bubba. The debil. Thing is, you don't know you call him up you really talkin' to him or one of dem soldiers he got, but that don't matter none. Dandy, you see, was tryin' to become a Travelin' Man."

Miss Maggie paused to spit. She had a big cracked cup she kept for the purpose, and now she reached it off the little shelf by the stove behind her and spat snuff juice into it. She wiped her mouth with the back of her hand, said, "You gonna do this right, thing Dandy wanted to do, you got to gets down in them bottoms where it's the thickest, and there's a crossroads."

"There's crossroads everywhere, Miss Maggie."

"Uh huh. But the best place to meet the debil or one of his soldiers is down in the deepest part of them bottoms, on a walkin' trail that crosses. And you got to be there right when it's gonna turn both hands up."

"Both hands up?"

"Hands on the clock, boy. Twelve midnight. You got to have you a good pocket watch keeps the right time. 'Cause you got to be on time. You got to be standin' right there in the center where the crossroads cross, and you got to be havin' you that peed-in whiskey with you."

"That what Dandy did?"

"They say he did. Say he went down in them bottoms with his peed-in whiskey and his fiddle and bow, stood at them crossroads, and sure 'nuff, right when he's checkin' the face of his turnip watch with a match, there's a tap on his shoulder.

"Now he jerks 'round fast, and there's the debil. He got a big ole pumpkin head and wear him a little black suit with shiny black shoes, and got a big ole smile, and he says to Dandy, noddin' at that whiskey bottle, ''At for me?' And Dandy, he says, 'Yeah it is, if'n youse the debil.' And this pumpkin head, he say, 'I'm what you might call his lead man, Bubba.'"

"Bubba?"

Miss Maggie paused to spit in her cup again. "Uh huh. Bubba. I always figured Bubba was probably Beezlebubba. You gets it. BeezleBUBBA."

"Oh, yes ma'am... Who's Beezlebubba?"

"It's just another name for the debil, Little Man. Like Scratch. It's probably a Northern name or somethin'. But this here fella, whether he's really the debil or the debil's man, I can't tell you. But whoever he was, he got the power to make the deal. So he takes that peed-in whiskey and drinks him a big jolt, and he say to Dandy, 'What is it you want?' and Dandy, he say, 'I want I can play this here fiddle better'n anyone they is.' And Bubba tell him, that's fine, he can do that, but Dandy gonna have to write his mark on a line."

"His mark?"

"Them can't write they name, they use they mark."

"Oh."

"So Bubba pulls out of his coat this big long paper, which is what them lawyers, who is a lot like the debil, calls a contact."

"Contact?"

"Yes suh, Little Man. A contact."

"Oh, a contract."

"All righty then, then it's that. But don't be correctin' me now. Ain't polite."

"Yes, ma'am."

"Then Bubba, he jerks the fiddle bow out of Dandy's hand, and it cuts him on the tip of one of his fangers. Then he has Dandy make his mark on the line with the blood on his fanger, and he says, 'Now here's your fiddle bow back. You done give me your soul for what I done give to you.'

"That's good with Dandy, and he goes to

play right there, and danged if that ain't a different bow in his hand than the one jerked from him, and a different fiddle. I mean it's the same, but it ain't. You follow me?"

I didn't entirely, but I said I did.

"So Dandy, he gets to playin' right there, and it's the most beautifullest sound you ever done heard. And when he looks up from hittin' a few notes, Bubba and that blood-marked contact...contract, is done gone.

"Now Dandy a happy man. He got the best fiddle playin' 'round. And the womens love him. He goes to dances, and them womens all around. He gets give free drinks and lots of folks tell him how good he is. It's the life for Dandy. Then he goes to this barn dance over'n Big Sandy, and he's playin' and people are dancin', and when he pauses to get him some rest, this stutterin' fella with a fiddle comes up and asks can he play and sang a bit. A song or two, you see.

"Dandy sees a chance to look even better. He lets this fella play. Figures that man ain't gonna match what the debil's done done for him, and if he sangs some, all that stutterin', he's bound to sound like a chicken workin' on a ear of corn. It gonna make Dandy look even better, see."

"Yes ma'am."

"So now, Dandy, he 'sides to really polish the apple, so he brings up this here fella and says how he's a man wants to play a song or two, sang a little. And he says how he ain't never heard him, but always wants to give a fella a

56

chance. So this nervous fella, who turns out is from a little ole town called Gilmer, gets up there, hits on his strangs with the bow, then cuts into it. And you know what, Little Man?"

"No ma'am."

"He good. He can play that fiddle like he part of it. And sang. He sang real purty, 'cause when he sangs, he don't stutter. So all them folks is dancin' and start'n to happy hoot and holler, and after one tune, this here fella, who I heard was named Ormond, he plays him 'nuther, then a 'nuther, and it's like one of the angels got hold of that fiddle bow, and pretty soon, ole Dandy, he done forgot. Ain't nobody missin' him."

"Bet that made him mad."

"Oooowweeeeee. All of a sudden, right in the middle of a breakdown, Dandy jump up with his fiddle and crack that Ormond fella right upside the head and knock him down. Then he go to beatin' on him. And he beat him till he done broke that fiddle all apart, and then he start to choke Ormond, and pretty soon, Ormond, he's dead.

"Well, now. People are starin' at Dandy, and he got death on his hands, and no fiddle. Busted it all to pieces. So he snatch up Ormond's fiddle and bow an run off through the back door 'fore folks can figure on what to do. Then they after 'em. But it's too late. He know them bottoms like the back of his hand, and he gone. He done become a Travelin' Man.

"Since it was a colored killin' a colored, white

law didn't go after him none, and all the colored 'round here wasn't in no place to do nothin', so Dandy, he get off on the other side of the bottoms, and he start at it."

"At what?"

"Travelin'. He kind of like a bum, you see. He go from house to house, tryin' to beg him a little somethin' to eat and such, and people hear about this fella travelin' around with a fiddle, playin' a tune or two for his dinner, but he ain't no good on the fiddle. No good at all. So folks that hear this, they don't figure on it being Dandy, 'cause Dandy, he can play good as a pig can eat. But it's Dandy."

"How come he can't play?"

"Comin' to that. You jumpin' ahead."

"Sorry, Miss Maggie."

"Where this Travelin' Man and his fiddle go, they's womens start turnin' up dead. You see, he got a bitter thing in him now. He always did want the womens to like him, but now he ain't got that goin' for him 'cause he ain't got no fiddlin' to draw them in, and it's boilin' him inside. Or, that's how I figure on it. Ain't no one really knows. But this is certain, for three years he wandered all over East Texas killin' colored womens and girls, and to the white law it don't mean a thing.

"But he finally gets him a little white girl, mistreats and kills her. Kluxers get on his tail, 'cause it ain't just about niggers killin' niggers anymore, you see. And he gettin' bolder and bolder, and he kills a white woman over near them honky-tonks in Gladewater, and the

Klan run him down and cut him where a man don't want to be cut, tar and feather him, hang 'im and light him on fire. And that's the end of Dandy on this here earth, and it one of the few times the Klan do us all a favor."

I thought about that for a while. I said, "But why couldn't he play the fiddle no more? If the devil gave him the power, wouldn't he be able to play?"

"I done some thinkin' on that. What I figure is that ole pumpkin head give him that fiddle and say you can play good on this here fiddle, that's exactly what he meant. That fiddle. When he smashed it up, and took a dead man's fiddle, a man learned to play it by hard work and not no pee in a bottle and a trip to the crossroads, he couldn't play no mo'. You see?"

I did. But I still had questions. "If you didn't see the devil, or the devil's man, how do you know he had a pumpkin head?"

"I knowed how he looked 'cause there's folks I know, includin' cousins, seen the debil and know what he and all his men look like. They can look different ways too. Might not have a head like a pumpkin all the time. Might have horns. Might look like a banker or one of them polatickans, but I'm just figure'n on how he might have looked that night. I'm colorin' the story some, but that don't mean it ain't true."

"And this woman me and Tom found, you think it's someone sold his soul to the devil done that to her? A Travelin' Man?"

"If'n you ain't sold your soul to the debil you wouldn't do such a thing, Little Man. It could be the debil himself. Sometime he like to do his own work."

"What about the Goat Man?"

"Little Man, I think the Goat Man might be the debil. I said he can look anyway he wants, and ain't them goat horns and hoofs jes like the debil? If'n I was the debil, them bottoms is where I'd be a runnin' 'cause they dark and wet and got all manner of thing in 'em. Let me gives you a word of smarts. You stay away from anything to do with what the debil likes, 'cause you get in with him he'll trick on you. You hear?"

"Yes ma'am."

"Now you need to run on. I got me some washboard'n to do."

"Yes ma'am. Thanks for the food."

"You welcome. Now you draw some water out of the well and water that ole hog of mine. And you come back and see me."

I went out, letting the screen door loose, not so that it would slam, but enough it would jar the flies that were on it.

I went out to the well, dropped the bucket and cranked it up, poured from it into the totin' bucket. I made several trips with the bucket to fill the hog's tub with water.

As I went away I remembered another time Miss Maggie told me about how flies are the devil's eyes and ears, and that got me to thinking.

When I turned my head to look back at her

house, the flies had already filled the screen again, and a big fat one was buzzing around my sweaty head.

I swatted at it, but it got away.

5

That night, back at the house, lying in bed, my ear against the wall, Tom asleep across the way in her own little bed made of crude lumber and nailed tight together by Daddy, I listened. The walls were thin. When it was good and quiet, and Mama and Daddy were talking, I could hear them.

"Doc Stephenson, the old pill roller, wouldn't even look at her," Daddy said. "Said if folks found out he'd had a colored in his office wouldn't nobody use him no more."

"That's terrible. What about Doc Taylor?"

"Well, I figure he's at least had some actual medical school. I guess they got medical schools in Arkansas or Oklahoma, wherever it is he's from."

"Missouri," Mama said.

"Anyway, he'd have come looked at her. He wanted to real bad, like it was some kind of

61

adventure, you know. But I didn't want to take the chance on him gettin' in trouble with Stephenson to do me a favor. Might go bad for him in the long run, mess up his doctorin' career. He's set up to take over Stephenson's practice when he retires in a year or so, he seems like a nice enough fella. I drove the body over to Pearl Creek to see a doctor there."

Pearl Creek was an all-colored town.

"She was in our car? I mean, didn't it foul the car?"

"It didn't hurt anything. After Harry showed me where she was, I came back, drove over to Billy Gold's house. He and his brother went down there with me, helped me wrap her in a tarp, carry her out, and put her in the car. We wrapped her up good. No leakage. I drove her over to Pearl Creek and they packed her in ice in the icehouse."

"I wouldn't be wanting any of that ice."

"Body was in pretty bad shape to begin with. Some pieces come off her. We had to throw the tarp away."

"And she was in our car? Dear me."

"I blew the odor out driving it home."

"Oh, my goodness."

"Doc Tinn, the colored doctor, he was out of town. Won't be back till tomorrow. He was out country deliver'n a baby. I'm gonna drive over there in the morning, see if I can learn somethin'. I don't know nothin' about this kind of murder."

"You're sure it's murder?"

"Well, honey, think about it. I don't suppose she cut herself up like that and ended up tied to a tree with wire."

"You're awful impatient, Jacob... Wire? She was tied with wire?"

"She was bound with a couple strands of barbed wire and a bunch of vines. Someone sure had enjoyed that wire part. They'd taken a piece of wood and fastened it to the wire and used it as a kind of crank so they could wrap it around the tree, loop it, and tighten it by twistin' that wood like a handle. Then I 'spect he messed with her."

"Surely not."

"I don't know much about these things, but I know she didn't fix herself to that tree. And as for people doin' these kind of things, well, two things come to mind. I had a fella tell me once about this Jack the Ripper guy in London. He cut women's bodies up. For fun. He cut pieces out of them. He messed with their womanly parts."

"That's got to be just some kind of story."

"That's history. They never caught him. He killed they don't know how many, but they never caught him or had no idea who it was. Then Cecil, at the shop, and bear in mind he'd rather hear himself talk about most anything than to let a room go quiet, told me when he was in the war in France, there was a fella that at night would roam the battlefield looking for someone alive, you know, hangin' on from wounds. Germans. And he'd do things with the bodies. Like a man would with a woman. Only in a different place."

"A different place."

"You know. There."

"You can do that?"

"If you're determined," Daddy said. "This fella, they could see him from the trenches. Had on an American uniform, and he was doin' these things to the bodies."

"They didn't stop him?"

"Wasn't no one crazy as he was. They wouldn't get out there on the battlefield, and they weren't gonna shoot their own. It was war. And way they was thinking then was at least he was doin' it to Germans. Cecil said you got so you thought different. War does that. He figured it was just punishment for the enemy. They could see this fella at night, one that was doin' it, and he'd wander among the dead an dyin' lookin' for someone to mess with, and Cecil said they didn't always have to be alive."

"He's lyin', Jacob. Got to be."

"Cecil said this fella would do this kind of thing, then disappear back into the trenches. They all had their suspicions who it was, but no one knowed for sure. They just saw his uniform, never got a good look at his face. Or if anyone did, they didn't come forward. Cecil said he saw him once, but he was just roamin' out there, like a ghost. Not doin' anything strange. Just lookin' over the bodies. He was surprised the Germans weren't shooting at him. Cecil said he never met anyone had actually seen the man doin' anything. Just seen him roamin'."

"Cecil didn't actually see him do nothin' then?"

"No. He just heard the rumors."

"So it could have been a made-up story? A lie told to Cecil and he told it to you."

"Could be Cecil lyin' right out. But say it ain't a lie. Think about it. Fella like that gets by with doin' them things in the war, and comes home..."

"But he was doin' it to men."

"Maybe 'cause they were available. Maybe he'd just as soon, or rather, do it to women. I ain't no expert on these matters. Far as I know, there **ain't** no expert on these matters. One thing I come to figure though. Way that woman's body was punctured by that barbed wire, figure the body was already dead when he put the wire to her. She'd been alive, it would have bled out, and those wounds didn't look to have drawn much blood. 'Course, river could have been up and washed it away, but I think she was dead awhile and he come back to play with her. Like an alligator will stuff its kill in a hole in the riverbank, come back when it's ripened some."

"No one would do that."

"When Jack Newman shot his brother-in-law while drunk and there were fifteen witnesses seen him do it, that wasn't so hard to figure. This... I don't know. It don't look like anything I've seen before. I got my ideas, but that's all they are. I'm hoping this Doc Tinn can help me out."

Mama and Daddy went quiet after that,

then a little later on I heard Mama say, "...I ain't exactly in the mood after that little bedtime story you told me. Sorry, hon."

"All right," Daddy said. Then came complete silence. I snuggled under the covers, overcome by something I couldn't quite put a name to. Fear. Excitement. A sense of mystery. They had talked about things I never even suspected could exist or happen.

I decided right then I was gonna be up early in the morning, see if I could get Daddy to let me ride with him over to Pearl Creek. I thought he owed me that. After all, I had found the body.

I lay there, drifting off, then it began to rain, softly at first, then hard. The sound of it helped put me to sleep.

"No. You can't go."

"But Daddy—"

"No ifs, ands, buts, or maybes. You can't go."

It was just daylight. I had hardly slept a wink last night, fearing I'd miss being up in time to talk to Daddy about the trip. But I didn't feel a bit tired. I was boiling with energy and excitement. I hadn't let on I had heard them talking through the wall. I had innocently asked Daddy what his plans were that day, and when he said Pearl Creek, I asked why Pearl Creek, and he told me had to check with the doctor over there about the woman's body I

66

had found. That's when I asked if I could go.

"I wouldn't be any trouble," I said.

"That may be, son. But I don't think you oughta go with me. This is grown-up business."

We were sitting at the table. Daddy was eating a couple of eggs Mama had fried up. He was poking the yellows with a big biscuit. I was having the same with a glass of buttermilk Mama had poured for me. She kept it cool by lowering the capped bottle down in the well and pulling it out when we wanted a taste.

I drank and ate quickly, fearing Tom would wake up, 'cause back then we were all early risers. Once Tom woke up, found out I was trying to go with Daddy, then it would darn sure be spoiled because Tom would want to go, and if Daddy didn't want me to go, he sure wouldn't want her to go. It was easier for him to say no to both of us than yes to one of us when we were both wanting the same thing.

'Course, he had already told me no, but I had learned that no didn't always mean no, right at first anyway. By the time Daddy got to the third no, then I knew it was best I shut up.

Mama was pouring Daddy coffee when she said, "Jacob, he done seen the body. Why not let him ride over with you. He don't have to see the body again."

That wasn't exactly what I had in mind, but if I could get Daddy to let me go, that would at least be a leg up. Who knew what I could work from there.

67

Daddy sighed. He looked at Mama, who smiled. Daddy said, "Well, I don't know. He's got chores."

"There ain't a lot to do this morning. I can do it for him. Me and Tom."

"Tom will love that," Daddy said.

"Just let him ride over. Won't hurt him none to know what you do."

Mama was standing behind Daddy, a hand on his shoulder. She looked at me and gave a slow wink.

Daddy didn't say any more on the matter right then, and neither did Mama, and I had learned when he was at a bar ditch of decision it was best to just wait it out. It meant his mind wasn't stone solid on a matter, but that things were being considered. It could go either way. If it went the way I didn't want, I might beg, plead, or whine, but once his mind was truly made up, I could forget it. There'd be no jumping that bar ditch.

Daddy finished a second cup of coffee, then had Mama pour him a third he could take with him. He looked at me, pursed his lips, said, "You can go. But you got to stay out of the way. You ain't doin' nothing but riding over and ridin' back, so get that in your head."

"Yes sir," I said.

Mama buttered me up a large biscuit, wrapped it in a cloth we used for a cup towel, poured me up another glass of buttermilk, gave them to me to eat on the way. We went out to the Ford, Daddy started it, and we were off.

It was exciting to ride in the car. We didn't

always use it. Saved gas that way, and according to Daddy saved on the engine. Besides, lots of places we wanted to go roads wouldn't take us there. You had to go on foot or by mule or wagon rut. But this day was a special day. 'Cause not only would the road carry us to Pearl Creek, but I was with Daddy and going on a trip of discovery.

The sun was starting to shine bright by the time we rolled out of the yard, and while Daddy drove and tried to drink his coffee, I ate my buttered biscuit, and for the first time began to feel that I had stepped over the line of being a child, and into being a man.

―――――◆―――――

It was a muddy trip, with the wet roads almost bogging us down a few times, but finally we came to Pearl Creek.

Pearl Creek was a real creek, and the name source for the town. The creek was broad in spots and fast running, and the bed of it was rich with white sand and a kind of pearl-colored gravel, hence the name. It was bordered by ancient and magnificent hickory trees and oaks, twisty, droopy willows with wrist-sized roots that worked out of the ground, wound around on the banks, looked like snakes and provided cover for the real thing.

On one side of the creek was the little town that was its namesake. To get there from our side, you had to cross a narrow, wood slat bridge, and when you did, the slats rattled beneath car tires, horse hooves, or wagon wheels like it was breaking apart beneath you.

Pearl Creek was all colored, except for old Pappy Treesome, who did not own but operated the sawmill by method of his sons, and ran the post office drop and the commissary with the aid of his wife.

Pappy had married a Negress and was scorned by the white community, accepted by the colored. In years past the Klan had waited on him as he rode his horse into town and they had taken him out, stripped and whipped him, cut off his hair, tarred and feathered him, shot his horse, run him into town on a rail held between the windows of two cars, and dropped him off in front of the commissary.

Rumor was Pappy had probably not been lynched because he had a relative in the Klan. Whatever the reason, the Klan decided a whipping, tar and feathers were enough. Pappy went back to living with the colored woman and from then on the Klan left him alone.

Pappy had children near as white as he was. It was rumored a daughter had gone up North to pass. The others, though light-skinned, weren't white enough or didn't care to be, and they were boys: James, Jeremiah, and Root. Two named from the Bible, and one, real name William, rumored to be nicknamed for the size of his equipment. He was also addled in the head, and known to expose himself from time to time. There really wasn't any malice in this, and he didn't expose himself with the intent to show anyone. He just liked fondling his own equipment, and he didn't have the brains to know it was against convention. For this reason, Root was kept pretty much to the black community. It was feared he might go about his hobby in front of white folks, and even if he didn't know better, the end result might be a lynching.

Pearl Creek was all about lumber. It was a sawmill community and the sawmill and the commissary were the world for most. The sawmill paid in money, but it mostly paid in tokens that could only be cashed at the commissary. It was a form of indentured servitude.

The land that was Pearl Creek had once been bottom land, and though it had been cleared of timber and built into a serviceable town, it was still soggy and mosquitoes loved the place. My Daddy used to say there were skeeters over there big enough to carry off a man and eat him and wear his shoes.

We didn't pass another car that day, as there weren't that many around in that part of the country then, but we did pass a few men on horseback, a boy walking, and three wagons drawn by mules.

Our car was like a rolling black beetle cooking in the sun, and by the time we crossed that little rickety bridge and arrived at boggy Pearl Creek, our clothes were stuck to us and we were red-faced and water poor.

We stopped in front of the commissary. It was a long tin-roofed building of weathered lumber with sheds out back. We got out and went over to the community water pump. This was the only place you could get running water in town, outside of the creek, and the sawmill ran dust off in that, and no telling what else. There were also a number of outhouses along the edge of the creek, and though there were many who believed long as water moved the mess along it was all right to drink, Daddy was suspicious of such and warned me to not drink out of the creek.

He said, "That ole stuff's got somethin' in it called microbes, Harry. They cling along the bank and on the bottom, in the moss, on rocks and such, and they get in the water and in you, and you get sick. I ain't never seen a microbe. But I don't doubt they're there, smaller even than seed ticks and chiggers."

The idea they could be microscopic was not something I think Daddy could entirely comprehend. He could imagine them small, but **that** small, probably not.

Daddy worked the pump for me. I ducked my head under and rubbed water over my hands and arms. Then Daddy took his turn while I pumped. Finished, he took out a pocket comb, carefully raked water from his short black hair, parted it, and gave me the comb. I made a few licks and gave it back to him and we went inside the commissary.

Daddy said, "Might as well grab a soda pop."

That was exactly what I wanted to hear.

The commissary was the center of Pearl

Creek, like it was in most sawmill towns, especially colored. East Texas was always slow to get a thing everyone else had. It wasn't until the forties that I remember there being electricity outside of towns, and then not all towns. Marvel Creek, as I've said, had some electricity, but that didn't expand or become common throughout the town and country-side until some years later.

The Rural Electrification Administration strung the wires from house to house, except for colored houses. Some coloreds got electricity a year or two behind everyone else, and some never did get it. If East Texas was last on the list to get the things everyone else already had, then the colored of East Texas got whatever it was long after the whites, and then usually an inferior version. Lincoln may have long freed the slaves, but the colored of that time were not far off living as they had lived before the Civil War.

Pappy ran a pretty good store. There was most everything you needed from food items to soda pops to furniture to cloth for clothes and curtains, hardware items, candles, soaps, hair oils, coal oil, and gasoline. I loved going in there to look and smell the smells.

Pappy Treesome was behind the counter drinking a Co'-Cola and eating on a rough-cut slab of bologna when we came in. When he saw Daddy he grinned. Minus teeth and with a mouthful of bologna, it wasn't a pretty picture. I'd seen better-looking mouths with hooks in them.

Daddy had known Pappy all his life, even before he married the Negress. Camilla was her name. She was a big plump woman who did wash work for a white family not far from Pearl Creek. She also did midwifing and once whipped two colored men with her fists on account of they had been picking on Root, talking him into exposing himself. It was said they only wanted to see the amazing instrument after which he was named, but it made no difference, Camilla didn't take kindly to it.

Pappy scared me a little. He was scarecrow lean with a shock of white hair that stood up like porcupine quills. Once in a while he wore store-bought teeth, but they clicked and clacked and slid around when he talked, as if they might have some place to go and were anxious to get there. Therefore, he mostly went toothless.

Another thing was the way he moved. He lunged and jerked about, as if invisible strings were tied to him and he were being pulled at random in two or three directions. Looking back, I suppose he had some kind of neurological or muscle ailment, but at the time he was said to have the jitters.

There were a few cane chairs thrown around a potbelly stove made from an oil drum, and after Daddy bought us Co'-Colas and popped the bottle tops with an opener, we sat there, drank, and relaxed a moment. The stove wasn't lit that time of year, but the log door was open and I could see ashes and bits of paper and peanut hulls customers had tossed inside. The commissary, even without the lit stove, was hot and oppressive with the tin roof gathering in and holding the heat like an oven.

If you didn't move too fast, got down low in your chair, and sucked slowly at your pop, it was almost pleasant.

Pappy came over. I said a polite hello, then tried not to look at him while I drank my Co'-Cola.

"Dey zay ooo god u ded gul in duh eyezouse, cozdabull," Pappy said, flapping his lips all over the place.

"That's right," Daddy said. He amazed me with his ability to understand Pappy Treesome. "It wasn't supposed to be common knowledge, but I guess that's too much to expect."

"Ron ere dis," Pappy said, and went over to wait on a fat colored woman in a dress made of hand-dyed flour sacks wearing a cardboard hat with colorful paper flowers on the crown.

We drank our Co'-Colas, and Daddy walked around a bit, looking at the furniture we couldn't afford, then he asked Pappy if we could buy some gas.

Pappy took us out back to a pump in a shed, unlocked the pump with a key, worked the handle, and filled a large tin tote can. Daddy poured the gas in the car, told me to take the can back to Pappy.

When I came back, Daddy was sitting behind the wheel, woolgathering. I realized then that he had been dragging his heels, looking at this and that in the store, getting gas when we may not have really needed it, just plain old stalling, not wanting to do what it was he was about to do.

Daddy sighed, started up the Ford, drove on around the little mud-rutted square, dotted here and there by buildings on stilts, or piles as they were sometimes called. This was, of course, designed to keep out the water when the creek rose. Mostly the buildings were homes and had gardens or hog pens out beside them, but there was a office that said PEARL CREEK STANDARD on it, and a lawyer shingle and a sign that said DENTIST. There was also a barbershop with a red and white pole out front.

Although the sawmill was full of working men, many of them with no more than three fingers, some missing hands, there were plenty didn't have work, and they were milling about or sitting on porch steps or in chairs. Most were gathered at the colored barbershop, like crows on a fence. They dressed in overalls and straw or felt hats, worn-out work shoes with laughing soles.

Old black women, some in dresses, some in overalls and hats like the men, were also visible. Kids ran about splashing mud, falling and sliding, screaming off toward the creek.

We stopped at a whitewashed house with a well-tended flower bed on one side, a little patch of garden fenced in with chicken wire on the other. In the garden were a dozen or so staked tomatoes, a few stalks of corn, a row of beans, a couple rows of peas, and four big white pattie squash that deserved flouring and frying. Four banty hens and a rooster were scratching about in the dirt near the garden, and a yellow dog, that looked as if it had just completed some kind of race, lay on its side panting from the heat.

As we got out of the car the dog moved its tail a few times, then stopped, lest it wear itself out with enthusiasm. The chickens scattered, and when we were on the porch, they converged again on the spot they had just abandoned, pecking away at nothing I could see, besides dirt.

On a hill barren of trees I could see and hear the sawmill grinding away as the mules worked the saws and the saws gnawed logs into lumber. Sawdust flowed down the hill and into the creek. The dust closest to the mill was butternut-colored, the older stuff, black and sludgy with age; it slid into the creek where it heaped up and was washed slowly away by the water.

Daddy took off his hat, knocked on the door and a moment later it opened. A plump colored lady in a tight-fitting blue dress stood looking out.

"I'm Constable Collins. Your husband is expecting me."

"Yes suh, he is. Come on in."

Inside, the house smelled pleasantly of pinto beans cooking. It was neat with simple furniture, some of it store-bought, most of it handmade from rough lumber and apple crates. There was a shelf of books on the wall. The most books I had ever seen collected together at one time, and perhaps the most I had seen in my life. Some were fiction, but most were books on philosophy and psychology. I didn't know that at the time, but many of the titles stayed with me, and years later I realized what they were.

The wood slat floor looked to have been freshly scrubbed and smelled faintly of oil. There was a painting on the wall. It was of a blue vase of yellow flowers sitting on a table near a window that showed the moon hung in the sky next to a dark cloud.

The house looked a lot nicer than our place. I guessed doctoring, even for a colored doctor, wasn't such a bad way to make a living.

"Jes 'scuse me for a moment so I can see I can find him," the lady said, and went away.

Daddy was looking the place over too, and I saw something move in his throat, a sadness cross over his face, then the lady came back and said: "Doctor Tinn's out back. He's waitin' on you, Constable. This yo boy?"

Daddy said I was.

"Ain't he just the best-lookin' little snapper. How're you, Little Man?"

That was the same thing Miss Maggie called me, Little Man. "Fine, ma'am."

"Oh, and he's got such good manners. Come on back, will y'all?"

She led us through the back door and down some steps. There was a clean white building out back of the house, and we went inside. We stood in a stark white room with a large desk and smelled some kind of pine oil disinfectant. There was a maple wood chair behind it with a suit coat draped over it. There were some wooden file cabinets, another shelf of books, this one half the size of the one in the house, and a row of sturdy chairs. There was a painting similar to the one in the house on the wall. It was of a riverbank, rich with dark soil and shadowed by trees, and between the trees a long thin shadow over the river.

The lady called out, "Doctor Tinn."

A door opened and out came a large colored man, older than Daddy, wiping his hands on a towel. He wore black suit pants, a white shirt, and a black tie. "Mister Constable," he said. But he didn't offer to shake hands. You didn't see that much, a colored man and a white man shaking hands.

Daddy stuck out his hand, and Dr. Tinn, surprised, slung the towel over his shoulder, and they shook.

"I suppose you know why I'm here?" Daddy said.

"I do," Dr. Tinn said.

Standing next to him, I realized just how large Dr. Tinn was. He must have been six four, and very wide-shouldered. He had his hair cut short and had a mustache faint as the edge of a straight razor. You had to really pay attention to see he had it.

"I see y'all met my wife," Dr. Tinn said.

"Well, not formally," Daddy said.

"This here's Mrs. Tinn," Dr. Tinn said.

Mrs. Tinn smiled and went away.

Daddy and Mama called each other by their first names, but it wasn't unusual then for husband and wife to use formal address to one another, at least in front of folks. Still, since it wasn't something I was accustomed to, it seemed odd to me.

"Have you looked at the body?" Daddy asked.

"No. I was waitin' on you. I thought instead of totin' her, we'd go on over to the icehouse for a look. Do what we gonna do there. I got some things I need, then we'll go. And I'll need you to tell me where the body was found. Give me some of the background."

"All right," Daddy said.

Dr. Tinn paused. "What about the boy?"

"He's gonna be on his own for a while," Daddy said.

My heart sunk.

"Well then," Doc Tinn said, taking his dark suit coat off the back of the chair. "Let's go."

6

The icehouse was a big worn-out-looking barn of a place with peeling paint that had once been white but was now gray. It had a narrow front porch of new lumber, the only new lumber on the building.

I knew that inside the icehouse would be lined with sawdust. Big blocks of ice would be stacked about. There would be a table for cutting up slabs of ice with a saw, and a scale to weigh it, and a chute to send it down into wagon or truck beds. The ice would be so cold if you put your hand on it, it would burn you, and cause the flesh to stick.

And there was the body. The body I'd found.

As we came to the icehouse, Daddy said, "I'll be damned."

Sitting on the porch, dressed in a dusty white suit with mud splashed on his shoes and pants legs, fanning himself with his straw hat, was Doc Stephenson.

There was a flat bottle of dark liquid on the porch beside him, and when he saw Daddy he took a swig of it and put it down. Doc Stephenson had a mouth that looked as if it did not want to open wide, lest tacks and nails fall out. His eyes made you uncomfortable, like they were looking for a place to stick a knife.

"What's he doin' here?" Daddy asked Dr. Tinn.

"Can't say as I know, suh," Dr. Tinn said.

"You don't need to sir me," Daddy said. "I won't sir you, you don't sir me."

"Yes suh... Very well, Constable."

At that moment, Doc Taylor came walking toward the icehouse. He was carrying a Dr Pepper and some sort of candy from Pappy's place. He looked sharp in his clothes, which were a little more special than we were used to seeing. Very-well-made slacks, the cuffs of which he had somehow managed to keep clear of mud, though with the shoes he had not succeeded. He wore a clean white shirt that was so soft-looking it seemed to be made of angel wings. He had on a thin black tie that glistened like the wet back of a water snake, and his soft black felt hat was cocked at a jaunty angle that made him look more like he was going to a dance than to examine a mutilated body. I wondered if he had on his chain with the dented coin attached.

"That there's Doc Taylor," Daddy said to Doc Tinn. "He's what I think they call an intern. He's with Stephenson 'cause he's thinkin' about retirin', and he thought he'd get to know folks so he could take his place. He's a little dandy, but he seems all right to me."

"I doubt he wants to know us folks," Doc Tinn said.

"I suppose you're right," Daddy said. "Let's get this over with, then."

Daddy turned to me, gave me a pat on the head, said, "See you later, Harry."

Dejected, I wandered up the street a ways, turned, looked back at the icehouse, watched Daddy and Doc Tinn go inside with Doc Stephenson.

It was confusing to me. I had heard Daddy say the doctor didn't want anything to do with the body because it was colored, but here he was, away from his office, down in colored town for a looksee. And he had Doc Taylor with him.

I was thinking on all this when I heard a squeaking behind me, turned to see an ancient, legless, colored man in a cart covered by a willow stick and tarp roof, drawn by a big glossy white hog fastened up in a leather harness. The old man was bald and his scalp was wrinkled like a leather bag that had been wadded up and smoothed out by hand. He could have hidden a pencil in the wrinkles on his face. There wasn't a tooth in his head. He looked much older than Miss Maggie. In fact, she was a girl compared to him.

He carried a thin green willow stick he was using to tap the hog on the hind quarters. The hog was grunting, trundling along at a pretty good gait. Walking beside the old man and his cart were two boys about my age, one colored, one white. Their clothes were even more worn-looking than mine. The colored boy's pants were gone at the knee and there wasn't any attempt there to hold patches. The white kid's pants were gone at one knee, and there was a cotton sack patch there that had been multidyed by life, most likely the dye consisting of grass stains, clay roads, dirty riverbanks, and berry stains.

I noticed folks that had been standing around were edging toward the icehouse, congregating outside of it like a bunch of blackbirds on a limb. I realized then the body in the icehouse wasn't much of a secret.

The old man in the hog-drawn cart pulled up beside me. He looked at me with his rheumy eyes and opened his toothless mouth to say: "How're you, little white boy?"

"I'm fine, sir."

The truth of the matter was he scared me. I had never seen anyone that looked that old, and certainly no one in that circumstance, minus legs and drawn about in a cart by a hog.

The white boy who had been walking along with him said, "I'm Richard Dale. I live on down the bottoms."

Richard Dale was a little older than me, I think. Thin of jaw, ripe of lips, with a nose that we used to call Roman. Some smart alecks used to say, "Yeah. It roams all over his face."

I told him I lived in the bottoms too, explained my part of the country. His part of the bottoms was on the other side from me. His section was called the Sandy Bottoms, because there was more white sand there than where we lived, which was rich with red clay and brown dirt.

84

The colored boy with him introduced himself as Abraham. He looked very energetic, as if he had been drinking lots of coffee and was expecting something big to happen, like a tornado, a flood, or tripping over a boxful of money.

Being all of the same general age, quick to bore, and a little tired of adults, we were immediate friends.

Abraham said, "Me and Ricky got some cards with nekkid women on 'em."

"But we ain't got 'em with us," Richard hastened to add, lest I might ask for him to lay them out for examination.

"Yeah," Abraham said, disappointed. "They in the tree house, and it ain't nowhere near here. We got nigger shooters too. I can shoot a tin can at maybe thirty feet."

A "nigger shooter" was a word for a slingshot made of shoe tongue, tire rubber, and a forked stick. The name was common, and Abraham had said it without shame or consideration.

"We hear they's a body in there," Abraham added. "A woman got murdered."

I couldn't contain myself. "I found the body."

"Say you did," Abraham said. "Naw. Naw you didn't. You pullin' our leg."

"Did too. That's my Daddy in there. He's the constable over our parts."

"This ain't his constablin' here," the old man in the hog cart said. He could hear right good. I figured he'd heard us talking about those cards

85

with naked women on them, and I was embarrassed.

Richard Dale said, "That's Uncle Pharaoh. He got his legs torn up and cut off 'cause of a wild hog. Hog is Pig Jesse. That ain't the wild hog. That's a tame one."

"I'm sorry," I said to the old man.

He looked at me like I was some sort of strange vegetable he had never seen before. "Sorry 'bout what?" he said.

"Your legs."

"Oh," he said. "Well, don't be. Didn't happen yesterd'y. I done got over it."

"Where'd you find that body?" Abraham asked, and I told all three of them the story. I finished with: "I thought since I found it and done seen it, Daddy might let me look again and hear what the doctor's got to say about it, but he wouldn't do it."

"That's the way it always is," Richard said. "Adults think they got to know everything and we ain't supposed to know or see nothin'. Hey, you want to go off and play?"

"No," I said. "I think I'll wait here."

Richard winked at me. "Let's play."

Abraham was smiling, and I wondered what it was they were after. I hoped they didn't want to smoke grapevine, or even tobacco, 'cause I never liked either a bit. Times I had tried they had made my stomach sick.

Richard leaned over close and said, "Me and Abraham know somethin' you might like to know about that body. Come with us."

I thought on that, but only for a second. They

told Uncle Pharaoh goodbye, and I went running with them, away from the crowd, toward the creek. They led me along the edge of the creek and up behind the icehouse to where the big chinaberry tree grew.

Richard whispered: "Me and Abraham we know everything there is to know about over here. There's a big hole in the roof up there, right over the front room, where they bring the ice out. There's a piece of tin over it, but it'll twist aside and you can see in. If you don't twist it too much, they won't notice 'cause the tree shades that spot. Won't be a bunch of sunlight slippin' in. 'Sides, there's all sorts of cracks in that roof anyway. Little sunlight here and there won't be noticed none."

"What if they ain't in that room?" I said.

"Then they ain't," Abraham said. "But what if they is?"

Richard led the way up the chinaberry tree, Abraham after him, and me following up last. The chinaberry was a big one, and several of the limbs branched over the top of the icehouse. We climbed out on those and onto the roof. Richard moved along the roof to a spot in the shingles with a tin patch. He used his hand to push the patch back. Cold air came up from the icehouse and hit us in the face, and it felt good. Above us, the clouds had turned dark, as if filling up with shadow to aid our cause.

We looked out at the crowd. Most of them could see us. Some of them waved. I thought: Boy, am I gonna be in for it. But it was worth the gamble. These folks had no reason to tell my Daddy anything. They didn't even know him. And like most colored, they pretty much minded their own business when it came to whites.

There wasn't nothing to see at first, but we could hear men talking. I recognized Doc Stephenson's voice. He sounded loud, and drunk. Just when I was getting cold feet, and thinking about climbing down, Richard put his hand on my shoulder, and into view came two colored men carrying a long, narrow, galvanized tub packed with ice and, of course, the body.

The corpse was covered with a big burlap sack, and soon as they set it down on the ice-cutting table, they removed the sack, and I got a good look.

Looking down on it, I felt strange. It was the same body I had found that night. But it had seemed ten feet tall and terrible then. Now it was small and bloated and sad-looking, and suddenly, a person. Someone's spirit had inhabited that body and it had been alive and had eaten and laughed and had plans. Now it was a pathetic shell of wasting flesh, minus a soul. I either smelled, or imagined I could smell, the decaying odor of the body rising up with the cold from the icehouse's interior.

In that moment, something else changed for me. I realized that a person could truly die. Daddy and Mama could die. I could die. We would all someday die. Something went hollow inside me, shifted, found a place to lie down and be still, if not entirely in comfort.

Her head was tilted back and slightly sub-merged in chunks of ice. The mouth was open, and missing teeth. Many of the remaining teeth were jagged or broken, and I immedi-ately realized they had been knocked out. The woman's breasts were split open and laid back and the blood had gone gray and was frozen.

For the first time I was seeing a woman's pri-vates, but there was really nothing to see. Just a triangle of darkness. The poor woman's knees were slightly bent and she lay with her left hip down and her right hip up. Her hands were out to her sides and cupped into claws. Her face was hard to make out. Things had been done to it. There were rips in her body where the barbed wire had torn it. There were cuts all over.

Doc Stephenson, sucking from his flask, wob-bled over to the body and looked down. He said, "Now that is one dead darkie."

The colored men who had toted the body out in the galvanized tub looked at the floor. Doc Stephenson punched the one on his right with his elbow, said, "Ain't it, boy?"

The man lifted his chin slightly, and without looking at Doc Stephenson directly, said, "Yas suh, she sho is."

It embarrassed me to see that colored man have to act like that. He was big and strong and could have pulled Doc Stephenson's head off. But if he had, he would have been swinging from a limb before nightfall, and maybe his entire family, and any other colored

89

who just happened to be in sight when the Klan came riding.

Stephenson knew that. White folks knew that. It gave them a lot of room.

I glanced out of the corner of my eye at Abraham. The look on his face had gone from boyish excitement to one I couldn't quite identify.

Daddy moved to look at the body then, and said to Doc Stephenson, "I thought you couldn't look at the body? Wouldn't."

"Not in town. Wouldn't a white person within a hundred miles have anything to do with me they knew I was hauling a colored into my place. A decent white woman sure wouldn't want to be examined in no place like that. No offense, boys, but colored and white need their separation. Even the Bible tells us that. Hell, you boys are happier when you don't have the worries we do. You're lucky, is what you are... Taylor here told me I ought to have a look. That we ought to come out and help you boys."

Doc Taylor grinned shyly; the dampness on his teeth caught the lamplight and made them shine.

Doc Tinn had not stepped forward. He stood slightly back of Daddy and Doc Stephenson, his head down, not quite knowing what to do with his hands, though I had an idea what he'd like to do.

Doc Taylor stood at the end of the table, looking at the body calmly, taking it all in.

Doc Stephenson looked the body over,

touched it, moved it slightly, said, "Looks to me a wild hog got her."

"Then tied her with barbed wire to a tree?" Daddy said.

Doc Stephenson looked at Daddy as if he were an idiot. "I mean before she was tied to the tree."

"You saying a hog killed her?"

"I'm saying it could be like that. They got tusks like knives. I've seen them do some bad things to flesh."

"Doctor Tinn," Daddy said. "Do you know this woman?"

Doc Tinn came forward, looked the body over. "I don't think so. I've sent for the Reverend Bail, though. He's supposed to be here already."

"What'd you do that for?" Doc Stephenson said.

"He knows most everybody in these parts," Doc Tinn said. "I thought he might could identify her."

"Hell, how you tell one colored woman from another is hard for me to figure," Doc Stephenson said. "I wouldn't think you boys could keep up with your wives. 'Course, maybe you don't try to."

Stephenson laughed as if everyone were in on the joke. He had no idea he was being rude. He believed so strongly that colored and white were truly different at the core, he thought it was evident to everyone.

I could see Doc Tinn's shoulders shaking. Doc Taylor's expression changed slightly.

He glanced at the floor briefly, then looked up again, focusing on the body.

Doc Stephenson said, "Now that I look at her better, I think a panther did it."

"A panther ain't any more prone to tying bodies to trees with barbed wire than a hog," Daddy said. I saw Doc Tinn's face change slightly. He had liked that.

"I know that," Doc Stephenson said, and his tone was sharper than before. "What I'm suggestin' is she was killed by a panther, then someone else came along, some colored boys, and tied her to a tree."

"What for?" Daddy asked.

"For fun. Why not? You was a boy once. You ever done somethin' foolish, Constable?"

"Lots of times. But I wouldn't have done nothing like that, and I don't know any boys would."

"Maybe not white boys. And listen here now, Tinn, I don't mean nothin' by it. I know you. You're all right. But colored and whites is different. You know that. Down deep you do. Hell, there's things that a colored can't help, and I think folks are wrong to hold every little thing you coloreds do against you. Boys wouldn't have meant nothing by it. It'd just be somethin' to do. You know, like finding a dead fish and draggin' it around."

"A dead fish ain't a woman," Daddy said.

"Yeah, but don't you think a couple little colored boys would have a pretty good time playin' with a naked colored gal?"

"Doc," Daddy said. "You been drinkin'. Why don't you go somewhere and get sober."

"I'm all right."

Doc Taylor, who had been silent, said, "Doctor, maybe you have had a bit too much to drink. I ought to get you home."

"What for," Doc Stephenson said. "Nothin' there."

I had heard how his wife had up and ran off from him, and since he always seemed mean as a snake to me, I couldn't say I blamed her.

"You could rest," Doc Taylor said.

"I can rest fine right here, anywhere I want to."

I saw Doc Taylor look at Daddy and shake his head, as if to indicate he was sorry.

"I don't want you here," Daddy said. "Go somewhere and get sober."

"What'd you say?"

"I don't stutter. Go somewhere and get sober."

"You talkin' to me like that in front of these colored boys?"

"These men haven't been boys in years. And I'm just talkin' to you, period."

"This ain't your jurisdiction no how."

"Did I say anything about arresting you? Now get on your horse and ride."

"I got a car."

"It's an expression, you jackass."

"Jackass. You callin' me a jackass?"

Daddy turned and moved close to Doc Stephenson. "I am. I'm callin' you a jackass. Straight to your face. Right now. Here. Ain't it bad enough we got a woman's been murdered, and not by no goddamn panther neither. Ain't that bad enough? We ain't supposed to be quarrelin' over her poor dead body. Get out before I put you out on the end of my shoe."

"Well, I never..."

"Right now. Go. Taylor, get him out of here."

Doc Taylor touched Doc Stephenson's arm, and Stephenson jerked it away. "I don't need no damn seein' eye dog."

Doc Stephenson, perhaps trying to show some defiance, took a big swig of his whiskey and wobbled off toward the door. Just before goin' out he turned and said, "I ain't for-gettin' you, Constable."

"Well, I almost done forgot you, and will, quick as you go out that door."

Doc Stephenson hesitated, then said, "I'll just leave you then. See what you can learn from that boy. I can't believe they even give the title Doctor to a colored. You ain't no doctor to me, nigger. You hear me?"

"Come on," Doc Taylor said.

"You leave me alone," Doc Stephenson said.

And out the door he went.

I looked at Richard, then Abraham. They both had big grins on their faces. We looked back down through the split in the roof.

"Sorry about him," Doc Taylor said. "His wife run off from him. He ain't got over it yet."

"He's not the kind that will."

"I talked him into coming," Doc Taylor said. "I thought he could help. And I guess I was curious."

"I appreciate you," Daddy said. "You better take care of him."

It was polite, but it was clear Daddy wanted Doc Taylor out of the icehouse too.

"Yeah," Doc Taylor said, and left.

Daddy said, "Doctor, would you like to examine and give me your opinion on the patient?"

"Yes, I would," Dr. Tinn said.

He set his bag on the edge of the table and opened it. He said, "Billy Ray, light me up a lantern, would you?"

Billy Ray, one of the colored men who had carried the body in, lit a lantern and brought it over to the table, as it was pretty dark inside the icehouse. The only other light was light from cracks in the roof and from a few breaks in the board siding.

The lantern made the room glow orange. Doc Tinn draped the lantern handle on a hook that hung from a rafter over the table. When he did that we moved back from our place at the hole, waited, then slid our faces back. I was afraid we'd make a shadow that would cause them to look up and see us, but with chinaberry limbs hanging over us, and that cloud across the sun, there wasn't a noticeable change. Least I wasn't aware of one. And the bottom line was curiosity ate up caution.

Doc Tinn pulled on a pair of big rubber gloves and poked the body with his big fingers. He took off the gloves, lit a match, held it close to her mouth and looked inside. He waved the match out, slipped on the gloves again, stuck a finger down her throat and worked it. He came up with a little something on his finger, wiped that on a cloth he took out of his bag. He stuck a finger up her nostrils, worked it around, wiped what he found on the same rag, then folded it.

He said, "I'm gonna have to cut on her to see the inside of her stomach."

"The inside of her stomach?" Daddy said.

Doc Tinn nodded. "I ain't maybe had the schoolin' Doc Stephenson's had, but I got my hunches."

"Well," Daddy said, "I know for a fact Doc Stephenson learned his doctor'n out of a book and he did his first doctor'n on horses and cows."

Doc Tinn grinned. "So did I."

Daddy grinned back, said, "Go on and do what you got to do."

"This won't be pretty."

Daddy, less humored now, nodded. "I know."

Doc Tinn took a tool from his bag, a scalpel, began cutting at the woman's chest and down to her navel. I thought at first I was gonna lose my breakfast, but I was just too mesmerized to turn away. Doc Stephenson wasn't entirely wrong. Boys were fascinated by a dead body, but not in the way he had suggested.

The cutting was odd in that there wasn't any blood. She was long dead and pretty well

96

frozen, but there was a hint of gas that rose up from the corpse and through the slit in the roof. It made me feel sick for a moment, then it passed.

I squinted when he started handling the sweet meats inside her. Finally he cut open something, reached in with his hand, took out some dark things, and put them on the table.

I turned away for a moment, saw that Richard and Abraham were still looking. I didn't want to be thought a weak sister, so I looked again.

Doc Tinn had Daddy open the front door to let in some more light. There were people out by the porch and Daddy had to run 'em off. They moved away reluctantly. They were looking up at us on the roof, but no one spilled the beans. I think they were glad someone was getting a look.

Doc Tinn went to work on the woman's privates, cut, probed around down there for a while, and Daddy moved across the room with the other two men.

This went on for some time, and finally the doctor stopped, rolled the body over, looked at it, rolled it on its back again, said, "Billy Ray. Will you or Cyrus bring me a pan of water and some soap and a towel?"

Both Billy Ray and Cyrus went away. Doc Tinn pulled off his gloves and lay them on the table. He said, "Now this is just my opinion, mind you."

"I appreciate it," Daddy said, walking up to stand beside him. "Go on."

"Wasn't no wild hog nor a panther done this."

"I never thought it was. Panthers don't normally attack people. It could happen, but it ain't normal."

"Panther. Wild hog. They don't work a body like this no how. This was a man done it."

"I figured as much."

"Used a real sharp knife. These cuts was made while she was alive. Mostly. But some was after. Look at her hands here." Doc Tinn reached down and took hold of one, lifted it, turned it so Daddy could see. "There's cuts on 'em, like she was tryin' to fend the fellow off. Also there's fingernail wounds. This means he did most of this while she was alive. See how she's buried her own nails into her palms, trying to deal with the pain. There's a stab here on her back, and a slash at the kidney area. None of these are deep, 'cept for the stab. It's pretty deep, and it was twisted to be pulled out. I think she tried to fight him off, he had a knife, he slashed at her, she put up her hands, they got cut, she turned to run, he stabbed her in the back, then slashed her, or maybe the other way around. She went down, and from the looks of the way she's been used...you know, down there...she was raped. She's all torn up, so she was forced. He got through with that, he cut on her some while she was alive. Her clitoris is missing."

"Her what?" Daddy asked.

"It's down there with her private parts. You rub it on a live woman and they get really excited."

98

"Yeah?" Daddy said.

"Yeah."

Doc Tinn said, "It's a little nub and it rolls under your thumb or finger. It's a thing a man ought to know, you know what I mean."

Daddy nodded again, as if contemplating a great mystery, or rather common information that had somehow been denied him. I filed it away in my own file cabinet, though at the time I wasn't sure it was something I'd ever need.

Daddy said, "He cut it off? This cli..."

"Clitoris. Did it just as precise as could be. And from the looks of the wound she bled good. Probably still alive through that too, though I don't know for sure. Lot of the other cuts and slashes and such I think he did after he choked her to death."

Doc Tinn leaned over the table. "See her throat there. Those bruises. Them are from hands. He finished up with her, I think he threw her in the river."

"How would you know that?"

"Well, I can't say for sure, but there ain't no river in her lungs, so she didn't drown. I know a little about drownings. Flood five years ago there was twenty-five people drowned. I seen what it did to bodies."

"Twenty-five people?" Daddy said. "Five years ago. I don't remember anything about that."

"Wasn't none of 'em white," Doc Tinn said.

"Oh," Daddy said.

"This woman was dead when she was thrown in. There's all kinds of scrapes on her forehead there, and there was a piece of gravel in one of her eyes, lodged in the corner there. River gravel. Body thrown in a river will mostly go face down, and the current will drag it along and scrape it up, like it's done on her forehead there. There was bits of river in her mouth, throat, and nose, but not in her lungs, so I figure she was dead already."

"Makes sense," Daddy said. "But if he threw her in the river, how does that account for her being tied to that tree?"

"Well now, Doctor Stephenson may be kinda right. Someone got the body out of the river and cut on it some more. Way her breasts are all cut up there, that was done afterward. You can tell 'cause there ain't no real blood wound. He was cuttin' on a corpse."

"Jesus Christ."

"Then he tied her to that tree with barbed wire, way you said your boy found her. Wrapped some vines around her and such, and left her there. I wouldn't be surprised he came back a few times and messed with the body. Your boy hadn't found it, he might have come back some more. I think he would have."

"You couldn't know that?"

"No. But like I said, some of them wounds was after death. It might have been done in one trip, but they're some with maggot eggs in them, and some not so many. The maggots was just gettin' started in some of them

100

wounds when your boy found it and you got her down before they was thick. Maggots don't just work one wound at a time. Flies get all over them wounds, lay eggs in them. Ones wasn't packed with eggs was because there wasn't time for 'em to."

Daddy considered on this for a moment. "Like you said, though. Stephenson could have been right. It could have been someone else found the body and did those things. It don't mean there was just one fella did it all."

"Uh huh, but what do you think? What's your gut tell you, Constable? Man did this in the first place is the more likely to do it some more. I think he threw her away, like she was garbage, threw her in the river, but then figured he hadn't got his fill, come back, got her out, and did the rest."

"How would he know where to find her? She could have washed downriver."

"She could have. But I figure he threw her in there, tied her out like a trot line. Look here. You see this around her ankle. See that friction. I think after he killed her he tied a rope around her and tossed her out. Maybe had some kind of weight tied to her. That way he knew where to find her. And just for the record, on her butt there, I think that's a turtle been nibblin'."

The sun came out from behind its cloud and it was bright enough to burn right through the leaves on the chinaberry tree, giving our immediate world a shade of green. I could see the shapes of our heads move across the woman's body on the table, and Daddy looked up as we pulled our heads back.

We didn't look again. We just sat there listening. Doc Tinn said, "You know ain't no one here gonna worry about her none."

I didn't hear Daddy respond. Doc Tinn continued.

"She's colored, but colored over here don't want no trouble. If it's one of our own did it, and we find out who it is, well, it'll get taken care of. We tell the whites a colored did it, well, ain't no tellin' who all will pay."

"Could be a white man done it."

"Even better reason colored won't get involved."

"Can you see to it she gets a proper burial, and let me know when?"

"I can. We got a graveyard that'll let anyone in."

"Yep. Dirt ain't particular."

"Nor the worms," Doc Tinn said. "And one other thing." He pulled a long pair of tweezer things out of his bag and picked something up lying between the woman's legs. "Soon as I went to work down there, this fell out. It was pushed up in her."

"What is it?"

"It looks like paper. It's so bloody and wet, there's no telling now, but that's what it looks like."

"He stuck paper up her?"

"Rolled up a small piece and put it there," Doc Tinn said.

102

"Why?"

Doc Tinn shook his head. "It means something to him. I couldn't begin to tell you what."

We heard someone else come in, speak, and I realized it was the Reverend arriving. After greetings, I heard the Reverend say in a high voice, "Uh huh. Oh, my God. That be Jelda May. Jelda May Sykes. She was a harlot, but she come around now and then to talk to me. She was always wantin' to do different and get salvation, but couldn't. She worked them juke joints way down yonder on the river. Take in both black and white trade I hear. She did some conjurin'."

"Conjurin'?" Daddy asked.

"She worked the juju. Magic spells and such."

"You don't believe that?" Daddy said. "You, a man of God?"

"Wasn't all bad spells she worked," Reverend said. "Poor, poor thing. Good Lord! Who cut her up like that?"

"Some of it was done by whoever killed her," Doc Tinn said, "and some I did as way of examination. Checkin' the cause of death."

"Ain't nothing like that need to be done after someone done had the indignities of death. Good Lord, what a mess. You ought not have done that."

"You know what kind of animal you're huntin'," Daddy said. "How it lives, how it kills, you got a better chance of catchin' him."

"Lord, poor Jelda May," the Reverend said. "She better off now. She in a better place."

"I hope you're right," I heard Doc Tinn say. Then me and my newfound pals eased toward the chinaberry tree and started down.

By the time we hit the ground and got around front, the crowd was starting to break up. Folks were mumbling back and forth, mad 'cause they hadn't learned anything, and the old colored man, Uncle Pharaoh, was moving his pig cart toward the commissary with, "Now get on, Pig Jesse."

"I got to go catch up," Abraham said when he saw Uncle Pharaoh. "He gonna need some help with some groceries and such."

"I'm with them," Richard said. "It was nice meetin' you, Harry," and they went away.

I felt abandoned and full of guilt. Daddy had told me to do a certain thing, and that was wait. I told myself that I had waited, but I knew I was splitting hairs. I had waited on the roof of the icehouse and seen what I wasn't supposed to see; heard what I wasn't supposed to hear. I didn't always do as told, but somehow, this time, I felt as if I had transgressed beyond forgiveness.

I tried to look innocent as Daddy, Doc Tinn, and the Reverend came out. I had not seen the Reverend enter, but it had to be him. He was a tall, very lean colored man with a flat nose and a look like someone waiting on something bad to happen so he could talk salvation. He wore black pants and shoes and a white shirt with yellow sweat stains under the arms. He had on a thin black tie that looked to be fraying about the edges and he was putting on a soft brown felt hat as he came out of the icehouse. The hat had a little bright red and green feather in the brim on the left side.

As they came down the steps, Daddy, slipping on his hat, looked over at me, and though he didn't say anything, his gaze made me nervous. At the bottom of the icehouse steps Daddy gave the Reverend something, turned to Doc Tinn and extended his hand. Doc Tinn, still unaccustomed to such, stuck out his hand quickly and they shook.

"I want to thank you for your help," Daddy said. "I may be talkin' to you again."

"It's all just opinion, Constable," Doc Tinn said.

"It sounded like reasonable opinion to me," Daddy said.

"Thank you, kindly, Constable."

They talked a little more with the Reverend. I saw Daddy reach in his pocket and hand the preacher something, but I couldn't make it out. Then he shook hands with him, turned around, and called to me.

"Son, let's go."

We walked over to Doc Tinn's house, ahead of the Doc, got in our car, and drove over to the commissary. Uncle Pharaoh was around front, sitting in his cart in the shade of his willow and burlap sack cover, drinking a Dr Pepper. His hog, Jesse, was lying in the dirt with the cart posts and straps still on him. He had his head just under the porch in the shade and was grunting away, eating some old moldy bread.

"Now that's a hog," Daddy said to Uncle Pharaoh.

"Mr. Constable, how you doin'?"

Uncle Pharaoh **knew** my Daddy. My heart sank. Would he mention that me and Abraham and Richard had climbed on top of the icehouse?

"How the world treatin' you, Mr. Constable?"

"Fair enough," Daddy said. "And you?"

"I could complain, but it wouldn't do no good."

Daddy and Uncle Pharaoh exchanged a small laugh, and Daddy lifted his hand as if to wave Uncle Pharaoh away, like he couldn't handle such powerful humor that time of day.

We went inside the commissary. I said, "You know him?"

"Son, wasn't it obvious I did?"

"Yes sir."

"He used to be the greatest hunter in all these bottoms until a wild hog tore up his leg. It's a critter they call Old Satan. He wanders these here bottoms. Big old boar hog. And ain't no one ever been able to kill him. He's mainly over here on this side of the county. 'Round here and over toward Mud Creek."

I started to ask if what Doc Stephenson had said about a wild hog tearing up that woman could be possible, when I caught myself.

"Sure are lots of towns named after creeks," I said.

"Yeah," Daddy said.

Abraham and Richard were inside getting groceries together for Uncle Pharaoh. They spoke to me and Daddy as we came in, then went on about their business.

Daddy bought us a slab of bologna, a box of crackers, some rat cheese, and a couple Co'-Colas. We sat on the front porch of the commissary where it was cooler and watched Jesse snooze with his nose in the shade and Uncle Pharaoh nurse his Dr Pepper. Daddy used his pocketknife to slice up the meat and cheese and he laid them out on the butcher paper they had come wrapped in. We ate the meat and cheese with the crackers and drank our pops. Wagons rattled by with fresh-cut lumber in them.

We sat quietly for a time, then Daddy said, "Son."

"Yes sir."

"I prefer you do as I ask. You get to be a grown man, you can do as you please. Long as it's within the law and within God's law, but as a boy, you do as I ask."

So he had seen me. "Yes sir."

We ate some more. I said, "You gonna give me a whippin'?"

"No. You're gettin' kind of old for that foolishness, don't you think?"

"I guess so."

"Well, you are. You act more your age, and I'll treat you your age. That a deal?"

"Yes sir."

"Being your age means listenin' to what I tell you. Or your Mama tells you. You got to show some good sense. I didn't want you to see all that."

"I done seen her, Daddy."

"I know, son. But that was an accident. This here, it wasn't none of your business. It was in a different light. Hear what I'm sayin'?"

"Yes sir."

"That poor woman was loved by someone somewhere, and it ain't good to have a bunch a people gaping at her like she's somethin' in a circus. She ain't got no control over what happens to her now, so we got to control it. Everything done there was to find out what we needed to know. And another thing, son, there's things you don't need in your head 'less you got to have 'em. You may not think that now, but believe me, there's things you don't need and they'll come back to you and they won't be pleasant. And by the way. I noticed you boys were up there soon as you climbed on the roof. Ain't none of you quiet. Just to let you know, them boys are pretty good boys. Uncle Pharaoh's the little one's grandpa."

"Abraham."

"Yep, Abraham. And the other one is Mr. Dale's boy. Mr. Dale is a pretty fair farmer. He wrestles at fairs for money. I hear he's good at that too. His boy's name is...let me see..."

"Richard."

"Yep, Richard. They ain't a bad couple to play with. And let me tell you something sad. Abraham, another few years, he and Richard won't play together. They won't even be together."

"Why, Daddy?"

Daddy looked over at Uncle Pharaoh, as if to make sure he was out of earshot. "'Cause the world ain't the way it's supposed to be. You figure on that, and I think the answer will come to you."

It already had. I said, "Daddy? Did you figure out who done that to that colored woman?"

"No. I don't really know more than I did, 'cept it was horrible. I don't know I'll ever know any more than I know right now."

"Why did Doc Stephenson come?"

"I don't rightly know, but I figure he wanted to be in on something like that, and not have it hurt his business none."

"He didn't sound like he knew much."

"I don't think he cared one way or another. He just wanted to be the one making the statements, not a colored doctor. I'd come to Doc Tinn anytime before I'd go to that pill-pushin' quack. Listen here. Whites and colored ain't neither one better or worse than

109

another. There's just men and women of whatever color, and some of them are worse than others, and some are better. That's the way to look at that matter. I'm an ignorant man, son, but I know that."

"Daddy. Miss Maggie says it's probably the Goat Man done it."

"How'd she know anything was done?"

I blushed. "I guess I told her."

"Well, I figure it's no big secret by now, but you want to keep talk like that to yourself when you can."

"Yes sir. She says the Goat Man might be the devil. Or one of the devil's servants. Like Beezlebubba."

"She means Beelzebub. But no. I done told you I don't believe there's no Goat Man," Daddy said. "I've heard tell of such all my life, but ain't never seen it. As for this fella done this being the devil's servant, well, she might have somethin' there. But I figure he's flesh and blood all right."

"Daddy, the one done that to that colored woman?"

"Miss Sykes, son. She had a name. We know it now."

"Yes sir. One did that... He still around?"

Daddy had the bologna in his hand, and was cutting it with the pocketknife.

"I don't know, son... I doubt it."

It was then, for the first time, I thought my Daddy might have lied to me.

It was hotter on the way home than when we'd left, and a lot of the water had dried up or at least caked into mud. It was thick in the road and it caused us to go slow.

We hadn't got more than a couple miles outside of Pearl Creek when a black Ford with dents all over it, sitting in the shade of a hickory nut tree, pulled onto the road and right up beside us, going fast enough to toss mud on us.

A red-faced man was sitting on the passenger side wearing a big white hat. He waved his arm out the open window at Daddy and pointed to the side of the road.

Daddy pulled over, said, "It's all right, son. It's the law over here. I know 'em. Wait on me, hear?"

As Daddy got out of the car, I slid over behind the steering wheel. Daddy went to the rear of our car, and the man on the passenger side of the dented Ford wearing the big white hat got out. He was big and solid. He was dressed in gray khakis and wore his sleeves rolled down and buttoned, as if it were the dead of winter. A badge was pinned on his shirt.

The driver, a fellow with a yellowish coloring to his features, wearing a tan hat with a near flat crown that made it look like the top to a butter churn, stayed behind the wheel chewing tobacco.

The man in the big hat shook hands with

Daddy. I could hear them real good. The red-faced man said, "Good to see you, Jacob. I heard tell you was constable over there in your county."

"I don't expect you're all that proud to see me, Woodrow," Daddy said, "so don't act like it."

The man laughed a little. He took off his hat and pulled a handkerchief out of his pocket and wiped sweat from the inside of it. His hair was even redder than his face.

"That Ralph Purdue with you?" Daddy asked.

The man Daddy called Woodrow didn't answer that question. He said, "Jacob, I got to talk to you. This here nigger murder. We heard about it."

"Who hasn't."

"Well, now, I could beat around the bush, but I ain't gonna do that. What I got to say is simple. Over here ain't your jurisdiction."

"If I was solvin' a crime, and it led me over here, you'd help me out, wouldn't you, Woodrow?"

"Oh, you know it. But, a nigger? Listen, Jacob, let me give you some advice—"

"I've heard it before."

"You heed it from me, okay?"

Daddy didn't answer.

"There's nigger murders, then there's white murders, and then there's nigger and white and white and nigger murders."

"Murder's murder."

"Let me put it like this. Niggers over here

don't want nobody meddlin' in their business. Not you. Not me."

"We're the law."

"Yeah, but a nigger woman gets killed down in the bottoms, that's one thing. It ain't like it's a good nigger. And it ain't like it matters much to us. One's gone, and that's all there is to it. It was probably one of her boyfriends. She didn't put out, or put out to someone else. It's always something like that.

"Jacob, you got some Christian ideas, and that's good. But niggers take care of their own. They like it that way, and we like it that way. They get in white business, then we take care of them. White man kills a nigger, that's our responsibility. A nigger kills a white man, that's sure our responsibility. But this..."

"Person's dead, they're dead," Daddy said. "Isn't that our responsibility?"

"There's some things been a certain way for a long time, and they ought to stay that way."

"I thought the Yankees whupped us," Daddy said. "And Lincoln freed the slaves."

"The Yankees didn't whup me. Jacob, what happened here seems obvious. Somebody got off the train, a nigger hobo ridin' the rails most likely, and he decided he needed some comfort. And he got with this nigger woman and didn't have the money. She probably tried to cut him. He ended up doin' her in and caught the next train out. Doc Stephenson, he sees it that way."

"That's funny," Daddy said. "He told me he thought a panther did it. Or a wild boar.

113

Or maybe a wild boar held her while the panther did it. I forget. When the two got through they tied her to a tree with some barbed wire."

"Jacob—"

"Since when is Doc Stephenson able to look at a body and know a hobo did it? Did the hobo leave him a note?"

"Goddamn you, Jacob! It's known far and wide all over this country you're a nigger lover, and you ain't careful you're gonna bring up another generation of them nigger lovers, and some folks around here have all the nigger lovin' they want. Over here, we take care of our niggers our way."

"I want to tell you something, Woodrow. When we were boys you fell off a barge and damn near drowned—"

"Don't hold that over my head."

"Got in that sinkhole and was almost sucked down. But you wasn't."

"And I've thanked you."

"You have. Thought you was real grateful about it. And even though you and I have our differences, I've always thought, when push come to shove, you was a fair man. But sometimes, I wish I'd have just gone on and let you go under. And if I could rightly figure for sure what you said about another generation of nigger lovers was some kind of threat on my family, I'd break your goddamn neck."

Woodrow turned red and put his hat on.

"It wasn't no threat. But you just keep in mind what I've said."

"Whatever it is you said, you keep in mind

114

what I just said. Take it to heart, Woodrow. I'm goin' home now."

"I ain't finished, Jacob."

"Yeah you are," Daddy said.

As Daddy walked away, Woodrow said, "You tell May Lynn I said howdy."

Daddy paused momentarily. I saw the arteries stand out in his neck, and for a moment I thought he might turn around, but he didn't. He kept coming.

I slid away from the driver's side and waited for Daddy to get in. When he was behind the wheel, I said, "Everything all right, Daddy?"

"Everything's fine, son. Fine."

I looked back and saw the banged-up black car was turned around and heading in the other direction, the man called Woodrow had his sleeve-covered arm hanging from the window.

◆

When we got home, Daddy let me out, turned the Ford around, and headed off. He didn't say where he was going. Just told me to tell Mother not to worry.

He didn't come back until nightfall, and he was quiet all night. After supper, he and Mama sat and read awhile, her from the Bible and him from a seed catalogue and then the *Farmer's Almanac*. But he seemed to be just going through the motions. I noticed that he had been on the same page for a long time. Once he looked over at Mother, sighed, then went back to glaring at the page, as if he wished to be absorbed by it, like a stain.

Me and Tom played checkers, and Tom, after me beating her four times in a row, got mad, turned over the checker board, and went out on the sleeping porch. There were a couple of cots out there, and when it was real hot, sometimes that's where me and Tom slept.

Normally, I wasn't of a mind to care a lot about how she felt, but maybe seeing that body had softened me. I went out on the porch. Tom was on one of the cots, her hands behind her head, looking up at the ceiling.

"It's just an ole game," I said, realizing I probably should have let her win one.

"That's all right," she said.

I sat on the other cot. We sat there in silence, listening to the crickets, some bugs banging up against the screen.

"That woman we found," Tom asked, "you think the Goat Man did that to her?"

"Doc Stephenson said he thought some kind of animal did it. Doc Tinn said he thought a man did it. Constable over there thought it was a hobo."

"How you know all that?" she said.

"I heard 'em talkin'."

"Is a hobo a monster?"

"It's a fella rides the trains by sneaking on."

"Well, that's a man, ain't it? You said an animal, a man, or a hobo."

"I suppose."

"But could it have been the Goat Man?"

116

"Daddy says it ain't. But if you put together what everyone says, it adds up to the Goat Man. Miss Maggie thinks it was the Goat Man."

Tom considered on that for a while, said, "Miss Maggie knows all kinds of things. Makes sense to me it was the Goat Man. We seen it, didn't we?"

"We did."

"I didn't see it real good. It was too dark. It looked pretty horrible though, didn't it?"

I agreed it did.

"I think about it sometimes," Tom said.

"I know." I thought about Daddy telling me I didn't need to talk about the body, but then again, hadn't Tom already seen it?

Heck, I was turning out to be a real blabber-mouth.

I told Tom what I had done, about climbing on the icehouse and looking through the hole. I told her what was said, and I embellished it a little, making myself the leader of the boys that climbed the chinaberry.

I also left out the part about being caught in the act of spying. That seemed to me to take the edge off the story and made me seem less clever than I wanted to be.

I also added, "Don't say nothin' about what I told you, or I'll be in a heap of trouble."

Me and Tom talked awhile, speculating on the Goat Man, and pretty soon we were starting to hear him creeping around at the back of the house, and maybe even calling to us in a kind of soft voice that mocked the wind. I got up and locked the screen door, but that

117

didn't keep us from being scared. Pretty soon every time a bug smacked up against the screen, I was sure it was the Goat Man scratching to get in.

Having scared ourselves to death, we gladly went inside to bed.

———————◆———————

That night, as I lay in bed, Jelda May Sykes came to me, all cut up. Not just the way I found her, but the way Doc Tinn had cut her, from breastbone to private parts. There was a big empty gap in her stomach except for one long intestine Doc Tinn hadn't pulled out. It hung out of the rip in her belly and dragged across the floor. She moved slowly, and finally stood by my bed, looking down at me. Her pubic hair and her cut-up womanhood was near my head. I had my eyes open and I could see her, but I couldn't move. Very carefully, very slowly, she laid her hand on my forehead, as if checking for fever.

I woke up in a sweat, and lay panting. I looked to see if I had awakened Tom, but she was still sleeping sound by the window that connected to the sleeping porch. She might have been frightened when she went to bed, but she sure seemed content enough now. She had even opened the window, which was a good thing, hot as it was.

The wind was soft and gentle, moving the curtains. It licked at Tom's dark hair and waved it about. I was certain I could smell death

118

and river water in the room. I checked about, to see if Jelda May had moved into the shadows, waiting for me to get comfortable again, but there was nothing there but the shapes of familiar things.

I folded my pillow and stuffed it under my head and took deep breaths, tried not to think about Jelda May Sykes. While I was doing that, I heard Mom and Dad talking behind the wall, just a buzz of words.

I slid over and put my ear against the wall and tried to pick up what they were saying. They were speaking soft, and for a moment I couldn't make anything out, but pretty soon I adjusted, shut out the sound of the wind coming through the window by putting a hand over my ear and pressing my other one tight against the wall.

"...you got to consider that except for stories I haven't never heard of a panther killing anybody," I heard Daddy say. "My belief is they probably have. Some say they don't do that, but I think any kind of critter can do that under the right circumstances. Even a family dog. But Doc Stephenson didn't have no reason to suspect that. He just wanted it to be that way."

"Why?" Mama asked.

"He didn't want no colored doctor making any kind of examination and maybe knowing something he didn't know. Everyone that's got the mind to admit it, knows Doc Tinn is a good doctor. Better'n most, white or black. That's all I can figure. And Stephenson was drunk, so I don't think that helped his judgment

119

none. He may have been showin' out for that intern, Taylor. Though I don't think Taylor was much impressed."

"What did Doc Tinn say?"

"He said she'd been raped and cut up. The cut-up part was obvious. He figured someone had come back after she was dead, probably the killer, and kind of played with the body."

"You don't mean it?"

"Uh huh."

"Who would do such a thing?"

"I don't know. I haven't even an idea."

"Did the doctor know her?"

"No, but the colored preacher over there, Reverend Bail, he knew her. Name was Jelda May Sykes. He said she was a local prostitute and a...he called her a juju woman."

"A what?"

"Some kind of witchcraft they believe in. She sold charms and such. She worked in the juke joints along the river. Picked up a little white trade now and then."

"So no one has any ideas who could have done it?"

"Nobody over there gives a damn, May Lynn. No one. The coloreds don't have any high feelings for her, and the white law enforcement let me know real quick I was out of my jurisdiction."

"If it's out of your jurisdiction, you'll have to leave it alone."

"Taking her to Pearl Creek was out of my jurisdiction, but where she was found isn't out of my jurisdiction. Law over there figures some hobo ridin' the rails had his fun with her, dumped her in a river, and caught the next train out. They're probably right. But if that's so, who bound her to the tree?"

"It could have been someone else, couldn't it?"

"I suppose, but it worries me mightily to think that there's that much cruelty out there in the world. I'd rather it just be one fella, not two, and if I had my real druthers, I'd rather it not be any. But as they say, wish in one hand and shit in the other and see which fills up first."

"Jacob!" Mama said in what sounded like a not entirely offended tone. And then she laughed a little. "Such language." Then: "What do they care if you chase this? Why are they so against it?"

"You know that much as I do," Daddy said.

"'Cause she's colored? But what would it matter to them if you wanted to chase it?"

"What if a white man done it?"

"Then he ought to pay."

"Of course. But not everyone sees it that way. They figure a colored woman who was a prostitute...well, she had it coming. If it was a colored did it, one less colored woman for all they care, so why bother and upset the old apple cart. If it was a white man, then they want it left alone. They figure a white man can have his fun with a colored, no matter what kind of fun it is, and he ought not have to pay for it no kind of way."

"When you dropped Harry off. Where did you go?"

121

"Into town to see Cal Fields."

When he said that, I felt knee high to a crippled June bug. My climbing on the icehouse had probably got me sent home early, and Daddy had been discontent enough with me to drive me all the way home and take the ride into town by himself.

"He's the newspaperman, isn't he?" Mama asked. She was talking about our weekly newspaper, the *Marvel Creek Guardian*. "The older man with the younger wife," she continued, "the hot patootie?"

"Yeah," Daddy said. "He's a good fella. His young wife ran off with a drummer, by the way. That doesn't bother Cal any. He's got a new girlfriend. But what he was tellin' me was interestin'. He said this is the third murder in the area in eighteen months. He didn't write about any of 'em in the paper, primarily because they're messy, but also because they've all been colored killings, and his audience don't care about colored killings."

"How does he know about them?"

"He gets along pretty well with the colored communities here about. He said he's got a nose for news, even if the newspaper he owns and writes isn't one that's worth all the news. He said all the murders have been of prostitutes. One happened in Pearl Creek. Her body was found stuffed in a big drainpipe down near the river by the sawmill. Her legs had been broken and pulled up and tied to her head and her body had been cut on. Like the one I seen today. Turned out nobody really knew

122

this woman, though. She had sort of drifted in and got a job in one of the cribs over there."

"Cribs?"

"That's where the prostitutes work, dear. It's a kind of house... You know?"

"Oh. I'm certainly gettin' an education. I didn't know you knew all this."

"I find out a lot doin' my little constablin'. Anyway, she was found and buried by some Christians wanted her to have a burial, and after a time no one thought much about it. It's the same old story. A colored murder isn't something the colored say much about, 'cept amongst themselves. They take care of their own when they can, 'cause the white law sure ain't gonna do much. In this case, wasn't no one really knew the woman and wasn't anyone suspected. Same thing was thought then that's thought about Jelda May Sykes. It was figured a tramp done her in, caught the train out."

"You said there were three."

"Other was found in the river. Thought to be a drown victim at first. Cal said rumor was she was cut on, but he can't say for sure if it's true. Might not be any kind of connection."

"When did these murders happen?"

"Best I can tell, the first one was killed January of last year. The other one, I don't know. Don't even know if it did happen. People could have been talking about something happened years ago and Cal caught wind of it. Or whoever told him might have misheard it. Or been yarn'n him. It's hard to tell when it comes to the colored community."

"Did Mr. Fields know about Jelda May Sykes?"

"He did."

They were silent for a while. Through our thin walls I could hear the crickets outside, and somewhere in the bottoms, the sound of a big bullfrog bleating.

"Jelda May's body," Mama asked. "What happened to it? Who took it?"

"No one. Honey, I paid a little down payment to have her buried in the colored cemetery over there. I know we don't have the money, but—"

"Shush. That's all right. You did good."

"I told the preacher over there I'd give him a bit more when I got it."

"That's good, Jacob. That's real good."

"By the way, the constable over there. You know who it is?"

"No."

"Red Woodrow."

"Oh. I didn't know that. Did you know that?"

"Yeah, I did."

"You didn't mention it."

"Didn't see any reason to. I never thought about it much until today when I seen him. I didn't want to mention it now—"

"Oh, don't be silly."

"—but I felt I ought to. I don't like to hide behind something bothers me. He told me to tell you hello."

"He did."

"I didn't plan to tell you. I don't know why I did."

"Honey, you can quit being silly. You know there wasn't nothing to any of that."

Their tone had changed. Had become almost formal. I wasn't sure what was different, but something was, and it had to do with Red Woodrow.

"He wanted me to stay out of things."

"It is his jurisdiction, isn't it?"

"Like I said, murder took place here. The only reason they have the body is I needed help from Doc Tinn."

"Red can be...well, testy."

"Wasn't the word I had in mind for him," Daddy said.

"Jacob, just forget him."

"I want to."

"His shirtsleeves?" Mama asked.

"He still keeps them rolled down."

They grew silent. I turned on my back and looked at the ceiling. When I closed my eyes I saw Jelda May Sykes again, ruined and swollen, fixed to that tree with barbed wire. And then she was gone, just faded away, leaving only her dark eyes, and then the dark eyes turned bright and I saw white teeth in the dark face of the horned Goat Man.

Suddenly, I was standing in shadow in the middle of the trail looking at him. He started coming toward me.

I ran, and I could hear him running right behind me. I was breathing hard, and he was breathing even harder, but not like he was tired. It was more the fast-paced breathing of someone planning something they would enjoy.

The shadows from the trees grabbed at me and tried to hold me, but I broke loose. Just as the Goat Man was gaining on me, about to put his hand on my shoulder, I reached the Preacher's Road ahead of him, and when I looked over my shoulder, he was gone. I was sitting up in bed, wide awake, staring at the wall.

It took me a long time to fall back asleep, and in the morning I awoke exhausted, as if I had been pursued all night by the devil himself.

After a while, things drifted back to normal for Tom and me. Time is like that. Especially when you're young. It can fix a lot of things, and what it doesn't fix, you forget, or at least push back and only bring out at certain times, which is what I did, now and then, late at night, just before sleep claimed me.

Daddy looked around for the killer awhile, but except for some tracks along the bank, signs of somebody scavenging around down there, he didn't find anyone. I heard him telling Mama how he felt he was being watched when he was in the bottoms, and that he figured there was someone out there knew the woods and river well as any animal and was keeping an eye on him.

But that's about all he said. There was nothing about it that led me to believe he thought those tracks were actually of the Goat Man or that the tracks belonged to the murderer. They could have been anyone fishing, hunting, or just fooling around. I didn't get the impression his sensation of being watched meant much either.

In time Daddy no longer pursued it. I don't think it was because he didn't care, or that he was concerned with what Red Woodrow thought, but more like there was nothing to find, and therefore, nothing to do.

Making a living took the lead over any kind of investigation, and my Daddy was no investigator anyway. He was just a small-town constable who mainly delivered legal summonses, and picked up dead bodies with the justice of the peace. And if the bodies were colored, he picked them up without the justice of the peace.

So, with no real leads, in time the murder and the Goat Man moved into our past.

The thing I was interested in was what had interested me before. Hunting and fishing and reading books loaned me by Mrs. Canerton, who was a kind of librarian, though it wasn't anything official. There wasn't an official library in Marvel Creek until some years later. Mrs. Canerton was just a nice widow lady that kept a lot of books and loaned them out and kept records on them to make sure you gave them back. She would even let you come to her house and sit and read. She nearly always had cookies or lemonade on hand, and she wasn't adverse to listening to our stories or problems.

I continued to read pulp magazines down at the barbershop and talked with Daddy and Cecil, though as usual, it was Cecil I enjoyed talking to the most. He certainly loved talking, and seemed to like my company. He was especially fond of Tom, always giving her a penny or a piece of candy, letting her sit on his knee while he told her some kind of whopper about wild Indians, people at the center of the earth, planets where the moon was blue and men lived in trees and apes rode in boats.

Daddy wasn't as much fun to talk to because he always led his conversation around to telling me how I was supposed to live life and giving me lectures on this and that. I figured I knew all that and he could save his breath. I had learned the best thing to do was to just sort of look interested until he ran out of steam.

Although the murder wasn't on my mind much anymore, one day at home something came up about it and the talk Daddy had with Red Woodrow. I don't remember exactly what it was, but Daddy said something about him, as if he were baiting some kind of hook, and Mama said he shouldn't be so hard on Red, and though Daddy didn't say anything to that, I could tell he didn't like any kind of defense of Mr. Woodrow. I could also tell my mother regretted she had said anything.

Daddy began working at home a lot, going into the barbershop now and then. He had left the key to Cecil, who he had come to rely on heavily.

On this day, he had me and Tom go out and set Sally Redback to harness and plow. After a bit he came and ran the middles, had me and Tom walk behind him and pick up chunks of grass that didn't get rolled good, turn them over, mash them with our feet so the roots would be exposed to the sun and die out.

He brooded for an hour or so over the thing with Red Woodrow, then gradually he ceased to mope and began to whistle. Lunchtime he told me to go to the house and bring back something to eat, as he was going to continue plowing.

Back at the house Mama packed a lard bucket with some cornbread and fried chicken, filled a fruit jar with pinto beans and put the lid on it. She put a couple bowls and some spoons with it all, jammed it in the bucket, had me go out to the well and draw up the buttermilk.

When I brought it back she poured the buttermilk into a couple of fruit jars and screwed rings and rubber toppers on them. Out of the clear blue, I said, "Daddy don't like Red Woodrow, does he?"

"Oh, I don't know," Mama said. "They used to be best friends."

I felt like I'd been poleaxed. "Best friends. You don't mean that, do you, Mama?"

"I do."

"They didn't sound like best friends when they was talking that day over at Pearl Creek."

"Daddy told me they talked. I think Red felt Daddy was horning in on his business."

"Was he?"

"Not really." She dried her hands and put the two jars of buttermilk into another lard bucket. "Daddy saved Red from drowning once."

"They talked about that," I said. "Daddy said how he had saved him from a suck hole."

"Yes. I was there. We were on a barge. I wasn't supposed to be there. Girls weren't supposed to do that sort of thing. Be out late swimming with boys. I shouldn't have been there."

"What happened?"

"Nothing really. Red jumped off in the water, got in a suck hole, your Daddy jumped in and pulled him out, was nearly drowned himself. He was a strong swimmer back then."

"How come they don't like one another?"

"Me, I guess."

"What about you?"

"Red was my beau, then I met your Daddy, and he became my beau. It happened on that

130

barge trip. That was long ago. We were very young then."

"So he didn't like that you liked Daddy better?"

"That's pretty much it. But I've felt bad about it some."

"Because you didn't go with him?"

"Oh, heavens no. But I hear tell all the time about how I broke his heart and it hardened him. About how he don't like women no more. Won't have anything to do with them. I don't mean he's funny or anything."

"Funny?"

Mama suddenly realized what she had said and that it wasn't something she wanted to discuss with me. Back then such matters were hardly mentioned, let alone discussed. Least not within family or polite company.

"Oh, nothing, honey. I just mean he got kind of mean-spirited about women and quit having anything to do with any of the decent ones."

"What about the not decent ones?"

I knew what I was doing, but I tried to present it in an innocent way.

"Well, I don't know about that," Mama said, and I noticed her face had gone red. "Now you run on. Take this on out to your Daddy before the food gets cold and the buttermilk gets warm. Tom don't like buttermilk, so let me get her some cold water."

I knew Tom didn't like buttermilk. Why was she telling me that?

Mama went out to the well with a fruit jar. I followed carrying the two lard buckets filled

131

with food and drink. Mama dropped the bucket in the well, started winching it up.

I said, "So Mr. Woodrow liked you, but you liked Daddy, and Daddy don't like that you liked Mr. Woodrow, and Mr. Woodrow don't like you didn't like him, and now he don't like other women?"

"Something like that," Mama said. "I liked Red. I just, well, it just didn't work out between me and him."

"I'm glad," I said.

She pulled the bucket up on the well curb, poured from it into the jar, and put a lid on it. "Me too," she said. "Now you run on."

"Mama?"

"Yeah."

"Why does Mr. Woodrow wear long sleeves rolled down all the time?"

"I'm sure I don't know. Now go on."

I put the water jar with the buttermilk jars, went on back to the field. Daddy and Tom had parked Sally Redback at the far end near the woods under a sweet gum tree. We sat under the sweet gum and ate. I stole side glances at Daddy from time to time and tried to think of him young and pulling Red Woodrow out of the water.

Actually, he was young when all this occurred, most likely in his thirties, but at my age he seemed ancient.

I wondered if that day he said he wished he hadn't saved Red Woodrow was on account of the murder and what Red Woodrow had said, or on account of Mama.

I had never really thought much about my parents having a life before me, or having to choose each other at some point. I just took for granted they had been together forever. The fact Daddy might be jealous of Red Woodrow was strange to me. It was a side of my father I had never seen or even suspected. I began to realize why he had never really taken a shine to Cecil. Cecil flirted with Mama, and Mama kind of liked it, and Daddy didn't.

◆

When the air had turned cool and the nights were crisp as a starched shirt and the moon was like a pumpkin in the sky, Tom and me played late, chasing lightning bugs and each other. Daddy had gone off on a constable duty, and Mama was in the house sewing.

Toby had actually begun to walk again. His back wasn't broken, but the fallen limb had caused some kind of nerve damage. He never quite got back to normal, but he could get around with a bit of stiffness, and from time to time, for no reason we could discern, his hips would go dead and he'd end up dragging his rear end. Most of the time he was all right, ran with a kind of limp, and not very fast. He was still the best squirrel dog in the county.

On this night he was in the house, something he wasn't supposed to be allowed to do, but when Daddy was gone Mama sometimes let him in and he would lie at her feet while she sewed.

So it was just me and Tom, and when we were good and played out, we sat under the oak talking about this and that, and in the back of my mind I was imagining the oak to be the Great Oak where Robin and his Merry Men met in Sherwood Forest. I had read of it in one of Mrs. Canerton's books, and it had made quite an impression.

As we sat under the oak, talking, I had that same feeling Daddy had spoken of when he was down in the bottoms, in the deep woods, the feeling of being watched.

I stopped listening to Tom, who was chattering on about something or another, slowly turned my head toward the woods, and there, between two trees, in the shadows, but clearly framed by the moonlight, was a horned figure, watching us.

Tom, noticing I wasn't listening to her, said, "Hey."

"Tom," I said. "Be quiet a moment and look where I'm lookin'."

"I don't see any—" Then she went quiet, and after a moment, whispered: "It's him... It's the Goat Man."

The shape abruptly turned, crunched a stick, rustled some leaves, and was gone.

It scared me to think the Goat Man could come as far as our house, knew where we lived, but our land was connected directly to the bottoms and we were a long way from the Preacher's Road.

"He must have followed us home that night," Tom said.

"Yeah."

"I don't like him knowing where we live."

"Neither do I."

We didn't tell Daddy or Mama what we saw. I don't exactly know why, but we didn't. It was between me and Tom, and the next day we hardly mentioned it. I think mentioning it made it too real. It was one thing to have seen the Goat Man in the bottoms, but up next to our house, that was another matter.

Besides, what would have been the point of telling Daddy? He didn't believe in the Goat Man. You couldn't believe in some things till you seen it or done it. Which made me think of that business about a woman's clitoris. Was that real? Or was Doc Tinn just yarning?

For a few days I slept with one eye open, then the urgency of it passed. That's one of the joys of being a kid. You can build up enthusiasm fast, and you can get over something just as fast.

A week after we saw the Goat Man the great rains came. Lightning danced along the skyline for two days, crackled and sparkled inside the cloud cover like lightning bugs caught up in a cheesecloth sack. Rain pounded the earth like Thor's hammer, stirred the river and turned it muddy. Fishing ceased. Plowing ceased. Daddy didn't bother trying to go into town to the barbershop at all. The roads turned to mud. The world turned wet and gray and all progress stopped.

With the rain came the wind, and on the third day of the great rain and the tree-bending bluster came a Texas twister.

A twister is a horrible, fascinating thing. One moment there's a huge dark cloud, then the cloud grows a tail. The tail stretches toward the ground, and when it touches it begins to cry and howl and tear up the earth.

Its winds can carry men and cars and buildings away as easily as a woman might tote a handkerchief. It can rip huge trees out by the roots and toss them about, knock a train off its tracks and tear it up like so much cardboard. It can pull worms from the ground, toss pine straw through tree trunks, fling gravel like bullets.

This twister I'm telling you about tore through the bottoms and laid trees flat all along the riverbank for about two miles, ripped a swath through the woods that killed wildlife, demolished shacks, sucked ponds dry, toted off the fish and frogs and rained them on houses three miles away.

Old Man Chandler, gray-bearded with a nose that lay slightly on his left cheek, it having got that way by him being butted by a goat when he was a child, lived about ten miles from us, directly in the path of the twister.

The twister came down and got him, carried him away, and he lived to tell the tale.

Later, down at the barbershop, he was quite a celebrity. For three or four days he sat and told his story all day long to the men that came in for a haircut or a shave, or to just sit and bull. We did considerable hair-cutting business during that time, and I made several pennies sweeping up, and Tom made two nickel tips just for being cute and sitting there sucking on a peppermint stick.

Way Mr. Chandler told it, he was in his outhouse taking his morning constitutional when he felt a popping in his ears, a sensation like his head being packed tight in sawdust, and a sound like a train roaring across his property, but since he wasn't within miles of a track, he knew that couldn't be.

Without rising from his business, he lifted a leg and kicked the outhouse door open just in time to see his shack go to pieces and leap skyward amidst a black tangled wind already filled with debris.

Before he could get a page torn from the Sears and Roebuck and apply it to that part of his body he'd just dirtied, the twister took the outhouse, peeled it apart around him, and away Mr. Chandler went, Sears and Roebuck catalogue in hand, his butt hanging out. On those rare occasions when women dropped by to hear the story, Mr. Chandler conveniently forgot to mention he was in the outhouse when the twister struck. The tale was slightly abbreviated then, with the storm tearing up the shack and the next minute he was up and in it.

He said he had no idea how long he was in the storm before he developed a sort of calm, realized he had lost the Sears and Roebuck catalogue as well as his pants. He said it was strange going around and around, like being in a suck hole. And he could see things in the funnel, spinning about. A cow, a goat head, fish, tree limbs, and lumber. And a naked colored woman. Her mouth wide open, screaming.

It was here in his story that he often got stopped, having stretched the credibility of some of the listeners. Key words that disturbed them were *woman, colored,* and *naked.* It wasn't that a woman couldn't be sucked up in a storm, or that she couldn't be colored and naked, but it seemed to some this was putting the lace on the panties.

I suppose the reason for this was simple. Nudity wasn't as common as it is now. These days, pick up a magazine, watch the TV, go to a picture show, and someone's always shucking or nearly shucking their drawers. Back then a woman's exposed ankle got men excited.

In my case, the cards like Richard and Abraham had talked about having, the covers of some pulp magazines, Tom bathing in the tin tub, and me likewise, were as close as I had ever gotten to nudity. And I'd only heard about the cards, never actually seen them.

Daddy was often chastised by certain church-minded folks for keeping pulps handy at the barbershop. But as my Dad always explained about the racy covers, it's just a little paint, folks. Nobody's naked.

But since nudity wasn't something thought of outside of the privacy of the home, the idea that Mr. Chandler had gotten a peek at a naked woman, and a colored woman at that, her being forbidden fruit, and it all coming together so conveniently with him having lost his pants, there was doubt among some that this ever happened, and that buried within this story was some sort of wish fulfillment.

You see, colored women weren't supposed to be something a white man would bother about, which of course everyone knew was a lie, but it was one of those polite lies back then. Like women only had sex to have children and everyone was a virgin when they married.

So the idea of a cow going round and round didn't throw them, but a naked colored woman, that was different. Then again, there were a few jokes about the pants-less Mr. Chandler and the cow, but modesty forbids I discuss such a thing.

Even with the ribbing and the doubt, Mr. Chandler stuck to his story. It was here he added in yet another fact. As he went round and round, he determined the woman was not screaming, but was dead, her mouth wide open as if to scream. Her feet were crossed behind her and her arms were crossed over her breasts, and no matter how the storm turned her, she stayed in that position.

Round and round Mr. Chandler and all that stuff went. Then he saw a mattress and a little brown dog, still alive, spin past him. He thought if he could grab hold of that mattress, then everything would be all right. Why he thought this he was uncertain, but it was some kind of plan.

He tried to swim on air toward the mattress, but couldn't. He and it tumbled around and around and finally it came within his grasp and he got hold of it and wrapped his legs around it.

He lost sight of the woman. Things got blacker, then abruptly there was light. Mr. Chandler felt as if he were gliding, hanging on to that mattress like some kind of Arab magician riding a magic carpet, and out into that brightening light he went.

But as Mr. Chandler said, "Soon as it got light, I went back into the dark."

He lost consciousness. When he came to he was clutching the mattress and was stripped of every stitch of clothes, except for his right sock and shoe. He was lying in a field of clover without a drop of rain or wind going on, and when he looked up there wasn't a cloud in the sky. The cow that had gone around and around with him lay in a crumpled mass some distance away, having hit the ground so hard it had been compressed to half its size. There were fish and some lumber and tree limbs sprinkled about. The little brown dog wasn't brown anymore. Most of its fur was gone. It looked like a large balding rat. It was wandering about barking wildly, not able to decide if it was scared to death or mad about being plucked. The colored woman was nowhere to be seen.

Mr. Chandler tore the cover off the mattress, wrapped his privates, started in the direction he figured would be town. He arrived some hours later, his rear end poking out the back of the mattress cover, his hair gone, and his beard plucked, wearing one sock, one shoe, and an amazed expression. He was followed by a stunned bald dog in an extreme nervous condition that barked at anything that moved.

After Doc Stephenson treated him for shock with his favorite cure—a snort of whiskey—and gave him some spare clothes, Mr. Chandler nested free at Cal Fields's house that night and for a week or so after. It was thought by members of the town that Cal did this not only out of love for his fellow man, but—being the entire staff of the newspaper—for the reason of getting the first real lowdown on Mr. Chandler's adventures, which appeared sanitized in the paper's next issue, two days early of its usual weekly appearance. It was a much sought after item, second only to Mr. Chandler himself, who as I said, made daily residence at our barbershop, along with the plucked dog that had become his constant companion.

My father listened attentively to the story, but like everyone else he was most interested in the nude colored woman Mr. Chandler had seen in the midst of the tornado.

"I just seen her a little bit," he said, "then she disappeared. I can't tell you much other'n she was a naked nigger, her mouth wide open. But she looked like a comely nigger to me."

At home the night after we first heard the story, I asked Daddy if he thought the tale was true. We were out on the screen porch, and Daddy was oiling the shotgun down. He studied the distance through the screen a moment, said: "Reckon so. I've known Chandler all my life. He's an honest man. And he tells the story pretty much the same every time he tells it. It don't read as good, but it comes across the same in the paper. I'm pretty certain that's what happened, or what he thinks happened."

"What about that colored woman?" I asked.

"That's what makes me believe him."

"It's like that woman I found, ain't it, Daddy?"

"'Spect so, son. She was most likely put down somewhere by her murderer. Probably in the river. And that ole storm picked her up and carried her off to who knows where. Maybe she was hid good, and God, he wanted her found, so he sent a storm to pull her out and show her to us."

"But she isn't found," I said.

"Yeah, well, you're right. Is this upsetting you, son?"

"No sir. He's still out there...ain't he, Daddy?"

"Depends on a lot of things that can't be figured right now. Depends on how long ago the body was put down. Depends on if the killer moved on after the killing."

"But you don't think so, do you, Daddy?"

"No, son, I don't."

"What you gonna do?"

"Nothing I can do unless the body turns up. I'm gonna drive out to where Mr. Chandler says he landed, where the cow was, and look around there tomorrow."

And he did. But he didn't find anything other than the cow and some junk. At the barbershop Mr. Chandler continued to tell the story for a full work week and half the next. The young doctor-to-be, whose full name we found out was Scott Taylor, told how Mr. Chandler had looked when he was treated, and that story got another week's worth of interest.

Then business dropped off and folks quit coming in for a repeat telling. Mr. Chandler returned to his property, and with the help of neighbors started rebuilding, beginning with the outhouse and a new Sears and Roebuck catalogue. He rounded out the work with a small shack made of crude lumber on the exact spot where the old house had been taken. It was Mr. Chandler's logic that since that spot had been hit once, it was unlikely to get hit again. He felt he'd paid his dues.

The dog went to live with him, and in time grew its hair back, which, according to local legend, came in snow white, just the way Mr. Chandler's did. I can't vouch for that. I don't remember ever seeing the dog again.

Shortly after Mr. Chandler abandoned the barbershop to rebuild his place and regrow hair, the body of the colored woman was found. It was discovered in a hickory nut tree next to a farmhouse. A child, hearing crows, looked up to see a mass of black birds nesting on a black body.

It was determined the body had been there for several days, and it was considered somewhat amusing that the family had walked about and under that tree all that time without so much as looking up, and might not have then, had there not been the cawing of crows.

Cecil pointed out that without the crows they might never have realized it was there until the body got so rotten it started raining meat in the yard. The image of raining meat seemed to please him, and he mentioned it several times.

As it turned out, the woman in the tree, her legs pulled up behind her and bound, her arms pulled across her chest, her hands over her shoulders, wrists tied to her ankles by rope, was named Janice Jane Willman.

She had landed in my Daddy's jurisdiction. I didn't know it at the time, but it was later discovered that a piece of paper had been rolled up and shoved deep in her ear.

Part Two

9

⬧

The year turned cool and crisp and the colored leaves were starting to drop. I remember that in the fall, me and Tom used to go down to the Sabine, find big leaves shaped like a boat, put them in the water, and watch the river take them away.

As I lie here now in my rest home bed, I think of those boats sailing smoothly and beautifully, the river bordered by great and bountiful trees, casting their shadows on the surface of the water, and I long to be there, or to be small enough to lie in one of those leaf boats and glide away.

But the beautiful woods are all gone now, cut down, cemented over with car lots and filling stations, homes and satellite dishes.

The river is there, but the swamps it made have been drained. Alligators have gone away or been killed off. The birds are not as plentiful, and there is something sad about seeing them glide over concrete surfaces, casting their tiny shadows.

147

All the wildlife you see is desperate. Possums and coons in garbage cans. Squirrels being fed from feeders. Befuddled deer standing next to the highway or eating corn put out by hunters.

What was once the bottoms is hot sunlight on cement and no mystery. Seasons are not as defined. One month, save for the temperature or the weather, is not too unlike the next.

Back then it was different. And that time of year, fall, was my favorite. Warm days, cool nights. Dark woods and a churning river. Leaves of many colors. The moon bright and gold.

———————◆———————

Every Halloween there was a little party in town for the kids and whoever wanted to come. It was sponsored by Mrs. Canerton, the widow who operated the unofficial library. It was held at her house.

The women brought covered dishes. Fried chicken, beans, and sausage. Cornbread and rolls. Squirrel and dumplings. Gravy and mashed potatoes. Pumpkin, mince, and sweet potato pies.

The men brought a little bit of hooch to slip into their drinks. The kids sometimes made ghost costumes from sheets and pillowcases. Some of the older kids slipped off, went down on West Street to mark up windows with soap.

Daddy drove us to the party. When we

arrived and stepped out into the main room of the house where the tables were prepared, Mrs. Canerton, who was surrounded by men, both single and married, came to me straight away, walking in a bouncing manner I'd never seen before.

Her hair, tied up and bound in the back, had slipped. A chestnut strand had fallen across her cheek, another across her long neck. Her white dress, dotted with blood-red flowers around the neck, fit her well, and in all the right places. I suppose now that dress would be considered modest. It showed very little, but suggested much.

"How's my favorite reader?"

"I'm fine," I said.

On some level, I realized that night that Mrs. Canerton was more than just a widow lady and, like my mother, pretty. And when she floated across the room in that white, red-flowered dress, she seemed magnificent.

Her breaking off from those men, including Cecil, and coming over to me right away, made me feel special. I could see they were all a little jealous, her having decided to give her time to me.

She took me aside and sat me down in the corner in a red-velvet chair. She sat across from me on a wooden chair and reached into her bookcase. She said, "Have you read Washington Irving?"

I said I had not. I found myself staring at her blue eyes, porcelain white skin, and full lips.

After explaining to Mrs. Canerton that I had not only not read Washington Irving, but didn't know who he was, she said, "Well, you ought to know who he is. And you will now. There's one story in here you'll especially like. About the headless horseman. With you not getting a lot of school, you and Tom need to keep up. At least with good books. I'll come out in a few days and you have this one read. I'll bring you some others."

"Thank you, ma'am."

Though I was glad to have the book, all my friends were outside playing, and that's where I wanted to go. Not only to play, but to get away from Mrs. Canerton. She was making me feel funny, her face close to mine, her breath sweet as a hot peach pie. I had grown warm and itchy all over.

Mrs. Canerton's men friends were anxious for her to be back as well. Cecil came over, winked at me, said, "Are you trying to steal my girl?"

He was wearing a stiff black suit with a shine to the knees and elbows. He had on a white shirt and a tired black tie.

"No sir," I said.

"Oh, that's silly," Mrs. Canerton said. "I'm not your girl, Cecil."

"There," Cecil said, giving me a falsely sour look. "You've done it. Stolen my girl. I think we should duel with sabers at dawn. The prize, Louise."

That was the first time I realized she had a first name.

"Quit being silly," Mrs. Canerton said, but it was obvious she was loving it.

Doc Taylor came over then, just sort of edged between me and Cecil and touched Mrs. Canerton's arm.

"I'll tell you whose girl she is," he said. "Mine."

The three of them laughed and floated back to the crowd of males that had gathered around the former Mrs. Canerton. I saw a number of other women on the far side of the room, dressed up and pretty, frowning in the direction of the pack, and I remember over-hearing a little later at the general store one of those women say something about how shameful it had been, Mrs. Canerton with all those men around like that, and she ought to be ashamed, but I thought it sounded like sour grapes to me.

I found Mama and gave the book to her. She was in the kitchen, sitting at the food-loaded table with the rest of the women, having what she called a hen party.

As I went back into the living room I saw Doc Stephenson sitting in a chair across the way. He was slouched down, looking drunk. I hadn't noticed him when I came in, but then again, I hadn't been looking. Mrs. Canerton had distracted me right away.

Doc Stephenson glanced at me briefly, his face turning even more sour. I figured he was still mad at my Daddy. Then Mrs. Canerton darted by with Cecil following like a puppy, the other men not far behind, Taylor being prominent, and Stephenson quit looking at me. He watched Mrs. Canerton meet some new guests as they came in. I couldn't tell if the way he was looking at her was with interest or anger.

I realized then every man in the room was watching her, like birds protecting a nest.

I went outside to play.

It was another fine cool night with no mosquitoes, lots of lightning bugs glowing and crickets chirping. Me and Tom got to playing hide-and-go-seek with the rest of the kids. While the boy who was it was counting, we went to hide. I crawled under Mrs. Canerton's house, and elbowed and kneed my way beneath the front porch, hoping I wouldn't get fussed at too much when Mama saw my clothes.

I hadn't no more than got under there good than Tom crawled up beside me. I hadn't worn a costume, but she had on her ghost outfit, an old white pillowcase with eyeholes.

"Hey," I whispered. "Go find your own place."

"I didn't know you was under here. It's too late for me to go anywhere."

"Then be quiet," I said.

While we were sitting there, we saw shoes and pants legs moving toward the porch steps. It was the men who had been standing out in the yard smoking. They were gathering on the porch to talk. In passing, I recognized a pair of boots as Daddy's, and after a bit of moving about on the porch above us, we heard the porch swing creak and some of the porch chairs scraping around, then I heard Cecil speak.

"How long she been dead?"

"Couple of weeks, maybe," Daddy said. "It's hard to say. Water and tornado didn't do the body any good."

"She anyone we know?"

"A prostitute," Daddy said. "Janice Jane Willman. She lived near all them juke joints outside of Pearl Creek. Maybe she picked up the wrong man. Ended up in the river."

"How'd you find out who she is?"

"I brought Doc Tinn and the Reverend Bail from over Pearl Creek to take a look at her."

"How'd you know she was from there?"

"I didn't. But they seem to know most everybody. Colored do most of their personal business over there, for obvious reasons. They both knew her. Doc Tinn had treated her for some female problems, and the Reverend had tried to save her soul, of course."

"I didn't know niggers had souls." I knew that voice. Old Man Nation. He showed up wherever there was food and possibly liquor, and never brought a covered dish or liquor. "And one less nigger ain't gonna hurt nothin'."

"She wasn't all colored," Daddy said. "She was part white. A mulatto. Not that that matters."

"Ain't no such thing as part white," Nation said. "A drop of nigger blood makes you a nigger. You shit in a snow bank, snow's ruined. It don't matter how white it was to begin with. You ain't gonna melt that and drink it."

"You know who did it?" Cecil asked. "Any leads?"

"No."

"Hell, a nigger did it." Nation again. "He'd have liked it better had it been a white woman. And mark my words, it will be you don't catch this sonofabitch. A nigger prefers a white woman he gets a chance. Hell, wouldn't you if you was a nigger? A white woman, that's prime business to 'em."

"That's enough of that," Daddy said.

"I'm sayin' it's comin', Constable. It's nothing yet, just niggers, but a white woman is gonna get hers."

"I don't get you," Daddy said. "You think colored kills colored it's all right—"

"It is."

"—and you don't care if anything's done about that, but now you're telling me this killer's got to be caught because a white woman might die. Which is it?"

"I'm just sayin' niggers ain't a loss."

"And what if the killer's white?"

"They still ain't a loss," Mr. Nation said. "But it'll turn out to be a nigger. Mark my words. And all this murderin' won't end at just niggers."

"I heard you had a suspect," Cecil said.

"Not really," Daddy said.

"Some colored fella, I heard," Cecil said.

"I knew it," Nation said. "Some goddamn nigger."

"I picked a man up for questioning, that's all."

"Where is he?" Nation asked.

"You know," Daddy said, "I think I'm gonna have me a piece of that pie."

The porch creaked, the screen door opened, and we heard boot steps entering into the house.

"Nigger lover," Nation said.

"That's enough of that," Cecil said.

"You talkin' to me, fella?" Mr. Nation said.

"I am, and I said that's enough."

There was a scuttling movement on the porch, and suddenly there was a smacking sound and Mr. Nation hit the ground in front of us. We could see him through the steps. His face turned in our direction, but I don't think he saw us. It was dark under the house, and he had his mind on other things. He got up quick like, leaving his hat on the ground, then we heard movement on the porch, the screen door again, and Daddy's voice. "Ethan, don't come back on the porch. Go on home."

"Who do you think you are to tell me anything?" Mr. Nation said.

"Right now, I'm the constable, and you come up on this porch, you do one little thing that annoys me, I will arrest you."

"You and who else?"

"Just me."

"What about him? He hit me. You're on his side because he took up for you."

"I'm on his side because you're a loudmouth spoiling everyone else's good time. You been drinkin' too much. Go home and sleep it off, Ethan. Let's don't let this get out of hand."

Mr. Nation's hand dropped down and picked up his hat. He said, "You're awfully high and mighty, aren't you?"

"There's just no use fighting over something foolish," Daddy said.

"You watch yourself, nigger lover," Mr. Nation said.

"Don't come by the barbershop no more," Daddy said.

"Wouldn't think of it, nigger lover."

Then Mr. Nation turned and we saw him walking away.

Daddy said: "Cecil. You talk too much."

"Yeah, I know," Cecil said.

"Now, I was gonna get some pie," Daddy said. "I'm gonna go back inside and try it again. When I come back out, how's about we talk about somethin' altogether different?"

"Suits me," someone said, and I heard the screen door open again. For a moment I thought they were all inside, then I realized Daddy and Cecil were still on the porch, and Daddy was talking to Cecil.

"I shouldn't have spoken to you like that," Daddy said.

"It's all right," Cecil said. "You're right. I talk too much."

"So do I. I shouldn't have told you I had a suspect in the first place. I didn't tell you to be quiet about it. I should have. I can't say I'm much of a policeman. I think I was talkin' so I could brag a bit. About what, I don't know. Feeling like I'm on the job, I guess."

"Still, I knew better."

"Let's forget it. And thanks for hitting Nation. You didn't owe me that."

"I did it because *I* owed him that. This suspect, Jacob. You think he did it?"

"No. I don't."

"Is he safe?"

"For now. I may just let him go and never let it be known who he is."

"Again, I'm sorry, Jacob."

"No problem. Let's get some of that pie."

On the way home in the car the windows were rolled down and the October wind was fresh and ripe with the smell of the woods. My belly was full of pie and lemonade and I was cozy and content. I was thinking of Louise Canerton, and I found myself wondering how she would look without her dress. The thought bothered me and I tried not to dwell on it. But I kept thinking about her bosom, her long legs and how they would feel beneath my hands.

Finally I prayed silently to God, but all the while I was thinking of her naked. I wondered if God saw her naked. He must. What did he think about that? Did he like what he saw? Was there no consideration for what he saw? Didn't he create her? If so, why did he make ugly people?

I believe it was at that point, although I didn't realize it at the time, my ideas of God and religion were starting to change, even erode.

As we wound through the woods along the dirt road that led to our house, I began to feel sleepy.

Tom had already nodded off with her dirt-stained ghost mask clutched in her hands. I leaned against the side of the car and began to halfway doze. In time, I realized Mama and Daddy were talking.

"He had her purse?" Mama said.

"Yeah," Daddy said. "He had it, and he'd taken money from it."

"Could it be him?"

"He says he was fishing, saw the purse and her dress floating, snagged the purse with his fishing line. The dress washed on by him. He saw there was money in the purse, and he took it. Figured a purse in the river wasn't something anyone was going to find, and there wasn't any name in it, and it was just five dollars going to waste. Said he didn't even consider that someone had been murdered."

"So you believe him?"

"I believe him. I've known Old Mose all my life. He practically lives on that river in that boat of his. He wouldn't harm a fly. Besides, the man's over seventy years old and not in the best of health. He's had a hell of a life. His wife ran off forty years ago and he's never gotten over it. His son disappeared when he was a youngster. Whoever raped this woman had to be pretty strong. She was young enough, and from the way her body looked, she put up a pretty good fight. Man did this had to be strong enough to...well, she was cut up pretty bad. Same as the other woman."

"Oh dear."

"I'm sorry, honey. I didn't mean to upset you."

"How did you come by the purse?"

"I went to see Mose. Like I always do when I'm down on the river. It was layin' on the table in his shack. I had to arrest him. I don't know I should have now. Maybe I should have taken the purse and said I found it. I believe him. But I don't have evidence one way or the other."

"Didn't Mose have some trouble before?"

"When his wife ran off some thought he'd killed her. She was fairly loose. That was the rumor. Nothing ever came of it."

"But he could have done it?"

"I suppose."

"And what about his boy? What happened there?"

"Telly was the boy's name. He was addle-headed. Mose claimed that's why his wife run off. She was embarrassed by that addle-headed boy. Kid disappeared four or five years later and Mose never talked about it. Some thought he killed him too. But that's just rumor. White folks talkin' about colored folks

159

like they do. I believe his wife ran off. The boy wasn't much of a thinker, and he may have run off too. He liked to roam the woods and river. He might have drowned, fallen in some hole somewhere and never got out."

"But none of that makes it look good for Mose, does it?"

"No, it doesn't."

"What are you gonna do, Jacob?"

"I don't know. I was afraid to lock him up over at the courthouse. It isn't a real jail anyway, and word gets around a colored man was involved, there won't be any real thinking on the matter. I talked Bill Smoote into letting me keep Mose over at his bait house."

"Couldn't Mose just run away?"

"I suppose. But he's not in that good a health, hon. And he trusts me to investigate, clear him. That's what makes me nervous. I don't know how. I thought about talking to the county boys that cover Pearl Creek. They have more experience, but they have a tendency to be a little emotional themselves."

"You mean Red."

"Yeah. He's rumored to be in the Klan, or was."

"You don't know that for a fact," Mama said.

"If he ain't got an official hood in his drawer," Daddy said, "you can bet he's got one in spirit."

"He ain't always been that way."

"No. But things change...things can happen."

Mama quickly changed the subject. "But if it's not Mose, who is it?"

"After I was told about Janice Willman, I went over and took a look at the body. Same sort of thing. She's been cut on, and tied with one leg pulled up to her neck, rope around her head and ankle. That seems to be a thing he does to every one of 'em, some kind of tie-up."

"Does that mean anything, tying them up like that?"

"I don't know. Doc Tinn thinks so. When I showed him this body and talked to him about it, he said he believes these fellas have a pattern. He'd done some reading on it, and he thinks they do pretty much the same thing over and over. Little difference here and there, but the same thing. Jack the Ripper did his killings the same, 'cept each one got more vicious than the last. Doc Tinn told me about some others he's read about, and now these. All cut up. All tied or bound up in some kind of way, and all of them in or near the river. Or they had been in the river. He calls them pattern killers. He said he hoped to write some kind of paper on it, but figures being colored he hasn't got a chance in hell of doing anything important with it."

"That doesn't explain why," Mama said.

"No. It doesn't."

I began to drift off again. I thought of Mose. He had white blood in him. Red in his hair. Eyes green as spring leaves. Skin dark as molasses. I had waved at him not so long ago. Sometimes, when Daddy had a good day hunting or fishing, he'd go by there and give Mose a squirrel or some fish. Mose was always glad to see us.

I thought of the Goat Man again. I recalled him standing below the Swinging Bridge, looking up through the shadows at me. I thought of him near our house, watching. The Goat Man had killed those women. Not Mose. I was certain of it.

It was there in the car, battered by the cool October wind, that I began to formulate a plan to find the Goat Man and free Mose. I thought on it for several days after, and I begun to come up with something that seemed like a good idea.

Looking back on it now, I realize just how foolish and wild it was. Inspired by one of Mrs. Canerton's books, *The Count of Monte Cristo*.

But my plan, foolish as it was, never came to pass.

———◆———

Next day Daddy went to the barbershop and Mama had me stay home with Tom to help her do the canning. We did that all morning and well after lunch. Late in the afternoon, Mama sent Tom and me out to play and she set about putting up the vegetables we had canned in the cabinets.

Although it's called canning, we did it in jars. It was a lot of work, sterilizing jars, packing them with cooked vegetables, sealing them with paraffin and lids, setting them aside. I was glad to get away from it all. Tom and I played a game of chase at the edge of the woods, and finally took to resting under the oak. Tom fell asleep in the chair there right away, and I walked to the well to get a drink of water. I was still cooking on my plan to rescue Mose, although I was beginning to wonder what I was rescuing him from. Where would I take him?

I cranked up the bucket and used the dipper to drink, and as I was putting it aside, I heard a car roll up around front. I thought it was most likely Daddy, maybe coming home early if the shop wasn't well attended, so I went around the edge of the house to see.

When I got there I saw the car was a black dented Ford. The man that got out was wearing a large gray cowboy hat and a holstered gun on his hip. He stood in front of the Ford with his right knee cocked forward and he was working the ground with the toe of his boot, way he had the day I first seen him. He wore a long-sleeve shirt with the sleeves buttoned down tight. There was a sweat ring around his neck. He was the same man Daddy had talked to outside of Pearl Creek. The one he had saved from a suck hole when they were both young. Red.

He saw me and smiled. "How're you doin', partner?"

"Okay," I said.

"Your Daddy here?"

"My Mama," I said.

"Yeah," he said, "well, that'll do. Tell her I'm here, will you?"

I went inside and told Mama. When she went to the front door and saw Red standing in the yard, I noticed a change in her expression. I can't describe it to you. It was surprise, but something else too. She reached up and gently touched her hair, then her hands dropped to her sides and she smoothed her dress.

"Red," she said.

"May Lynn. You're as lovely as ever."

She colored slightly. "Jacob isn't here."

Red stood in the yard and looked around, as if Daddy might appear out of the afternoon air. "Say he ain't."

Of course he wasn't. I had already told him Daddy wasn't in.

"Well now, maybe we could chat a few minutes," Red said. "He be in soon?"

"Yes," Mama said. Then added: "Very soon."

"May I come in?"

Mama hesitated. She looked at me. She said, "Harry, run on with you. We're gonna do a little grown-up talk."

I hesitated, but went out on the screened back porch and sat in the swing. When Red came in and Mama shut the door, the air draft made the door to the screen porch push open a bit. I got up to shut it, pushed it almost to, then hesitated. I knew it wasn't polite to listen in on other people's conversations, but I couldn't help myself.

"Well, sit down," Mama said. She sounded uncomfortable and unsure of herself in her own house. I had never known her to sound like that before.

"Thank you," Red said. I heard chairs

164

scrape, then there was a long moment of silence.

Mama said, "I could make some coffee."

"No. That's all right. He'll be back soon?"

"I can't say exactly. He cuts hair until there isn't any to cut."

"It's been a long time, hasn't it?"

"Yes, it has."

"Nice house."

"Thank you. It isn't much really. Jacob and I built it. I nailed down the floors myself. My Mom and Dad helped us."

"Floor looks sturdy," Red said.

"Thanks."

"How are your mother and father? I haven't seen them in years."

"They moved to North Texas few years back. Mama went there to be near my sister Ida. Ida was ill and had children to take care of. Ida got better, but Daddy died."

"I'm sorry. How's your Mama?"

"Spunky as ever. We've been writing each other a lot. She may move back to be near us."

"I see. I guess that's good."

There was a long silence. A bumblebee buzzed behind me, and I turned to see him at the screen, bouncing up against it.

Mama broke the silence. "Could you tell me what it is you want, and I can tell Jacob?"

"I really should talk to him myself."

"Is it about this murder business? The colored women?"

"Yeah."

"Jacob says you don't want him bothering with it."

"First of all, the body wasn't in his county."

"It was found in the bottoms here."

"Yes, but he had the body brought to Pearl Creek. To have a bunch of niggers tell him what had happened to her. You don't have to be one of the city boys to know what happened to her."

"But he wanted to know who she was, as well as what happened to her."

"Doc Stephenson could have told him."

"Doc Stephenson is a drunk, and a fool. And a lot less likely to know who she is."

"He knows every nigger in these parts. He ain't got nothing against niggers. And neither do I."

"Stephenson is still a drunk and a fool."

"I don't want to argue with you, May Lynn. There was a time—"

"If the body was found here, under Jacob's jurisdiction, what's it matter, Red? What business is it of yours? You say it isn't Jacob's business, but it seems it's more his business than yours. He drove her to your county to identify her, but she was murdered here."

"We don't want the niggers stirred up, May Lynn. That's all. They got to know their place, and when Jacob starts treating them with the same concern, the same respect as white folks, then you could have problems."

"You really believe that?"

"I do... There's a rumor Jacob's arrested a nigger for the murders."

"That's not true."

"Story goes he's hidin' this nigger out. What I want to say to Jacob is this. Give the nigger up. 'Cause he don't, it'll go bad for him."

"Jacob hasn't arrested anyone for the murder. And if he has, what would be the problem with that?"

"None. We just want him to give the murderer up."

"Just a few minutes ago you didn't care about a colored being killed. Now it's a concern."

"I'm concerned a white woman—like yourself—could be next. A nigger gone on a streak like that, he won't be satisfied with just black women. He's gonna want a white one before long. One he killed had white blood in her."

"Now it matters because she had white blood. I always thought folks like you thought a drop of colored blood made a person colored, no matter how much white was in them."

"Well, I don't think that. There are degrees. White blood can dominate. It's the way you look makes you a nigger. How you live."

"A life is a life, Red. Dark skin. Light skin. Anything in between. That's what concerns Jacob."

"Way it looks, May Lynn, is Jacob's got the man did these murders and he's protectin' him 'cause he's a nigger."

"You know that's ridiculous."

"I don't know that. Doc Stephenson claims Jacob's pretty tight with the niggers."

"Doc Stephenson's an idiot."

Red laughed. "He may be at that. I'm here

to help, May Lynn. I owe Jacob. I'm here to warn Jacob."

"I don't think you are. I think this has to do with somethin' else besides him pullin' you out of a suck hole."

"It does. I owe him for another reason. And there's you. I don't want nothing to happen that could come down on you too."

"That's considerate of you...now. Considering."

"I was a damn fool..."

"Sssshhhhh," Mama said. "Don't speak of it."

Red was silent for a while. After what seemed like a change of seasons, he said, "I want Jacob to know it could get so folks come to see him."

"Are you talking about the Klan?" Mama asked.

"I'm just sayin'..."

"Red. I heard you'd turned bitter. That you was sympathetic to that bunch of sheet-wearing cowards—"

"Careful with your words, May Lynn."

"I don't need to be careful. I would have never thought it of you. I knew you when we were young, Red. I knew you to carry food down in the bottoms to that poor old colored lady, Miss Maggie."

"We was just kids."

"That woman practically raised you, Red."

"She was just a nigger worked for my Daddy. I fed Daddy's dogs too."

"You know she more than worked for your

168

Daddy. You suckled at her breast. Played with her kids like they was your own kin. Then your Daddy got old and so did she. She was almost your mother. She was more of a mother than your mother. And she was more of a wife to your Daddy than your mother."

"That's enough!"

I heard a slam, as if a hand had been slapped on the table, a chair slid back. I pushed open the door and rushed in.

"You okay, Mama?"

"Yes, hon. I'm okay."

Red was standing at the table, his hat in his hand. His face red as his hair, his knee cocked forward slightly, turning the toe of his boot against the floors he'd not too long ago bragged on. He glared at Mama. "You done come to be just like Jacob," Red said.

"And you'd be lucky if you were anything like him," Mama said. "You got somethin' in you always been there, Red. It wasn't just me turned you like they say."

"You didn't help."

Red looked at me. His hand shook as he put on his hat.

"There was a time when I thought I might should have done different than I did, Red," Mama said. "For just a moment. But I come to a understanding with myself long ago that I was wrong about that. Still, I considered you a good man, Red. Today, I don't know. I do know this. Jacob is ten times the man you are or ever will be."

Red opened his mouth as if to speak. He looked at me and the steam went out of him. He trembled slightly.

"I could say somethin'," he said.

"You could. And if you must, say it. But I've said my somethin', and I've got one more thing to say. I see you're still wearin' your shirts with the sleeves rolled down."

There was a movement in Red's face that frightened me. But it was just a twitch, then it was gone.

"You tell Jacob what I said, hear? He's been warned. I've paid my debt."

"You think that's paying a debt, you're wrong, Red. Let me tell you somethin'. Now you've been warned. Don't you ever step foot on this property again. You hear?"

"I hear."

Red went to the door, turned, looked at me and Mama. "That's a fine-looking boy you got there, May Lynn. And you got that little girl out there too. So innocent. I believe she's gonna look a lot like you. Already starting to get your face. I hate to think of you bringing them up to think niggers are the same as us. It'll just bring them grief, put them on the same level as the niggers. You too, May Lynn."

"Good day, Constable," Mama said.

Red unconsciously rubbed his left hand along his right sleeve, went out without shutting the door, got in his dented black Ford and drove away.

A thin plume of dust followed after the car and drifted in the air long after he was gone.

11

Mama made me swear not to tell Daddy about Red's visit. She said she wanted to do it. Word it right so he didn't get angry and go off half-cocked. I didn't worry much about that. Daddy could be a little impatient at times, and I had seen him angry, but I hadn't never seen him go off half-cocked.

That night I listened with my ear close to the wall to find out what Mama told Daddy about Red, but they were whispering so light I couldn't make anything out but their bedsprings making noise. I drifted off to sleep finally, and when I awoke the next morning I remembered faintly dreaming of the Goat Man.

It was a Monday, and Daddy was off from the barbershop. He had already gotten up and fed the livestock, and as daybreak was running like a broken egg yolk through the trees and the birds were calling out that they were in search of breakfast, he got me up to help tote water from the well to the house. Mama was in the kitchen tending the wood stove, cooking grits, biscuits, and fatback for breakfast.

When we came in she smiled and he kissed her on the cheek and ran his hand down her back. She gave him a quick peck on the mouth and a wink.

We left out then for another bucket of water, and about halfway to the well, I said, "Daddy. You ever figure out what you're gonna do with ole Mose?"

He paused a moment. "How'd you know about that?"

"I heard you and Mama talkin'."

He nodded, and we started walking again. We got water and started back to the house. He said, "You ain't mentioned you know anything about that, have you?"

"No sir."

"Good boy."

"So what have you decided to do with Mose?"

"I haven't decided. I can't leave him where he is for good. Someone will get on to it. I'm gonna have to take him to the courthouse, or let him go. There's no real evidence against him, just some circumstantial stuff. But a colored man, a white woman, he'll never get a fair trial. I guess I'd done let him go, but I got to be sure myself he didn't do it."

"I thought you said the woman was colored. Or part white."

"You was listenin' from somewhere at Mrs. Canerton's house, wasn't you?"

I admitted it.

"Well, let me tell you somethin'. That woman was white. She didn't have a drop of colored blood that anyone knowed of. She was dark-lookin' 'cause she was bloated and dead and up there in that tree for the wind and rain to hammer on. Folks that found her just thought she was colored, way her skin had turned. Around here, someone gets a good burn in the sun and it turns brown, there's someone whisperin' there's colored blood in 'em. Hell. I thought she was colored too. Body gets like that, you can't tell much about skin or race or nothin'. Death puts us all even, boy."

"Mr. Chandler said she was colored."

"She's dark-skinned, son. Just like I said."

"But you said—"

"I threw that in to keep from stirrin' people up. You put white and colored in the same sentence, folks start to stir."

"You did put white and colored in the same sentence. You said she was part white."

"You're right." Daddy paused to take his pipe out of his pocket, stuff it with tobacco, and light it. "I'm not sure that was smart, son, but I was playing the odds. I said she was colored, no one cares. Had I said she was white, there'd have been lynchin's all over this county. But she's got white blood, it gives most folks pause, makes some folks see her as a human being. On the other hand, she's not so white they'd get worked up over it. It's a sad state of affairs, but that's how it is."

"How'd you find out she was a white lady?"

"Thinking she was colored, I drove her body over to Pearl Creek to see if Doc Tinn or Reverend Bail knew who she was. They did, but not because she was colored. She was white and had a bad reputation and mostly

173

worked the colored section over Pearl Creek. That gave her a worse reputation. A white woman that'll lie down with coloreds don't get the respect of one will lie down with her own kind. And a woman like that don't get much to begin with. She hoboed to get to Pearl Creek from Tyler, rode the train back when she could catch it. Did most of her work at the dance joints and about. But, word gets out— and it will eventually—that she was white, well, it won't matter she was a woman none of the so-called self-respectin' men over here would have given the time of day, even if they might have given her a dollar. Them same men are gonna be up in arms, ravin' about how a colored killed her and how all white womanhood is in danger."

"Ain't it in danger?"

"Womanhood in general is in danger, son. Anyone could be in danger with a killer like this. But I think it's mostly women he's after. I'm just sayin' she'd gotten killed by a train or drowned by accident, wouldn't have been no mournin'. But folks like Nation think maybe a colored had his way with her, well, Mose and every colored boy over twelve might end up bein' lynched."

We carried the buckets toward the house.

"You said you got to be sure Mose didn't do it, but you don't think he did, do you, Daddy?"

We were on the back porch now. Daddy set his bucket down. I set mine down too. "It's like I've opened this box and I don't know how

174

to close it. Mistake I made was mentioning it. That was pride talking."

"You were proud of arresting Mose?"

"I was proud of the fact I was doin' somethin'. So far in this whole business all I've done is look at a couple dead bodies, talk to a few folks, and that's it. I don't know no more than I did when I started. 'Cept these women got names, and I figure they got loved ones. Worse thing about it, I don't even know for sure. I didn't try to find any of the families or go see 'em. I was gonna do any real investigatin', that's what I should have done. It's what I ought to do. Mistake I made was arrestin' Mose in the first place, then tellin' I'd arrested someone. And I did that on account of Doc Stephenson."

"How's that?"

"He was in the shop. He came in to get Cecil to cut his hair. He used to come in now and then for me to do it, but after that little event over in Pearl Creek, he only has Cecil do it. I guess my pride got to me, him thinkin' I didn't know what I was doin', and Cecil gettin' the bulk of the customers, so I shot my mouth off like I was talkin' to Cecil."

"But you was talkin' to Doc Stephenson?"

"Afraid so. And it come back to haunt me at Mrs. Canerton's."

We took the water inside, poured it up in the pitchers and one of the washtubs where Mama kept extra water throughout the day, then started back.

We came to the well and Daddy rested his

bucket on the curbing for a moment. He turned to me and said, "You know why I haven't seen any of the folks of these women got murdered?"

I shook my head.

"'Cause one's colored, Harry, and the other is a prostitute. I don't really know no colored people, 'cept Mose. I talk to a bunch of 'em, and like 'em okay, and I think a bunch like me okay, but I don't know 'em, and they don't really know me. Hell, I don't really know Mose. All me and him ever talked about was fishing and the river and now and then tobacco. I guess I don't want to know no prostitute's mother or Daddy. Down deep, I think I may be just like everyone else. And you know what, Harry?"

"No sir."

"That bothers me."

Daddy dropped the bucket into the well. When it splashed, he began cranking it up.

"You ain't like everybody else, Daddy. You don't hate colored."

"Down deep, like I said, I ain't so sure. I have my feelings."

"But you and Mama, you're different than the others."

"There's lots of folks feel like we do. It's just the ones feel the other way got bigger mouths and they're meaner. Let me tell you somethin', son. When I was a boy every word out of my mouth about the coloreds was nigger this and nigger that. I fished on the river as a boy a lot, and there was this colored boy down there, and he was catching big ole catfish. I was jealous of him. The idea of a colored catchin' those big ole fish, and me not able to catch anything. I'm ashamed to tell it, but I was gonna beat him up one day. I was down there, and there he was near my spot, pullin' them fish out like they was trained to jump on his line.

"He looked over at me, and said, 'Sir, I got some good bait I done made myself, you want some?'

"I took some, and I still didn't have any luck. But we sat there on the bank and we talked, and by the end of the day I knew somethin' I'd never known before."

"What was that?"

"He was just like me. He had a mean old Daddy too. Old man had killed half a dozen folks, all colored, so not a damn thing had been done to him, and the boy was afraid of him. I was afraid of my old man. He taught me how to make the bait, how to take blood and cornmeal and a little flour dough, and knead it all together in little balls and let them harden, then fasten them to the hook just right.

"Me and him didn't become best friends, but I quit thinking about what color he was. It got so I looked forward to goin' down there and fishin', just so me and him could talk.

"Well now, a white girl come up dead and naked in the river, and somehow, and I don't remember how, it was decided this boy, name was Donald, was the one did it. I didn't hear nothin' about it happenin' at the time, but one afternoon I was comin' home from squirrel

177

huntin', and I hit over there on what some folks are callin' Preacher's Road, and there was this big crowd, and when I worked my way in there, they had Donald in a wagon bed, and they had nailed his hands and feet to that bed and they had castrated him.

"He saw me, son. Looking out of that crowd at him. I still remember his eyes. They looked to me as big as saucers. He looked at me, and he said, 'Mister Jacob. Can't you help me?' I stepped back into the crowd, son. I was thirteen years old and I didn't know what to do, and here was a boy my age dying and calling me Mister and beggin' me to help.

"They set the wagon on fire and finished him. And it wasn't two days later they found a trail of that little girl's clothes, and they was followed to a little camp where they found some more of the girl's belongin's, and a dead colored man. But there was the girl's goods, her little purse and such. Now, I don't know that fella did it, but I can be pretty sure Donald didn't. I figured the crowd was mad, and the cry went up a nigger did it, and they found them one. Poor Donald. I 'spect it was that man they found that actually done it."

"How'd he die, Daddy?"

"Just died, I suppose. Another thing. They took that man's body and dragged it through the woods, dragged it down Preacher's Road and all over and finally cut it loose and set fire to it. The damn corpse, mostly bones, laid beside the road for a month before animals or someone dragged it off.

"Donald's old man. The mean sonofabitch. He was finally killed trying to rob a house in Mission Creek. He come through the window and was shot. I remember thinkin', good riddance. Donald, he was a good kid. He wasn't no worse than any kid that age, and he was killed like that. Burned a memory, Harry, that's what I'm tryin' to tell you, and it ain't a memory I like worth a damn.

"Bottom line is, I ain't so pure, Harry. I didn't do a thing to help Donald."

"Daddy, wasn't nothing you could do."

"I like to think that's the truth. But I ain't never been the same since. I don't hate no one because of their color if I can help myself. Sometimes bad things wash back on me, but I try, Harry. I try.

"As for your Mama. Well, she's always been that way. Some people can just see a thing is true right off. Your Grandma is like that too, and she passed it on to your Mama, and your Mama helps me understand it when I ain't always willin' to. It's easy to hate, Harry. It's easy to say this and that happens because the colored do or don't do one thing or another, but life isn't that easy, son. Constablin', I've seen some of the worst human beings there is, both white and colored. Color don't have a thing to do with meanness. Or goodness. You remember that."

"Yes sir, I will."

"You see, Harry, there ain't no future in the way things been. A change has got to happen if people are gonna live together in this

179

country. Civil War's been over seventy years or so, and there's still people hatin' folks 'cause they're born in the Northern or Southern part of these United States.

"And the only difference for colored now is the masters can't sell 'em. Mose just missed being a slave, but he ain't never had nothing but white folks on his butt. That's why he went off to live in the woods like he done. To get away from white folks. And you know what, he trusts me. Or seems to. I go over to check on him, he's glad to see me. He thinks I'm protectin' him."

"Ain't you?"

"He'd been more protected had I left him alone. I think I partly arrested him 'cause he's colored and had that white woman's purse.

"Part of me, not a good part, was bothered by that. Him havin' that white woman's purse and him bein' colored. Even if he did find it. I was a boy, he taught me how to put bait on a hook so it wouldn't come off. How to skin catfish with a pair of pliers. How to tell directions in the woods and where all the good fishin' holes are, and how to look for new ones. He ain't never showed me no signs of being a killer, and I arrested him right away."

"You was just goin' on evidence, Daddy."

Daddy smiled like his lips might run off the side of his face, poured the well bucket's water into the tote bucket.

When we finished with the water, Mama had breakfast on the table, and Tom was sitting there with her eyes squinted, looking as if she were going to fall face forward into her grits.

Normally, there'd be school, but the schoolteacher had quit and they hadn't hired another yet, so me and her had nowhere to go that day.

I think that was part of the reason Daddy asked me to go with him after breakfast. That, and I figured he wanted some company. He told me he had decided to go see Mose.

We drove over to Bill Smoote's. Bill owned an icehouse down by the river. It was a big room really, with sawdust and ice packed in there, similar to the one at Pearl Creek. People came and bought ice by car or by boat on the river. He sold right smart of it.

Up behind the icehouse was the little house where Bill lived with his wife and two daughters, who looked as if they had fallen out of an ugly tree, hit every branch on the way down, then smacked the dirt solid. They was always smilin' at me and such, and it made me nervous.

Behind Mr. Smoote's house was his barn, really more of a big shed. It looked like it had fallen down once, then been blown back together by a high wind. That's where Daddy said Mose was kept. We pulled up at the house and Daddy went up and knocked on the door. A ragged, big-breasted, teenage girl with dirty blond hair answered.

Daddy said, "Elma. Your Papa in?"

"Yes sir, I'll git 'im."

A moment later Mr. Smoote was on the porch. He was a porky man in greasy overalls. He was missing several teeth and wore a big straw hat with dark sweat stains where the crown met the brim. He liked to curl his upper lip and spit tobacco through a gap in his teeth. He did that almost immediately, smacking a wad of tobacco in the sand around the porch.

"I come to see him," Daddy said.

Mr. Smoote nodded. "All right. Let's go on up there and get it over with. Someone come up on us, find out I'm housin' that nigger, it could be trouble."

"I appreciate you doin' this, Bill."

"I owe you some. You sure this nigger's okay to have around here? I mean, he killed somebody, I don't like him around my family. I got girls."

We stepped off the porch and started walking toward the barn.

"Bill," Daddy said, "I just brought him in for questioning, you know that. I can't take him into town. Folks find out, it'll be trouble. Your littlest girl could whip Mose's ass."

"Well, he might use an axe."

"Bill, you've known Mose long as I have. What do you think?"

"It's hard to figure a nigger."

Daddy didn't answer that. He said, "I really appreciate you, Bill."

"Well, it's like I said. I owe you."

When Mr. Smoote opened the barn door the sunlight barged in. Dust floated up and made me cough. The sunlight poking through the dust motes made it seem as if I were seeing the barn and its contents through a veil. There was a smell about the place. Old hay. Sweat and soured sewage. The sewage part obviously came from a nasty-looking black can with flies humming around it.

In one corner, sitting with his back against a hay bale, was Old Mose. I hadn't seen him in a time, and I was shocked by how small he'd become. He wasn't any taller than me, and not as wide. His arms were like sticks and the skin didn't fit; it was loose enough to be double-wrapped. His patched overalls, gone nearly white from wear, flapped around his bony legs when he stood up. He grinned at us. He had a few teeth and a couple of them weren't black. He bowed his head and it wobbled in our direction as if it hung there by a loose screw. His eyes were squinted, trying to accustom to the light. When he finally widened them, I was reminded that they were green as emeralds. They were the only part of him that seemed alive. His reddish black complexion, odd combination of freckles with kinky, red hair gone gray, made him look like some kind of gnome from a book Mrs. Canerton had loaned me. I couldn't imagine when Mose had gotten so old.

"Missuh Jacob, I'm sho glad to see you,"

Mose said. His voice was like a crippled man trying to rise up on crutches.

As Mose shuffled toward us, something dragged and thumped against the ground, stirring up dust. It was a chain and it was attached to a cuff of metal around his ankle, just above where his small foot poked sock-less into a worn-out shoe. The chain was attached to the barn's central support post.

"Goddamn," Daddy said, then turned on Bill. "You've chained him."

"I owe you, Jacob. But like I said, I got a family. Girls. Mose always seemed a good nigger to me, but a favor only goes so far. He stays here, he wears the chain. Hell, he's got it all right. He eats good cookin' and shits in a can over there. I have it emptied every day. And he don't want for water."

I could see Daddy was exasperated, but he sighed and said, "All right. Let me talk to him, just me and my boy."

"Your boy can know what I can't?"

"If you don't mind, Bill."

"I mind, but I'll do 'er. Jacob, you get this nigger out of here pretty damn quick."

"That's the plan," Daddy said.

Mr. Smoote left out, leaving the barn door slightly open. Daddy went over and touched Mose's shoulder.

"I don't unnerstan', Missuh Jacob," Mose said. "You knows I didn't do nuttin' to no white womens. No coloreds neither."

"I know," Daddy said. "Let's sit down."

Daddy sat on the hay bale and Mose dragged

his chain and sat on the other side of it. I went and leaned against the post that the chain was fastened to. From that angle, way the light was slicing in, I could see Mose's ankle had been bleeding. There was a brown cake of blood below the metal cuff, just above where his shoe started.

"I didn't mean for this, Mose," Daddy said.

"Yessuh," Mose said. "I 'spose not."

"I'll get you out of here."

"Yessuh. Missuh Jacob?"

"What, Mose?"

"How come you done me like this?"

"The purse, Mose."

"I fount it, Missuh Jacob. I tole you that."

"Yeah."

"I wouldn't hurt no white womens. I wouldn't hurt nobody 'cept a fish, a coon, a possum. Somethin' to eat. And I don't eat no white womens. Coloreds neither."

"I know."

"You know, Missuh Jacob, but here I is."

Daddy looked at the dirt floor.

"I could have run off that firs' night, but I stayed here 'cause you asked me to, Missuh Jacob. Next day, him and a boy came put the chain on me."

"I thought you having the purse was evidence. Not that you did it, but that it was some kind of evidence."

"You done got that purse, Missuh Jacob. You don't need me."

"Wait a minute. Boy? What boy helped chain you?"

185

"Jes some white boy."

"Okay, Mose. Listen here. I'm gonna get this chain off of you, and I'm gonna let you go. We're gonna take you home. Hear?"

"Yessuh. I'd like that, I would."

Daddy got up. "Stay here a minute, son."

Daddy went out. Mose looked at me. He smiled. "You 'member that ole grennel you and me caught?"

"Yes sir."

"Had them teeth like a man. It really scart you. 'Member that?"

"Yes sir."

"I cooked it up fer us. 'Member that?"

"Yes sir."

"It was good too. You don't cook 'em right, they taste jes like cotton. But I done it good. We ate it on a stump down by the river. My boy was little, me and him used to do that. Sit down by the river and eat."

I started to ask him about his son, but considering all Daddy had told me, I thought it might not be the best idea. No use dredging up more bad things for Mose to think about.

"You still got that coon dog?" I asked.

"No, Missuh Harry, I don't. That ole dog done gone on to his rewa'd. He was nigh on fifteen year ole when he done up and died. He couldn't see none last year of his life. I had to hand-feed 'im. He couldn't eben smell no mo.'"

Daddy and Mr. Smoote came in. Mr. Smoote had a hammer and chisel. "Get that off of him," Daddy said.

"You takin' him away?" Mr. Smoote asked.

"I am. And don't mention he's been here. Just keep on keepin' it a secret."

"We even then?"

"Yeah. And Bill, you tell that boy you hired to help put this chain on not to say nothin' either."

"I done told him that."

"I mean it. I told you not to let no one know Mose was here, and you done told a boy."

Mr. Smoote made a noise in his throat like a hog makes when it pokes its nose into slop and snorts. He went over to Mose, put the chisel against where the cuff had been squeezed shut and pinned. He struck off the pin with one whack of the chisel and hammer.

Daddy helped Mose up from the hay bale. "Let's get you on home," Daddy said.

———◆———

From our house it's no big problem to walk through the deep woods, hit Preacher's Road, take the trail down by the river to Mose's shack. By car it took longer. We had to travel some distance. At first Mose and Daddy just sat, but after a while they talked fishing. It wasn't until we were on the Preacher's Road and nearly to the trail that the subject of the murder came up again.

"It gonna be okay now, Missuh Jacob?" Mose asked.

"You just go on about your business, Mose. I got the purse. You told me what you know. I'm sorry I bothered you."

"Well, I guess you had to do it."

"I'm sorry you had to stay at Bill's."

"He done all right by me. 'Cept that chain. He fed me all right, but he didn't empty that ole mess can much as he said."

"I didn't figure he did," Daddy said.

We drove onto the trail that led down to the river. The trees were close and limbs lapped over the top of the car and bathed us in shadow. Daddy had to drive slow and careful because the trail was full of washouts and slippery with leaf mold.

We drove down a good ways, parked, left the car, and walked down to the river with Mose, over to his shack. A cool wind was blowing off the brown churning river and it felt good, but carried with it the faint aroma of something gone to rot.

"You need to come fish, Missuh Jacob," Mose said.

"It's been a while."

"Sho has. You 'member when them ole Davis brothers down the river there poisoned the water with all them green walnuts, killed all them perch and bass. Even some of them big ole catfish?"

"I do."

"I remember how mad you was. You said, ''At ain't no way to do no fishin',' and you walloped one of 'em. You 'member that?"

"Sure."

"You and me, we never did go in for them green walnuts or dynamitin', did we?"

"No, we didn't, Mose. We just fished the

way you're supposed to. With a pole, line, hook, and patience."

"Yessuh, we did."

"Dem Davises you know they eventually turned they boat over and one of 'em drowned an other'n got snake-bit."

"I heard that."

"Now that's somethin', ain't it, Missuh Jacob."

"It is."

"Now they ain't no Davis brothers."

We walked him to his shack. He was limping as he went. When we got there he pushed the unlocked door open. It didn't look any better inside than Mr. Smoote's barn, except there wasn't the smell and as many flies. It was just one room with a window near the door, and a window on the opposite side. One window had glass in it, the other just a thin strip of yellow oilcloth.

Mose went inside and we stood in the doorway.

"You gonna be all right, Mose?" Daddy asked.

"Yessuh, Missuh Jacob."

"You got somethin' to eat?"

"I got couple cans a stuff. I'll fish me up somethin' too."

Mose got a small can off a shelf and pulled the lid free. He stuck his fingers in the black mess inside, bent over and rubbed it on the spot where the chain had cut his ankle. It was axle grease. Lot of folks used it back then to lubricate sores or help stop bleeding from minor wounds.

When Mose was finished with that, he limped over to one of the two chairs he had and sat down at a small wood plank table. He looked even smaller than he had looked at Mr. Smoote's place.

"All right, then," Daddy said. "Well, you take care, Mose."

"Yessuh. And you come to fish, bring the boy."

"I will."

As we were climbing into the car, Daddy said, "Ain't no doubt, this hasn't been my finest hour."

12

s we bumped up the trail toward Preacher's Road, I said, "What favor did you do Mr. Smoote? He didn't sound like he was real grateful."

"He don't like to think about it, son. One of his girls, the oldest one. She's about nineteen now...we didn't see her today."

"Mary Jean?"

"That's the one. I caught her with a colored boy, son. If you know what I mean."

I blushed. Daddy had never talked to me about such things.

"I ain't never told nobody but you. Not even your Mama. And you ain't never gonna say, 'cause I'm askin' you to keep your word, and I know you will. I figure there's some things a man ought to be able to tell his son he don't have to tell no one else and can't."

"Yes sir. Is that why he chained Mose?"

"Part of it. He don't let that girl out of the house hardly no more. He's afraid she'll get with the colored. He figures she's got a fever for it. I figure she's just a little slutty to begin with, and that probably wasn't her first time to dally. Colored or white, I can't say. I don't think Mary Jean's all that choosy."

I filed that away.

Daddy added, as if reading my mind, "You stay away from that gal, hear? She might have some kind of disease."

"Yes sir. I don't want nothin' to do with her... Daddy, what about the colored boy?"

"She didn't even know him. She met him down by the river, fishin'. She'd gone down there to do the same. They got to talkin' about things, and I guess she figured she could talk to him about stuff she couldn't talk to a white boy about. People figure colored haven't got the morals whites got. But it ain't that way at all, son. There's just as many good coloreds as white, and just as many sorry. Most, white or colored, ain't quite on one side altogether. They're a mix. A good person is one where the mix turns out mostly for the better. But she got to talkin', and he got to talkin', and well, pretty soon they was doin' more than talkin'. I was out lookin' for Mrs. Benton's cow. Widow lives up on the hill behind Bill. She come to me askin' for help, so I went to lookin'. What I found was Mary Jean and that colored boy. I run him on. Told him not to come back. Mary Jean didn't know his name, so that wouldn't gonna come up. I told her to dress, and I took her home."

"And told her Daddy?"

"I wasn't gonna say nothin'. She told her Daddy. Just to hurt him, I figure. She's got a mean streak in her, but then again, so does her Daddy. He's walloped her hide pretty often."

"Daddy, you've walloped us some."

Daddy was quiet for a moment. "You think so? I raised big welts on you, son?"

"No sir."

"Have I whupped you just to make myself feel better?"

"I don't think so."

"I whupped you for things you didn't do?"

"Once. I didn't drop that cat down the outhouse. Tom done that."

"You didn't tell me that."

"She was little. She didn't know no better."

"So you took the whuppin' for her?"

"Yes sir."

"I can admire that. But you've been corrected, boy. Not beat. Stung, but not injured. And I don't spank as a matter of course. I think hard on any spankin's I give you."

"There was that time we put salt in your

coffee, and you took a swig and we laughed and you jerked us up and got us both. You didn't consider much on that one."

Daddy laughed. "That one didn't deserve considerin'. I knew darn well who done that."

I turned back to the subject. "So Mary Jean told her Daddy what she did to hurt him?"

"Way I figure it. Bill wanted to kill the boy, but I told him I didn't know who he was and didn't remember how he looked. Far as he's concerned they all look alike anyway, so he didn't have no trouble buyin' that.

"And she wasn't raped. I told him I seen what was happenin', and it sure wasn't rape. Not the way she was laughin'."

"So Mr. Smoote knows you know and he wants to make sure you don't say 'cause he don't want folks to know his daughter was with colored."

"That's about the size of it. I don't intend to say no how. And I've told him that. I figured I asked a favor of him he'd do it 'cause he owed me. But Bill ain't smart. Askin' that boy to help him chain Ole Mose. He didn't think that one through."

◆

That night I couldn't sleep, got up carefully so as not to wake Tom, and still wearing my nightshirt slipped out onto the sleeping porch. I thought I might sleep there, but instead I ended up going out to the well in my bare feet and pulling up a bucket of water and using the dipper to get a drink. I took my time about it, listening to the crickets saw on their legs.

When I got back to the sleeping porch, Mama was there. She was sitting in the swing, wearing her quilted nightgown. I thought I might have awakened her, or that she was going to fuss at me for being up, but instead she patted the seat beside her and I went over and sat down.

"Couldn't sleep?" she asked.

"No," I said.

She put her arm around me. "Me either. What you thinkin' about?"

"Nothin' really."

"Oh."

"You?"

"Everything all at once. That's why I can't sleep. Sometimes things jumble together. I get to thinkin' about what I'm going to fix for breakfast or dinner or supper. I wonder if the mule's gettin' too old to plow and if the weather's gonna spoil the fall crop. I wonder if times gonna get any better, and I think about the mistakes in my life, and I think about you and Tom."

"What about me and Tom?"

"No one thing. Just thinkin'."

"Mama?"

"Yes."

"Did you tell Daddy about Red?"

"No, I didn't."

"Why?"

"It's hard to explain. I guess it's because your Dad wouldn't like the idea of Red comin' around and I don't want to start no trouble between 'em. They don't like each other anyway, and yet they do."

"How's that?"

"Ain't nothin' worse than two friends fallin' out. Underneath it all, there's still the old feelin's they had for one another."

"I think it's gone. Daddy don't like Red."

"There's still the old memories, and that makes not likin' each other all the worse and all the harder. It was me made the two of them not like each other in the first place. Then your Daddy savin' Red like that, and them both courtin' me, well, it made things difficult when me and your Daddy got together. They never could patch things up."

"How do you mean?"

"I can't explain it. But that's why your Daddy was mad at Red... People do foolish things, Harry. Things they wish they hadn't done, but you can't take them back. You have to live with them, get over them or work around them."

"I don't think Daddy felt foolish about what he was doin'," I said.

"I didn't mean your Daddy."

"What do you mean?"

"Someday, maybe I can explain it to you better."

"Red still likes you, don't he?"

"I guess he does. Or did until our little talk."

"Is it like that with you? I mean like you say it is with Dad and Red?"

"Maybe. A little. Just a little. I think I like some memories better than I like some nows. You know what I mean?"

"I don't know, Mama… What did you mean talkin' to Mr. Woodrow about Miss Maggie and his Daddy?"

"Miss Maggie was Red's Daddy's mistress."

"Mistress?"

"That's kind of…well, Harry, this is embarrassin'. But it's when a man is married, and he ain't supposed to be but with his wife, but he don't always do that. And he's got him a woman on the side."

"Miss Maggie was his woman on the side?"

"That was many years ago. She was a young woman then."

I had a difficult time imagining Miss Maggie young.

"Red's got a half-brother and a half-sister by her. Or maybe it's two half-brothers or two half-sisters. I'm not sure. He knows that, but he never acted like he did. He don't claim 'em. When he was little, that ole colored woman was like his Mama. His Mama was a cold woman, and didn't have much to do with Red nor his Daddy. I think that's why his Daddy took a mistress. But it was really more like havin' a slave than a mistress. I don't know how else to explain it, Harry."

"I understand."

"Harry, you're gettin' to be a young man. Figure that's why your Daddy took you with him today. He wanted your company. Did you enjoy it?"

"Yes ma'am."

"Your Daddy and me got hopes for you and Tom. Jacob come from a real ignorant family, Harry. He don't want that for you. He wants you to have a chance. Remember that when you feel like he's pushin' you a little too hard. He's afraid you'll end up like him."

"I think I could do a lot worse."

Mama put her arm around me. "So do I, Harry."

Suddenly Toby barked and a voice called loudly: "Jacob. Come out."

"Who was that?" I asked.

Mama said, "Sit tight."

She got up, started through the house. I disobeyed her immediately and followed.

"Jacob," the voice called again. "Come out."

Through the windows and curtains I could see there was a brilliant light outside, a moving light, gnawing at the darkness.

Mama pulled back the curtains and looked. There were a dozen men on horseback, dressed in white robes. They were carrying torches. One man was standing on the ground, his horse being held by a mounted rider. On the far side of our road blazed a cross about eight feet tall.

Toby had come up on the front porch, and he was barking in as ferocious a manner as he could manage.

"Run get your father," Mama said.

I started that way, but Daddy was already coming. He wasn't wearing any shirt. He was carrying our double-barreled shotgun. He leaned the shotgun beside the door, went out on the porch.

Toby continued to bark. Daddy said, "Hush, Toby," and after one more bark, just to show he wasn't any lapdog, Toby went quiet. Mama called him softly and he came inside the house, growling under his breath.

I could smell the gasoline the cross had been doused with. I watched the flames whip at the air like a bloody sheet in the wind.

"You boys done missed Halloween," Daddy said.

The robed man with the torch said, "We command you now, pilgrim. Tell us where we can find the nigger you arrested."

"You don't do worth a damn trying to hide your voice, Ben Groon," Daddy said. "I'd recognize it anywhere. You don't command me nothin'. You hear?"

"Turn over this nigger you got, Jacob. You can't protect him."

"First of all," Daddy said, "I ain't got no one in custody. Second of all, I wouldn't turn him over if he was on the porch with me. Take that cross with you, and leave out. And by the way, I recognize you, Nation, just the way you sit that horse. And that means them two dumb boys of yours are bound to be with you. So that's four I know right there."

Daddy called to me. "Hand me that gun, son."

I was standing just inside of the doorway. I handed him the shotgun. He took it quickly, stepped off the porch, leveled it at the man he said was Groon, the general store owner. I had a hard time picturing him under that sheet.

"Pull that thing down and take it with you," Daddy said.

There was a moment's hesitation. Daddy cocked the shotgun. You could almost hear their butts grabbing at their saddles.

Groon spoke in a cracked voice, "Better go on and take it down. He said he ain't got no nigger."

The white hoods looked back and forth at one another. Finally one produced a rope, tossed it over the top of the burning cross, dragged it out of the ground and started down the road with it, the cross flinging sparks and flogging flames.

The others left out, except for the man holding Groon's horse, and Groon himself. The rider presented Groon with his reins, and thundered off down the road.

"It's one tight brotherhood, ain't it?" Daddy said. "Groon, step up here on the porch."

"We done tore the cross down, Jacob."

"I know. Step up here."

Groon came over, leading his mount.

"Tie your horse," Daddy said.

Groon tied it to a porch support post.

"Lift that hood off."

Groon lifted it, revealing his bald head. He looked half the size he had out there by the cross with the pointed hood on. I realized he wasn't any taller than me, and only a little bigger. He appeared to be a silly adult who had been wearing a ghost costume.

"Now, come on in the house."

"Jacob..."

"Just do it."

Mama put Toby outside as Mr. Groon came in, just in case he might decide to take a nip at his ankles.

Daddy led Mr. Groon through our main room where the kitchen and dining table were. He took Groon into his and Mama's bedroom, mine and Tom's room, then out on the sleeping porch, all of us tagging behind, trying to figure what in the world was going on.

We ended back up in the main room. Daddy said to Groon, "See any colored folk?"

Groon shook his head.

"Good. You tell your friends that. Now sit at the table."

Groon was starting to shake. I was pretty darn nervous myself.

Daddy said, "May Lynn, would you mind gettin' the cake out of the pantry?"

Mama looked at Daddy as if he had just decided to use her kitchen for an outhouse, but she got the cake out and put it on the table.

"And if I could trouble you for some plates. And some forks." .

Mama got out the plates and forks. She looked at Daddy as if he were ready to be put in a home for crazy folks.

"Now," Daddy said, still holding the shotgun on Groon, "everyone please sit at the table."

I did, and Mama did. Daddy lowered the

shotgun, opened it. No shells flew out. It was empty. He made note of this to Groon, who let out a sigh of relief.

"Now, Groon. I want you to have some of this cake. May Lynn is the best damn cake baker in these parts. And I want you to note that everything here was made from supplies we bought at your store."

Groon looked at Mama. Mama tried to smile, but it didn't quite work.

We all ate cake.

When Groon was finished, Mama said, "You like another piece, Mr. Groon?"

"Yes ma'am, I would."

———————◆———————

I don't know how late Daddy and Mr. Groon talked, but it was late. I finally tuckered out and drifted to the sleeping porch with Mama. We sat together on the swing there, and when I woke she was gone and I was lying on the swing with a pillow under my head and a blanket over me. The sun was coming up and our rooster crowing. I went into the kitchen. Daddy and Groon were still in there, sitting in front of greasy plates, well sopped of eggs and fatback grease. Mama was pouring coffee.

"You like some eggs and biscuits, Harry?" she asked.

I told her I would, and sat down at the table. Tom came wandering in, rubbing her eyes. Sometimes she could sleep through a marching band. She looked at Mr. Groon, who still sat at the table wearing his robes, his hood pushed back. In the morning sunlight, his hair looked even thinner and whiter and the bald spot was a soft, smooth cream color. I could see liver spots on the back of his hands.

"You got on a ghost suit, Mr. Groon?" Tom asked.

He smiled at her. "I guess I do, missy." He stood up, stretched out his hand to Daddy. "You won't have no more trouble from me."

"Fair enough," Daddy said.

"Good cake, and a good breakfast, Mrs. Cane. Thank you."

Mama nodded.

Groon got up and went outside. Daddy went with him. The air still smelled faintly of gasoline and burnt wood. Toby was lying on the porch. He shifted slightly and put an eyeball on Mr. Groon. Mr. Groon leaned forward slowly and extended his hand to Toby. Daddy said, "It's all right, Toby."

Toby sniffed at the hand, then lay back down, satisfied.

"Maybe we ought to walk your horse down to the barn, get some grain and water," Daddy said.

"That'd be good," Mr. Groon said.

"I'd like you to look around out there. See there's no colored hiding there."

Groon nodded.

"Son," Daddy said, "clean that up, will you?"

He was talking about a big pile of horse manure Mr. Groon's horse had left. "Yes sir," I said, and went to get the shovel.

As I went around the house to where the shovel was leaning against the outside wall, I heard Daddy say: "Ben, wasn't any shells in that gun, but I want you to know, I had some in my pocket."

———◆———

Later that day, I walked down the road following the path of the dragged cross. Eventually, I came upon what was left of it. The rope had burned through and the remains of the cross lay in the center of the road. It was a black-charred ruin, but still obviously a cross.

As I stood looking, a sharp wind came along and kicked ash off of it and some of it stuck to my shirt, the one Mama had made of bleached flour sacks. The one that was almost snow white, not from design, but from wear. And even though Mama washed it afterward, using good lye soap, it never came completely clean.

Somewhere, even now, after all these years, and me long grown out of it, I still have that shirt. Folded up in a trunk in storage, motheaten and turned yellow, with stains the color of ancient dried blood dotted just above and below the left shirt pocket.

Part Three

13

⬩

The other night, here in the home, under warm blankets with sleet slanting in hard against the window, I drifted off and awoke to the sound of a horn blaring, and though the horn had a different noise than those on the old cars, when I heard it, I awoke immediately thinking of Grandma.

I may have even called to her, for in that moment, with the sound of the horn still in my ears, and me slowly realizing the sound had come from out on the highway near the home, I was reminded of her enthusiasm. She liked her horn, and was known to honk it at the slightest reason.

I awoke thinking of her, and tears rolled down my cheeks. Not only because of her memory, but because I was even more reminded of then, and suddenly I was pulled into now, and I do not like now, for I am old. So very old. Older than she got to be. And I'm not sure a person ought to live to be too old. For when you can't live life, you're just burning life, sucking air and making turds.

Perhaps it's not age, but health that matters. Live long and healthy, it doesn't matter. But live long and unhealthy, it's a living hell. And here I lie. Not doing well at all.

Only the past seems to matter now; only it seems to be alive; only it can support my soul.

———◆———

It was about two days after our encounter with the Klan that Grandma come to live with us. She drove up in a dusty black Ford with a cracked windshield and a rabbit hung up on the front bumper. She was honking her horn like she wanted a train to move.

Women drove cars back then, but it wasn't real popular among men folks down in the bottoms, especially if the woman was older, and therefore figured to be more dignified. Driving was considered masculine, like smoking, cussing, chewing, and fighting.

Grandma did a little of all of those. She and my grandfather had been one heck of a couple, and now that he was dead and gone, and Grandma was nearing seventy, I assumed she'd be calmer and older-looking.

But on the day she arrived, and we ran out to see who it was—Toby gimping around the edge of the house to join us—she got out of the car looking the same as always.

She was a little heavy, but really quite pretty

for an older woman, tall and strong-looking. Her hair was a mixture of brown and white and she had it up in a tight bun. She wore lace-up brown men's work shoes with a kind of sack dress that was once green but had faded to gray.

"Hey, there they are," she said as we came out of the house. "My whole pack of heathens. Oh, my God, is that Tom?"

Tom was peeking out from behind Mother's dress. She had only seen Grandma when she was little and had not been old enough to appreciate what a whirlwind the old lady was. "Come here to me," Grandma said.

"I don't wanna," Tom said.

Grandma tossed back her head and bellowed. "Ain't she just the cutest little rascal."

Toby was so startled by that laugh, he started barking.

In one smooth action, Grandma reached to the ground, grabbed a dirt clod and tossed it at Toby. Most of the clod came apart before it reached him, but it made him scuttle under the porch, where he continued to bark until Daddy hushed him.

Grandma latched her eye on me now. "You, boy, come here and give me a hug."

I went. Grandma always overwhelmed me, but there was something about her that made you feel safe and confident. She was strong. She picked me off the ground and set me down so hard on my heels my back teeth shook.

She then proceeded to hug my Dad, actually picking him up as well, then she grabbed

209

at Mama, who feinted and said, "Now calm down, Mama. I ain't like them boys. I can't take all that liftin' up."

Grandma laughed, grabbed Mama, and gave her a wet kiss on the cheek. Grandma, contrary to the fact she chewed tobacco and smoked and drank coffee all the time, had all her own teeth and they were as white as the ivory on a piano. She said she used a frayed willow branch and baking soda to clean 'em, but I think a lot of it was just natural. I doubt she ever had a cavity. She chewed peppermints all the time for breath freshener and kept chunks of them in a paper bag in her purse.

"Honey," she said to me, "get that rabbit out of the bumper there. Take it out back and clean it and bring it in and I'll fix us some dinner."

She was talking about the noon meal. Lunch was something Yankees in cities ate. We called the late meal supper.

I looked at Daddy, not knowing what to do about that rabbit. He said to Grandma, "June, ain't that rabbit a little ripe?"

"Aw, hell no. I hit it about two or three miles down the road. Jumped right out in front of me. Probably still warm. You still like my rabbit and dumplin's don't you?"

"Well, yeah," Daddy said.

"Good then," Grandma said. "We got us a free dinner. Now shut up, Jacob. Get the rabbit, honey."

I got it. Daddy put his arm around me. "Let's go on out back and skin it," he said.

Grandma put her arm around Mama's shoulders. Tom clung to Mama's dress, lest Grandma get her hands on her, and they all went in the house.

"That, son," Daddy said, "is a human tornado."

———◆———

As we finished up the rabbit, which was really good-tasting, Grandma, who had been talking almost the entire time, even while eating, said, "I love and miss Grandpa, but I'm glad he's dead."

"Don't say that!" Mama said.

"Was he in a lot of pain?" Daddy asked.

"No. No. Thank goodness for that. But he took to singin' gospel songs. He'd just burst out in one from time to time, and he couldn't carry a tune in a syrup bucket with a lid on it. It was miserable. And you couldn't shut him up. I figured it was time for him to go just so I wouldn't have to listen to that."

"Mama," my Mama said. "That's terrible."

"Naw, it ain't. He didn't have no mind to speak of, and he wouldn't have wanted to just carry on. He was a smart man before the old age took him. I ever start talkin' to myself, or heaven forbid sing a goddamn gospel song—"

"Mama, your language."

"—just go on and shoot me in the head. Pass them biscuits. And, Harry, pass the gravy, and don't put your thumb in it this time."

211

We ate rabbit and sopped up gravy with big fluffy biscuits Grandma had cooked, and they were better than Mama's. After dinner we were all too weak to go out in the fields and work, and Daddy pronounced, in honor of Grandma's visit, except for those chores that couldn't be put off, a day of rest. As for the barbershop, well, when he didn't show Cecil knew what to do. It was best that way, Daddy trying to work the farm and being a constable and all.

It was a warm November day and cloudy. It and a full belly made me feel sleepy. I went out on the sleeping porch with Tom and we sat in the swing and talked.

"She reminds me of that witch in Hansel and Gretel," Tom said.

"Naw. She's all right. You just don't know her. You give her some time. She's more fun than Mama and Daddy, and she gets in trouble more than we do."

"Really?"

"Oh yeah. When you was little we used to live with her and Grandpa. They moved off though, and Grandpa died."

"I know that. I went to his funeral too."

"You don't remember that, do you?"

"I heard tell I went."

"I remember it. It was a long ride up there and back."

"She gonna stay?"

"Probably."

"That means our room is her room, don't it?"

"We can lay claim to the sleeping porch, most likely."

I thought about that. There were a couple advantages. It was cool in the summer, and if you slid over next to the wall under Mama and Daddy's room, you could hear them talkin' even better than in our room.

Drawback was, in the winter it was cold as a well digger's butt. Most likely we'd end up putting our pallets down in the kitchen then.

"Was Grandpa crazy too?"

"Might near. But he was quieter."

"Well, I guess that's somethin'," Tom said. "She talks loud enough to shake dust off the ceilin'."

Grandma come out on the sleeping porch then. She said, "Anybody for fishin'?"

Daddy had followed her out. He said, "I don't let them go off fishin' much. Not these days."

Grandma looked at him as if he had spoken an obscenity even she was offended to hear. "Why not?"

"We've had a few problems of late," Daddy said. Then, in a nutshell, he told her about the murders. He didn't mention the Klan's visit or Mose.

"They'll be with me, Jacob. I'll take 'em fishin'."

"I don't know."

"Come on, Daddy," Tom said. "I done forgot how to fish."

"You can't let somethin' like that run their lives," Grandma said. "I brought along my shotgun. I'll take it with me."

Daddy had doubts, but he said, "Don't go off a long ways. There's some close fishin' holes."

"I know where they are," Grandma said. "Mose showed us all them holes. Is Old Mose still alive?"

"Yes," Daddy said.

"He still live in that same shack?"

Daddy nodded. "I'd prefer you not go off that far."

"All right then," Grandma said. "Can they go?"

"Long as you're with them. And stay pretty close to the house."

◆

Grandma put on some overalls. Me and Tom dug some worms and put them in a coffee can, got poles and fishing business together, and with Grandma toting a double-barrel twelve-gauge, we went into the woods, heading for the river.

The woods smelled sour that day, and the way the trees rose up and the sun shone down, it was like being in some kind of cathedral with light coming through stained glass. Dried pine needles crunched under our feet and colored leaves were blowing past us thick as raindrops.

I still felt full and sleepy, but the walk was starting to invigorate me. Grandma walked us down to the river and we picked a spot with a big wash in the bank and gathered up there, put worms on our hooks. We started fishing, and pretty soon, Grandma started talking.

"You remember me, Harry?"

"Yes ma'am. I remember when you moved off. I remember you good. Grandpa too."

"Well, I'm glad to be back now."

"I don't remember you," Tom said.

Grandma laughed. "I suppose you don't."

"I'm sorry about Grandpa," I said.

"Me too. I couldn't stay there near his grave though. A grave is just a grave. The man is in my heart. I love my daughter Earlene, but I had to get back to East Texas. They ain't got no trees up there near Amarillo."

"No trees?" Tom asked.

"They call some of 'em trees, but they're more like bushes. And they ain't got the rivers and the creeks like we got down here. Ain't got the critters we got. And it's harder to make you somethin' to eat. Can't grow nothin'."

"Daddy says times are hard here," I said.

"They're hard all over. But here ain't nothin' like North Texas, and those poor people in Oklahoma and Kansas."

"How do you mean?"

"Well, Harry, they ain't got the soil we got here to begin with. You can drop a seed in the ground here and it'll grow... Look there, I got a bite... Damn! Took the worm off my hook. Danged fish are smarter than you think."

Grandma pulled up the line and Tom put another worm on it.

"It was rough up there in North Texas.

215

One day they had somethin' growin'. Corn, cotton, peas, and such, then it got dry. Didn't no rain come and the ground got crusty as a scab. A few clouds floated around to tease us now and then, but they wouldn't give up water. Finally they quit jokin' us and just went away altogether. Everything got baked. Corn yellowed on the stalks, ears shriveled up like caterpillars on a hot piece of tin. Taters rotted in the ground, or when they were dug they were like pine knots. Not fit to eat, even if you boiled them from here till next Sunday, put salt and pepper all over 'em, and beat 'em with a hammer. Cotton wouldn't grow and the peas burned up.

"Dirt got so dry it turned like face powder. Wind come along, all blue norther and wild, picked up the dirt, made a cloud of it, and blew it around. Then there was grit in everything. 'Tween your teeth, in the crack of your butt, twixt your toes, in anything you had to eat and drink. That ole wind worked dirt out from under rocks and sucked all the goodness out of the soil, leavin' just sand that would run through your fingers like water. Then there were the grasshoppers."

"We got grasshoppers," Tom said.

"'Course you do. But they ain't starvin' to death here, and they ain't eatin' everything green or brown that's got some life in it. They came from all over, them hoppers. They ate what was left growin'. Ate the leaves off the bushes, ate them things they call trees up there. And they was always gettin' in your hair. It was a mess. Then them dark clouds of dust that hung around got caught up good on the constant wind, and the sky turned black as preacher sin, 'cept for where the sun bled through like a bloody, seepin' head. All that dirt blowed away, all the decent topsoil toted off to God knows where. Then all them folks started headin' out to California for pickin' jobs. Went out there in old cars and trucks as worn out as the crops and the people in 'em."

"Pickin'?" I asked.

"Fruit and berries, Harry. Whatever they got grows out there needs pickin'. There's Okies goin' by the hundreds out that way. Texans too. I figure they're just chasin' that dirt blowed away, like chasin' a dream. Anyway, they all went west, and I figured I'd go the other way."

"What about Aunt Earlene?"

Grandma cast her fresh worm out into the water.

"She and her husband was dead-set for California. They done been told it's the Promise Land, and they believe it. I figured I didn't want to get that far from Texas. I want to die in Texas. East Texas anyway. Least I'll be in damp ground and not some dusty hole. I like to think a worm can live in this dirt, and if it and all its friends eat me, then I at least get carried all over East Texas."

"That's awful, Grandma."

She laughed. "Well, I don't think so. I'd rather be the turds the worms leave than slow rot in dry ground. Here the earth's held down by trees and roots and kept damp by creeks,

217

rivers, and a high-up waterline. 'Cause of that, I wanted to be here. And I hadn't had no real time with you and Tom. Earlene's boys are in their teens, and they've got plans of their own, and I hope long as I live never to pick another ball of cotton nor another berry neither, 'less I'm just pickin' for myself to eat."

"I'm almost twelve."

"What?"

"You said Aunt Earlene's kids are in their teens. I'm almost in mine."

"He is old," Tom said.

"I suppose he is," Grandma said. "But your Mama and Daddy have kept you close to the house, Harry. They ain't made you work like Earlene's young'ns had to work and are gonna have to work out there in that California. I think they won't find it near as promisin' as they think. I tried to tell 'em, but it's their business, you know."

"I'll work."

"Know you will. But you don't need to work like them... Why ain't you gettin' any schoolin'?"

"School ain't got a teacher."

"Say it ain't. Well, I've done some teachin' from time to time. Not that my English is all that good, but it can get better when I want it to. I wasn't so dead-set on doin' little to nothin' right now, I'd be your teacher. I can do that anyway. Back at the house. We can do readin', writin', and 'rithmatic without any ole teacher. I can teach you and Thomasina a few things."

"We ain't gonna start right away, are we?" Tom asked.

"Naw."

"Lookee there, Grandma," I said. "A big ole cottonmouth moccasin."

A black head was poking out of the brown water, slipping close to the bank. A moccasin always made my skin crawl.

Grandma picked up the shotgun and let loose with one barrel. The moccasin's head disappeared.

"Never could stand those nasty sonsabitches," Grandma said.

The leaves had fallen on and all around us, almost thick as a blanket.

Tom, full of biscuits, rabbit, and gravy, warmed by the soft earth and made cozy by the blowing leaves, curled up and tried to listen for a while, but was soon fast asleep.

Grandma said, "Ain't she precious."

"When she's asleep."

"Harry, your Daddy sure didn't want to talk about Mose much. Is there somethin' wrong about Mose?"

"No ma'am."

"You're lyin' to me, Harry. I can tell. But I bet it's 'cause you're doin' it for your Daddy. That's an understandable lie."

I didn't contradict her. I took a keen interest in my fishing pole.

"Your Daddy wants you to keep a secret, I figure there's a good reason. Jacob's a good man, if a little hot-tempered."

"Daddy? I ain't never seen any real temper.

219

He's fussed at me and Tom from time to time. And he poured water on my head once for sassin' Mama, and we've got some spankin's for stuff we done, but I ain't never seen him really lose his temper."

"He's got it. I guess truth is he ain't hot-tempered, he's just bad-tempered. He don't lose his temper easy, so hot ain't right. But it's a bad one when it goes off."

I doubted this too, but didn't say anything.

"Hope you don't never see it, 'cause it's an ugly thing. And hope you don't have it your-self. A temper really ain't worth nothin'. Jacob's prideful too. In a good way mostly. But somethin's always tamperin' with your pride, and if you got too much of it, it ain't pride no more. It's prideful. Take a fall from that, it's hard to get up. I've seen it. But there ain't no better-meanin' man than your Daddy."

"Grandma. Do you know Red Woodrow?"

"You met him?"

"Yes ma'am."

"He used to be one of your Mama's suitors. She had a lot of 'em. It might be hard to figure now, lookin' at me, but so did I in my day. But your Mama had them all on a string. Your Daddy and Red. But she met Red first, and they were pretty serious."

"Really serious?"

"Uh huh. But Red he had ways. Just a little off center. Folks said he done mean things to animals, but I don't know that's true. People like to talk, especially they don't like someone. One thing's for sure, his home wasn't none too good. Not just poor folks. Hell, we were all poor and are poorer now for the most part. But his Daddy whupped him, and his Mama she liked to go with the men."

"Mama said he was raised mostly by Miss Maggie?"

"What raisin' he got that woman done it, but he didn't get much. She wasn't in any position to do it, and her being colored, that didn't give her a lot of say. Red mostly raised himself up, and it wasn't a good raisin' lots of the time."

"Mama said he had two half-brothers by Miss Maggie."

"That's the story. I don't know there's anything to it."

"When Mama met Daddy, was that when she quit seein' Red?"

"Like I said, she had 'em both on a string. But when she met Jacob, there was sparks. Then they went on some barge ride, somethin' your Mama wasn't supposed to be on, by the way. I'd told her to stay home, but she run off and didn't listen. Somehow, Red ended up in the water in a suck hole, and your Daddy saved him. After that, Red and your Daddy, who had been good friends, never did see eye to eye. And your Mama lost interest in Red. He turned kind'a rough. Or maybe the true Red just showed up. He started tattooin' on his arm the women he'd conquered."

"Conquered?"

"Was intimate with. You know what I mean, Harry?"

"Yes ma'am. I think so... He did it himself? The tattooin'."

"Yep. With something sharp and some charcoal. He'd put their name and a date for when... You know. It was crude-lookin' and a crude subject. He got so he wore his shirt-sleeves rolled up so you could see who was on his arm and the date he done what he did."

"You'd think women wouldn't have nothin' to do with someone like that," I said.

"Men and women are hard to figure, Harry."

"He wears his sleeves rolled down now, even in hot weather."

"Good. Maybe he ain't so proud of it now."

"Was he like that you think 'cause he was raised hard?"

"That sure had something to do with it. But let me tell you somethin'. Your Daddy, his family, they weren't so good neither. Jacob turned out good. So that ain't no excuse for Red. Your Daddy's mother died when he was eight years old. The old man never did cotton to schoolin' much, and when the wife died, he took Jacob out of what schoolin' he was get-ting and put him to work in the cotton fields. Lot of folks did that back then with their kids, and they do it now. Had to make a livin'. It was survival. But the old man took to beatin' on your Daddy, and bad. Once your Daddy got sick in the cotton fields. Got hurt actually. Fell somehow, hit his head on a rock and blood come out of his ears. I was a young woman then, just married to your grandfather, so I heard about it. I didn't see it, but knew some did see it, since it happened right out in front of God and everybody.

"Your Daddy had a spotted pinto pony. I remember it like it was yesterday. He rode it home, and fell off in the yard, he was so hurt. Jacob's Daddy took a horse whip, and beat that boy like he stole somethin', sent him running back to the fields, chasin' him the whole way. And he made Jacob put in a day.

"Your Daddy's Daddy married again. Or really he took to shackin' up. The woman was Red's mother, and Red come to live with them for a time, and they were like brothers, your Daddy and Red.

"But Red's mother took up with some other fella about nine years later, run off with him, and left Red with the old man and Jacob. Not that she ever cared about Red for one moment. She had a couple other kids too. Girls, I think. They were by Red's Daddy. I don't know whatever happened to them. He also had some kids by that colored woman, Miss Maggie. Or so they say.

"Your Daddy grew real close to Red. Kind of a protector. Jacob's Daddy was gonna beat Red over somethin', and Jacob, who was sixteen or seventeen at the time, picked up a board and told his Daddy his beatin' days were over. And the old man backed off.

"So, Jacob saved Red twice. Once from a beatin', and once from drownin'. Jacob left home that day, and so did Red. Wasn't long after that Red started seein' your Mama, then of course your Daddy met her and things changed. They were like brothers, Red and your Daddy, and there ain't nothin' worse than kin or near kin fallin' out."

"What happened to my Grandpa? Daddy's Daddy?"

"Somebody killed him."

"I never heard Daddy say that."

"What's he say about his Daddy?"

"Nothin'."

"Well, then you ain't heard him say nothin', and inside that nothin' is this somethin'. He was murdered."

"Who done it?"

"No one knows. He was found in his bed, his throat cut from ear to ear. He worked at the sawmill when he wasn't drunk. He'd already lost three fingers there, and he wasn't makin' any real money, just scratchin' shit with the chickens. So there wasn't nothin' there for anyone to rob."

"Grandma, I thought ladies weren't supposed to cuss."

"They aren't. And it ain't nice to interrupt a story. Like I was sayin' about your Grandpa. It's more likely in my mind someone killed him because he was a rotten sonofabitch. That's a harsh thing to say, Harry, but them's the stone-cold sober facts. I figure he rode one of them coloreds out at the mill a little too hard, and the man waited until he went to bed, slipped in, and cut his throat. Wasn't nothin' stole no one knew about. Then again, wasn't nothin' in the house besides corn liquor and some crackers anyway. Whoever

224

done it, it couldn't have happened to a dirtier bastard than that old man. He may have been your Grandpa, Harry, but you're lucky you didn't never have no truck with him."

"Daddy says when someone's killed, people always think it's a colored. It don't have to be a colored killed my Grandpa, does it?"

"No. 'Course not. But I hope it was. 'Cause he deserved to die by a colored's hand, way he treated them. Hell, he just deserved to die."

"Grandma?"

"Yes."

"Was Mama's name tattooed on Red's arm?"

"That isn't somethin' I'd know about, Harry."

"Grandma, Daddy says you've always been good to colored. He says that ain't like most folks. Why do you feel that way?"

"First off, I don't know what good to colored is. I try to treat people right, but I'd be a liar I said I treated them just the same. I don't spend that much time with them, and I ain't got any real colored friends. I don't know that much about the lives of the ones I do know. So all I can say is I don't hate colored. That's somethin' worth sayin', though. Let me ask you a question."

"Okay."

"Do you hate colored?"

"No ma'am."

"Why don't you?"

"I don't know... I guess Daddy and Mama."

"It was the same for me. Someone somewhere figured some truth out and passed it along. I got it. Your Mama got it, and now you got it. And Jacob, well, he once told me how he come by his thinkin'."

"He told me the story," I said.

"Did he tell you that we all, no matter what we think, slide a little backward now and then? Did he tell you somethin' comes up missin', and there's a white man and a colored man standin' nearby, most of us are gonna think it's the colored that did it? That he's the one shiftless? Ain't none of us that damn good, Harry. We all got a lot of learnin' to do."

"But a colored man could have stole it, couldn't he?"

"He sure could have. But it ain't the thing to expect of him just because he is colored. You get what I'm sayin', Harry?"

"Yes ma'am."

We fished for a time, then Tom woke, shook off the blanket of leaves, and we moved to another place.

I was sort of worried Grandma would try to take us off to where Mose was. I could tell she was curious about what was going on there, but she fooled me. We stayed pretty close to the house, even though we changed spots two or three times, and by nightfall we had caught a dozen fish or so and Grandma had shot the head off another moccasin.

We got back to the house about supper time. I cleaned the fish, which were mostly hand-sized perch, and Grandma fried them up with hush puppies. She also made a pie with fig preserves, Mama not believing it could be done and taste right.

We ate the fish, all the while being told to watch for bones by Grandma and Mama, then we sucked down the pie, which turned out delicious. Afterward, we went out on the sleeping porch to sit or swing or lie on the floor until we had digested enough to move again.

14

Next day the fun was over and we were back to regular. We did chores, and after lunch Grandma brought out one of her cardboard suitcases. Inside were six books. The Bible, *Ivanhoe*, *Huckleberry Finn*, *Last of the Mohicans*, *The Red Badge of Courage*, and *Call of the Wild*. She had me read aloud to her from *Ivanhoe*.

She kept saying how she just loved bein' read to.

When I finished a chapter, it was Tom's turn. Tom had a lot of trouble with the words, and I wanted to just go on and read it because the story was so good, but Grandma insisted

Tom do it. Tom got about halfway through the chapter and gave up.

Grandma said, "That was real good, Tom. You just need more time for the big words."

She gave the book back to me, and I caught on to what was happening. We were being schooled. I didn't say anything. I just read. I liked reading. I liked the book. Grandma made the whole thing fun. By the afternoon, she asked if Mama, Tom, and me would like to drive into town and visit Daddy at the barbershop.

Mama declined the trip, having wash she wanted to hang, and though Grandma volunteered us to help her, Mama insisted we drive on into town and visit without her.

We drove along at a fast clip with the windows down. The wind picked up the scent of the woods and the earth and filled the car with them.

Grandma said, "I just love the smell of dirt. I like it best when it starts to smell right before a rain. There's somethin' about an oncomin' rain gives the earth a real fine smell. That's another thing about North Texas. Dirt, wet or dry, didn't smell right."

We weren't long at the barbershop before Grandma got bored. She was willing to argue with the customers on nearly anything that came up. Religion. Politics. Farming. The Depression. She even got on Cecil's nerves, and he generally liked to talk about most anything. She thought he cut hair a little too close, and even suggested a superior form of wrist movement for stropping his razor.

When she finally tuckered out arguing, she took to reading one of the pulp magazines, and pretty soon she was criticizing the writing. I could tell Daddy, Cecil, and the customers were glad when she made up her mind to go over to the general store and take us with her.

I was nervous about going over to Groon's store, but when we got there, he greeted us like family. He didn't bring up our recent encounter with him except to talk about Mama's chocolate cake.

"She bakes a good'n," Grandma said, pursing her lips, "but she always put a little too much sugar in it, and not enough egg to make the icing."

"Oh," Mr. Groon said.

"I'll fix some sometime and bring you a slice," Grandma said.

"That would be right nice of you, ma'am," Mr. Groon said. "Since my wife died, I don't do much cooking that matters. Just a little to get by, and it ain't worth much."

Grandma bought a few small items. Staples for Mama: flour, coffee, cornmeal, and finally a couple of peppermint sticks for me and Tom. We went out to the car and placed our boxed items inside, except for the peppermints, which me and Tom took to sucking right away.

"Ain't there anything else to do around here?" Grandma asked.

"No ma'am. Not really. 'Cept go see Miss Maggie. You was sayin' you knew her."

"I know who she is, but I don't believe

229

we've ever exchanged words... Well, hell, let's go see her. She might be up better for conversation than these men folks. They can't stand to be disagreed with. There ain't a thing they don't know. They ain't even half the cussers they think they are neither."

Since I hadn't heard anyone cuss around Grandma, I wasn't certain how she had drawn those conclusions, but thought it was a pretty good bet she could cuss with the best of them. As for them not knowing as much as they thought, well, they hadn't had all that much time to express themselves. Grandma was always talking.

We left her sacks in the car; unlike now, you could do that. It was rare then, even in hard times, that anyone would steal from you, unless it was a banker. There were, of course, the Pretty Boy Floyds of the world, but it wasn't like now where everything has to be under lock and key. A thief was usually from somewhere else other than where you were.

We came up on Miss Maggie hanging out her wash. She had on her big black hat. She heard us coming, looked over her shoulder.

"Howdy there, Missuh Harry. And who that you got with you?"

"This is my Grandma," I said.

"My name's June. I hear yours is Maggie."

"Yes'm, that's right."

"Don't ma'am me," Grandma said. "Makes me feel a hundred years old."

Miss Maggie cackled. "I am a hundert years old."

"Naw you ain't."

"Yes'm. I am too. I might be a hundert and two, but I done lost me some track on it."

"You don't look a day over seventy," Grandma said. "I see you're hangin' out your drawers."

"Yes'm. They got to have air'n. My drawers might even need a little extra air'n."

"Least your drawers ain't wide enough to stretch and jump on."

Miss Maggie cackled. "You somethin', Miss June."

There was a basket full of wash and clothespins setting on the ground. Grandma plucked out some clothes, grabbed up a handful of clothespins. She put one of the pins in her mouth, and somehow holding three more in one hand, she pinned the piece up, grabbed another and pinned that.

When she had used the pin in her mouth, Grandma said, "I been up the barbershop my son owns, talkin' to the men there, and I can tell you straight out, ain't a one of 'em knows a damn thing."

Maggie grinned. "Ain't that the truth, Miss June."

Grandma grabbed more wash and started hanging. "They think they know everything there is to know, but they don't know which end of themselves the crap comes out of."

Miss Maggie laughed. "You is one cutup, Miss June. Yes, you is."

A short time later we were sitting in Miss Maggie's house, at the table, eating buttermilk pie, and Grandma and Miss Maggie were arguing over a chocolate and buttermilk pie recipe. I had never heard of such a combination, but then again, I'd never had fig preserve pie until the night before either, and it had been like a slice of heaven.

It was hot in there because of the wood stove. The front door was open, and I could see out the screen. There were no flies this day, but in the distance I could see a black and yellow butterfly playing above the hog pen. I was seeing it and not seeing it. I was thinking about *Ivanhoe.*

Pretty soon Grandma and Miss Maggie were up cooking together, arguing all the while, banging pans, pouring this and that, Miss Maggie showing Grandma where the cooking stuff she needed was, and telling her what's what on how to use it.

Grandma told her how she had been cooking for over sixty years, and Miss Maggie said how she started cooking regular when she was four, and hadn't never stopped, and how she was a hundred years old or more.

Grandma sideswiped that by telling how she'd cooked for twenty men at a time, and Miss Maggie upped that one by telling how she used to cook for a logging company, cooking for well over three hundred men, three times a day, breakfast, dinner, and supper.

Before too long, both of them, covered in flour and sugar, were poking pies in the oven, building up the wood, stoking the fire, and letting the pies bake.

They went outside and brushed flour off, came back in, sat at the table, and went right back to it.

"You done put your buttermilk in too heavy," Miss Maggie said.

"You poured in too little," Grandma said. "Pie'll be dry."

"You got too much buttermilk, you can't taste the chocolate right."

"Use too little, you might as well have done gone on and baked a chocolate pie."

"Hard as chocolate is to come by, you got to play with it some, add a little ginger to give it a right taste."

"Ginger don't help chocolate none at all," Grandma said.

"We'll just sit here and wait on them done pies," Miss Maggie said.

While we waited, Miss Maggie said, "That boy there done told you about seein' that Goat Man?"

Grandma looked at me and raised an eyebrow. "Goat Man?"

"Yes ma'am," I said. "Me and Tom seen it."

"Now, I know you probably didn't want nothing said, but I wanted your Grandma to know there's been things goin' on in them bottoms. She'd want to watch for you."

"I heard there was some murders," Grandma said.

233

"Uh huh," Miss Maggie said. "But they wasn't just no common murders. And I ain't talkin' out of school here, child," she said, looking at me, "it's all over colored town here, and over in Pearl Creek, which ain't nothin' but coloreds. This here is one of them funny murderers. A Travelin' Man, maybe."

"Travelin' Man?" Grandma asked.

Miss Maggie told her the story she had told me, but a truncated version.

"Ah, tush, ain't no such business," Grandma said.

"Well, that boy there, he done see the Goat Man hisself. And that Goat Man is probably a Travelin' Man."

Grandma looked at me.

"Just like I said, Grandma. Me and Tom seen it. It had horns."

"You must have seen somethin' else and thought it was a Goat Man."

I shook my head. "No ma'am."

Grandma pursed her lips. "Well, you say you seen a Goat Man, then that's what you think you seen. I haven't got any doubt on that. But that don't mean that's what it was."

"Whatever you believe, you best keep them young'ns out of them woods," Miss Maggie said. "Well, I do believe them pies is ready."

Tom and me was set up as judge, and they were both delicious, neither better than the other, just different. We declared it a tie. Both Grandma and Miss Maggie were happy with that. We ate half of each pie. Then Grandma said we had to go. Miss Maggie put all the pie in one metal pan and wrapped it with brown paper.

"This way, you got to bring my pan back," Miss Maggie said, "and I could sure tolerate the company. I like my mule, but ole mule doesn't say much."

"Kind of like some men I've known," Grandma said.

Miss Maggie chuckled over that. We got our pie, said our goodbyes, and went out of there.

On the way home Grandma drove a little more slowly than usual, which was good news for a couple of slow stray dogs and a startled squirrel.

Grandma quizzed me about the murders. I told her what I knew. Like Miss Maggie said, wasn't any of it a secret, and she'd done told Grandma pretty much what I knew. I even told her about the body I found, and before I could help myself, I was telling her about being on the roof of that icehouse, looking down, seeing that poor dead woman.

"Well, now," Grandma said. "This ain't nobody gettin' off a train at random, 'less they're somebody lives close, catches that train to get into the area where they can do what they want to do. How many random hoboes you think gonna come through and do the same thing?"

"I don't know Daddy thinks that," I said. "Whites are pretty sure a colored is doin' it."

"Wait a minute. That's what's goin' on with Mose, ain't it? Somebody thinks he did them murders. That's why your Daddy's so hush-hush about him... Ain't that it, boy?"

"I don't know," I said.

"You just said yes," Grandma said. "You don't tell a lie worth a damn."

I thought about what she had said about Red's tattoo and Mama. Neither did she.

———◆———

Late that afternoon, when Daddy got home, Grandma was laying for him. She kind of directed him onto the back screen porch with Mama, and I sidled over to the door to listen. After a moment, Tom saw me and asked what I was doin'. I hushed her and waved her over. We both put our ear to the door.

We couldn't catch all that was being said, but I could hear my name coming up, and Grandma explaining I wouldn't tell her nothing, but she said she "deduced it from cir-cumstances."

I heard them moving toward the door. Me and Tom slid over to the table and sat down. When Mama, Daddy, and Grandma came in we were sitting there, our hands folded in front of us. Daddy looked at us and said, "Y'all just sittin'?"

"Yes sir," Tom said. "We was talkin'."

"Say you were," Daddy said. He reached over and got me by the shoulder. "Come with me."

We went out the front door and started walking down the road. Daddy said, "Grandma told me she figured out about Mose."

"Yes sir."

"She said you didn't tell her nothin'."

"No sir."

"I want you to know I believe that. You can't hide a darn thing from that woman. Too nosy, and too smart."

"She's a lot of fun, Daddy."

"In some ways," Daddy said. "I want you to know I appreciate you tryin' to not let your Grandma know, and I want you to know I know you kept shut about it."

"Yes sir." I was actually thinking: well, mostly.

"You hungry?"

"Yes sir," I said, even though I was still full of pie.

"Let's walk back and see if we can get Mama to rustle us up some supper."

15

It must have been about two days later, early morning, just before daylight, when we were awakened on the sleeping porch by a pounding on the front door. It sounded as if someone had a log and was ramming it. It didn't even budge Tom, who could sleep sound as a fence post.

I leaped up, pulling on my overalls, and ran into the kitchen. Daddy was already there, one overall strap in place, the other dangling, a pistol in his hand. He went to the window, looked out, grabbed up a lantern, lit it, and with his pistol in his right overall pocket, opened the door.

In the distance we heard a car gun. I looked out the window. Down the road I saw taillights. One of the lights had been busted, showing both tinted red glass and raw yellow light. The car sped from sight, dust swirled up to be tinted by the red and yellow, then that was gone, and there was only the moon to illuminate the dust, make it gold and fairy-like till it settled to the ground.

I saw Toby, who wasn't quite as alert as he had once been, come limping around the side of the house, barking shrill enough to pop your eardrums. He hobbled down the road in the direction of the car, then made his way back to the house, looking embarrassed.

Stuck in the door with a red-handled pocket-knife was a note. Daddy pulled the knife out and brought the note inside. He lay the note on the table and looked at it while he folded up the red-handled pocketknife and dropped it in his overalls next to the pistol.

Mama drifted in from the bedroom, her hair hanging, her face marked with concern. She looked at the note. So did I. It had been written in thick black pencil. It said:

MOSE IS IN TROUBLE. YOU OUGHT TO GO SEE TO IT.

Daddy didn't say a word, he just hurried to get his shoes. I went out on the back porch and put on my own, slipped out the back way, got in the car, lay down in the back floorboard, up close to the seat.

It wasn't a couple minutes before I heard the car door open and slam, heard Mama yell, "Jacob, you be careful. It could be some kind of setup." Then the car was rolling.

I knew I had fixed myself up for a well-deserved walloping, but I felt as if I was a vital piece in these events, and to not have me in on it was playing a checker game without all the checkers.

After a while, the car bumped and slammed, and I was banged up and down hard enough to bruise my ribs. I knew then we was off the main road, on the path that led to the river and Mose's shack. Eventually the motor quit and Daddy got out.

I waited a moment, sat up, looked over the seat, out the windshield. We were parked near the river, up the path a piece from Mose's shack.

It was early morning still, and the rising ruby and amber sunlight tumbled through the trees like nectar busted from exotic overripe fruits.

In front of Mose's shack and beside it was full of cars, wagons, horses, mules, and people. The river was stained by the morning sun, and the people in the yard were stained the same colors as the sky and the river.

I recognized a number of folks in the crowd. Some were friends of my Daddy. Many of the others I had seen around. I suspect there were nigh on forty people there.

The crowd broke open, and out of it came Mr. Nation, his two boys, and some other man I'd seen around town before but didn't know. They had Mose between them. He was being half dragged. I heard Mr. Nation's loud voice say something about "damn nigger," then Daddy was pushing through the crowd.

A heavyset woman in a print dress and square-looking shoes, dark hair knotted on top of her head, yelled, "Hang that coon."

I don't actually remember getting out of the car, but suddenly I was down there in the middle of the crowd, next to Daddy. When he looked down and saw me, his eyes went wide, but he didn't have the time to deal with me.

"Hold on here," Daddy was saying.

The crowd closed around us, except for a gap that opened so Mr. Nation and his bunch could drag Mose into the circle.

Mose looked ancient, withered and knotted like old cowhide soaked in brine. His head was bleeding, his eyes were swollen, his lips were split.

When Mose saw Daddy, his green eyes lit up. "Missuh Jacob, don't let them do nothin'. I didn't do nothin' to nobody. You said I was gonna be all right."

"It's all right, Mose," he said. Then he glared at Mr. Nation. "Nation, this ain't your business."

"It's all our business," Nation said. "When our women folk can't walk around without worrying about some nigger draggin' 'em off, then it's our business."

There was a voice of agreement from the crowd.

"I only picked him up 'cause he might know something could lead to the killer," Daddy said. "I let him go."

"Bill here says he had that woman's purse," Nation said.

A couple of men in the crowd stepped aside, and there was Mr. Smoote. He stood wringing his hands, looking like a boy who had been caught pulling his rope to a underwear picture in the Sears and Roebuck.

"Bill, you sonofabitch," Daddy said.

"Boy was with me that day I chained him," Mr. Smoote said. "He's the one told."

"And because you're such a Samaritan, you come out here to stop it," Daddy said.

Mr. Smoote said, "I come here to see justice. I shouldn't'a hid him out. And wouldn't have, had you not been the law."

"Justice?" Daddy said. "This is a lynch mob. Justice is a day in court."

Mr. Nation grinned. "Who you think's gonna be the jurors, Mr. High and Mighty? Let's just save the time and money of a trial, right here, right now."

"I'm the law here," Daddy said.

"Not today, you ain't," Nation said.

"Let him go."

"In the old days, we took care of bad niggers prompt like," Nation said. "And we figured out somethin' real quick. A nigger hurt a white man or woman, you hung him, he didn't hurt anyone again. You got to take care of a nigger problem quick, or ever nigger around here will be thinkin' he can rape and murder white women at will."

The crowd grew tighter around us. I turned to look for Mr. Smoote, but he was gone from sight.

"There's no evidence against him," Daddy said.

"Had her purse, didn't he?"

"That doesn't mean he killed her to get it."

Mr. Nation said, "You ain't so high and mighty now, are you, Jacob. You and your nigger-lovin' ways aren't gonna cut the mustard around here."

"Don't take your personal grudge on me out on Mose. Turn him loose."

"He ain't gonna be turned loose, except at the end of the rope."

"You're not gonna hang this man," Daddy said.

"That's funny," Nation said. "I thought that's exactly what we were gonna do."

"This ain't the Wild West," Daddy said.

"No. This here is a riverbank with trees, and we got us a rope and a bad nigger."

"He's an old man," Daddy said.

"Yeah," someone in the crowd said, "and he ain't gonna get no older."

One of Nation's boys had slipped off while Daddy and Mr. Nation were talking, and when he reappeared, he had a rope tied in a noose. He slipped it over Mose's head.

"Please, Missuh Jacob," Mose said. "I ain't hurt nobody."

"I know," Daddy said. He stepped forward then, jerked the rope off Mose. The crowd let out a sound like an animal in pain, then they were all over Daddy, punching and kicking. I tried to fight them, but they hit me too. Next thing I knew I was on the ground and legs were kicking at us, then I heard Mose scream for Daddy. When I looked up they had the rope around the old man's neck and were dragging him along the ground, him clutching at the rope with his hands, his old body making ruts in the muddy grass on the riverbank.

Daddy and I got up and staggered after the crowd. My eye was starting to close where someone had kicked me. I saw Daddy reach in his pocket for his pistol, but his hand came out fumbling. He looked around on the ground, but if the pistol had fallen out, someone had picked it up.

"Stop," Daddy yelled. "Stop it, goddamnit!"

They dragged Mose over to a clutch of oaks. One man threw the rope over a thick oak limb. In unison the crowd grabbed it and began to pull, hoisting Mose up. The rope slid over the limb like a snake, made a cutting sound. Hemp puffed up smoke as it rubbed tight against oak bark. The limb creaked. Mose pulled at the rope with his hands, trying to work it free of his throat. He couldn't get his fingers between it and his neck. His feet kicked.

Daddy staggered forward, grabbed Mose's legs, ducked his head under, and lifted him. Nation blindsided Daddy with a kick to the ribs. Daddy went down and Mose dropped with a snapping sound, started to kick fast and spit blood-tinted foam. His eyes turned red and his face puffed. Daddy tried to get up, but the crowd began to kick and beat him.

I ran at them, yelling, swinging, striking anyone I could hit. Someone clipped me in the back of the neck. The world jerked and I couldn't stand. I couldn't kneel. I couldn't do much of anything. I saw the sky going up fast through the limbs and leaves of the oak, then I was looking up at the bottoms of Mose's feet. Last thing I saw were holes in Mose's shoes and cardboard inside them to plug the holes; it had gone damp and was starting to come apart. I could see the flesh of his foot through one of the holes where the cardboard had torn and slipped. The hole was directly over me. It seemed to widen and drop around me, then I was lost within it.

When I came to Daddy was still unconscious, on the ground near me. Mose hung above us, his tongue long and black and thick as a sock stuffed with paper. His eyes bulged out of his head like little green persimmons. Someone had pulled his pants down and cut him. Blood dripped from between Mose's legs, onto the ground.

The crowd was gone.

On hands and knees I threw up until I didn't think I had any more in me. Hands grabbed my sides. I was figuring the crowd had come back and were gonna hang me and Daddy, or give us more of a beating. Then I heard Mr. Smoote say, "Easy, boy. Easy."

He tried to help me up, but I couldn't stand. He left me sitting on the ground and went over and looked at Daddy. He turned him over and pulled an eyelid back.

"You did this," I yelled at Smoote. "You leave my Daddy alone. You hear? Leave him alone!"

He ignored me, and suddenly I was glad for his assistance. I said, "Is he...?"

"He's all right. Just took some good shots."

Daddy stirred. Mr. Smoote sat him up. Daddy opened his eyes.

"That boy told," Mr. Smoote said. "I come with 'em, but I didn't mean for nothin' to happen. I didn't try and hang him. You ain't gonna tell about...you know, are you?"

"You stupid, simple sonofabitch," Daddy said. Then his eyes turned to Mose. He said, "For Christ sake, Bill, cut him down from there."

16

Two afternoons later Mose was buried on our place, between the barn and the field. Daddy made him a wooden cross and carved MOSE on it, swore when he got money he'd get him a stone.

A couple black folks Daddy knew who knew Mose came out, but the only whites there were our family. There was some didn't have no truck with what was done to Mose, but they didn't want it known they'd show up at a colored man's funeral.

At night, when I closed my eyes, I saw Mose hanging, his pants down, cut, bleeding, his eyes and tongue bulged, that rope around his neck. It would be some time before I could lay down and not have that image jump immediately to mind, and some years before it didn't come back to me on a regular basis. Funny things would set it off. Just seeing a rope, or a certain kind of limb on an oak, or even the way sunlight might be falling through limbs and leaves.

Even now, from time to time, it comes back to me clear, as if it happened day before yesterday.

Part Four

◆

From my window is a view of a great oak tree. One evening, in early spring, propped in a wheelchair, looking out, just as evening shadows fell like tangles of black and blue cloth, as the birds gathered in the boughs of the oak like Christmas ornaments, preparing for sleep, I thought I saw Old Mose hanging there.

His body seemed very real in that moment, a twisting shadow amongst other shadows, but it was clearly his shape, and there was the dark line of the rope. But when I blinked, he and the rope were gone.

There were now only the shadows beneath the tree filled with birds, and there was the night descending, and another day of spring was slowly draining away.

No shadows now, not even beneath the trees.

Daddy wanted to quit being a constable, but the little money the job brought in was needed too badly, so he stayed at it, swearing anything like this came up again he was gonna quit.

But for the most part he *had* quit. He was constable in name only. It was as if he were fading right before our eyes. He had been washed out to some dark and infernal sea, and there he floundered, then ceased to flounder, merely drifted on a single crumbling plank left from the wreck of his life. His life having crashed and shattered upon a reef named Mose.

Many of those at the lynching had been Daddy's barbershop customers, and we didn't see them anymore at the shop. As for the rest, Cecil cut most of the hair, and Daddy was doing so little of it, he finally gave Cecil a bigger slice of the money and only came around now and then. He turned his attention to working around the farm, fishing and hunting, and not doing much of any of those.

Mama and Grandma tried everything to bring him around. Patience. Anger. Encouraging words. Right out mean remarks. They could have been talking to a duck. Only the duck would have startled at least.

When spring came, Daddy showed minor improvement. He went to planting, just like always, but he didn't talk about the crops, and I didn't hear him and Mama talking much, but sometimes late at night, through the wall, I could hear him cry. There's no way to explain how bad it hurts to hear your father cry.

Daddy stayed in the bedroom a lot. He mostly ate his meals alone, when he ate. He spoke, but the words were dry and crinkled, like dead leaves. If he sat outside, and saw us coming, he got up and moved away, as if we had caught him doing something embarrassing.

The house changed. It had never occurred to me before that, but a house is a shell like a body, and like a body, it's the spirit inside it that makes it whole. And if we, the family, were the spirit, part of us, a great and powerful part of us, was ailing.

Grass actually began to grow up through the porch, and the hard ground around the house began to fall off and wash away and turn to sand. The well water tasted less sweet. Wild dogs killed our chickens.

Only Grandma was a light in the dark. She was ever energetic, tried to be fun, but Daddy's darkness hung over the house like a tree about to fall. One day, as we put flowers on Mose's grave, Toby limping along beside us, I asked Grandma if Daddy would soon be better.

She thought about it before she answered. That was unusual for her. She was usually quick to respond, and knew exactly what she thought about a matter, exactly what she wanted to say.

She put her arm around me. "I believe he will, Harry. But your Daddy's received a blow. It's not all that different than a fellow I knew named Boris Smith out there in North Texas. He was kicked in the head by a mule. He didn't change right out, but he got sort of strange and stayed that way a long time. One day, he brightened and came out of it."

"What made him better?"

"Well, for one thing, the mule died. That cheered him up. But I don't think it was that simple."

"You think Daddy got hit too hard by them folks?"

"You were both hit too hard. But no, that's not what I mean. Your Daddy got kicked in the soul, sweetheart. So did you. But you're young enough to see daylight. Jacob ought to be, but I think the kick to him was a little harder. He felt he saw it coming and stepped right into it."

"But he'll be all right?"

"I'm gonna tell you I think so. But I ain't gonna lie to you, Harry. I don't know. Boris, he got all right in time. But it took a long time. His was a physical injury, so you might say it's harder to recover from that. I'm not so sure. A kick in the soul can take it all out of you forever. Lot of them Dust Bowl folks just pretty much laid down and quit. Most of them took a chance, went somewhere to try again. They had hope. Some of 'em will find out their hope ain't hope, just a lie, and they'll lay down and quit. Some of them will get up and try again. Your Daddy's like that. If he can get up, he will. I just don't know when."

"It's like everything's fallin' apart," I said.

"I know," Grandma said. "But we've got to be strong. Not only for your Daddy, but for the family. You and me, we can pull this through."

254

"Think so?"

"I do."

"How?"

Grandma was quiet for a moment. "I don't know exactly, but these murders, all this business with Mose, they're connected in more ways than one. I know your Daddy gave you a trust, Harry, but now might be the time to break that. Mose is gone. I know about the murders. Is there anything you can tell me? Maybe I can help. And if we can help, that sure won't hurt your Daddy."

She was right. I had kept my word, and now it seemed to me it was no longer necessary. I told her all that I knew. I did choose, however, to leave out the part about Mr. Smoote's daughter.

When I finished telling her the story, Grandma said, "This Nation. He seems to pop up at all this business. And his two boys. You say they're just like him?"

"Except even more snivelin'."

"Miss Maggie, I bet she knows a little somethin' on everybody in town. Wouldn't you say?"

"Yes ma'am."

"Come on then."

Grandma drove her car over to Miss Maggie's place. Miss Maggie was sitting on the back porch fanning herself with a church fan. When she saw us come up, she grinned around the teeth she had left.

"Well now, if it ain't Miss June."

"Howdy, Maggie," Grandma said. "You got any coffee on?"

"No, I ain't, but I can sure git it on."

Grandma and Miss Maggie had theirs black. Miss Maggie poured me a half cup, put cream in it out of a can, and a lot of sugar. She placed it on a cracked saucer. We took our coffee out on Miss Maggie's porch.

Grandma talked about some general things, then skillfully turned the conversation to the Nations.

"Them Nations," Miss Maggie said. "They's a bad lot. But mostly cowards. They throwed Old Man Nation out of the Klan 'cause he too stupid."

"That tells us somethin'," Grandma said. "It ain't like you're dealin' with a bunch of Edisons there in the first place."

"Oh, they's people in ole Klan you wouldn't believe. I use'ta work for a white man was Klan, and he was right smart and jest as nice to me as could be. But he in the Klan. Cleanin' his house, I fount his robes. He go on to make a judge."

"Another kind of robe," Grandma said.

"Uh huh," Miss Maggie said.

"Maggie," Grandma said, "I'm gonna tell you somethin' that's supposed to just be family business. But I'm gonna tell you about it, 'cause I think I can trust you, and maybe you can help me and Harry here out. His Daddy, this thing with Mose—"

"Po ole Mose."

"Yeah," Grandma said. "Well, Jacob, he's a good man—"

"Oh, Lord yes. I know Missuh Jacob done all he could. He ain't a bit like his Daddy."

"You knew his father?" Grandma said.

"Yes'm, I knew him. Real well. No disrespect to the boy, it bein' his grandfather and all. But I don't miss him none."

"No one else is missin' him much either," Grandma said.

"There's peckerwoods right proud of themselves, goin' out and gettin' 'em an old nigger can hardly stand up and hangin' him. No disrespect to you and Missuh Harry."

"None taken. Wasn't any way Mose did any of this. I knew him too. Many years ago. Me and my husband used to fish with him. He taught Jacob and Harry both to fish."

"He thought a lot of Missuh Jacob and Missuh Harry. He used to come see me sometime."

I noticed that Miss Maggie's eyes were teary.

"Me and him was kind of together oncet. After his wife run off. But his boy needed him a lot. Wasn't right in the head. Liked to run off and live in the woods. I tole him didn't matter none. Me and him could take care of that boy better'n jest him. But he didn't want to move off from down there on that river, and I just couldn't do it. Go there, I mean. I got my place here. Then the boy disappeared, and there was them rumors 'bout Mose killin' him, or some such. But wasn't nothin' to it.

We didn't never go back like we was, but he stopped by from time to time. You know what I mean."

"I know," Grandma said.

I didn't. I thought about it. I guessed maybe he stopped in like us now and then for coffee.

"I wish't I could'a gone to his fun'ral."

"We didn't know who to invite," Grandma said. "Couple folks Jacob knew who knew him come out. We'd have known, we'd have come got you."

"I 'preciate that. They's lots of things 'bout me I ain't made no point on, though. So ain't no way you'd have knowed."

"Don't suppose you have any idea who could have done these murders. Ones Mose was blamed for."

"I knew, I'd said other time we was talkin'."

"Not even rumors?"

"Rumors was what got Mose hung up like that."

"I see your point."

"I think it be a Travelin' Man, just like me and Missuh Harry talk about."

"And if it isn't a Travelin' Man?"

"Anyone could be a Travelin' Man, he sell his soul. I'd keep my eye on them Nations. One of them boys... Don't remember which'n, but one of 'em is crazy. They all crazy, but he's the craziest. Starts fires. Raped couple colored gals in the past that folks know 'bout. Wasn't nothin' could be done 'bout it. No one wanted to do nothin' 'bout it. Missuh Jacob, he tried, but the girls and their families wouldn't talk.

258

Klan done come to see 'em, tole 'em it best jest to stay hush of it. There's a little light-faced, freckled colored boy over there on the other side of the river belong to a girl ain't no more than sixteen. She was thirteen when it happened. That boy, he a Nation's child. Old Man Nation, he thought it was funny. Just his boy sowin' his oats on a nigger. And ain't none of what I'm tellin' you is rumor. Everybody know it... These ain't things to be talkin' in front of a boy."

"Normally, I'd agree with you," Grandma said. "But me and Harry want to find who's doin' all these murders. We got to do it. Jacob, he's not doin' so good now. Life isn't treatin' him good. He sees this as his fault."

"I don't know we want to be meddlin' with no Travelin' Man. And I'll tell you now, you ain't never gonna set things right. Ain't nothin' 'round here ever gonna be on the plumb."

"Come on, Maggie. It's a flesh-and-blood man done this. I was thinking maybe you could ask around. You know people I don't."

"You mean coloreds."

"I'm not privy to them. I don't want nothin' from nobody except to boil down all the lard, and get to the bottom of this. Find out who's killin' these women."

"I do what I can. You drink another cup of coffee?"

"I surely would," Grandma said.

"Miss Maggie," I said. "You know Red Woodrow, don't you?"

'Course I knew the answer, but I wanted her take on things.

"I do."

"He hasn't been a big help," Grandma said. "He didn't want Jacob meddlin' in dead colored business."

"That what he said?" Miss Maggie asked.

I told her what I had heard when he spoke to Daddy, and then when he spoke to Mama.

"Little Man," Miss Maggie said. "Everything ain't exactly as it looks all the time. I prac'ly raised that boy. He know better than that... Red, he come here to see me from time to time. Brings me groceries."

"Red does?" I said. "Red Woodrow?"

"He the one," Miss Maggie said.

Grandma and I sat silently for a time.

"Things he says..." I said.

"Sometimes folks mouth-say things they hear, but their heart, that's what talk for how they really is."

"And how does his heart talk?" Grandma asked. "His voice seems to want to keep Jacob out of finding out who done these things."

"I ain't gonna talk on it anymore," Miss Maggie said. Suddenly it had grown uncomfortable on the porch; it was as if a wave of cold air had blown in, wrapped around us, and was squeezing us like a jungle snake.

"I need to go on and rest," Miss Maggie said. She stood up slowly. She didn't mention the coffee again. We thanked her, returned our cups to the table inside. Miss Maggie disappeared behind a curtain that she had hung up to separate her cooking and eating quarters from where she slept. She went behind the curtain and didn't come out.

We left, closed the door quietly, and walked back to the car.

———————◆———————

On the way home in the car, Grandma and I talked awhile.

"What was wrong with Miss Maggie?" I asked.

"I don't know, Harry. But it might be somethin' we ought to know."

"And it might be meddlin', Grandma."

"You're right about that. It's a surprise to me. I didn't mean to hurt her feelings. I guess, having helped raise Red she's got an investment there. And knowing how he turned out..."

"He brings her groceries."

"He cares for her, Harry, but that doesn't mean he sees her as a full person. People feed and water mules, but that doesn't mean they value their opinion."

"They don't have an opinion."

"Yes, but humans do. Tell you what. Let's put this Miss Maggie business aside, and figure what we do know. You stop me I get any of it wrong, or it ain't the way you see it. Murderer ties his victims up. Sometimes in kind'a odd ways. He's killed three women we know about, maybe four. Is that the way it is?"

"Yes ma'am. I think so."

"And they're all colored? Except for one. They were all put in the river or were found near it."

"Except for the one blown around by the tornado, but she could have come from the river. Storm went through there, so it makes sense."

"The colored doctor you was tellin' me about..."

"Doc Tinn."

"Doctor Tinn thinks whoever kills these women comes back to bother their bodies. How am I doin' so far?"

"Okay."

"Question is, why?"

"Killer's crazy?"

"Somethin' to that, I guess, Harry. But if you had some idea why, then you could maybe ease in on who's doin' it. 'Course, there may not be any reason. But I'm one of them thinks there's damn near a reason behind everything. Even crazy folks have reasons. They may not be logical to us, but there's some kind of reasonin' there. I guess unless you're so damn crazy you don't know who you are or what day it is. But a fella like this, he's around here amongst us, seemin' normal. So somethin' sets him off, or there's some kind of thing cookin' in his head that makes it all seem logical. And maybe he can't help himself. He might not even want to do it. Another thing is, we got to figure it's someone likes the river or can get to it easy. Someone who knows the area down there, or how to get these women off by themselves. Someone is bound to have seen somethin'."

"Mose was like that," I said.

"Like what?"

"He lived by and liked the river."

"So he did."

"And there ain't been another murder since he was hung."

Grandma nodded. "But you and me don't think it was Mose, do we?"

"No ma'am, not really. Be easier if it was."

"In a way. Then again, that may be why your Daddy gets worse and worse. He don't want no one murdered, but he's got to wonder, it's all stopped now, so was it Mose? Was he protectin' a guilty man? And he's got to wonder too, if it wasn't Mose, who is it? And if he'd caught the real culprit, wouldn't none of this happened to the old man."

"Guess Daddy mentioning at the Halloween party that someone was arrested kind of got the ball rolling. That's why he feels so guilty."

"Yeah, but he didn't say who he had or where they was, did he?"

"No ma'am."

"Mr. Smoote, or the boy helped put on Mose's chains, or both of 'em, could have talked, couldn't they? And probably did. That solves how anyone knew Mose was a suspect and where he was being kept. We don't have to think on that one too hard. Either by intention or stupidity, they couldn't keep their mouths shut. Next thing is someone comes by and warns that Mose is going to be hung. Who would do that?"

I shook my head.

She continued. "Could be someone got the word, wanted to save the old man. That's the obvious idea, now ain't it?"

"Yes'm."

"But say it's the murderer, and he wants to save Mose 'cause he knows Mose ain't the one?"

"But why would a murderer save Mose?" I asked. "That seems like just what he'd want, someone else to take the blame."

"Maybe the murderer can't help himself. He's driven by somethin' else. He don't want no one else to take the blame... This Groon. Maybe he warned your Daddy."

"He could have."

"Maybe he heard and wanted to help your Daddy and Mose out. Maybe he didn't want to see an innocent man die for something he knew the fellow didn't do."

"'Cause he did it?"

"I ain't sayin', just speculatin'."

"But Mr. Groon?"

"Again, I'm just speculatin'. I've read some detective books, and if there's one thing I know from them, it's everyone is a suspect. Excluding me and you, Tom, your Mama and Daddy, of course. Think about this. You didn't expect someone like Groon to be in the Klan either, did you?"

"No."

"Another thing. Groon. Ain't that a Jewish name?"

"I don't know."

"I knew some Groons out in West Texas, and I know they was Jewish. Name sounds German, but it ain't. It's Jewish. Oh, I guess this fella you're talkin' about could be German, but these folks I knew weren't German. They was practicin' Jews... If this here Groon is a Jew, won't that be ironic?"

"Ironic?"

"Kind of plays back on itself. That's what it means. You see, Klan don't like Jews neither. But this fella, he's been in the community so long, they don't even consider him Jewish. Probably goes to a Christian church."

"He's a Baptist, like Mama," I said.

"You said you saw a car with a busted taillight drivin' off after leavin' the note?"

"Yes ma'am."

We drove along in silence for a moment, then Grandma said, "I'm turnin' this bucket around."

We drove to Groon's store. Out back of it, under a huge pecan tree, his black Ford was parked. Grandma eased up behind it and stopped. She leaned toward the windshield, squinted her eyes for a look.

"He's got both taillights," she said. "Could have fixed it. Wouldn't take much. I've fixed a taillight myself. Where would he get parts for a taillight around here, Harry?"

"There ain't a garage here," I said.

"Who mechanics?"

"Everyone 'round here pretty much does his own work," I said. "It's something serious, they

265

take it to Tyler. That's where he'd have to get parts."

"Less he had some spares," Grandma said. "And he's sure had plenty of time to fix it."

"Yes ma'am. I guess so."

"We ain't gettin' anywhere, are we, boy?"

"No ma'am."

"You say this Doc Tinn had some ideas on this kind of killer?"

"He seemed real smart, Grandma. Lot smarter than Doc Stephenson."

"Why don't we go see him?"

"I don't know, Grandma... I mean, you know, a white woman in colored town, talkin' to a colored man."

"I can take care of myself."

"Yes ma'am... I mean, Doc Tinn. You and him talkin', and him bein' colored and thought to be uppity 'cause he's smart and a doctor... Bad words gets out... It could be like Mose."

"You got a point, Harry. But I'm thinkin' selfish. I want to help Jacob. And we ain't gonna get Doc Tinn in no trouble... Pappy Treesome still there, runs the general store?"

"Yes ma'am."

"Then there's a way."

Grandma turned the car around, and we headed for Pearl Creek.

18

We drove over to Pearl Creek, and as we neared Grandma said, "Here's how we'll do it, Harry. We'll go to the general store. Say we're low on gas, which we are, and we'll buy some. We'll go in the store and get soda pops, but before we do that, you run over to Doc Tinn's place... Said it was close, right?"

"Yes ma'am."

"You run over there, and you tell him I'd like to speak with him at the store. Bring his wife if he wants. That way ain't nobody gonna blame him for messin' with me. He comes to the store, I want to ask him some questions only I think he can answer. Tell him we're tryin' to clear Mose's name and help Jacob. We're tryin' to get the real killer. Okay?"

We arrived in Pearl Creek just as black rain clouds were rolling in. Their shadows fell over the road and over the general store, moved on, were followed by even darker shadows that pooled over everything and hung there.

"That's what I meant about East Texas," Grandma said getting out of the car. "You don't go long without rain."

Only it wasn't raining, just clouding. I went inside and talked to Pappy Treesome. He took me out back and filled me a can with gas. He walked with me around front, jerking his body this way and that. When he saw Grandma they hugged.

"How're you doin', you ole horse thief," Grandma said.

He was wearing his store-bought teeth today, so I could understand him, even if there was an occasional click and pop from the teeth slipping.

"I was real young when I stole that horse," Pappy said.

"When you was young is farther back than I can count," Grandma said.

While they were talking, I eased off to Doc Tinn's place, and Grandma went up the steps into the general store with Pappy. I heard Pappy's plump wife, Camilla, yell out, "Ah, Miss June, you ain't aged a day."

"Uh huh," I heard Grandma say, "and neither has no one else."

I went over to Doc Tinn's house and knocked on the door. His wife answered. She said, "Yes, sir."

I explained who I was and asked if I might see Doc Tinn, if he wasn't busy. He wasn't. She let me in the house and Doc Tinn was sitting in a rocking chair in the living room, reading a book. He put the book in his lap, smiled at me.

"How're you, little sir? How's your Daddy?"

"That's what I've come to see you about," I said.

Doc Tinn and his wife, both dressed as if going to church, walked with me to the general store. Inside Grandma was chatting with Pappy and Camilla. Pappy was his usual jerky self, standing behind the counter, his upper body wagging off in one direction, only to be pulled in the other as if by unseen hands.

Camilla was on our side of the counter, wearing a dress made of enough potato sacks to have contained all the Irish potatoes in the county and a pretty good batch of the sweet potato crop. She was sitting on a stool laughing at something Grandma had just said.

The sacks her dress were made from had been bleached and dyed blue, but the bleach hadn't done a good job and the dye hadn't taken, or was washed out; her outfit had gone gray leaving the faint impression of a potato sack brand visible at the top of her butt; the words reminded me of bugs riding the rolling hocks of a pig on the run.

Camilla's hair was highly greased and two long knitting needles were plunged through a knot at the top of it. When the light caught the tips of the needles, sparkles jumped, suggesting extreme sharpness. Rumor was, Camilla wore the knitting needles for self-defense.

Grandma was sitting on the stool next to Camilla, close enough they could exchange elbow jabs between funny remarks. All three were drinking Co'-Colas.

I introduced Grandma to Doc Tinn and his wife, and gradually Grandma eased away from her friends toward the Tinns, and we sat where Daddy and I had sat the day he had come to look at the body. I took a wooden chair with cloth wrapped on the arms to make it more comfortable, and left the stuffed chairs and a couch to the adults.

The little door that had been fixed into the stove was closed this time and a brown dog with a white spot on its nose lay in front of it. Since there was no heat, I assumed his lying there was out of habit. The dog saw us, got up, and wandered over to me with its head down. When it walked it limped. I noticed that part of its right front foot had been cut off in some kind of accident. I patted it and it lay its head in my lap for more attention. I stroked its nose.

Grandma gave a little background on Daddy to Doc Tinn, who listened intently, nodding his head now and then. I found it embarrassing, and wouldn't have told about how lost Daddy was these days, but no one asked me. Grandma had her own methods.

When she was finished, Doc Tinn shook his head. "That's a real shame. I like Jacob. I really do."

"That's one reason we've come to you. We're trying to get a handle on who done these murders."

"Ma'am, I knew, I'd have told somebody."

"We know that," Grandma said. "What we want to know is if you know what kind of person done these murders."

"I heard you talkin' to Daddy," I said. "I was on the roof of the icehouse. Things you told him, seems to me you know a lot about this kind of thing."

"I knew you was up there. So did your Daddy. Not right away. But we come to know it."

"You should have called those boys down," Mrs. Tinn said.

"They done seen what they seen," Doc Tinn said. "Wasn't any undoing that. As for these murders, nobody knows a lot about this kind of thing. You mind hearin' all this, dear?"

"My heart and stomach is a little too delicate for it, but my curiosity is strong as steel. I'll stay."

"Well now," Doc Tinn continued, "I don't know anything at all. Not really. But I do some reading, and I've given it some thought. This kind of killer, he don't kill 'cause he don't want to pay his john bill, you know what I mean?"

Grandma nodded.

I thought on it. John Bill? I had no idea what he was talking about.

"He enjoys hurting people. Like that de Sade. The idea of them sufferin' makes him happy."

"That's hard to imagine," Grandma said. "Surely he can't want to do this kind of thing. He's got be driven to do it."

271

"You're right. He is driven. But he wants to do it. He likes doing it."

"You don't know that," Grandma said.

"Ma'am, you asked me my opinion. That's all I can give."

"I'm sorry, Doctor. Please continue."

"I have a book in my house called *Psychopathia Sexualis*, by a fella named Richard Krafft-Ebing. It's a morbid curiosity, I suppose, but it interests me. It tells a lot about people who enjoy being hurt—"

"They want pain?" Grandma asked.

"Yes. De Sade discussed it in his books."

"I haven't read them," Grandma said. "I don't know that I would want to."

"You're probably right, ma'am. And there are those who enjoy giving pain. It gives them control over people they might not normally have control over. Or, maybe they just like the idea of power."

"These women," Grandma asked. "They're prostitutes?"

"Seems that way."

"Isn't that control enough?"

"That's control by permission. He wants complete control. It's also possible he experienced something bad in his life, saw something affected him. Got him so he feels he's got to do this. Someone else might not be affected by this thing happened to him, but for some reason, his basic nature, the intensity of the event, he has been changed. And, in the case of our man, not for the better. There's another thing mentioned in the book. Fetishism."

272

"What?" Grandma asked.

"Obsession with certain things."

"I'm obsessed with peppermints, but I don't kill people."

Dr. Tinn smiled. "Fetishes like, say...an obsession with shoes. He might only pick victims that wear a certain kind of shoe. Or they're of a certain type. Or maybe he likes to have relations with a woman while she wears a certain kind of shoe."

"Like prostitutes?" Grandma asked.

Doc Tinn nodded. "That could be it. Could be he likes to leave a little somethin' that means somethin' to him. Say when he was young, he got all confused on sex and hurtin'. It happens. Could be he keeps some of their clothes or shoes after he does his murders. Could be because they're colored. Prostitution may just make them available and it hadn't got a thing to do with their color or their way of makin' money."

"But one of the victims was white," I said.

"That's the one got Mose hung," Doc Tinn said. "I knew Mose. He didn't have anything to do with any of this business. Lot of things make him look good for it. Mose was on the river. Had a boat. Went up and down the river all the time. Purse was found on his table. Also the fact his wife and son ain't around no more and no one knows where they are. And there hasn't been another murder. But Mose was too old and not strong enough.

"Whoever this is, they might be doin' this

'cause they don't like the way some women carry themselves. Maybe thinks any woman he can have, or has had, isn't worthy to live. Wants to enjoy the woman's favors, but soon as he does, she's no longer on a pedestal. She isn't the Virgin Mary any longer. Or in the case of the prostitutes, he already hates them for what they are."

"Way he ties them up," Grandma asked. "Anything in that book on that? Could it tell us somethin'?"

"We're back to fetish. Bondage. Control. Humiliation. He likes all them things, I figure. He could be someone knows ropes and how to tie them. You know your Dad brought that dead white woman over for me to look at? He didn't know she was white at the time. You know that?"

"Yes sir," I said.

"Knots tied on her was like loggers use when they don't have chains. Have to use ropes. Small operations. But that don't tell you much. Darn near every man in the county and bunches outside have worked logs some. I've seen men use them same kind of ties for trussin' up a dead hog to be carried. And on a smaller scale I've seen similar ties used to fasten on hooks to fishin' line. I've used them myself. Used to be everyone knew how to tie a good knot."

"If Mose didn't do it, you think since there hasn't been a murder, fella's moved on?" Grandma asked.

"Possible. But I doubt he's quit murderin'.

He'll do it again, wherever he goes, and there's a chance he was doin' it somewhere else before he come here."

"But he could just work it out of his system?"

"Who am I to say. I doubt it. Unless they get too old. Or they're in jail or a nut house or somethin'."

"Any guess about the color of this man?" Grandma asked. "Any guess about anything?"

"Outside of what I told you, I can't say. Maybe someday someone will make a science of this. I've tried to learn what I can out of curiosity, but what I know ain't much."

"There was a warning about Mose being lynched," Grandma said, and she gave Doc Tinn some of the details. "Figure whoever's been doin' this didn't want an innocent man to die for what he done. His conscience got the best of him."

"You're a credit to Christian thinking," Doc Tinn said. "But I think he didn't want someone else to take credit for what he done. He's right proud. Kind of signs all his work, so to speak. Same kind of ties and cuts. Does it all along the river, or takes them to the river. He feels comfortable there."

I thought: Like the Goat Man.

"I don't think this fella's got a conscience. Least not the way we think of one. But he ain't no monster in his ever-day life. He's normal like. Not someone you'd expect."

"Unless it's Mr. Nation," I said. "Or one of his boys. They're monsters."

Doc Tinn rubbed his chin, then nodded. "I

know them. That young one, Joshua, he likes to set fires. And Esau, the older one, he's hired couple of colored boys to take him out boat fishin', and they say he's took the fish he's caught and thrown 'em out on the bank and just stomped them. Had a real delight in it. So, you could be right. It could be any one of them Nations, and I wouldn't be surprised. People got that much hatred and meanness in 'em, it's got to come out somehow."

It had begun to rain. We could hear it pattering on the tin roof.

"And there's another thing I been thinkin'," I said. "Red Woodrow."

"You're thinkin' on some harsh things for a boy," Doc Tinn said.

"Yes sir," I said. "Me and Tom found the first body, and I've been in touch with everything since. I feel I'm part of it."

"Red's the law," Grandma said, "so he's got access to information and people. He could get a woman off by herself easy. Say to her it's law business. Coloreds, they've got no say against the law. And Red's known as someone that isn't too fond of women. And he hates colored."

Doc Tinn studied the air for a moment, as if trying to decide if certain information should be revealed.

"Listen here," he said. "I'm gonna tell you somethin' I shouldn't. And I got it on rumor, but it's worthwhile knowin', considerin' we're all meddlin' here. And this ain't even well known in the colored community, but once when Miss Maggie took ill she come to me, and she had to spend three days at our house, she come down with such a case of the pneumonia. She got to talkin', and she told me somethin' I maybe shouldn't tell now, but considering what happened to Mose, and what's goin' on, it might be best you know. I got to have your word, though, that you ain't goin' to spread it around. I don't need the reputation as a gossip."

Grandma and I agreed.

"Red, he ain't white. Least not totally."

"What?" Grandma was leaning forward in her chair now, as if being closer to Doc Tinn might make everything clearer.

"Red's Daddy thought he put three children in Miss Maggie's belly," Doc Tinn said. "Two girls and a boy. All three of them children turned out white-lookin'. Red's two sisters was raised in the black community until they was four or so. Miss Maggie seen they could pass for white, and she had relatives help them girls. They went up North somewhere. Story is, and it might not be true, is them girls was adopted by white folks wantin' babies, and they don't even know them girls are colored.

"Red, bein' a boy, well, old man Woodrow wanted him at first. He was raised as his son, and his wife had to claim she gave birth to him. They kept it hid somehow."

"Red know he's got colored in him?" Grandma asked.

"No. And I don't know it for sure. I'm tellin' things I've heard. But I believe 'em. Red,

277

he loves Miss Maggie 'cause she darn near raised him. He just come up thinkin' he was white and she was his nanny and wet nurse."

"Wait a minute," Grandma said. "You said Mr. Woodrow thought he put three children in Miss Maggie's belly. Thought?"

"You're a good listener and a smart lady," Doc Tinn said. "The third child, the youngest, that was Red. But in this case, it wasn't old man Woodrow who put him there. It was Mose."

At that moment, it was as if the roof had fallen in on us.

"Mose was part white," Grandma said.

"Yes," Doc Tinn said.

"And Red was a kickback to that part of Mose."

Doc Tinn nodded.

"You look real close, 'cept for the size, Red and Mose were the spittin' image of each other. Red hair, freckles, and them leaf-green eyes. And there's another thing she told me. Mose, his Daddy was the old man Woodrow's Daddy."

"Any way Red could have known?" Grandma asked.

"Not unless Miss Maggie told him. I don't think she'd have told me had she not been half delirious. She's proud of him. He made somethin' of himself. Then again, he don't know he's colored, don't know Miss Maggie's his mother. She ain't totally happy about all that."

"Why doesn't she tell him?" I asked.

"She thinks way things are is best, I figure.

He gets treated a lot better as a white man than a black."

I knew then why Miss Maggie had not wanted to talk about Red the other day. Why she had become so upset.

"Once again, I mention this only because Red Woodrow is puttin' the pressure on folks here in the community to keep what they know in the community. He don't want colored business flowin' into white business. But it ain't all hatred on his part. He may not know he's colored, but in spite of what he says, he's got a good streak. He's thinkin' it gets out more, whites are gonna get upset more, and it's the coloreds gonna suffer. Things ain't always how they look."

"And the killer?"

Doc Tinn shrugged. "I don't know any more than I told you. But if it's like some other murders, like the Jack the Ripper murders in England, he's gonna grow bolder, and more violent. Right now he's takin' women he don't think matter. But he may not stay doin' that. He might decide any woman is fair game. Man like that, he's playin' games with the law and everyone else. He don't think he can be caught. He don't think he's doin' anything wrong."

———— ◆ ————

By the time Grandma said her goodbyes and her and Camilla poked and laughed at each other a bit, the rain was coming down hard, slamming on the tin roof like someone was beating it with a chain. The air was heavy but cool with the rain. Outside the store's open door you could see it splattering in the mud street, running ruts across the road. It was growing darker by the moment.

"Y'all ought to wait it quits rainin'," Camilla said.

"I don't want my daughter to worry about us," Grandma said. "Besides, we'll take it easy."

We rushed out to the car, and by the time we were inside we were soaking wet, and chilly. Grandma started off. I said, "Did we learn anything, Grandma?"

"I don't know, Harry. In the detective books they just keep askin' questions of people, and finally someone tells someone somethin' that matters. We did hear some interestin' stuff, but I don't know it helps any. Time will tell."

Just outside of town, something stumbled through the rain, out into the road and stopped.

It was a naked black man. He was holding his privates, shaking them at the car, as if it were something he might use to flail the hood. He had his mouth open and seemed to be making some kind of sound, but over the motor and the rain, it was impossible to hear him.

Although I had never seen him before, I knew immediately who it was by reputation.

"Root," I said.

"What?" Grandma said.

"That's his name. He's harmless."

"You mean Camilla's boy William?"

"They call him Root now," I said. "He ain't right in the head."

Root stumbled out of the road, releasing himself, throwing his hands to sky, talking to the heavens. He wandered into the woods with his hands up and disappeared.

"Well, my goodness," Grandma said. "He's certainly...large."

19

In the dark rolling wetness of the rain, Grandma lost sight of the road and we found ourselves driving toward the woods. Trees seemed to leap at us.

By the time Grandma realized her mistake, we were sliding on grass and mud. The car turned sideways, slid in slow motion, as if on greased glass, and came to a stop with the rear end gently bumping against a sycamore tree.

"Goddamnit!" Grandma said.

She tried to drive the car out, but the more she tried, the more the tires churned the grass into mud, and the deeper they buried.

"We're stuck, Harry. We got to walk."

"I can walk, Grandma. I'll get Daddy to come back and get us."

"I got us into this, I can walk out and get wet with you."

"You don't have to."

"I know, but it's what I want. The idea of sittin' and waitin' don't appeal to me. Look under that seat there."

I reached under me. There was a pretty good-sized wooden box with a latch.

"Open it up," Grandma said. "Let's see what all I still got in it."

There was a flashlight, small pistol, some first-aid stuff, matches, a box of .32 shells, and a road flare.

"You tote that for me," Grandma said.

I locked the box, we got out and started walking. The rain was very hard, and soon it turned to ice. Hail in the middle of the summer, and it was pounding us so violently, we took a trail off the road and wandered into the woods, hoping the trees would give us some respite against it.

It was dark and the air was blurred by rain and hail, but it didn't take long before I realized the trail we were on led to the Swinging Bridge.

I told Grandma as much.

"That means we aren't far from Mose's shack," Grandma said. "We can hole up there."

I thought about that. I remembered the shack being surrounded by townfolks. Not far from the shack, Mose had been strung up. I didn't want to go down that trail to the shack, but the hail didn't leave us much choice.

As we broke out of the trees into the clearing that led down to the river and to Mose's shack, the hail hammered us as if trying to drive us into the ground. It was knocking knots on my head and the rain was chilling me to the bone. It was dark as night now, and Grandma took the flashlight out of the box and we used that as we hurried down the hill that led to the shack. We burst in through the half-open door. A raccoon, startled at our presence, jumped back and hissed at us.

Grandma pushed me along the wall and left the door open, the startled coon didn't want to leave. Grandma took a chair and poked it and it ran out the open door, disappeared into the rain and hail. I almost felt sorry for it.

After Grandma closed and bolted the door with the wood bar, she poked the flashlight around. The place had been turned inside out. Mose's few clothes were strewn about. There was flour dumped and a few tins and broken jars of food lying on the floor. I didn't know if the mob or animals had done that after Mose's death.

Lying on the floor, next to a broken jar of food that had gone rotten, was a photo of a colored woman in a frame. There was also a loose picture of what I figured was Mose's son, the one that had gone out and never come back. It was stuck in the frame with the picture of the woman, just pushed into the edge of it. The picture had faded considerable. The boy appeared to be about eleven. I looked at the picture real close, realized it was a white boy's picture cut from a Sears and Roebuck catalogue, the features colored dark with pencil. I wasn't exactly sure what that was about. Not then. Not now. The woman was very dark and her features were not particularly distinguishable. I set the frame on the table.

In the corner of the room was a simple wood frame with a mattress on it and some covers strewn across it.

"Kind of smells in here," Grandma said.

"Well, it ain't Mose's fault. It didn't stink when he lived here."

Grandma put her arm around my shoulders. "I know, Harry."

The storm grew more violent, dark and thundery with cuts of lightning slashing through Mose's two windows.

"I'm exhausted and cold, Harry," Grandma said. "It's gonna be a little wait. I'm gonna to lay down. There's room for two."

Grandma sat on the edge of the bed, gave me the flashlight. She suddenly looked her age.

"You all right, Grandma?"

"Of course. I'm just old. And my heart gets kind of tired now and then. Beats funny. I rest a bit, I'll be all right."

Without another word, she lay on the bed and pulled a cover over her. I took the spare one and put it over my shoulders and sat in a chair at the little table. After a while I got up and picked up the canned goods and put them in the shelf. I put the photo and the Sears and Roebuck cutout in the center of the table. I sat in the chair again with the blanket around me, turned out the flashlight, and closed my eyes.

I hadn't been sleepy, it being midday and all, but there was something hypnotic about the pounding rain and hail, the darkness. I could hear water leaking through the roof as well, dripping in a far corner of the shack.

I focused on that sound and fell asleep to it.

———◆———

I was dreaming of Mose. Of how they must have beat on his door until he opened it, and then they pulled him out. Then Daddy showed up and he thought he was going to be all right, but he wasn't. The fear he must have felt, the pain of strangling, feeling his life flying away from him, and for no reason at all, other than the color of his skin.

I jumped awake to a knocking sound.

I jerked my head around, looked at the rain-streaked window, and yelled, "Grandma!"

Grandma came awake. "Harry? Harry?"

"The window."

She looked. There was a dark face in the window, horns on its head. It was looking in the glass at us, tapping with its knuckles. Rivers of rain fled down the glass, blurring the face.

The Goat Man.

Grandma sprang awake, tried to get hold of the box she had placed by the bed. She managed to kick it and slide it under the table.

The face went away. The door shook. The wooden bar held. There came a noise from outside like someone trying to talk with a mouthful of mush. The door was tugged harder, and for a moment I thought it might break free.

I crawled under the table, got the box, opened it, gave it to Grandma. She pulled out the .38. "Go away, goddamnit! Go away or I'll start shootin' through the door."

This didn't discourage the Goat Man. He shook the door some more, and Grandma, in spite of her threat, did not start blasting through the door.

Finally the door ceased to shake. I got a glimpse of him as he passed the window. A heartbeat later I turned to a sound behind me. The second window was without a glass. There was only a yellow oilcloth pulled over it. A dark hand with long broken nails worked its way through, past the oilcloth, moved about as if trying to get a hold by which to pull himself inside. Grandma stepped forward and whacked the hand with the gun barrel.

There was a howl. The hand leaped away and was gone. We listened for a while. Nothing. Grandma eased over to the window, pulled back the oilcloth. Wet wind whipped inside and chilled the room. Grandma cautiously leaned against the wall and looked out the window. She went to the other side of the oilcloth,

286

lifted it again, looked out that way, and hopped back with a scream.

"Damn!"

She had hold of her chest as she backed toward the table.

"He was out there. Soon as I looked he ran away."

"The Goat Man," I said.

"I almost believe it," Grandma said.

"He had horns, didn't he?"

"He had... He had somethin'."

Grandma pulled up a chair and we both sat at the table, the little revolver lying in the center next to the frame with the pictures in it.

◆

I suppose it was an hour later when the hailstorm stopped, and a little later after that when the rain slowed and the sky lightened.

"It could have been Root," Grandma said.

"With horns on his head?"

Grandma didn't respond to that. We waited a while longer, then, carefully, Grandma had me lift the bolt on the front door and open it. She stood with the pistol ready.

The Goat Man didn't jump in on us. We both breathed a sigh of relief. Grandma got her box, and we went out of there, back into the rain. The rain was softer now and the sky was much lighter. The air smelled fresh, like a baby's first breath. The bottoms themselves were beautiful. The trees lush, the leaves heavy with rain, the blackberry vines twisting and tangling, sheltering rabbits and snakes. Even the poison ivy winding around the oak trees seemed beautiful and green and almost something you wanted to touch.

But like the poison ivy, looks could be deceptive. Under all the beauty, the bottoms held dark things, and I tell you true, I felt greatly relieved when we reached the Preacher's Road.

We stopped at the car, tried it another time, but no deal. It was stuck and proud of it.

There was nothing to do but walk home. The rain quit and the sunlight turned hot. It was very muddy. My shoes and pants bottoms were caked with it. So were Grandma's shoes and the hem of her dress.

"Next time I'm wearin' pants," she said.

And she meant it. It was just the sort of thing she'd do and it would start a scandal. Back then, the idea of a female, unless they were a kid like Tom or some movie actress, wearing pants wasn't even considered.

When we finally walked onto the porch the sun was starting to slip on the other side of high center. Mama opened the door. She was beside herself.

"Are you okay?" she said. "Where you been?"

"We run off the road," Grandma said.

"You shouldn't have walked all that far, Mama. How's your heart?"

"Fine. I ain't an invalid, you know."

Both us changed clothes while Mama fixed us something to eat, a couple of rewarmed biscuits and some salt pork. Grandma even told Mama part of the truth. She said we had gone for a ride and ended up sliding off the road and staying in Mose's old shack. She didn't mention we had gone to Pearl Creek, that we had seen Root, and his root. She didn't mention the Goat Man.

It was my idea to hook Sally Redback up with a single tree and some chains, go back and pull the car out, but Mama nixed that idea, saying Sally was too old for that sort of thing, and the strain might kill her.

It was decided, instead, I would ride Sally into town and get Daddy, who had as of late gone back to the barbershop to hit a lick at working. He'd come in as if he had never left, or perhaps as if he had never come home. He'd go into the bedroom, or outside, and sit in the chair beneath the great oak and whittle a large stick to splinters.

Since I was going into town I decided, while I was at it, I would return a book to Mrs. Canerton, maybe get another.

I put a bridle, reins, and saddlebag with the book in it on Sally, and Tom, who was disappointed she had missed out on our adventure, insisted on riding with me. I let her hang on the back, and Sally bounced us into town.

At the barbershop I noticed Daddy's car wasn't there, but Cecil's truck was and the shop was open. We dismounted and went inside. Cecil was sitting in the main barber chair reading a pulp magazine. I hadn't seen him in

289

a while. He looked tired, but happy to see us. He got out of the chair, came over to greet us, picked Tom up and sat back down in the chair and held her in his lap.

"My goodness, you've grown," he said.

"I'm two inches taller than last year," she said.

"And heavier," Cecil said. "You'll be a woman soon."

I came over and stood beside them, not wanting Tom to get all the attention. I noticed up close that Cecil had a thin line of rash on the back of his neck, just above his collar.

I wanted to interject myself somehow. "You still seein' Mrs. Canerton?"

"From time to time," Cecil said, pushing Tom's hair out of her eyes. "But she hasn't been as friendly lately."

"I'm going to see her today," I said. "Return a book she loaned me."

"Tell her I said hello," he said.

I had almost forgotten my mission. "Where's Daddy?"

"Well, he's not around just now."

"Where is he?"

"Actually, he's at my place."

"Why?" Tom asked.

"He wanted to relax."

I could tell something wasn't right. I said, "I'll go over to your place and check on him."

"Tom can stay here," Cecil said.

"Naw," Tom said. "I'm goin' too."

"He really wanted to be alone," Cecil said.

"This here is an emergency," I said.

"It might be best you went and got him," Cecil said. "Tom could help me clean up here, make a nickel."

"A nickel," Tom said. "You got a whole nickel?"

"You'd have to earn it," Cecil said. "There's work needs to be done. Sweepin' and such. Cleanin' that mirror, wipin' them hair oil bottles down."

"I'll go on then," I said.

Cecil nodded. I slipped out the front door and untied Sally from the tree by the barbershop, started on over to Cecil's house. By the time I got over there the sun was creeping down the horizon like a smear of sweet potato sliding off a navy-colored plate.

I had only been to Cecil's house once, when Daddy had wanted him to come into work early. He had given me directions and sent me over there, but I remembered the way easy.

Cecil's house was just on the edge of town, back amongst some trees, and it wasn't much to look at. A two-room gray shack with a rusty tin roof and a bunch of sweet gum trees around it; a limb from one of them had grown in such a way it lifted a corner of the tin roof as if its intent was to peel it off and peek inside. The porch was rotted in spots and there were gaps in the wood where the ground showed. The ground around the house was littered with sweet gum balls.

Daddy's car was parked out to the back of the house, not far from the outhouse. The driver's side door was half open. Leaning against a tree out back were the wooden side boards Cecil sometimes used for his truck, and his fishin' boat was up on bricks to keep from rotting.

I tied Sally to a tree, closed the car door, went on the porch and called out for Daddy. He didn't answer. I pushed at the door and it came open. There was a faint stink inside. I walked in and looked around. A wood stove, chintz curtains over a window, a table, couple of chairs. No Daddy.

The second room had a curtain over the door. I pulled it back, and that's where the stink was coming from, and the stink was Daddy.

He was lying on the bed asleep, blowing out his breath in such a way his lips trembled. The room was full of the stench of his breath, and the stench on his breath was alcohol. There was a tall bottle lying by the bed. It had turned over and whiskey had poured out of it.

I stood there looking at him, not knowing what to think. I had never seen my Daddy drunk. I knew he liked a drink now and then, but just a drink. Yet, here he was, knocked out on the bed with an empty whiskey bottle lying in the dust.

I knew then why I had seen him around less, and why he always got away from us when he could. He had been drinking regularly. Where before I had been sympathetic, I was now disappointed.

I began to understand what Mama was going through, and I marveled at how well she had held up and kept it from us. Grandma probably knew as well. Suddenly, I saw those women, who I had always loved, in an even brighter light.

I stood over Daddy, almost wanting to hit him. I decided not to try and wake him. He wouldn't be any good if I did get him up, and I didn't want to see him awake the way he was. I didn't want him to see the disappointment in my face, and I didn't want to see it on his.

I went out of the room quietly, closed the front door, and rode Sally back to the barbershop.

When I got back, Tom had done most of the cleaning Cecil had wanted, and he had sent her over to the general store to bring us back Dr Peppers and peanut patties, his treat.

When she was gone, he said, "I didn't want you to know."

"He's been slippin' into town to drink a lot, hasn't he?"

Cecil nodded. "He goes over to my place now and then. I thought it best he was gonna drink, he didn't do it anywhere where he could be seen. He sobers up before this usually. I don't really know what to say to him. He hasn't had it easy."

"It's not easy on anyone," I said.

"Don't be too harsh on him, Harry. He's a good man. He's just down. It's no trouble to kick someone when they're down."

"I'm not kickin' him," I said. "I come into town to get some help to pull Grandma's car out of a ditch."

"It's not like the business is pourin' in today," Cecil said. "I'll help you, you want. We can use your Daddy's car."

Me and him had put a small plan together. I was to go by Mrs. Canerton's with Tom, to keep her away from Daddy, and he was going to walk over and get Daddy's car, leading Sally as he went. He said there was some good grass out back of his house, and he'd put her on a long rope where she could have it till we come to get her. He would then meet us out front of Mrs. Canerton's in Daddy's car. I figured he was hoping he would see her.

Me and Tom knocked on Mrs. Canerton's door, but she wasn't home. I put the book on the porch swing, sorry not to get a new one from her.

Me and Tom sat on her front porch and waited on Cecil, drinking our Dr Peppers, eating our peanut patties. It wasn't long before Cecil showed. He didn't get out of the car. We went and got in.

"Ain't Daddy around?" Tom said.

"He's about business," Cecil said. "We'll see him later."

We drove off toward Preacher's Road.

◆

It was dark by the time Grandma's car was pulled out of the mud. There was nothing but for me to drive it home, following Cecil in Daddy's car.

Tom rode with Cecil. He let her sit in his lap and steer some, but that didn't last long. She soon moved to her side. Cecil was friendly, but he wasn't stupid enough to let her wreck.

I followed, steering a little too hard, causing the car to go way too far to one side, then the other, but we made it home without me running off in another ditch or meeting a tree head-on. I even managed to pass a car without scaring the other driver too much.

By the time we stopped off at the house and I rode back with Cecil in Daddy's car to get Sally, it got dark and the moon looked like a mashed potato in the sky, rain clouds running over it like burned gravy.

We got to Cecil's, Daddy was gone. I don't know where, since he didn't have a car, but he had slipped off. The whiskey bottle wasn't by the bed anymore. If nothing else, he was a neat drunk.

"Your Grandma can bring your Daddy into town tomorrow to get the car," Cecil said. "I'll have it over to the barbershop bright and early. I think it's better you just take the mule on home, not try and drive at night. You ain't got the experience, Harry."

"Thanks."

"It's okay."

We walked out on the front porch. I felt awkward and didn't know what to do with my hands. Finally I offered one to Cecil. He took it and we shook. I got Sally Redback and started for home.

It was dead dark, and as fate would have it, the wind had picked up. I went by Mrs. Canerton's to see if I could give back the book, but the lights were out and the book was still on the porch swing. I was nervous about leaving it there, lest the rain should start up again and blow water on it. I got the book, put it in Sally's saddlebag, mounted up.

I rarely ever was out this late by myself, so I decided to take advantage of it. I rode Sally over to Miss Maggie's. Unlike Mrs. Canerton's, there was a light in the window. There was also a car in the yard. I couldn't see it good, as its rear was to me. I rode Sally into a clutch of trees and waited a moment, trying to decide if I should bother her or go home. I had come to the conclusion I ought to just go on home, when I looked up to the sound of the car door slamming. The car started up. The tail-lights showed. One of them was broken. It was the same car that had sped away that time we got the message about Mose.

The car looped fast around the house, right through Miss Maggie's yard, came around the side, between some trees. I tried to get a look, saw a man in a hat, and that was it. The car hit the dirt road, flashed its broken taillight at me, and was gone.

I started to chase after it, but that idea went away quick. Sally couldn't keep up with that car, not even a little bit. She'd fall over dead if I pushed her to even try.

I got off Sally, tied her to a tree, walked toward Miss Maggie's. I felt something in the air I can't explain. Maybe it was just the car that had set me on edge, but it was as if the night were filled with needles and the cool points of them were sticking in my skin.

I walked quietly up on Miss Maggie's porch. I turned to look toward the mule pen. The mule was there. The hog was in his pen, lying down in a mud pit it had made in one corner.

The screen was closed, but the door was slightly open. I could see the kerosene lamp sitting on top of the wood stove. I had never known her to keep it there.

I called her name.

No answer.

I knocked.

Still no answer.

I called some more. And when she didn't answer this time, I opened the door and eased inside.

"Miss Maggie," I tried some more.

I went over to the little curtain, still calling her name. I eased it back. The light from the lamp spilled inside, giving a greasy orange glow to the bed.

Miss Maggie, wearing one of her potato sack gowns, was lying on the bed, her hands extended above her in praise Jesus position, her wrists were bent against the wall, causing her thin black hands to fold downward as if she were dumping something from them. Her eyes were open.

I felt a tightening in my stomach, then a sourness. I called her name. I went over and touched her gently on the shoulder. I could feel that she was warm, but she didn't respond.

"Miss Maggie," I said, and began to cry.

I stepped out of there and pulled the curtain back. I went over to the lamp and blew it out.

I went out on the porch and stood there for a long moment, considering the night. The night had nothing to say. I walked back to Sally as if in a dream. I untied her and mounted. I started riding toward home.

I didn't push Sally too hard, but I rode at as good a gait as she could carry me without wearing herself down. In the meantime, I was mentally trying to put something together; I was trying to figure on the broken taillight.

A man jumped out of the dark and grabbed Sally's bridle.

———◆———

"Harry," Daddy said. "I'm sorry, boy. I didn't mean to scare you. I think someone stole the car. I was walkin' home, 'side the road. Saw you comin' 'round the curve. I was afraid you'd get away from me."

"You're drunk," I said.

"I was," he said, and let go of Sally's bridle. "I ain't now. I've walked it off."

"I thought you slept it off."

298

For a moment, from the cock of his head, I knew he thought I had said too much. But he eased his posture, let it go.

"Car ain't stolen," I said. "It's back at Cecil's house. We had to use it to pull Grandma's car out of a ditch. I come over there to get you, but you was sleepin' it off."

"I'm sorry, Harry."

"Miss Maggie," I said. "She's dead."

"What?"

"She's dead. I was goin' home, to find you. I thought maybe you might have got back. I was hopin' you wouldn't be too drunk to do somethin' about it. Not that anything's gonna do Miss Maggie any good."

"She was old, Harry," Daddy said, practically leaning on Sally.

I told him about the car, about the tail-light.

"All right," he said. "I'm climbin' up there."

He pulled himself up on Sally with some difficulty, and we rode back to her place.

Inside, Daddy lit the lamp, pulled back the curtain, sat on the edge of the bed and took a look. First thing he did was use his hand to close her eyes. He touched her skin.

"She feels a little warm."

"She was real warm when I found her," I said.

He held the lamp close to her face. "Someone's had their hands around her throat. And that there pillow on the floor. I'd figure that ended up over her face. She was murdered, Harry."

He turned to look at me when he said that,

and his face in the light of the lantern looked as if it were made of wax.

I guess something in my face showed him something he didn't want to see.

"I don't know much of anything anymore, son," he said, "but I do know that."

Part Five

20

Only our memories allow that some people ever existed. That they mattered, or mattered too much. No one speaks of Old Maggie anymore. I can't say I know anyone who remembers her but me. Remembers her cooking, which if I think about hard enough, I can taste; remembers her stories, strange and wonderful, and told without doubt.

Then perhaps that is conceit. She has family somewhere. They might be alive. Old as, or older than me.

They could remember.

But they can't remember my memories.

Maggie.

Gone now.

Murdered.

And the seasons change as if nothing ever happened.

We went back and got the car at Cecil's, him and Daddy not saying much, then with Daddy driving slow and me riding Sally, we went home.

All the way home I thought about poor Miss Maggie, and that the last time I had seen her she had been upset. I got all my crying out on that ride to the house so I wouldn't be crying in front of the family when I got home.

At the house Daddy sat at the table drinking coffee, Mama sitting beside him, and he tried to figure on Miss Maggie's murder.

I told him about the car I had seen with the broken taillight, the same that had sent us the message about Mose. I also told him how when Grandma and I had last seen Miss Maggie, I had mentioned Red Woodrow and she had gotten upset. Grandma told him we had heard rumors Red was really Miss Maggie's son.

Daddy seemed amazed at this.

"Me and him was once like brothers," Daddy said. "I think I'd have known such a thing."

"Well," Mama said. "It was that old woman who raised him, so it's possible."

Daddy nodded. "But, since she did, why would he kill her?"

"I'll tell you why," Grandma said. "Accordin' what Harry here told me, he didn't care for coloreds. He seen himself as white, and he seen himself as superior, then one day maybe Miss Maggie told him. For whatever reason, she just told him. He couldn't stand the idea, and he killed her."

"If she told him," Daddy said, "and say he realized Mose was his Daddy, and he had Klan connections, and it was him tried to warn us about Mose, then why would he turn around and kill Miss Maggie?"

"I got that one too," Grandma said.

"I figured you had an opinion on it," Daddy said.

"Say he did find out, and from his Klan connections he heard that someone had told Mose was bein' held as a suspect, and say he then knew what they were gonna do to the old man. Say just the day before he was all for it, then he found out the old man was his Daddy. He sent you the note, tryin' to stop it. But he didn't, and say Miss Maggie then said somethin' to him about that, about how he let his Daddy die by not steppin' in and just stoppin' it on his own, or helpin' you. So, in a rage, he killed her too."

"That sounds possible," Daddy said.

"Thing to do, hon," Mama said, "is go see Red. See if he's got that busted taillight."

Daddy nodded. Tom crawled up in his lap and put her arms around his neck. He patted her softly on the back.

———◆———

Next day Daddy went looking for Red, but it turned out he was nowhere to be found. He hadn't been doing his job, and no one had seen him in a week. His car was missing.

Couple days later a fella huntin' over in the next county found it parked down in the woods on a little trail. It wasn't really a trail big enough for the car, but it looked to have been driven down it fast and wild. It was scratched on all sides from brush and limbs. It had a missing taillight.

It wasn't concrete, but it seemed Red had murdered Miss Maggie, and he had been the one to warn us about Mose. Grandma's theory seemed to make sense.

There was still another mystery.

Miss Maggie was buried at the back of her property in a cedar chest that was donated by Mr. Groon. It was simple but lots of folks showed up, both black and white. Miss Maggie was well liked.

A paper was found in her house that had been written out for her and her name was signed on it, scrawled out in poor letters. She wanted her mule and hogs to be given to folks could use them, and she wanted friends to come and pick the house clean. That was done right away, even before an owner for the mule and hogs could be found. Also in this will of hers was the plan to sell her property and give the money to Red Woodrow.

The property was sold all right, but Red Woodrow never did come and collect it.

Mystery was, day after Miss Maggie was buried, the body was dug up. Wasn't nothing but a hole left in her yard, and to the best of my knowledge, to this day no one knows what became of it or why it was taken.

After the business with Miss Maggie, it got around town that maybe Mose hadn't been the killer of all them women, and it had been Red, and in a final rage he had killed Miss Maggie.

'Course, ones sayin' this didn't know she was his mother or that Mose was his father, or that it looked as if he had given Daddy a warning note about the lynching. All this Daddy kept to himself.

What Daddy let be known was I had seen the car at Miss Maggie's, and thinking something suspicious I had gone and got him and he had investigated. Where he fudged a bit was he didn't let on I had discovered the body. He was afraid it might point to me somehow.

The supposed reasons Red killed Maggie were as many as the ants on the ground. A popular one was that Red, who had some reputation as being a bit crooked, had stolen the money she had buried at her house.

This led to speculation as to why money from her property had been left to him in her will. Some said he made her write it that way, but that didn't explain the mule, the hogs, and her household items.

Years later, when the story got around that Red was Miss Maggie's son, the particulars changed some. It was said by some Red come back and got the body and buried it private like. There were other rumors that a colored voodoo man came and dug it up to use the body parts, and it was even said by some that Miss Maggie's wilted, dried hand had been turned into a hand of glory. There were those over the years claimed to see it, just like they'd know one dried black hand from another.

At the barbershop one day, while me and Tom was there with Cecil, I remember Mr. Evans speculating as Cecil clipped at the hair above his ears. Mr. Evans was one for speculating. Like Grandma, he read murder mysteries and saw himself as quite a detective, though the only detecting he'd ever done was trying to puzzle out a story in one of the magazines at the barbershop.

He was a short, fat, bald man with a habit of pursing his lips when he was making a point, or setting up a mystery.

"Say Miss Maggie had her money buried, or hid out, and Red found out about it."

"How?" Cecil asked.

"Some nigger knew somethin' and told him. You know, somethin' about Miss Maggie, and he got it figured, and maybe Red picked him up for somethin'. You know, a crime of some kind."

"Picked who up?"

"Some nigger. Ain't you listenin'. No nigger in particular. Just a hypothetical nigger. And this here nigger, to lighten his load with the law—"

"What'd he do?" Cecil asked.

"He didn't do nothin'. He's hypothetical. Anyway, this fella, he knew about the money and told Red where it was supposed to be, and Red went to get it, and it wasn't there. So he tried to make Miss Maggie tell him, and he accidentally killed her."

"If'n I was him," said Mr. Calhoun, a normally quiet man in overalls, "it'd be that hypothetical nigger lied to me got a beatin'. Not some poor ole nigger woman."

"You people are impossible," Mr. Evans the Great Detective said.

"Did Red get the money?" Cecil asked.

"I don't know," Mr. Evans said, "but I'd wager he did. He maybe had someone else help him. A woman. And he dumped his car and they went off in hers."

"Why would he dump his car?" Cecil asked.

"Harry here had seen it and thought it would be recognized," said Mr. Evans.

"How did Red know he'd seen it?"

"He must have seen Harry," Mr. Evans said. "Hell, I ain't got that part figured out yet. But give me a day or two."

Besides this version of events, there were others. Some said Red not only killed Miss Maggie, but was the Bottoms Killer, as the murderer had come to be known.

But this wasn't a popular theory. It had too many things against it. Miss Maggie wasn't mutilated or tied, for one. Second, there were those that figured white men didn't go in for that kind of horrible killing. And thirdly, most were certain the real man responsible had been lynched. Their conclusions as to why it had to be Mose were simple. There hadn't been another murder like the ones in the bottoms since.

Many didn't even think Red killed Miss Maggie.

'Course, that left a series of questions. Why was Red's car at Miss Maggie's? Why had he disappeared? Why was his car found in the bottoms, run off in the woods like that?

There were answers given for all of these. Like he found the money and run off somewhere to spend it. Hadn't folks heard him say he wanted to go abroad someday?

Bottom line was, no real conclusions were come to, and finally it became an "unknowable nigger murder." Wasn't anyone besides Daddy concerned about it. More people were concerned about Red.

Had he actually been abducted by the Bottoms Killer? Maybe he had found some clues to the killer's identity, and the killer had gotten rid of him.

No matter Red hadn't been concerned about the killer before, this became a popular theory, right up there with him having found the hidden money and gone off to Paris or some such.

There was even a rumor that one of his friends got regular postcards from him under a disguised name and that the cards came from exotic places all over the world. It was also said some of the cards had lipstick stains on them, kisses he had asked his girlfriends in all those countries to stick to the cards with their soft red lips.

'Course, since these cards were supposedly coming in over a short time from all over the world, this wasn't an entirely convincing story.

I think the fact that Daddy didn't come up

with any answers just made things worse than before. For a few days there he had been his old self, but his investigation had stalled at Red's car being discovered and then nothing else.

The whole thing settled down on him heavy as a boulder, and he fell back to the dark place where he had been lying for so many months, and unlike before, he didn't even bother to dodge us when he was on a drunk, and pretty soon the whiskey bottles showed up at the house in plain sight.

Grandma took the hard line with him, calling him this and that, but it didn't budge him.

Finally, he moved out to the barn with his bottles and it was as if he didn't exist anymore. Oh, he got some money from the barbershop, though now Cecil was getting the bulk of it, and he did a little work around the place, but the plowing was left to me and I wasn't real good at it.

We were scratching for a living like never before.

If things weren't difficult enough on the farming scene, it started in raining real hard, beating on the ground worse than that day Grandma and I had been trapped in Mose's shack.

With it pouring like that, there wasn't any real plow work to be done. The rain went on for days, gushed through our fields, washed away our topsoil, carried plants with it, or beat them down in place.

Grandma said it was the darnedest thing yet.

311

She'd already been through everything drying up and blowing away, now she was having to go through everything turning wet and washing away.

The rain turned to flooding and the Sabine flowed high and wide and fast, swirling mad water in brown foamy heaps. The river even changed its course by churning away weak standing banks and uprooting and toting off trees, some of them large enough to have built the front end of Noah's Ark.

But eventually it passed. The rain quit, the black sky cracked open, showed blue behind it, as well as the sun in all its hot golden glory. In fact, it turned hot as hell and dry as Arab sand; mud heaped up in hard crust, like scabs healing all over the earth.

At night the dark sack that held the skies was burst open and the stars fled from it and glowed like frightened animal eyes all across the black velvet heavens.

The river ceased to roar, murmured instead, like a man sleeping contentedly, his belly full of cornbread and beans. Earth stopped dropping off the banks, the ground turned solid again, and the river flowed comfortably within its new boundaries, happy as if the skies had never mistreated it.

———◆———

Clem Sumption lived some ten miles from us, right where a little road forked off what served as a main highway then. You wouldn't think of it as a highway now, but it was the main road, and if you turned off of it, trying to cross through our neck of the woods on your way to Tyler, you had to pass Mr. Sumption's house, which was situated alongside the Sabine River.

Clem's outhouse was on the bank of the Sabine, and it was fixed up so what went out of him and his family went into the river. Lot of folks did that, though some like my Daddy were appalled at the idea. It was that place and time's idea of plumbing. Daddy thought it was not only nasty, but lazy. To have a proper outhouse you had to have the fortitude to dig a proper hole. A very deep hole. When the hole was packed, you dug a new hole, moved the outhouse, filled the old hole, and started about packing the other.

The lazy way, you backed an outhouse up to the river's edge so your waste dropped down a slant and onto the bank. When the water rose, the waste was carried away. When it didn't, you did your best to stay downwind. Big blue-green bottle flies collected on the dark mess like jewels shining in rancid chocolate. In the dry season if a sudden wind picked up, the stink could bowl you over.

During the flood, Mr. Sumption and his boys used pieces of lumber that fit into grooves on the side of the outhouse so it could be lifted and placed in an area safe from the rising waters.

What they did to relieve themselves during this time I'm uncertain, but when the flooding passed, they moved the outhouse to a location near its original spot.

As the river lowered, it was discovered that the mess from the outhouse had not completely washed away, but was now parked in a big dark hill under the outdoor convenience's new slip-and-slide position.

But before I continue with events, it's necessary to point out Mr. Sumption ran a little roadside stand where he sold vegetables now and then, and on this hot day I'm talking about, he suddenly had the urge to take care of a mild stomach disorder, and left his son, Wilson, in charge of the stand.

After doing his business, Mr. Sumption said he rolled a cigarette and went out beside the outhouse to look down on the fly-infested pile, maybe hoping the river had carried some of it away. But dry as it was, the pile was bigger and the water was lower, and something unusual lay in it.

Mr. Sumption, first spying it, thought it was a huge, bloated, belly-up catfish. One of those enormous bottom-crawler types that were reputed by some to be able to swallow small dogs and babies.

But a catfish doesn't have legs.

Mr. Sumption said even when he saw the legs it didn't register with him that it was a human being. It looked too swollen, too strange to be a person. But it was, and it was a woman. Her legs were crossed and tied at the ankles. One of her arms was pulled behind the back, stretched out and tied so tight to her feet it had caused the back to bow slightly. The other arm was tied in such a manner it looked as if she were reaching over the shoulder to scratch the small of the back, but the hand, from the wrist on, was gone. The cord was bound around the forearm, and was tied off to the other arm.

Mr. Sumption eased carefully down the side of the hill, mindful not to step in what his family had been dropping along the bank all summer. He saw the woman's bloated body lying face down in the moist blackness, and the flies were as delighted with the corpse as they were with the waste.

Mr. Sumption saddled up a horse and arrived in our yard a short time after that. I was out trying to knock some splashed mud off of some tomato plants so they might stand up and not rot, when he showed up.

Mr. Sumption rode right up to the edge of the field, jumped off his horse, and started calling to me. Toby barked at him a few times, but it was a friendly bark. He knew Mr. Sumption.

I hurried through the field to where he stood, and he started in on how he had to see Daddy. Even though Daddy had taken to drinking, folks thereabouts didn't know about it, least most didn't. He kept it pretty much at home. I hated that Mr. Sumption might see Daddy that way; we had done a pretty good job of hiding it.

But there was nothing for it but Daddy had to be told. I asked Mr. Sumption to wait,

315

and I went to the barn to get him. He was lying on a bed he had made with an old blanket and some hay, and he had his head propped up with Sally Redback's saddle. He was awake, and he turned his head as I came in. I thought I saw something pass along his face that might have been shame or embarrassment or both. Then again, it could have just been a bellyache.

I suspected he wouldn't even bother, but when I told him Mr. Sumption had found a body, and it was tied up, he got up quick, knocking over his whiskey bottle, not bothering to pick it up. I didn't bother either. Daddy went out ahead of me. I watched the whiskey run out of the bottle and into the dirt.

To this day, I've never so much as taken a drink.

Daddy was a little sick-looking, like a man coming off a long bout with the flu, but he hurried ahead of me, through the field, and met Mr. Sumption at the far end.

When he told Daddy what he had found, Mr. Sumption rode back and Daddy followed in the car. I wanted to come, but Daddy insisted that I stay. There was a part of me that felt I was no longer subject to what Daddy wanted. He had given up the respect I had for him long ago, but I waited. Maybe I just didn't want to be with him.

Later I learned Daddy and Mr. Sumption pulled the body out of the pile using a hoe and a rake, dipped it in the river for a rinse. Something a modern forensic-trained officer of the law would avoid these days. But back then, Daddy had never heard of forensics. I don't even know if the word existed.

After fishing the body out, they were shocked to see the face of Louise Canerton buried in a mass of swollen flesh, one cold dead eye open, the other half closed, as if she were winking.

On closer examination, they discovered the body was very cut up, and one of the breasts had been sliced open and sewn back together with fishing cord. Something was visible between the stitches. Daddy used his knife to cut the cord free and to poke out what was inside. It was a wad of paper. Like was found in the others. And like the others, it was too far gone for him to figure what it was. He wrapped it in a handkerchief and put it in his pocket.

The body arrived at our house wrapped in a tarp. Daddy and Mr. Sumption hauled it out of the car and toted it up to the barn. Me and Tom were out under the big tree, waiting, and as they walked by carrying their burden, we could smell that terrible reek of death and defecation through the tarp.

Daddy and Mr. Sumption were in the barn for a short time, and when they came out, Daddy had an axe handle in his hand. He also had a straighter back and a more determined stride. His eyes, though not clear, looked hard and brittle like dark beads of glass. He walked briskly to the car. I could hear Mr. Sumption arguing at him. "Don't do it, Jacob. It ain't worth it."

We ran over to the car as Mama came out

317

of the house, calling Daddy's name. But Daddy wasn't listening. Nothing seemed to register. It was as we always said about a determined mule. He had his nose forward and his ears back.

Daddy calmly laid the axe handle in the front seat, and Mr. Sumption stood shaking his head. Mama climbed into the car and started on Daddy. "Jacob. I know what you're thinkin'. You can't."

Toby had sidled up to Mr. Sumption, and Mr. Sumption, knowing he was defeated as far as influence with Daddy went, bent down to scratch him behind the ears.

He hollered out once more, but like he didn't really mean it. "Don't do it, Jacob."

Daddy started up the car. Mama called, "Children. Get in. You're not stayin' here."

Maybe she thought our presence would slow Daddy down, I don't know. But we jumped in just as Grandma came out of the house. She took in the situation, immediately pushed her way into the car, and Daddy, hardly mindful of our presence, roared off, leaving Mr. Sumption standing in the yard either bewildered or resigned.

Mama fussed and yelled and pleaded all the way over to Mr. Nation's house. Daddy never said a word. When he pulled up in Nation's yard, Mr. Nation's wife was outside hoeing at a pathetic little garden, most of which had been washed downhill by the recent rain.

Mr. Nation and his two boys were sitting in

rickety chairs under a tree, cracking pecans and eating them.

Grandma, who had begun to put it together, said, "Oh hell."

Before Daddy could get out of the car, Mama grabbed the axe handle, but he carefully took it from her hands and got out of the car with it, started walking toward Mr. Nation. Mama was hanging on his arm, but he pulled free. He walked right past Mrs. Nation, who paused and looked up in surprise.

Mama started after Daddy again, but Grandma grabbed her, said, "Might as well let things be. He gets like this, he's like Achilles after Hector. You know that."

Mr. Nation and his boys spotted Daddy coming. Mr. Nation slowly rose from his chair, pecans falling out of his lap. The expression on his face was akin to discovering you hadn't buttoned your fly and were standing in a room full of church women.

"What the hell you doin' with that axe handle?" Nation asked.

The next moment what Daddy was doing with that axe handle became abundantly clear. It whistled through the hot morning air like a flaming arrow and caught Mr. Nation alongside the head about where the jaw meets the ear, and the sound it made was, to put it mildly, akin to a rifle shot.

Mr. Nation went down like a wind-blown scarecrow. Daddy stood over him swinging the axe handle. Mr. Nation was yelping and putting up his arms in a pathetic way. The two

319

boys came at Daddy. Daddy turned, swatted the older one down. The younger one tackled him.

Instinctively, I started kicking at that boy, and he came off Daddy and climbed me. But Daddy was up now. The axe handle sang. The boy went out like a light, and the other one, who was still conscious, started scuttling along the ground on all fours like a crippled centipede. He finally managed himself upright and ran for the house.

Mr. Nation tried to get up several times, but every time he did that axe handle would cut the air, and down he'd go. Daddy whapped on Mr. Nation's sides, back, and legs, until he was worn out and had to back off and lean on the somewhat splintered handle.

When Daddy got his wind back, he was at it again. Some of his sense had returned however, and he began to use the flat of the handle, banging it against Nation.

Finally Nation rolled on his back, lifted his hands in front of his face, and began to cry. Daddy stopped in mid-swing. The demon had gone out of him. I knew now what Grandma meant when she said Daddy had a temper.

Nation, ribs surely broken, lip busted, spitting teeth, bawled, lay there with his feet and hands up like a dog that had rolled on its back to impress its master.

When Daddy got his wind back, he said, "They found Louise Canerton down by the river. Dead. Cut the same way and tied as them others. You and your boys and that lynch mob didn't do nothin' but hang an innocent man."

"You're supposed to be the law?" Nation said, spitting blood. "You ain't supposed to do nothin' like this."

"If'n I was any kind of law, I'd have had you arrested for what you did to Mose, but that wouldn't have done no good. No one around here would convict you, Nation. They're scared of you. But I ain't. I ain't. And if you ever cross my path again, I swear to God, I'll kill you and beat your corpse daily till there ain't nothin' left of it. You just be glad this old handle wasn't as sturdy as some I got."

Daddy tossed the shattered axe handle aside, said, "Come on." I started back to the car. Mama, Tom, and Grandma joined us. Mama put her arm around Daddy's waist, and he returned the favor.

As we passed Mrs. Nation, she looked up and leaned on her hoe. She had a black eye, a swollen lip, and some old bruises on her cheek. She smiled at us.

Grandma said, "Good day to you."

———◆———

When the beating was over and we were home, Daddy explained to me whose body had been found. I sat on the screened-in porch and looked out at nothing and thought about Mrs. Canerton. Tom sat with me, doing the same.

Mrs. Canerton wasn't just some poor unfortunate we didn't know, she was someone we knew and really liked. It was hard to believe the woman I had seen at the Halloween party, all beautiful and pursued by every eligible man there, was now in our barn wrapped in a tarp, cut up like those other women.

It was a stunning blow.

As we sat there, Daddy came out on the porch. He pushed his way between us. He had a dried sweat coated with whiskey smell. He said, "Listen, kids. I know I haven't exactly been right. But you can count on one thing. I'm through with all that. I've been an idiot. I'm on my feet now, and I'm gonna stay there. I'll never touch another drop of whiskey, or any strong drink, long as I live. Hear me?"

"Yes sir," we said.

"First thing tomorrow, we're gonna start gettin' these fields in shape, and the day after that I'm gonna start back regular at the barbershop. I ain't exactly been settin' a good example, and I ain't got no excuse for it but my own self-pity. And you know what? I thought maybe Mose might have done it after all. I couldn't figure how logically, but with the murders stopped, it crossed my mind."

"Mine too," I said.

"All right then. Let's get back to being what we're supposed to be. A family."

"Daddy?" Tom said. "You're gonna go back to bathin' regular, ain't you?"

Daddy laughed. "Yes, honey, I am."

21

Daddy was true to his word. I never seen nor heard of him taking a drink again. He went back to work in the fields and back to work at the barbershop. And in short time his spirit filled up the house again.

But on this very day I'm telling you about, he heated up water and took a bath on the back porch in a number ten tub.

Rest of us waited in the kitchen. You'd have thought we was waiting for Lazarus to rise, and I suppose in one sense we were. Because when the back door opened and he come into the house, it was as if he was a man reborn.

He stood tall. His face was shaved close. His skin looked clean and pink. His hair was slicked back and he had on a fresh suit of clothes and held his best tan hat in his hand.

He took Mama in his arms and kissed her, hard, right in front of us. Mama and Daddy were always affectionate, but you didn't see anything like that right in front of us, not the way that kiss was.

When Daddy and Mama separated, smiling, he put on his hat, looked at me, said, "Harry, I need you to come with me."

"Me too," Tom said.

"No, baby girl. Just Harry. He's near a man, and I might need him."

I can't tell you what that meant to me. I climbed in the car with him and we drove over to Mrs. Canerton's.

———◆———

The doors to Mrs. Canerton's house were unlocked, but that wasn't so strange back then. People didn't lock their doors like now, there wasn't a need.

Daddy looked through the rooms while I stood in the parlor looking at the books in the shelves, thinking about how enthusiastic Mrs. Canerton had always been about them. I saw a number that I had read. I felt worse by the moment.

When Daddy came back from looking, he shook his head. "Ain't no sign of a struggle nowhere. She's just gone. She could have been out and was nabbed by this fella, or maybe she know'd him and went with him without no trouble. And if that's the case, it could be a number of folks, 'cause she know'd everyone and was kind to everyone."

We went out back where she kept her car. It was missing.

"Well now, that's somethin'," Daddy said. "Means she went off in her car and either picked this fella up, or he was with her."

"Cecil might know," I said. "He was seein' her some."

"I was thinking the same thing."

We went over to the barbershop. It was empty except for Cecil. He was sittin' in Daddy's barber chair reading a detective magazine.

Cecil seemed surprised to see Daddy all spiffed up and neatly dressed. "How about givin' me a haircut, Cecil?" Daddy asked, removing his hat.

Cecil got out of the chair and flipped the magazine on the table with the others. "Certainly. You're lookin' good, Jacob."

Daddy climbed in the chair. Cecil pulled a sheet over Daddy to catch the hair, and went to work. "Did you know about Louise?" Daddy asked.

"Well, me and her ain't exactly visitin' these days. What about her?"

"She's dead, Cecil."

The scissors quit snipping. Cecil came around to the front of the chair and looked at Daddy. "No?"

Daddy shook his head. "Afraid so. I didn't mean to drop it on you so blunt, but there ain't no other way to tell it. Found her body in the river. She was got by that maniac."

"It wasn't Mose," Cecil said. "You said it wasn't Mose."

Cecil went over and sat in one of the customer's chairs, absently clicked the scissors a few times.

"I thought me and her might be together, you know. But it didn't work. She didn't want to get serious. She quit seein' me. I still thought about her. I think I might have been in love with her. Good God. How'n hell could that happen? She wasn't a river whore."

"I thought maybe you might have heard of someone was seein' her might not have been on the up and up. Maybe you knew or suspected somethin' suspicious goin' on."

"No. Jacob, would it be all right I didn't cut your hair? I don't feel so good."

Daddy nodded. "That's all right, Cecil. I got things to do. I just thought you might could help us and I could get a haircut in the meantime. I'm cleaning myself up. I'll be comin' in more regular. I know that affects your money, but I wanted you to know."

"I'm glad for you," Cecil said, snapping the scissors. "Jesus. Louise."

"You rest a bit," Daddy said, flicking off the sheet and rising. "Not like there's a rush on customers. You don't feel up to it, go home a while."

"I'm all right. I'll just sit a moment."

Daddy put on his hat, said, "All right then."

Me and Daddy went outside. When we were out to the car, Daddy said, "Run back in there and get a bottle of that coconut hair oil, will you, son? I'm gonna clean myself up, I might as well smell good all around."

I went back for the hair oil. Cecil was in the barber chair with a magazine.

He lowered the magazine when I came in. He said, "It's a hell of a thing, ain't it?"

"Daddy wants some hair oil," I said.

"Sure. He uses that coconut kind. It's on the end of the shelf there."

I got it, said goodbye, and went out.

I felt horrible about Mrs. Canerton, but I felt good that Daddy was doing so much better. I liked the idea of him smelling good for Mama.

<hr />

We drove out to Mr. Sumption's. When we pulled up in his yard, he came out of his house and walked out to the car. Daddy got out and stood by it. Mr. Sumption said, "You didn't kill him?"

"No," Daddy said. "But it wasn't from want of tryin'."

"I can't think of a sorrier sonofabitch than Nation. Doin' what he done to that old colored man, and bein' proud of it. Hard to figure on a man like that."

"And we won't waste time doin' it. I want to apologize just leavin' you in the yard like that."

"It was a short walk, Jacob."

"We want to look around some, Clem. You don't mind, do you?"

"Not at all."

I think Mr. Sumption thought he'd go with us, but Daddy, without really saying it, made it clear he meant just the two of us.

As we walked down to the outhouse and the river, Daddy said, "We washed her off, Harry, but that was most likely a mistake. There were probably things could have been learned from the body. If I had any education, I'd have thought of that. All I was thinking was here was this nice lady in all that mess. Unclothed. Cut up. Tossed out like garbage."

We climbed down the bank and stood near the mound of waste. It stunk something terrible. Flies rose up in a blue-black cloud. The water, though no longer high, was still tumbling along at a rapid brown clip.

"It's funny the good stuff goes in a belly, sure comes out rotten," Daddy said.

"He dump her here, Daddy?"

"I don't think so. This is just where she ended up. Body ain't that long dead. Few days."

"Maybe about the same time Miss Maggie was killed?"

"Could be."

"That night, I went by Mrs. Canerton's. Tryin' to return a book. She wasn't home. You think she could have been dead then?"

"It's possible, Harry. Way the river looks, she could have been dumped down a spell, and with all that floodin', carried up to here. I doubt the killer come through Clem's yard and dumped her. It's possible, but it seems more risky than he'd have to be. So far, he's been dumpin' down deep in the bottoms."

"You know what I was thinkin'?" I asked.

"That Miss Maggie and Mrs. Canerton were killed about the same time. And you seen that car of Red's, and we found his car and he's missin'. You're thinkin' he could have done it. That right?"

"Yes sir."

Daddy took his pipe out of his shirt pocket,

stuffed it and lit it. "I guess Red could have killed Miss Maggie 'cause she told him the truth and he didn't like it, but that don't mean he killed Louise. 'Course, it's quite a coincidence, ain't it?"

"Red could have left his car and took a boat downriver, Daddy."

Daddy nodded, lifted a leg, thumped his pipe against the bottom of his shoe. "He could have at that. Thing is, I can't imagine Red doin' this kind of thing. I've known him a long time. He might have killed Miss Maggie, and that's hard enough to believe... Jesus, I can't believe he was actually colored. Way he looked."

"It's what Doc Tinn told us."

Daddy tucked his pipe into his pocket, looked out at the river. "Doc Tinn seems like a fella not prone to gossip. Now I think on it, things kinda fit. And the way Red felt about colored, and findin' out he was colored, he could have lost it. He could have found out some time ago in fact, and this led to the rage of him killin' them colored women."

"Not all of them were colored," I said.

"Yeah. But I'm thinkin' it set him off."

I told him then what Doc Tinn had told us about these kinds of killers, his thoughts on them.

Daddy listened carefully, bent, picked up a stone and tossed it into the river. "Why don't you and me walk the trail yonder."

We climbed the bank and took the trail along the river. It was narrow and we had to

329

push limbs and brush out of our way. The trees were thick and dark and held water from the rains; they leaked it as if they were rain clouds.

I watched Daddy out of the corner of my eye. His tan hat was damp with the water drops and they had fallen on the shoulders of his shirt, creating a dark wet mantle. He looked big again to me, as if he had gained three inches in height from just a short time ago.

It wasn't easy to see the river, and yet we could hear it rumbling like a contented lion a few feet away, behind and below the thick growth of trees and brush. It gave off a smell of decayed fish, wet dirt, and aromas unidentified, mixed with the sweetness of the pines.

"What are we lookin' for, Daddy?"

"I don't know."

We walked along the river for an hour or two, shoving our way through the brush from time to time, looking at the river, trying to find I didn't know what.

As we walked, Daddy said, "Doc Tinn said somethin' to me about when a body gets dragged in the river, it gets scratched up along the belly, 'cause that's how it flows in the water. Louise, she wasn't cut up like that. Just the knife work of that nut. All along in front of Clem's house, and for a couple miles along here, ain't nothin' but sand. All this stormin', water must have carried gravel with it, but if she ain't cut up bad, that means she might not have been thrown in the river before the sand bottom. There ain't but one other area that's that smooth with sand, it's miles up, and there's plenty of gravel in between."

"I don't get it, Daddy."

"She had to have been chunked in the water along the sandy bottom, or, with all this flooding, and the river pushin' on her, she'd have had gravel marks."

"For sure?"

"Well, no, but I figure it's a logical stretch."

"So this here is the sandy section?"

"Yep. I'm bettin' she didn't go any farther than that. Another thing, there ain't but two or three good spots she could have been dumped. Rest of it's just like we're goin' through now, all that thick brush and trees on either side of us. A man was determined enough, he could have done it by fightin' these bushes. But if it's like I suspect, someone knows the river, I figure he picked one of the good spots."

The sunlight was weak in the thickness of the woods, and as we walked, and it grew later, it became weaker yet. Where the forest broke above and the limbs didn't wind, it fell through in gold red globs like busted apples dipped in honey.

The trail finally thickened and the trees gave way to a wide swath that wound down to the river in a sandy sink that disappeared in the water.

"Normally, this here is so clear, you can see bottom."

You couldn't see bottom now. The water was filthy and foamy, carrying tree limbs and hunks of bark down it lickity-split.

"I don't know what there would be to see," I said.

Daddy grinned. "Me neither. But I got me a hunch that our killer not only took Louise's car, but he got rid of it. He took enough of a chance drivin' it with her in it, or makin' her drive. But he killed her, he got rid of it. I wouldn't be surprised he done it one of them spots I'm tellin' you about. You could drive a car through that wide trail over there, right up to the bank. Ain't but two or three more spots on this sandy stretch you could do that."

"He got rid of the car, how'd he get home?"

"I ain't got that all figured out, son. But I figure him for one that plans. In the past, he ain't taken the victim's car. Fact is, them others didn't have any. This time looks as if he did. Well, he comes down here, kills poor Louise, dumps her in the river, tied up like he likes, then he had to get rid of the car. He could have run it off in the river, or just left it."

"Red's car was just left."

"That's right," Daddy said. "I tell you what, son. Comin' out of that bottle, I'm feelin' like I can truly think a little again. You don't hate me, do you boy?"

"No sir," I said. "Not even a little bit."

"Good. Then everything's all right."

We walked down the wider trail a piece. Come back to the river, got on the narrow trail alongside it again. It wasn't long before we come to the next spot in the river. It was kind of like the other sandy slide, but here you could see where brush had been broken down, washed over by the water. The sun shining on the broken brush made the bits of sand caught up in it twinkle like grit-ground diamonds.

Down in the river you could see the roof of a car. It was, of course, Mrs. Canerton's.

"You was right, Daddy."

"Reckon so," he said. "It's probably the first piece of truly successful detective work I've ever done."

<hr>

It was the next day before Daddy had some men help him pull the car from the water. Inside they found two water-soaked books, *The Time Machine* and *White Fang*. They also found a metal flask containing a partial of whiskey, and a bottle of headache pills that the label said was prescribed by Doc Stephenson.

Daddy's theory was Mrs. Canerton was bringing me out two new books to read, and that whoever killed her had followed in his car, and either coaxed or ran her off the road. It could have been someone she knew. Someone she would easily stop for.

From there, whoever it was killed her and dumped her and her car. Most likely his own car was nearby, and it was easy enough then for him to return home in his own car.

It seemed logical, and it made me ill.

If Mrs. Canerton had been bringing books out to me, then I felt partially responsible.

Everything seemed to be coming down on me like an anvil.

Just a short time before I had been a happy kid with no worries. I didn't even know it was the Depression, let alone there were murderers outside of the magazines I read down at the barbershop, and none of the magazines I read had to do with killers who did this kind of thing. And Daddy, though a good man, sincere and true, if briefly distracted, was no Doc Savage.

In the detective magazines the cops and private eyes saw a clue or two, they put it together. Cracked the whole case wide open. In real life, there were clues a plenty, but instead of cracking the case open, they just made it all the more confusing.

Bottom line was, no one really knew any more than they did the night I found that poor woman bound to a tree with barbed wire.

I had learned too that the people I knew, or thought I knew, had problems and lives. Mama and Daddy had a past. I had seen Daddy fall off the wagon, and suspected at one time Mama had fallen off as well, only it was a different wagon; the fall from it recorded by a tattoo on the missing Red Woodrow's forearm.

I found out my Daddy had a terrible temper. I found out Mr. Nation could beg and cry and his boys could run fast.

Miss Maggie was Red's mother and Red might be a killer. But had he killed Miss Maggie and Mrs. Canerton? And if so, why? And where was he now?

People I knew had turned out to be strange and savage. They had hung Mose and kicked and hit me and my father.

I wouldn't have been surprised right then to discover the moon could be reached by climbing to the top of the highest tree, and with a good pair of scissors you could snip it in half.

22

We all went to Mrs. Canerton's funeral. Me and my family stood in the front row at the Bethel Baptist Church. Cecil was there. Just about everyone in town and around about, except the Nations and some of the people who had been in the lynch mob that killed Mose.

Even Doc Stephenson showed up, stood in the back and looked more disappointed than sad. Doc Taylor showed up as well. He sat next to Doc Stephenson with his hands in his lap, his face as blank as the wind. It was said he was taking it very hard; that he and she had recently become a serious item.

Within a week Daddy's customers at the barbershop returned, among them members of the lynch party, and the majority of them wanted him to cut their hair. He had to go back to work regularly. I don't know how he felt about that, cutting the hair of those who had beaten me and him that day, that had killed Mose. But he cut their hair and took their money. Maybe Daddy saw it as a kind of revenge. Maybe he was easy to forgive and forget. And maybe we just needed the money.

Mama took a job in town at the courthouse. She rode in and back with Daddy. That left Grandma with us, and she had developed a habit of driving into town a couple times a week to annoy the men at the barbershop and to go over and visit with Mr. Groon.

They rode around town and throughout the country together. He sometimes drove her all the way over to Tyler just to eat dinner at a cafe and go to a show.

As was the habit with things, talk about the murders died down. Daddy dried out the pulp paper he had removed from Mrs. Canerton, but like the others it was too far gone. And even if it hadn't been, it was hard to see how it could mean anything.

Mose was no longer mentioned. It was as if the poor man never existed. Some still wanted him to be the killer, in spite of Mrs. Canerton turning up like she did. The most common story now was Red had done it, then gone off some-where, never to return. No one claimed to be getting postcards from him anymore. Just goes to show you how fickle people are.

The world slipped back to about as normal

as it would ever be again, though to my eyes it was never as sharp and clean and clear as it had been, and nothing I could do would ever completely bring it back.

As for the murderer, me and Tom weren't so convinced it was Red, or that it was over. We still had it in our heads it was the Goat Man. And on a day when Mama and Daddy were at work and Grandma had spiffed up and gone into town to flirt with Mr. Groon, we decided to head out to Mose's shack, carrying the shotgun.

That's where the Goat Man had last been seen, and I was determined to find out more about him, maybe capture him. There was a part of me that wanted to be a hero. To that end we took along the shotgun and some good strong rope.

Looking back on all this, it seems damn foolish. But at the time it made perfect sense. We thought we could hold the Goat Man at bay with the shotgun, or maybe wound him, then tie him up and bring him in.

Then again, could the Goat Man talk? Could he confess? Did he speak English? Did he have supernatural powers? We suspected he might, and to that end, we also took along the Bible. I had read somewhere, probably in one of those magazines at the barbershop, if you held up the Word, evil would cringe.

Me and Tom had made this plan to kill or capture the Goat Man the night before, after sitting around for days thinking about it.

As soon as Grandma's car had rolled out of

sight, we lit out for the woods. I carried the shotgun. Toby slinked along with us, and even with his injured back, he made pretty good time.

We also had a notion the Goat Man didn't have any powers by day, and if we could find his lair, he could be killed. How this notion had been formed is hard to say, but we had come to believe it as certain as we believed Daddy would crack a stick over Nation's noggin faster than a chicken can peck corn, and that the Word could be held up against evil.

We worked our way deep into the woods where the river twisted wild and loud between high banks and higher trees, where the vines and brush wadded together and became next to impenetrable.

We walked along the bank, looking for a place to ford near the Swinging Bridge. Neither of us wanted to cross the bridge, and we used the excuse that Toby couldn't cross it, but that was just an excuse.

We walked a long ways and finally came to the shack where Mose had lived. We just stood there looking at it. It had never been much, just a hovel made of wood and tin and tarpaper. Mose mostly set outside of it in an old chair under a willow tree that overlooked the river.

It looked to have weathered badly since that time Grandma and I had been trapped in it and we had seen the face of the Goat Man at the window.

The door was wide open.

"What if the Goat Man is waitin' inside?" Tom asked.

"I'll cut down on him with this here shotgun," I said. "That's what."

"Maybe we ought to peek in a window first."

That sounded like good advice, but we couldn't make out much in there, just enough to assure us the Goat Man wasn't lurking about.

It was a bigger mess inside than before. Toby went inside and sniffed and prowled about till we called him out of it. We went inside and looked around. Light came through the yellow paper over the paneless window, and wind whipped in with it. The window that had glass had been broken out, probably by kids, and from that direction the light was weak.

The framed photograph with the Sears picture stuck in the frame was knocked off the table, and I picked it up. With the door open rain had run in and ruined it, meshing the Sears photo to the photograph, blurring the whole thing into a kind of mush. I put it on the table, laying it face down this time.

"I don't like it in here," Tom said.

"Me neither."

When we went out, I made sure to close the door good.

We walked around the house, to the side facing the river, and finally down to the water. Looking back at the house, I noted there was something hanging on a nail on the outside wall.

It was a chain, and from the chain hung a number of fish skeletons, and one fresh fish.

We went over and looked at it.

"It looks like it's just been hung up there," Tom said. "There's still water drippin' off of it."

The fish bones along with the fresh fish showed me someone had been hanging fish there on a regular basis, and for some time, like an offering to Mose.

On another nail, strings tied together, was a pair of old shoes that had most likely been fished from the river. Hung over that was a water-warped belt. On the ground, leaning against the side of the house, below the nail with the shoes, was a tin plate, a bright blue river rock, and a mason jar. All of it laid out like gifts.

I took the dead fish down, all the old bones, and cast them into the river and put the chain back on the nail. I tossed the shoes and belt, the plate, rock, and mason jar into the river.

"What'd you do that for?" Tom asked.

"I think that fish was still alive. It don't need to suffer. Ain't no one gonna come get it and cook it."

"We could."

"But we ain't."

"You throwed all that other stuff away too. That seems kinda mean, Harry. Someone is hanging it here like a gift."

"I know," I said. "That's why I done it. Not out of meanness, but so the gifts would seem to be taken."

I couldn't really explain it. It just seemed like the thing to do.

Mose's old boat was still by the house, laid up on rocks so it wouldn't rot. A paddle lay in its bottom. We decided to take it and float it downriver to where the briar tunnels were. We loaded Toby in the boat, along with our shotgun, pushed it into the water and set out. We floated the long distance back to the Swinging Bridge and under it, watching to see if the Goat Man might be lurking about. Our idea that he was afraid of daylight was fading, and we had begun to feel nervous, and just a bit foolish.

We had been a lot braver planning than doing.

In shadow, under the bridge, deep into the bank, was a dark indention, like a cave. I imagined that was where the Goat Man lived, waiting for prey.

The thing to do, of course, was beard him in his lair. But we didn't. We didn't say a word. We just paddled on by.

We paddled gently to the riverbank where we had found the woman bound to the tree. There was no real sign she had ever been there. It seemed like a dream.

We pulled the boat onto the dirt and gravel bank and left it there as we went up the taller part of the bank, and into the briars. We hadn't discussed this, but we wanted to see the spot where we had found the first body, where we had been frightened in the tunnel of briars.

The tunnel was the same, and it was clear in the daytime that the tunnel had, as we suspected, been cut into the briars. It was not as large or as long a tunnel as it had seemed that night, and it emptied out into a wider tunnel, and it too was shorter and smaller than we had remembered.

There were little bits of colored cloth hung on briars, like decoration. There was a red strip and a blue strip and a white strip with little red flowers on it. There were pictures from the Sears and Roebuck catalogue of women in underwear and there were a few of those playing cards like I had heard about. The briars were poked through the pictures where the women's crotches were.

In the middle of the tunnel was a place where someone had built a fire, and above us the briars wrapped so thick and were so intertwined with low-hanging branches you could imagine much of this place staying dry during a rainstorm.

We hadn't seen all those pieces of cloth and paper that night, but they, or ones like them, might have been there. Dry as the place was, during all that raining and flooding, it couldn't have remained completely dry. Someone would have to have been adding fresh material to it from time to time.

Toby was sniffing and running about as best his poor old damaged back and legs would allow him. He was peeing on one spot, then another, leaving his mark all over. He was as agitated as if the briars were full of squirrels.

"It's like some kind of nest," Tom said. "The Goat Man's nest."

A chill came over me and it occurred to me that if that was true, and if this was his den instead of the cave under the bridge, he might come home at any time. I told Tom that, and we called up Toby and got out of there, tried to paddle the boat back upriver, but couldn't.

We finally got out and made to carry it along the bank, but it was too heavy. We gave up and left it by the river. We walked past the Swinging Bridge and for a long ways after that till we found a sandbar. We used that to cross, went back home, finished the chores, cleaned ourselves and Toby up before Mama and Daddy and Grandma came home.

We thought about what we had seen all day, and considered telling Daddy, but since we weren't supposed to have gone anywhere, our young minds were at an impasse. What would have seemed obvious to someone older didn't seem all that obvious to us.

That night, as me and Tom were out on the sleeping porch, whispering, Grandma came out. We went quiet. She said, "You two been actin' like conspirators all day. I'm too nosy to let it go."

"It ain't nothin'," Tom said.

"I believe it is somethin'," Grandma said, seating herself on the swing between our beds. "Why don't you tell me. I promise I ain't gonna tell your Mama and Daddy."

We, of course, were dying to tell someone. I looked at Tom, she nodded. I nodded back.

Tom said, "You swear not to tell, less'n your head falls off and gets covered in ants."

Grandma laughed. "Well, I wouldn't want that. So I swear."

We told her all about it. When we finished she said, "You ain't the only detectives. And since all three of us are detectin', we need to make a pact right now. We're gonna keep what we know between us."

"I don't know," I said. "Daddy might need to know some of this."

Grandma considered. I knew enough about her to know she was the one that always wanted to be in the know. So it was no surprise to me when she made her proposition.

"Tell you what. Let's keep it to ourselves, unless, or until, we got enough evidence your Daddy can use. That fair enough, kids?"

We agreed it was.

"Then we'll make a pact to that effect, lest our heads fall off and get covered in ants."

We swore it.

Grandma said, "I was in town today. I went over and visited Mr. Groon. He's such a nice man."

"You visit him a lot," Tom said.

"I suppose I do."

"Then you don't think he had anything to do with this mess?" I asked.

"Heaven forbid. No, I don't."

"He's in the Klan," Tom said.

"Was," Grandma said. "Me and him talked, and he brought up the little incident here on his own. He said he dropped out. And he is

344

Jewish. Said he joined up with them boys without really thinkin'. He thought they was out for right doin'. He saw a movie once called *Birth of a Nation*, and in that the Klansmen were good fellows. But after the other night, out here with your Daddy, and Mose gettin' hung and all, he got to figurin' that for the grace of God should they figure on the fact he's a Jew, he could have been on the end of that rope. He got out of the Klan. Burned his robes."

"Grandma?" Tom asked. "Is he your boyfriend?"

"Hardly... Well, not yet. It could happen that way."

Tom giggled. "Grandma. You're too old."

"Just by your standards, young lady. What y'all say we look at this shack of Mose's tomorrow, and that cave and that briar tunnel too."

———◆———

Next morning, when Mama and Daddy left for work, me, Grandma, Tom, and Toby climbed in Grandma's car with her shotgun, and she drove us over to Mose's shack. About halfway there, I remembered that I forgotten the Bible.

I had a hunch about Mose's old shack, and I wanted to check it out. But my hunch was wrong. There was nothing new hung from the nails, or leaned against the wall outside. But there was something curious. The boat we had left on the bank was back in its place atop the rocks with the paddle inside.

We told Grandma about that.

"Well, I'll swan," she said.

We looked around the shack for a while. It was the same as yesterday, except the water-meshed photograph in the frame had been set up on the table, and the faded Sears and Roebuck cutout of a little boy colored in pencil was nowhere to be found.

When I told Grandma that, she said, "Someone visits here, that's for sure. Question is, why? Tell you what, let's take the boat and see this place of yours," Grandma said.

Grandma got in the boat, me and Tom pushed it into the water, and with me paddling, Tom sitting in the front of the boat playing guide, we made our way to the briar tunnel. It was a pleasant trip. The day was warm, the river was running swift, and the water was dappled with the shadows of overhanging trees.

On the shore I saw a huge water moccasin basking on the twisted root of a big willow tree. Frogs plopped off the bank and into the water. Little black bugs darted about on the surface of the river as if they were Northern ice skaters. Twice I saw turtle heads poke out of the water to see if we were edible, then bob out of view.

When we docked the boat and got up there in the tunnel, it was dark in spots, but there were streamers of light shining in and the edges of the lights were like the sharp blades of archangels' swords, and the light showed the bits of cloth and the paper cut from the catalogues. Grandma looked around, touching the bits of cloth and paper.

She said, "I don't judge this to be any kind of killer's nest. Some kids, boys most likely, have made them a playhouse. They got them some colored cloth and some pictures to spice up the place."

"But some of them pictures are of women in their underwear," I said.

"You don't look at them same pictures while you're out there in the outhouse, Harry? You just use that catalogue to wipe on?" Grandma asked.

I blushed.

Tom gave me a look that told me I hadn't heard the end of this.

"You can see where he built him a fire," I said.

"Kids or hoboes could have built a fire," Grandma said. "And if you think about it, why would the killer want a fire? I don't think he stays down here. I think he lives among us, or near us."

"He built it so he could see at night," Tom said.

"I guess that's possible," Grandma said. I could tell she had already made up her mind.

"But he could come here," Tom said. "He could use this place."

"You could be right," Grandma said. "But I think you'll find kids are makin' 'em a playhouse here. Hoboes might be usin' it to hide out."

"Ain't it far in the woods for hoboes?"

"Who's to say?" Grandma said. "Let's see we can get this boat back, and be back home when your Mama and Daddy get off work."

"Aw," Tom said. "We got plenty of time."

"Yeah," Grandma said. "But we're goin' anyway."

We went back to the boat, ready to carry it upriver, but when it came down to brass tacks, Grandma decided not to bother.

"Mose is dead," she said. "And we ain't gonna have good luck paddling against the current. Carryin' it will wear us down. We'll just leave it. Besides, whoever brung it back last time might do the same."

We started walking. All the way to where we could cross over in the shallows, and all the way back to the car, I had a feeling that someone was moving silently between the trees, looking at us through the leaves, peeking out from the shadows. But every time I looked, I didn't see anything but the woods and the leaves and river.

———◆———

That night I lay in bed and tried to think on things, and I kept coming back to this. Grandma was a grown-up, and a smart one, but she wasn't no better detective than Daddy, and he wasn't worth a hoot, and he'd tell you so. Me and Tom wasn't so good either, but both of us had come to one decision. The murderer was the Goat Man, or what Miss Maggie called a Travelin' Man.

Thinking on Miss Maggie I felt sad again. There wouldn't be any more of her fine cooking, or her wonderful stories. She was gone. Murdered in the very home where I sat with her many a time and she had laughed and called me Little Man.

And Mrs. Canerton. She might have died because she was bringing me books. She might have been in the wrong place at the wrong time. I knew it wasn't my fault, but a feeling of guilt passed through me just the same.

Poor Mrs. Canerton had always been so nice. All those books. The Halloween parties. The way she smiled. Her breasts in that dress last Halloween night. White and pure, with a collar touched with little red roses.

As I drifted off to sleep I thought of telling Daddy about the Sears catalogue pictures and the cloth and such in the briar tunnel, but I had made Grandma a promise not to tell. I wasn't sure I should have made that promise. I was thinking about going back on it, or begging off of it, when sleep overtook me.

When I awoke the next morning, none of it seemed so all fired important, and in time Grandma seemed to forget all about it. She had found something new to occupy her. Mr. Groon. She even took to doing what a lot of folks thought was unladylike; she stayed around his store, visiting with him, helping him stock shelves and such, and for no pay at all.

From time to time, me and Tom slipped off and went down to Mose's old cabin. Now and then there would be a fish on the nail, or some odd thing from the river.

I reasoned that someone was bringing Mose gifts, perhaps unaware he was dead. Or maybe they had been left there for some other reason.

We dutifully took down what was there and returned it to the river, wondering if maybe it was the Goat Man leaving the goods, and if so, why would he do it? Could a monster like that have liked Mose? Could they have been an offering to the devil, like in Miss Maggie's story about the Travelin' Man? It wasn't peed-in whiskey, but who was to say if the devil liked fish and junk from the river?

When we looked around for sign of the Goat Man, all we could find were prints from someone wearing large-sized shoes. No hoofprints.

Sometimes we both sensed someone watching us. I always brought the shotgun with me, hoping that old Goat Man would show himself, give me just one shot. All the detective work in the world couldn't do what one shotgun blast could.

Then a thought hit Tom one day while we were down on the river.

"What if the devil ain't bothered by no shotgun?" she said.

I hadn't considered that. But I should have. After all, he was the devil.

We went away from there, less sure of ourselves, shotgun or no shotgun, and we didn't go back for a long time after. For the next few days I wondered if fresh fish and things from the river were on them nails, and what did the provider think when they weren't gone when he came back? Or had he been watching us all along from the concealment of the woods? It was a mystery too large for my mind, and finally, I had to tuck it aside.

23

As the summer moved on, it got hotter and hotter, and the air was like having a blanket wrapped twice around your head, and sometimes it seemed as if the blanket was on fire and filled with smoke.

Got so you hardly wanted to move midday, and for a time we quit slipping off down to the river even to fish, and stayed close at home.

That Fourth of July, our little town decided to have a celebration. Me and Tom were excited because there were to be firecrackers and Roman candles and all manner of other fireworks, and, of course, plenty of homecooked food.

Even more exciting was the fact they were gonna have a moving picture show.

Folks still thought about and talked about the killer from time to time, but most had settled on Red as the culprit, and since his car had been found and his house seemed to have been left pretty much as it always was, rumor got around that Daddy had been close to figuring out he was the one, so he'd took off.

The story seemed to satisfy people because it's what they wanted to believe. It was easier to lie down at night, or trek out to the outhouse beneath the moonlight, or check on your trot lines, if you thought the killer was long gone.

Women could lie a little easier in their beds, even if they had taken to locking doors and windows, something not done before the coming of the Bottoms Killer.

Even Daddy and Mama and Grandma had come to believe it had been Red. It seemed reasonable.

Me and Tom kept our eyes peeled, expecting the return of the Goat Man at any moment. We figured he was just lying out there in the woods waiting till things settled down, till folks least expected it, then he'd strike.

But on the day of the Fourth, a day of ice cream, fireworks, and a picture show, we dropped our guard. We had dropped it before, of course, and nothing had happened. And how could anything happen on a hot Fourth of July with all the wonderful things we had to look forward to?

The town gathered late afternoon before dark. Main Street had been blocked off, which was no big deal as traffic was rare anyway. Tables with covered dishes, watermelons, fresh-churned ice cream on them were set up in the street, and after the Baptist preacher said a few words, everyone got a plate and went around and helped themselves.

I remember Daddy telling Mama that he was grateful the tables were well stocked, not only because there was plenty of food, but that it had hastened the preacher through his sermon. The Reverend was known to be an eager and accomplished eater.

I ate a little of most everything, zeroing in on mashed potatoes and gravy and mince-meat, apple, and pear pies. Tom ate pie and cake and nothing else except watermelon that Cecil helped her cut.

There was a circle of chairs between the tables and behind the chairs was a kind of makeshift stage. There were a handful of folks with gui-tars and fiddles playing and singing; the men and women folks would gather in the middle of the closed-off street and dance to the tunes. Mama and Daddy were dancing too, and Grandma and Mr. Groon. Doc Taylor was holding Tom's hands, and he was dancing with her. He was so big, and she was so small, it's like when you pick a dog's front paws up and make him hop around on his back legs. He looked happy, though rumor was he was fret-ting hard over Louise Canerton.

I kept thinking Mr. Nation and his boys would show, as they were always ones to be about when there was free food or the possi-bility of a drink, but they didn't. I guess that was because of Daddy. Mr. Nation might have looked tough and had a big mouth, but that axe handle had tamed him, and Mr. Sumption had seen that word had gone around town about it, and long after my father died, there were still those who talked about that beating as if they had seen it, and in time it joined in with the story of Mr. Crittendon's hogs and eventually attained a position in local mythology.

As the night wore on, the music was stopped and the movie was shown. It was an older one. Silent and full of cowboys and gunplay. The tent under which it was reeled was full of yells and hoots and young drunk men talking for the voiceless characters.

Finally, late in the night, fireworks were set. The firecrackers popped and the Roman candles and rockets exploded high above Main Street, burst into burning rainbows that pinned themselves against the night, then fizzled.

Tom had deserted Taylor, who had found a young woman to dance with—Miss Buella Lee Birdwell—and was sitting on Cecil's knee, clapping and keeping time to the music, bouncing up and down, waiting for the next big slap of colors against the smooth night sky.

I remember watching as one bright swath did not fade right away, but dropped to earth like a falling star, and as my eyes followed it down, it dipped behind Cecil and Tom. In the final light from its burst I could see Tom's smiling face, and Cecil, his hands on her shoulders, his leg riding her up and down as it kept time with the music. And nearby, next to a table loaded with food, stood Doc Stephenson, hands in his pockets.

I had noticed him earlier, moving among the dancers but not dancing himself, just weaving through as if he were threading them with himself. Now he stood wearing his usual grim face, looking at Tom on Cecil's lap, his face slack and beaded with sweat. Above and beyond him the sky exploded with color.

———◆———

When we got home late that night we were all wide awake, and we sat down for a while under the big oak outside and drank some apple cider. It was great fun, but I kept having that uncomfortable feeling of being watched.

I scanned the woods, but didn't see anything. Tom didn't seem to be bothered. Mama, Daddy, and Grandma didn't show any signs either. Still, that didn't soothe me.

Not long after a possum presented itself at the edge of the woods, peeked out at our celebration, and disappeared back into the darkness. I felt a sigh of relief.

Daddy and Mama sang a few tunes as he picked his old guitar, then he picked while Mama and Grandma sang a couple songs together. From time to time Toby howled.

After that Grandma, Mama, and Daddy told stories awhile, Mama sitting in his lap as they did so. Daddy knew one about an old gunfighter who had been buried with his horse. Supposedly no one but him had ever ridden it, and when he was wounded while being pursued by the law, he killed first his horse and himself rather than be caught or have his horse ridden by another man. The posse found him buried him on the spot with the animal, and Daddy said he had relatives claimed there were times of the year when they could see that old bandit riding his horse down the road at a dead run, and then when it got to where he and the horse were buried, it would disappear.

Grandma said her grandmother told stories of a pigeon appearing in a room when someone was about to die. And upon the moment of their death, the pigeon would fly up and away to the ceiling, and would cease to be seen, but for moments after you could hear the beating of its wings. Her grandmother said the pigeon came to carry the soul away.

Mama told one about how up in the Ozarks a panther had chased a woman and her baby in a buckboard one night. The woman could see the panther gaining on them in the moonlight. It ran right alongside the horses, nearly panicking them. Thinking quickly, the mother began throwing pieces of the baby's clothing out along the road to distract it with its human smell. When the panther ceased to maul the clothing, and would reappear, running close to the carriage and the horses, the lady would toss out yet another piece. Finally, she was down to tossing out her own clothing, and finally she was able to gain pacing ahead of the cat. But when the lady, nearly naked, arrived at the house of a relative, she found to her horror the back of the carriage was scratched out, and the cradle where the baby had lain was empty.

After the stories we took turns going to the outhouse, Tom having Grandma walk out with her, and me wanting her to walk with me, but being too proud to ask. I did my business quickly, in the dark, in the stink, an owl hooting somewhere, a Sears and Roebuck catalogue clutched in my hand.

Finally, we washed up, said our good nights, and went to bed.

———◆———

As I lay on my pallet that night, I decided to slide over and put my ear to the wall. I hadn't done that in some time, but this night I wanted to hear my Mama's and Daddy's voices; I wanted to feel that they were once again connected, and that all was right with the world.

I listened for a while, and they talked of this and that, then they begin to talk softer and I heard Mama say: "The children will hear, honey. These walls are paper-thin."

"Don't you want to?"

"Of course. Sure."

"The walls are always paper-thin."

"You're not always like you are tonight. You know how you are when you're like this."

"How am I?"

Mama laughed. "Loud."

"Listen, honey. It's been a while since I been right... You know... And really, you know, I need to. Don't you want to?"

"Sure."

"I want to be loud. What say we take the car down the road a piece? I know a spot."

"Jacob. What if someone came along?"

"I know a spot they won't come along."

"Well, we don't have to do that. We can do it here. We'll just have to be quiet."

"I don't want to be quiet. And even if I did, it's a great night. I'm not sleepy."

"What about the children?"

"It's just down the road, hon. Grandma's here with them. It'll be fun."

"All right... All right. Why not?"

Thunder rumbled. I heard Mama say, "Oh, Jacob. Maybe that's a warnin'. You know, we ain't supposed to."

"Be fruitful and multiply."

"I don't think multiplying is what we need."

I heard Daddy laugh, and Mama giggled.

I lay there wondering what in the world had gotten into my parents. Their room went silent, and not long after I heard the car start up, and glide away down the road.

Where could they be going?

And why?

It was really some years later before I realized what was going on. I had begun to learn about sex, of course, but I wasn't so well versed in it that I understood what was going on between grown-ups, especially my own parents. I just couldn't imagine that, them

358

making love. I suppose the main reason they drove off that night was that the idea of doing something a little different, making love in a car appealed to them. That way, for a moment they were just two lovers enjoying each other's bodies in a romantic setting.

I contemplated it for a time, then nodded off, the wind turning from warm to cool by the touch of oncoming rain.

Some time later I was awakened by Toby barking, but it didn't last and I went back to sleep. After that, I heard a tapping sound. It was as if some bird were pecking corn from a hard surface. I gradually opened my eyes and turned in my bed and saw a figure through the screen door. It was just standing there, looking in.

Though it was cool, the storm was still in the distance, and there was no cloud cover, and the moon was bright. In that moment of awakening, in the glow of the moonlight, I realized there was a huge hole cut in the screen and that the latch had been undone.

It was then that sleep wore away completely and I realized it wasn't a dream. I sat bolt upright on my pallet, looking at the shape beyond the screen.

It was dark with horns on its head, and one hand was tapping on the screen's frame with long fingernails. The Goat Man was making a kind of grunting sound.

"Go away!" I said.

But the shape remained and its gruntings changed to whimpers. The wind blew, and the shape seemed to blow with it, coast to the right of the screened porch and out of sight.

I jerked my head toward Tom's pallet, and saw she was gone.

I got up quickly and ran over to the screen, looked at the hole that had been cut in it. I pushed the screen open, stepped out on the back steps.

Out by the woods I could see the Goat Man. He lifted his hand and summoned me.

I hesitated. I ran to Mama and Daddy's room, but they were gone. I dimly remembered before dropping off to sleep they had driven off in the car, for God knows what.

I opened the door into Grandma's room. "Grandma!"

She sat upright as if jerked up on a string. "What in hell?"

"The Goat Man, he got Tom."

Grandma tossed back the covers and rolled out of bed. She had on her nightgown and her long hair fell well below her shoulders, framing her face like a helmet.

She ran out on the porch. She saw the empty pallet, the cut-open screen.

"Get your Daddy," she said.

"He and Mama ain't here."

"What?"

"They went off in the car."

Grandma was considering that, trying to put it together. I said, "Look Grandma, out by the woods."

The Goat Man was still there.

"Keep an eye on 'im. I'm grabbin' my shotgun and my shoes."

Moments later Grandma reappeared with her shotgun, her shoes on her feet. I had slipped into my overalls and pushed my feet in my shoes while I was waiting. The Goat Man had not moved. He was waving us on.

"The sonofabitch is taunting us," Grandma said.

"Yeah, but where's Tom?" I said.

I could see Grandma's face drop, and there in the moonlight, netted by the shadow of the screen, she suddenly looked ancient, almost hag-like.

"Come on," she said.

She pushed open the screen door with the stock of the rifle, started racing toward the Goat Man. She moved very fast. The wind caught at her white gown and flicked it about her and the moon danced blue beams off the barrel of the shotgun. She looked like a wraith burst loose from hell.

I rushed after Grandma, and found it hard to keep up. The Goat Man ducked into the shadows, silent as thought.

As I ran, I began calling for Tom, and Grandma picked up on it and started doing the same, but Tom didn't answer. I tripped and went down. When I rose to my knees I saw that I had tripped over Toby. He lay still on the ground, just inside the woods. I picked him up. His head rolled limp to one side. He whimpered softly, his back legs kicked desperately. Blood leaked from his head where he had been whacked.

After all he had been through he had had his head battered, and was probably dying. He had barked earlier, to warn me about the Goat Man, and I hadn't listened. I had rolled over and gone to sleep, and the Goat Man had come for Tom. Now Toby was injured and dying and Tom was missing, and Mama and Daddy had gone off somewhere in the car, and the Goat Man was no longer in sight.

And for that matter, neither was Grandma.

I didn't want to leave him to bleed and die, but I had to help Grandma find the Goat Man and Tom. I put Toby down easy, pushed back the tears, ran blindly into the woods, down the narrow path Grandma had taken in her pursuit of the Goat Man. I fully expected at any moment to fall over Grandma's or Tom's body, but that didn't happen. I finally began to catch up with Grandma. She wasn't moving so fast now. She was limping, breathing hard. Her nightgown had been ripped by limbs, and so had her hair. She looked absolutely crazed.

"Hon, you got to follow," she said. "I can't go another step... I got to sit and rest... I ain't as tough as I thought. He went through them brambles there. You got to hurry... Take the shotgun."

"I don't want to leave you here."

"You got to follow him, find Tom. You got the gun. He ain't got none, but I seen he's got a knife. A big'n, strapped to his side. You make him tell where Tom is, hear? Oh, Jesus, I feel like I'm gonna die. My heart's actin' up. Go...go, Harry."

Grandma collapsed to the ground on her butt, her chest heaving as if pumped with bellows. As Grandma lay down, I snatched up the shotgun, darted through the brambles, broke out onto a narrow pine-straw-littered trail. The moonlight danced through the boughs overhead and lit up the path. I could see where the Goat Man had pushed back limbs, even broken a few, as if he wanted me to inspect the direction he had gone.

There was enough moon for me to see where I was going, but not enough to keep every shadow from looking like the Goat Man, coiled and ready to pounce. The wind was sighing through the trees and there were bits of rain with it, and the rain was cool. Gradually the moon was being bagged by rain clouds.

I didn't know if I should go on, or go back and get Grandma and try and find Mama and Daddy. I felt that no matter what I did, valuable time was being lost. There was no telling what the Goat Man was doing to poor Tom. Had he tied her up and put her at the edge of the woods before coming back to taunt me at the window? Maybe he already done what he had wanted to do to Tom, and now he wanted me too.

I thought of what had been done to all those poor women, and I thought of Tom, and a sickness came over me, and I ran faster, deciding it was best to continue on course, hoping I'd come on the monster and would get a clear shot at him and be able to rescue Tom.

It was then that I saw a strange thing in the middle of the trail, prominent in the moon-light breaking through the trees. A limb had been broken off, and it was forced into the ground. It was bent to the right at the top and whittled on to make it sharp. It was like a kind of arrow pointing the way.

The Goat Man was having his fun with me. I decided I had no choice other than to go where the arrow was pointing, a little trail even more narrow than the one I was on.

I went down it, and in the middle of it was another limb, this one more hastily prepared, just broken off and stuck in the ground, bent over at the middle and pointing to the right again.

Where it pointed wasn't hardly even a trail, just a break here and there in the trees. I went that way, spiderwebs twisting into my hair, limbs slapping me across the face, and before I knew it my feet had gone out from under me and I was sliding over the edge of an embankment, and when I hit on the seat of my pants and looked out, I was at the road, the one the preachers traveled. The Goat Man had brought me to the road by a shortcut and had gone straight down it, because right in front of me, drawn in the dirt of the road, was an arrow. If he could cross the road or travel it, that meant he could go anywhere he wanted. There wasn't any safe place from the Goat Man. That story about the road stopping him, about him not being able to leave the bottoms, it was all wrong.

The Goat Man could do anything he wanted to.

I picked up the shotgun I had dropped, ran down the road. I wasn't even looking for sign anymore. I was heading for the Swinging Bridge and across from that the briar tunnels. I supposed he could have Tom under the bridge, in the cave, but in spite of what Grandma had said, I knew those tunnels were his nest, and I wanted to find him there, and I wanted to shoot and kill him. I wanted Tom to be okay. I wanted to be a hero. I wanted not to be dead. I wanted that a lot. Then I wondered if a shotgun blast could stop the Goat Man. I had thought on that before and wondered, but now, chasing him like this, him leading me on, I certainly wondered it more than ever before.

As I ran, I became more certain that the place

I was being taken was the briar tunnels, and that Tom, for better or worse, was there. Those tunnels were where he had done his meanness to those women before casting them in the river. By placing that dead colored woman there, he had been taunting us all, showing us not only the place of the murder, but the probable place of all the murders. A place where he could take his time and do what he wanted for as long as he wanted.

I felt confident of my conclusions, though I could base them on little more than intuition and childish fantasy. I wished then I had pushed my ideas on Daddy, but I hadn't, and now I had to deal with the consequences.

When I got to the Swinging Bridge, the wind was blowing hard and the moon showed itself to the world in patches. The bridge lashed back and forth, and I could easily visualize myself being tossed through the air, a stone snapped from a sling. I decided I'd be better off to go down to Mose's cabin and use his boat to make my way to the briar tunnel.

I remembered we had left the boat along the shore, and my heart sank momentarily, then I thought of how it had been returned before, and ran down there hoping.

When I got there, the boat was in its spot, but when I put the shotgun inside it and tried to push it out in the water, it bogged in the sand and I couldn't move it. I struggled a full five minutes, unable to budge it, bursting into tears.

I took a deep breath. I had no choice but the

bridge. Way the boat was bogged down, there was no way I was going to move it by myself, and I knew in my heart where the Goat Man had taken Tom.

As I raced past the cabin, up in the woods I saw the nose of some kind of vehicle sticking out of the brush, the rest of it tucked between trees. It occurred to me that it might be Mama and Daddy for a moment, but a quick look and I could tell it wasn't their car. It was a truck. It really didn't matter. It could be someone down on the river with a boat, running night lines, or hunting possum or coon.

I turned and ran behind the shack on my way back to the bridge, saw something that grabbed my attention. It was hanging from the nail on the back of the cabin. It was a hand and part of a wrist. Something bright dangled from the hand.

My knees sagged. Tom. Oh God. Tom.

I went over to it slowly, bent forward, saw with relief the hand was too large to be Tom's, and it was mostly rotten with only a bit of flesh on it. In the shadows it had looked whole, but it was anything but. The rotting hand was in a half fist and it was holding a little chain; the chain was draped through its bony fingers, and in the partial open palm on a pad of darkening flesh I could see what it held was a bullet-dented French coin.

Taylor's coin.

I was trying to reconcile this with the Goat Man, figure on how it had all come together, when there was a hand on my shoulder.

As I jerked my head around, I brought up the shotgun, but another hand came out quickly and took it from me.

I was looking straight into the face of the Goat Man.

———◆———

The moon rolled out from behind a rain cloud, and its light fell into the Goat Man's eyes. They shone in his red-black face like cold emeralds. They were the same color as Mose's eyes.

The Goat Man made a soft grunting sound and patted my shoulder. I saw his horns were not horns at all, but an old darkened straw hat that had rotted, leaving a gap in the front, like something had taken a bite out of it, and the tips the gap had made had been turned up by time, wind, and rain.

It was just a straw hat. A blasted straw hat. No horns.

And those eyes. That skin. Mose's eyes. Mose's skin.

In that instant I knew. The Goat Man wasn't any Goat Man at all. He was Mose's son, the one wasn't right in the head and was thought to be dead. He'd been living out here in the woods all this time, and Mose had been taking care of him, and the son in his turn had been trying to take care of Mose, by bringing him gifts he found in the river, and he was still doing it, even if Mose was dead and gone. He was just a big dumb boy in a man's body, wandering the woods wearing worn-out clothes and shoes with soles that flopped.

The Goat Man turned and pointed upriver. I knew then he hadn't killed anyone, hadn't taken Tom. He had come to warn me, let me know Tom had been taken. Now he was pointing the way. I just knew it. I didn't know how he had come by the hand or Taylor's chain and coin, but I knew the Goat Man hadn't killed anybody. He had been watching our house; maybe he thought of himself as a kid. Hadn't aged a day in his head. The sensation I had felt earlier hadn't been any possum watching us, it had been the Goat Man. He had been in the woods and had seen what happened with Tom, and now he was trying to help me.

I broke loose from him, ran back to the boat, tried to push it free again. The Goat Man followed me, put the shotgun in the boat, grabbed the end of it, and together we pushed it out of the sand and into the river.

I splashed into the water with the Goat Man. He grabbed me suddenly and stuck me in the boat, pushed on out until the current had it good.

I watched as he waded back toward shore and the cabin. He stood on the bank looking at me, like a friend who hated to see his playmate go away. The wind snapped at his old hat and plucked at his clothes as if to remove them.

I picked up the paddle and went to work,

369

trying not to think too much about what was being done to Tom.

Dark clouds kept passing over the moon, but none grabbed it and held it. It peeked out every now and then, like a frightened child looking out from beneath warm blankets. The raindrops became more frequent as the wind grew hard and slightly cool with dampness.

I paddled so hard my back and shoulders began to ache, but the current was with me, pulling me fast. I passed a whole school of water moccasins swimming in the dark. I feared they might try to climb up in the boat, as they liked to do, thinking it was a floating log and wanting a rest.

I paddled quickly through them, spreading the school. One did indeed try to climb up the side, but I brought the boat paddle down on him hard and he went back in the water, alive or dead I couldn't say.

As I paddled around a bend in the river, where moss hung down from trees like curtains, and as I paddled through the moss, fighting it the way you might a thick swath of spiderwebs, I saw where the wild briars grew, and in that moment I had a strange sinking feeling, like carrying a bucket full of water and suddenly having the bottom drop out of it.

The feeling came not only for fear of what I might find in the briar tunnels, but fear I might find nothing at all. Perhaps I was all wrong and the Goat Man did indeed have Tom. Possibly in Mose's cabin, hiding her there, waiting until I was out of sight. But if that was true, why had he given my gun back? Then again, he wasn't bright. He was a creature of the woods, same as a coon or a possum. He didn't think like regular folks.

All of this went through my head and swirled around and confused itself with my own dread and the thought of actually cutting down on a man with a shotgun. I felt like I was in a dream, like the kind I'd had when I'd had the flu some years before and everything had whirled and Mama's and Daddy's voices echoed and there were shadows all around me, trying to grab at me and pull me away into who knows where.

I paddled to the bank, got out, pulled the boat on shore best I could. I couldn't quite get it out of the water since I was so tuckered out from paddling. I just hoped it would hang there and hold.

I got the shotgun, went up the hill quietly, found the mouth of the tunnel just beyond the tree, where me and Tom and Toby had come out that night.

It was dark inside the briars. The moon had gone behind a cloud and the wind rattled the bone-like stickers and clicked them together. Bits of rain sliced through the briars, mixed with the sweat in my hair, ran down my face, put salt in my mouth, and made me shiver.

July the Fourth, and I was cold.

Or was it the fifth now? I remember thinking that. Is it the fifth, and knowing full well I shouldn't think that at all. I had to keep my mind sharp.

As I sneaked down the tunnel, through the briars I could see an orange glow leaping, could see a shadow moving before the glow. And I could hear a crackling sound, like dry leaves being wadded up in a big man's hand.

I trembled, eased forward, came to the end of the tunnel, and froze. I couldn't make myself turn into the large tunnel; the one that was cave-like and held pieces of paper with pictures of women on them, and cloth. And it came to me in a rush. The cloth I had seen, white with something red on it. It was the trim on the dress Mrs. Canerton had worn the night of the party, and then, I assumed, the night of her murder.

Suddenly, it was as if my feet were nailed to the ground.

I pulled back the hammer on the shotgun, slipped my face around the edge of the briars, and looked.

There was a fire going in the center of the tunnel, in the spot where Tom and I had seen the burn marks that day, and I could see Tom lying on the ground, her clothes off and strewn about, and a man was leaning over her, running his hands over her back and forth, making a sound like an animal eating after a long time without food. His hands flowed over her as if he was playing a piano.

He picked up a Sears and Roebuck catalogue off the ground, tore out a page, tore it again. I could see in the firelight it was a picture of a little girl. He rolled the picture up carefully, very tight, and gently placed it on the ground. I thought of the others, with those pieces of paper stuck into them, and I thought of Doc Tinn and his talk of fetishes.

A huge cane knife was stuck up in the dirt near Tom's head, and Tom's face was turned toward me. Her eyes were wide and full of tears and blood-red flickers from the fire. Tied around her mouth was a thick bandanna. Her hands and feet were bound with rope, and they were twisted at horrible angles. It looked as if she would break at the slightest touch.

As I looked the man rose and I saw that his pants were undone and he had hold of himself. He was walking back and forth before the fire, looking down at Tom, yelling, "I don't want to do this. You make me do this. It's your fault, you know? You're getting just right. Just right. Tonight, you were just right."

The voice was loud, but not like any voice I'd ever heard. There was all the darkness and wetness and muddiness of the bottom of the river in that voice, all the decay of dead fish and snakes and tossed garbage, the sewage from the on-bank outhouses.

I hadn't been able to get a good look at his face, but I was sure from the way he was built, and from seeing that chain in Mrs. Canerton's hand, that it was Doc Taylor. I figured she had grabbed at him while they fought, got hold of his chain, and he cut her hand off, not knowing the chain had gone with it.

Slowly he turned, and the way the fire

caught his hair, I realized I was wrong. It wasn't Doc Taylor. It was Mr. Nation's son, the older one.

Then he turned to where I could see him good, and it wasn't Nation's boy at all. I had merely thought it was because that's the kind of person I expected.

I stepped fully into the tunnel, said, "Cecil."

The name came out of my mouth, without me really planning to say it. Cecil turned, and when he saw me his face was like it had been earlier, when Tom was being bounced on his knee and the fireworks had exploded behind him. It was neither happy nor sad, but dreamy, like a man waking from something he couldn't quite figure.

He let go of his privates, let them hang out for me to see, like some kind of display at Groon's general store.

"Oh, boy," he said, his voice still husky and animal-like. "It's just gone all wrong. I didn't want to have to have Tom. I didn't. But she's been ripenin', boy, right in front of my eyes. Every time I saw her, I said, no, you don't shit where you eat. But she's ripenin', boy. And I thought I'd go to your place, peek in on her if I could, then I seen her there, easy to take, and I knew tonight I had to have her. There wasn't nothing else for it."

"Why?"

"Oh, son. There is no why. I tell myself I won't, but I do. I do."

He eased toward me.

I lifted the shotgun.

"Now, boy," he said. "You don't want to shoot me."

"Yes sir. I do."

"It ain't something I can help. Listen here. I'll let her go, and we'll just forget about this business. Time you get home, I'll be out of here. I got a little boat hid out, and I can take it downriver to where I can catch a train. I'm good at that. I can be gone before you know it. I come out here in a truck with my boat, but I'll leave the truck for you. You're gettin' old enough for a truck. You should have a truck. I'll leave it for you. It's up above Mose's shack."

"You're wiltin'," I said.

His pee-dink had gone limp.

Cecil looked down. "So I am."

He pushed himself inside his pants and buttoned up as he talked. "Look here. I wasn't gonna hurt her. Just feel her some. I was just gonna get my finger wet. A little smell. I'll go on, and everything will be all right."

"You'll just go down the river and do it again," I said. "Way you come down the river to us and did it here. You ain't gonna stop, are you?"

"There's nothing to say about it, Harry. It gets out of hand sometime."

"You killed those people, Cecil. I trusted you. My Daddy trusted you. We all trusted you."

"Nothing I can say, Harry."

"Mrs. Canerton. I thought you liked her."

"I do. I did. I like Tom. I like them, and I

try to leave them alone. The ones that matter. I went for the prostitutes. Thought that would hold me. But I didn't want them. I wanted something...fresher. Louise, she was so nice.

"I didn't mean to kill Louise. I wanted her, and she didn't want me. She didn't want to be tied. I swear, I wasn't gonna hurt her. But she didn't want me. We got to arguing, then I saw that chain and coin around her neck, and I thought of that silly little doctor having some of that, and she was mine, and I grabbed at her throat, at his damn coin, and her hand came up, got tangled in the chain, and I had the cane knife."

He pointed at it where it stuck up in the ground next to Tom. It was a wicked-looking thing, and the firelight brightened its edge and made it appear to be coated in blood.

"I had it," he said, "and I swung it. Cut off her hand. Damnedest thing. We was on the edge of the river. I told her I wanted to show her somethin', see. That got her down here. And so we were on the edge, and"—he laughed slightly—"the damn hand, it popped right off and into the river. Can you imagine that..."

"I know the Goat Man found it."

"Goat Man?"

"You're the real Goat Man. You're Miss Maggie's Travelin' Man."

"You're not making any sense, boy."

I wanted him away from the cane knife. "Move on around to the side there," I said.

Cecil slipped to my left, and I went to the right. We were kind of circling each other. I got over close to Tom and I squatted down by her, still pointing the shotgun at Cecil.

"I could be gone for good," Cecil said. "All you got to do is let me go."

I reached out with one hand, got hold of the knot on the bandanna and pulled it loose. Tom said, "Shoot him! Shoot him! He stuck his fingers in me. Shoot him! He took me out of the window and stuck his fingers in me."

"Hush, Tom," I said. "Take it easy."

"This hurts. Cut me loose… Give me the gun and I'll shoot him."

"All the time you were bringin' those women here to kill, weren't you?" I said.

"It's a perfect place. Already made by hoboes. Once I decide on a woman, well, I can easily handle a woman. I always had my boat ready, and you can get almost anywhere you need to go by river. The tracks aren't far from here. Plenty of trains run. It's easy to get around. I used my truck to bring the boat down."

"You told where Mose was? You told Mr. Nation."

"Your Daddy gave me a lead. And Smoote, that idiot, who do you think cuts his hair? He was all worked up about that colored man in his barn, and he got to talkin', and I didn't mean to do anything with it, but hell, lots of people knew about it 'cause of his big mouth, and it was just a matter of time. All I had to do was let it slip to couple folks I figured wore the hoods."

"But why?"

"He took the blame, and I'd quit. I really wanted to, you know. I wanted to marry Louise, settle down, cut hair, live like your Daddy. Maybe even have some kids. But I can't do it, Harry. I tried, but I couldn't do it. I thought I had it beat, then Louise took a shine to that boy doctor. It all snapped."

"Just go on and shoot him," Tom said.

I squatted, got hold of the cane knife, ran it against the ropes that held Tom with my left hand and kept the shotgun tucked to me with the right hand.

"Sometimes friends make you mad, don't they? They do wrong things. But they don't mean to. I didn't mean to. I couldn't help myself."

"We ain't talkin' about stealin' a piece of peppermint here. You're worse than the critters out there with the hydrophobia, 'cause you ain't as good as them. They can't help themselves."

"I tell you, neither can I. You don't know what I saw in the war. It was horrible."

"You was the one killin' them Germans way you told Daddy about, wasn't you?"

"Your Daddy told you about that, huh? Yes. It was me. It was a relief. Pretty soon, I wasn't scared anymore. When I was home, I was always scared. My Mama, she liked me. She liked me a lot. And she liked to tie me up like her Daddy tied her when he had her. I learned that from her. The tying. But I didn't like being tied. She did. I liked the tying. We were quite a team till I overdid it. That was in Arkansas. I went away to the war then, and I learned to kill more. To enjoy it. And when I came back... Well, I just naturally found it burned off tension. I'm tellin' you, Harry. I can't help it. I tried to keep it to people that didn't matter."

"Like anyone matters to you," I said, sawing without much success at the ropes.

"You're gonna cut me, Harry," Tom said.

The fire crackled, bled red colors across Cecil's face. Some of the rain leaked in through the thick wad of briars and vines and limbs overhead, hit the fire, made it hiss.

Cecil said, "You're like your Daddy, ain't you? Self-righteous."

"Reckon so."

"My Daddy'll whip your ass," Tom said.

The cane knife was sharp, but just too hard to handle, and Tom was starting to cuss and going on about letting her loose and giving her the shotgun. I finally tossed the cane knife down, got my pocketknife out and opened it with my teeth.

Cecil eased toward me.

"Don't come no closer, Cecil. I'll shoot your legs out from under you."

"Shoot his pee-pee off!" Tom yelled.

The pocketknife was easier for me to handle. I finally got the ropes loose and Tom sat up rubbing her wrists.

"It's all right now, Tom."

"It will be when we shoot his pee-pee off."

I stood up, raised the gun, and Cecil flinched. But I couldn't cut him down. I wasn't raised to kill a human being. I couldn't even shoot a squirrel or catch a fish if I thought I wasn't gonna eat it, and I damn sure wasn't gonna eat Cecil.

Just wasn't in me to shoot a fella in cold blood. He needed it, no doubt, but no matter how hard I tried, I couldn't bring myself to do it. I figured if I blew his knee off to cripple him till I could get Daddy, he'd end up bleeding out slow, and dying anyway. The idea of letting buckshot fly into human flesh overwhelmed me, made me ill, and took my common sense away.

I didn't know what to do with him. I decided I had no choice but to let him go, tell Daddy, and have him try and hunt him down. If I went to tie him up, I was certain he'd turn the tables, and I was afraid if I tried to take him back at the point of a gun, he'd outdo me somehow.

Tom was pulling on her clothes when I said, "You'll get yours eventually."

"Now you're talkin', boy."

"You stay over yonder, we're goin' out."

He held up his hands. "Now you're using some sense."

Tom said, "You can't shoot him, I can."

"Go on, Tom."

She didn't like it, but she turned down the tunnel and headed out. Cecil said, "Remember, boy. We had some good times."

"You ain't never done nothing with me but cut my hair, and you didn't know how to cut a boy's hair anyway." I turned and went out by the tunnel. "And I ought to blow one of your legs off for what you done to Toby."

"He hurt Toby?" Tom said. "Gimme that gun."

She made as if to grab it, and in the same moment Cecil stepped forward. I pushed Tom aside and brought the shotgun up.

"I thought you was wantin' to go your own way."

He smiled. "I am, Harry. You can't fault a fella for tryin'."

"I can," I said. "Tom. Go!"

We hustled through the tunnel, and I listened for him following, looking back now and then, but I didn't hear nor see any sign of him.

We come out of the tunnel and went past the tree where the first body had been found, and down to where I'd pulled the boat on shore. I figured if we went through the woods he might get us, but if we took the boat down-river it would be hard for him to track us, if that was his notion.

I was hoping it wasn't.

When we got down to the river, the boat, which I hadn't been able to pull up completely on shore, had been washed into the river by the rain-dappled current. I could see it in the distance, flowing away at a rapid pace.

"Damn," I said.

"Was that Mose's boat?" Tom asked.

"We got to go by the bank, to the Swinging Bridge."

"It's a long ways," I heard Cecil say.

I spun around, and there he was up on the

higher bank next to the tree where me and Tom had found the body. He was just a big shadow next to the tree, and I thought of the devil come up from the ground, all dark and evil and full of bluff. Maybe Cecil wasn't the Travelin' Man after all, but in fact was Beelzebub himself, one Miss Maggie told me about.

Cecil stepped out from behind the tree, and the moonlight caught the blade of the cane knife, made me think of a story I had read once about Death and his scythe.

"You got a long ways to go, children. A long ways."

I pointed the shotgun at him and he slipped behind the tree out of sight, said, "A long ways."

I knew then I should have killed him. Or at least taken the cane knife. Now, without the boat, he could follow alongside us, back up in the woods there, and we couldn't even see him.

Me and Tom started moving brisk-like along the bank, and we could hear Cecil moving through the woods on the higher bank above us, and finally we didn't hear him anymore. It was the same as that night when we heard the sounds near and in the tunnel. I figured it had been him, maybe come down to see his handiwork at the tree there, liking it perhaps, wanting it to be seen by someone. Maybe we had come down right after he finished doing it. He had been stalking us, or Tom maybe. Could be he had wanted Tom all along.

We walked fast and Tom was cussing most

of the time, talking about what Cecil had done with his fingers. The whole thing was making me sick.

"Just shut up, Tom. Shut up."

She started crying. I stopped and got down on one knee, let the shotgun lay against me as I reached out with both hands and took hold of her shoulders.

"I'm sorry, Tom, really. I'm scared too. We got to keep ourselves together, you hear me?"

"I hear you," she said.

"We got to stay the course here. I got a gun. He don't. He may have already given up."

"He ain't give up, and you know it."

"We got to keep moving."

Tom nodded, and we started out again. Pretty soon the long dark shadow of the Swinging Bridge was visible across the river, and the wind was high, and the bridge thrashed back and forth and creaked and groaned like rusty hinges.

"We could go on down a ways, Tom, but I think we got to cross by the bridge here. It's quicker, and we can be home sooner."

"I'm scared, Harry."

"So am I. Can you do it?"

Tom sucked in her top lip and nodded. "I can."

We climbed up the bank where the bridge began and looked down it. It swung back and forth. White foam rose from the dark water below, rolled away and crashed over the little falls into the broader, deeper, slower part of the river, but on this rainy, windy night, even that flowed fast.

The woods seemed quiet, yet full of something I couldn't put a name to. Now and again, in spite of the rain, the clouds would split and the moon would shine down on us. The rain was growing stronger, and I knew before long there would be only clouds and lots of rain and little to no moonlight. That would only make matters worse.

Like that other time, I decided to cross first, so if a board gave out Tom would know. When I stepped on the bridge, the wind and my weight made it swing wide, and I darn near tipped into the water. When I reached out to grab the cables, I let go of the shotgun. It went into the water, making no sound over the roar of the water.

"You lost it, Harry," Tom yelled from the bank.

"Come on, just hang on to the cables."

Tom stepped onto the bridge. It swung violently, nearly tipped again.

"We got to walk light," I said, "and kind of together. When I take a step, you take one. But if a board goes, or I go, you'll see in time."

"If you fall, what do I do?"

"You got to go on across, Tom."

We continued, having gotten the movement right, because we weren't wobbling as badly as before. Still, it was slow work, and I began to suspect we might have been better off traveling down the bank until we could cross in the shallows. But that route was dark, the trees grew close to the water, and it would have been easy for Cecil to have snatched us.

But now, on this bridge, going slowly, the wind and rain blowing, I found myself reconsidering. But, of course, there was no going back. We had the same distance to go to cross that we did going back. And I no longer had the shotgun.

I turned, looked down the length of the bridge, past Tom. I didn't see anyone tryin' to follow.

It was slow going, but it wasn't long before we were six feet from the other side. I began to breathe again. Then I realized after we crossed the bridge we still had a ways to go till we got to the wide trail, then the road. But there wasn't any road would stop Cecil or anyone else. It was just a road. If we got that far, we still had more distance to travel, and Cecil would know where we were going, and Mama and Daddy might not even be home yet. As for Grandma, I didn't know if she had gone back to the house, in search of Mama and Daddy, or driven off for help. For that matter, she could still be lying where I had left her.

I thought if we got to the road, I might try and fool Cecil by going the other way. The drawback was it was a longer distance in that direction to anyone's house, and if Cecil figured what we were doin', we could be in worse trouble. I decided the only thing to do was to head straight home and stay cautious.

While all this was on my mind, and we were about to reach the opposite bank, a chunk of the bank moved and the shadows that clustered around it moved too. Cecil, looking as if he had crawled through a working cotton gin, stepped into view holding the cane knife.

The look on his face said it all. He had us. I tossed a glance over my shoulder at Tom. The look she gave me back was one that expected some kind of answer.

I thought maybe we could turn back, but before I could make the decision, I glanced at Cecil, saw him stick the cane knife in the dirt beside him. Staying on solid ground, he took hold of both sides of the cables that held the Swinging Bridge, said, "I beat you across, boy. Hurried down and crossed in the shallows, like you should have done. Then I just waited. Now you and little Tom, you're gonna have to take a dip. I didn't want it this way, but that's how it is. You see that, don't you? All I wanted was Tom. You give her to me right now, let her cross to this side, you can go. By the time you get home, me and her, we'll be on our way, and I'll keep goin' from there. That's all the deal I can offer, Harry."

"You ain't got your dough done in the middle," I said.

Cecil clenched the cables hard and shook them. The bridge swung out from under me and I found my feet hanging out in midair. Only my arms wrapped around one of the cables was supporting me.

I jerked a look at Tom. She had fallen and was grabbing at one of the board steps. As she clutched it, I could see bits of rotten wood splintering, throwing splinters into the moonlight. Tom's feet swung out into nothingness. The board creaked. She groaned. The bridge sighed in the wind and the rusty old cables screeched like a rat being slowly crushed to death by a boot heel.

Cecil shook the cables again. I hung tight, my feet swinging way out. I tried to pull up and get my feet back on the slats, but the bridge had tilted, and every time I tugged, it merely leaned with me, the cables being flexible, shaken, and wind-driven.

The board Tom clung to didn't give, just shed more wood; she was holding nothing more than a thin fragment bolted to the lower cables on either side.

I glanced toward Cecil, saw another shape lurch out of the shadows; a huge one, with what looked like horns on its head.

Mose's boy, Telly.

Telly grabbed Cecil around the neck and jerked him back. Cecil spun loose, hit him in the stomach. They grappled for a moment, holding each other's biceps, pushing and pulling.

Cecil got loose, losing some of his shirtsleeve in the process. He snatched up the cane knife, slashed it across Telly's chest. Telly let out with a wail, leaped against Cecil and the both of them went flying onto the bridge.

When they hit, boards splintered, and the bridge swung violently. There was a snapping sound, followed by a hiss as one of the cables broke in two, whipped out and away from us like a lash, then dropped into the water.

Cecil and Telly plummeted past us into the Sabine. Tom dangled for a moment from the bridge slat, then it cracked, but before it could break all the way and drop her, the remaining cable snapped, and we tumbled into the fast-rushing water after them.

———◆———

I went deep, surfaced in choking foam, bumped into Tom. She bellowed and I grabbed her shirt collar. The water churned us under again. I struggled to bring us up, all the while clinging to Tom's collar. When I broke the surface of the water, I saw Cecil and Telly in a clench, riding the blast of the Sabine over the little falls, shooting out into deeper, calmer waters.

Then we were part of the falls, and over we went, and the water covered us, and I clung hard to Tom's shirt collar. I felt as if I blacked out for a moment, then we rose up and I came to as the night air hit me.

I tightened my grip on Tom, started trying to swim toward shore. It was hard in our wet clothes, our clinging shoes, tired as we were, and that damn current.

Tom wasn't helping herself a bit. She had gone limp, letting the water pull her. I thought several times I wasn't going to make it, or that, worse, I would let go of Tom to save myself, but I clung to her until my fingers lost feeling.

Eventually my feet were touching sand and gravel. I waded onto shore, Tom in tow. I collapsed on my knees. Tom rolled over and puked.

I fell forward and rolled on my back and gasped in cool draughts of air. My head was spinning. Absently, I realized it had quit raining.

I raised my head, glanced out at the water. The moon, happy to be shed of rain clouds, cast a glow on the Sabine like grease starting to shine on a hot skillet. I could see Cecil and Telly gripped together, a hand flying up now and then to strike, and I could see something else all around them, something that rose up in a dozen silvery knobs that gleamed in the moonlight.

Cecil and Telly had washed into that school of water moccasins, or another just like them. Had stirred them up. Now it was like bullwhips flying from the water, lashing the two of them time after time.

They washed around a muddy bend in the river struggling with each other, accompanied by the lashing snakes, and even before they had completely gone from sight the clouds came again and the moon went away and in the shadows of the trees overhanging the river, they were lost from sight.

———◆———

When I was able to stand, I realized I had lost a shoe. I got hold of Tom, pulled her farther up the bank. We lay there for a moment, still recovering.

Finally we felt strong enough to move, and we staggered toward the gap in the trees that led to the road. My bare foot found every sticker in existence.

When we got to the Preacher's Road, I stopped, sat down, and picked the stickers out of my foot as best I could. I took off my other shoe, and we started walking toward home. The rain came in earnest now, not letting up at all. No more moonlight, just night and rain so dark it was hard to stay on the muddy road.

It took us a long time, but as we neared home, we heard Mama in the yard, calling our names.

When she saw us she let out a roar of relief, ran toward us with her hair wet in her face, her nightgown clinging to her like a satin glove.

———◆———

When we arrived that night, Daddy was off in the woods looking for us, and Grandma was in bed, ill from excitement. Toby, who I thought had died, was in the house, lying on a makeshift pallet Mama had made for him. She had also bandaged his head. She called him a hero. When he saw us, his poor pathetic body managed to make his tail work, and he beat it a few times to let us know he was glad to see us.

Near dawn, wet and tired, Daddy arrived, found us sitting at the table telling Mama and Grandma all about it. When he saw us, and we came to him, he dropped to his knees, took us both in his arms and began to cry.

Next morning they found Cecil on a sandbar. He was bloated up and swollen from water and snake bites. His neck was broken, Daddy said. Telly had taken care of him before the snake bites.

Caught up in some roots next to the bank, his arms spread and through them, his feet wound up in vines, was Telly. The cane knife wound had torn open his chest and side. Daddy said that sad old straw hat was still on his head; it had somehow gotten twisted up in his hair, and that the part that looked like horns had washed down and was covering his eyes.

I wondered what had gotten into Telly, the Goat Man. He had led me out there to save Tom, but he hadn't wanted any part of stopping Cecil. Maybe he was afraid. But when we were on the bridge, and Cecil was getting the best of us, he had come for him.

Had it been because he wanted to help us, or was he just there already and frightened? I'll never know. I thought of poor Telly living out there in the woods all that time, only his Daddy knowing he was there, and keeping it secret just so folks would leave him alone, not take advantage of him because he was addle-headed.

In the end, I remember mostly just lying in bed in what had become Grandma's room, our old room, for two days after, nursing all the wounds in my foot from stickers and such, thinking about what had almost happened to Tom, trying to get my strength back.

Mama stayed by our side for the next two days, leaving us only long enough to make soup. Daddy sat up with us at night. When I awoke, frightened, thinking I was still on the Swinging Bridge, he would be there, and he would smile and put out his hand and touch my head, and I would lie back and sleep again.

During the day he took a side of the barn down and used the planks to close in the sleeping porch. He said he'd never feel safe with anyone sleeping out there again. I missed the old porch, but it was best he did what he did. I could have never lain out there again, closed my eyes for a good night's sleep.

It was nearly two years later before he replaced the boards he had taken from the barn.

Over a period of years, picking up a word here and there, we would learn that there had been more murders like those in our area, all the way down from Arkansas and over into Oklahoma and some of North Texas. Back then no one pinned those on one murderer. The law just didn't think like that in them days. The true nature of serial killers was unknown.

It's all done now, those long-ago events of the nineteen thirties.

Epilogue

◆

Alittle side note. About six months after
the conclusion of these events, a hunter,
a man my Daddy knew named Jimmy St.
John, discovered a strange thing. Interestingly
enough, it was near where Red's car had
been abandoned, but the only way you could
have found what he found was if you dropped
your flashlight while out coon hunting,
climbed down the riverbank where it had
been dropped, and discovered there was a gap
in a clutch of trees, and if you looked up
just right, you could see it.

It was what looked like a tar baby; a scarecrow thickened with tar hanging from a rope
fastened to a limb over the river.

Next day he told Daddy about it, and Daddy
drove over there. I didn't get all the facts
then, but over the years they were pieced
together.

A body covered thick in pitch, the eyes
open, but gone, of course, just sockets filled
with insects, had a rope embedded in its tar-

covered neck, and the other end was fastened around a limb. Daddy said he could see that the man had thrown the rope over the limb, fastened it around his neck, and leaped off the riverbank. He said he wondered what it was like for someone to decide such a thing, to do it in that manner.

I think Daddy, during his darkest hours, might have considered death himself, but doing it like that, so lonely and so strange...

There were two huge barrels of tar there, and they were on what had once been a fire, but was now nothing more than washed gray ash. The cans were blackened and the lids were off, and there was a flat board covered with the stuff.

Daddy determined that the man had heated the tar, and then, deliberately, plastered the scalding hot stuff to himself, put the rope around his neck, and swung out over the river.

Having come to trust him, Daddy took the body to Doc Tinn, who did his best to clean it up. A large part of the flesh had been preserved by the tar, so that when it was taken off with paint remover and such, it was easy to see that one arm was self-tattooed with a list of women's names. I never asked Daddy if Mama's name was actually listed there, but I had my suspicions.

Across the chest was a new crude tattoo that read, NIGGER.

Daddy put it together this way. Red loved Miss Maggie like a mother, but when he discovered she was his mother, he lost his bearings, his position in life. He was no longer a good white man looking after a poor colored woman, he was colored himself. He then tried to save Mose, his father, and when he couldn't, and when he decided his life had been duped, he went to Miss Maggie. Maybe he thought she would say it was all a joke, or something of that nature. It's impossible to know. Or maybe Red decided to get rid of the one person who he knew knew for sure he wasn't white.

Again, we'll never know. But the guilt of who he was, and what he had done, caused him to torture himself with a crude tattoo cut into his chest, hot tar, and a slow choking death.

Maybe the Klan done it. Having discovered Red was black and that he had an arm tattooed with the names of near a dozen white women. Or maybe it was because they knew Red had tried to save Mose.

No way to know for sure. Life's like that. It isn't like one of Grandma's murder mysteries. Everything doesn't get sewn up neatly.

Like that damn picture colored with pencil in Mose's old shack.

What was that about?

Could Mose have done that?

Since he didn't have a picture of his boy, had he made one to go with his long-lost wife? Just colored in one to remind him he had a son?

Or had Cecil put it there?

He liked to put those little rolled-up pieces of newspaper in the bodies, hang up those pictures out of the Sears and Roebuck, for whatever reason. He had left them with his victims. Did he in some way consider Mose a victim of his; a man punished for his crime? He hadn't had a chance to put the paper on the body, so had he placed it in the cabin?

And what was on those other pieces of paper? Pictures of women? Did he blame those pictures for what they made him do? Lust and murder?

For a time, here in the home, before he stroked out, there was a retired psychiatrist, and I told him my story of that time, and asked him about those pieces of paper. He had no set answer, but thought they might even have been clippings about women from the papers. Maybe crimes that had to do with women.

He said it could be a lot of things, but none of those things were really an answer.

I didn't know then what it was about. And I don't have any better idea now.

There's not much left to tell. Just some general business. I was a hero for a while, then things settled down and we went to doing what everyone else was doing.

They finally got a schoolteacher, and before long they had several and we were attending regular. I made it all the way to the tenth grade. Tom finished the whole thing up, and even went on to college some years later.

But after that night in the bottoms, Grandma never fully recovered. It was like the anxiety took it out of her, made her old and wrecked her heart. She saw Mr. Groon a bit, but that didn't take. She got sick, stayed in bed for a year or so, then one morning she just didn't wake up.

We were living then in a new house on five acres Daddy bought in town. There was already a small cemetery back there, a family plot for some family long gone and forgotten, though those who had owned the house and the land had kept it up out of respect. We did the same. Grandma was buried back there under a huge oak tree that still grows, or did when I was there some ten years ago, back when I could get around. The grave has broken down and blended with the land. That's exactly what Grandma wanted, to be consumed by and dumped all over East Texas by earthworms.

Toby's buried somewhere out there as well.

After the events I've told you about, Toby lived another five years. He had run of the new place, inside and out. One morning Daddy let him out for his morning constitutional. He limped down the steps and out of sight. By nightfall he hadn't returned. Next morning Mama found his body not far from where Grandma was buried.

As for our old place, well, Daddy sold it. He just couldn't crop it anymore, and he wanted to be closer to the barbershop. Mose's grave got lost among trees and brambles, and now there's a parking lot and savings and loan built over it. It's like he never existed.

Daddy quit being constable. He wasn't no good at it anyway. He went to full-time hair cutting, and gradually times got better and he did well until the cancer. Fortunately, when it came, he went fast. He was sixty-two years old. Mama, as if Daddy were calling her, followed close behind.

Tom was killed by a drunk driver in nineteen sixty-nine. She grew into a woman lovely as our mother, made a kindergarten teacher. Her husband was a jackass. He ran off when she got pregnant, and was seldom heard of again.

Tom was driving my worthless nephew into Houston to see a doctor about shaking his drug habit when it happened. It was a head-on collision. Tom died instantly.

My nephew, named Jacob after my father, got a bruise on his head, recovered, and lived long enough to impregnate several women, poison the lives of numerous people with his drug and alcohol problems, and finally, almost mercifully, ended his life with a drug overdose in nineteen seventy-five.

Doc Tinn and his wife moved off to Houston sometime in the sixties. We really didn't have much association with each other. I never saw or heard from them again.

Pappy Treesome's boy Root was castrated and burned by the Klan in nineteen thirty-nine. When Pappy died and Camilla became an invalid from a stroke, Root was on his own more, and turned out he wasn't so harmless. He committed a half dozen rapes on colored girls, for which not a thing was done, it being determined by white and black alike they had it comin'. I'm not sure why they had it comin', other than they were female and he was male and he wanted to satisfy himself.

Finally Root made a bigger mistake in the eyes of white society than the rape of colored girls. I don't know where it happened, or the circumstances around it, but he exposed himself to a white woman, and he was done in. Daddy once said he estimated Root had the mind of a five-year-old.

Old Man Nation lived a drunken life and made trouble throughout it. It didn't catch up with him, though. He lived until he was eighty or more and died in his sleep.

His wife, long run off, was never replaced, and the two boys... Well, I don't exactly know what came of them. They moved off. I heard tell that one of them died in a fishing accident, but I don't know that's the truth, and if it is, I don't know which one of them it was.

Doc Stephenson, I have no memory of him going. Just one day he wasn't there, and Dr. Taylor was. When I was twenty-two I became marshal of Marvel Creek. Its first. Before that there had just been a constable for the area, but the place, though never big, had grown and felt it needed its own personal law.

When World War Two started up I enlisted, but they wouldn't take me. Years earlier, Sally Redback, stung by a hornet one day while I was plowing her, had kicked back in terror, catching me on the side of the cheek, causing damage to my right eye. I recovered with only a small scar, but it affected my vision. It was presumed I wouldn't be able to shoot a rifle. I tried to explain I could shoot left-handed, but at that point in time they weren't scrambling for soldiers, so I ended up staying home.

In the course of my marshaling duties, I met a lovely young woman named Eleanor Piggle—no joke. She ended up in Marvel Creek after her folks arrived from California. They had fled the Dust Bowl from Oklahoma and had come to East Texas, having found no Promised Land in California.

Doc Taylor delivered both our children, and pronounced Eleanor dead eleven years ago. Her big sweet heart just gave out.

James, my first boy, grew up to fight in Vietnam. He died there. William, who was a little younger, went to law school and does well. He helps pay for a lot of my care; he moved me to his home in Houston, then when I decided I was too much of a burden, he helped me find a rest home to finish off my days. He didn't like the idea, but to tell the truth I prefer it.

The family comes to see me twice a week, and more if I want. His wife, Coreen, is like a daughter to me, and my grandchildren are wonderful.

But time is wearing. It takes away the spirit. And though I love my son, his wife, and my grandchildren, I have no desire to lie here day after day with this tube in my shank, waiting on mashed peas and corn, and some awful thing that will pass for meat, all to be handfed to me by a beautiful nurse who reminds me of my long dead wife.

So now I close my eyes with my memories of those times. The bad things that happened aren't nearly as memorable as the good. When I sleep I find myself in our little house next to the woods and the Sabine River. I can hear the crickets and the frogs and the moon is bright and the night is cool. I'm young and strong, full of piss and vinegar.

Each time I visit now, close my eyes to go there, I hope when I awake I will no longer be of this world, but one where Mama and Daddy, Tom and Grandma, perhaps even Mose and the Goat Man, and of course good old Toby, will be waiting for me.

Visit THE ORBIT, the official drive-in theater of champion MOJO STORYTELLER Joe R. Lansdale, located on the web at www.joerlansdale.com. Free stories changed weekly.